Women in Sunlight

Also by Frances Mayes

Under Magnolia

Bella Tuscany

Every Day in Tuscany

Swan

In Tuscany (with Edward Mayes)

A Year in the World

Bringing Tuscany Home (with Edward Mayes)

The Tuscan Sun Cookbook (with Edward Mayes)

The Discovery of Poetry

Sunday in Another Country

After Such Pleasures

Hours

The Arts of Fire

Ex Voto

Frances Mayes

WOMEN IN SUNLIGHT

A NOVEL

CROWN
NEW YORK

Copyright © 2018 by Frances Mayes

All rights reserved.
Published in the United States by Crown, an imprint of the Crown Publishing Group, a division of Penguin Random House LLC, New York.
crownpublishing.com

CROWN and the Crown colophon are registered trademarks of Penguin Random House LLC.

Grateful acknowledgment is made to Random House, an imprint and division of Penguin Random House LLC, for permission to reprint an excerpt of "Leap Before You Look" from *W. H. AUDEN COLLECTED POEMS* by W. H. Auden, copyright © 1945 and renewed 1973 by W. H. Auden. Reprinted by permission of Random House, an imprint and division of Penguin Random House LLC. All rights reserved.

Library of Congress Cataloging-in-Publication data is available upon request.

Hardcover ISBN 978-0-451-49766-6
Ebook ISBN 978-0-451-49768-0
International Edition ISBN 978-0-525-57436-1

Printed in the United States of America

Book design by Elina Nudelman
Jacket design by Elena Giavaldi
Jacket photograph: Simone Becchetti/Stocksy

10 9 8 7 6 5 4 3 2 1

First Edition

For Rena Williams

Walk on air against your better judgment.

—Seamus Heaney, "The Gravel Walks"

Contents

I

Arrivals

BY CHANCE, I WITNESSED THE arrival of the three American women. I'd been reading in my garden for a couple of hours, taking a few notes and making black dots in the margins, a way to locate interesting sentences later without defacing the book. Around four thirty on these early darkening days, some impulse toward dinner quickens, and I began to consider the veal chops in the fridge and to think of cutting a bunch of the chard still rampaging through the *orto*. Chard with raisins, garlic, and orange peel. Thyme and parsley for the tiny potatoes Colin dug at the end of summer. Since the nights were turning chilly, I put down my book, grabbed the wood-carrier from the house, and walked out to the shed to fetch olive tree prunings for the fireplace grill.

Yet another escape. I am putting off writing about Margaret, my difficult and rigorous friend, whose writing I admired. Oh, still admire, but this project feels more like trying to strike mildewed matches—I keep rereading instead of writing. I've read her *Stairs to Palazzo del Drago* a dozen times.

A book can be a portal. Each one I've written firmly sealed

off one nautiline chamber (Is *nautiline* a word? Meaning pertaining to a nautilus?), and then opened into the next habitable space. Always before, my subjects chose me. I'm the happy follower of fleeting images that race ahead, sometimes just out of sight, of lines that U-turn and break like the downside of heartbeats. Isn't *boustrophedon* the ongoing form of writing that mimics the turns an ox makes when plowing a field?

At times, writing conflagrates, a vacant-lot fire started by bad boys. That's when I'm elated. But this time, I chose my friend as the subject. I feel as I did in college, slugging out a research paper on "The Concept of Time in T. S. Eliot's *Four Quartets*." I enjoyed the work but immediately felt humiliated by my limits.

I'm easily distractible. Those shriveled apples on the third terrace, still golden and dangling as brightly as in the myth of the three graces, lure me to make a galette. Fitzy has burrs in his silky hair and needs brushing. My own hair has turned unruly. I would like to have a few friends over for polenta with mushrooms and sausage, now that the *funghi porcini* are sprouting under every oak tree. My mind surfs over endless diversions.

When you're propelled by a sense of duty, you're easy to derail.

As I picked dried branches from the woodpile, I looked down from the upper olive terrace as Gianni, the local driver, turned sharply into the long drive of the Malpiedi place across the road, his white van crackling over dry stubble. Malpiedi—Bad Feet. I've always loved the Italian names that remind me of ones my friends and I adopted when we played Wild Indians in the vacant lot by my family's house in Coral Gables. Wandering Bear, Deer Heart, Straight Arrow. One friend chose Flushing Toilet. But here it's Bucaletto, Hole in the Bed; Zappini, Little Hoe; Tagliaferro, Iron Cutter; and stranger, Taglialagamba, He Cuts the Leg—maybe a butcher specializing in leg of lamb? Cipollini, Little Onion; Tagliasopra, Cut Above; Bellocchio, Beautiful Eye—how alive those names are.

Early in my years in Italy, fascinated by every syllable, I used to collect them. In hotels when there were telephone books, I'd read the names at night for the pleasure of coming upon Caminomerde, Chimney Shit—there's a story there—and Pippisecca, Dry Pipe (or Penis). The sublime Botticelli? Little Barrel.

The Bad Feet are gone now. I attended the wake for Luisa, the wife, who had an erotically decorated cake at her last birthday— figures like those feasting frescoes from Pompeii in the Naples museum, where the phallus is so large it's carried forth on a tray. Passing by their table in the restaurant where she was celebrating with friends, I was shocked to look down at the garish pink and green cake everyone was laughing over. After that, I was embarrassed when I saw plump, stoop-shouldered, rabbit-eyed Tito, her husband. She died of diverticulitis, some sudden rupture I couldn't help but think was caused by too much cake, and Tito followed all too shortly. He did choke, but on pork *arista*, with no one around to perform the Heimlich. I try not to imagine his rheumy eyes popping out of their sockets. The daughter, Grazia, who snorts then brays when she laughs, painted some rooms, put in a dishwasher, and listed the house for lease before she went to live with her failing aunt in town. (I later learned that the rental terms included an option to buy after one year.) Grazia was not coming back to rattle around in the big stone house that was cool in the summer and cool in the winter. I missed them as neighbors. I even missed the years of Grazia's squealing violin practice, Luisa's piano, and Tito's sax. Hours of sour notes wafting up the hill. We'd lived parallel lives on the same slope for eleven years, and then within six months the house stood empty, with the kitchen shutter banging in the night when the *tramontana* blew in from the Alps.

I've always loved their house—its big square self, rooted firmly on a long flat spur of our terraced hillside, and the great double *portone* with sphinx-face doorknockers popular from the time Italy was ransacking Egypt. Over the door, the fanlight's fanciful iron curls, twisted around the letter *S*, the initial, I suppose, of the person who built such a solid structure three hundred years ago. If you cut away the jasmine vines, you'd see VIRET IN AETERNUM, It Flourishes Forever. A prideful motto. The house's name—Villa Assunta. Perhaps it was finished around the holiday Ferragosto, when the Virgin Mary assumed into heaven. Six big square rooms up, six down. Afterthought bathrooms but okay.

I would sometimes take Tito and Luisa a basket of plums when my trees were dripping with them. As their door swung open, a splash of light pooled on the waxed bricks. At the end of the hall I saw the great large-paned window full of splayed green linden leaves, and in winter angular black limbs like a dashed-off charcoal sketch.

DOWN IN THE OLIVE GROVE, I saw Gianni's van weave in and out of sight. Through silvery trees, glimpses of white, scree of trees, flash of white. He descended the rough drive, pulling into the weedy parking spot beside the house, where Luisa often used to leave her blue Fiat Cinquecento ragtop open to the rain. I always wanted to use that image in a poem but it never fit.

Three women got out, hardly the three graces as they dragged carry-on bags and clumsy backpacks and totes. Gianni hauled out four mastodon-sized suitcases and struggled each one to the door. I couldn't hear the women, who appeared to be exclaiming and laughing. I supposed they were here for an autumn vacation. There's a certain kind of traveler who shuns the hectic summer months and arrives for the season of more solitude. I hoped they would not be noisy; sound travels in the hills. If their husbands are arriving and boozy dinners ensue, there could be chaos. Who are they? Not young. I could see that.

My own arrival here, *Dio*—twelve years ago, seems as vivid as yesterday. I stepped out of the car, looked up at the abandoned stone farmhouse, and I knew, what did I know? *This is it. This is where I invent the future.*

Could they be thinking the same? And Margaret, too, my subject, my lost friend, once arrived long, long before me at her golden stone house below the tower of Il Palazzone (big *palazzo* indeed), not knowing what life she might find. What she did find immediately was a huge, squealing pig left shut in the lower level by the farmers/former owners (peasants, she called them) as a gift.

Margaret was a firm exile, not like me, a come-and-go one, and in her embroidered slippers and Venetian black devoré velvet coat, nothing like these latest arrivals in magenta, orange, saffron puffy down jackets and boots.

The one in the electric magenta hoists a dog carrier out of the van's rear door. She kneels and releases a small toffee-colored yapper that starts up right away running in circles around all of them, almost lifting off the ground with joy. So, I guessed, since they've brought a dog, they're not here for a brief holiday.

Gathering more fire starter, I fell into sort of a reverie. Their gestures and movements below me seemed suddenly distant, a static tableau. Some latter-day illustration for a medieval book of hours: under a dapple-gray sky, the stalwart house catching late rays, stones gleaming as if covered with snail tracks; the windows' mottled glass bouncing back the sunlight as mirror. Between Villa Assunta and me, elongated shadows of cypress trees stripe the village road. As if behind veils (for the afternoon light here turns to a pale, honeyed transparency), the slow-motion women walk toward the door, where Gianni fumbles with the iron key that used to hang by a tattered orange ribbon on a hook inside the door. I knew they'd soon inhale the old-book smell of the closed house. They'd step in and see that hall window back-blazed with golden linden leaves, possibly would stop to take in a breath. *Oh, so that's where we are.* Why did tears sting my eyes?

Oh, Luisa, you never did get that craggy mole taken off your chin, never even plucked the coarse spike of hair that I weirdly had the impulse to touch. Too late; you are gone (what, a year?), and Tito, too, with his huge phallus or not, his meek smile, and now almost totally erased are the many seasons in the great old *cucina* with a fireplace big enough to pull up a chair, pour a smidgen of *vin santo*, and tell stories of the war, when many local men walked home barefoot from Russia. That flaky Grazia could have had the yard cleared up a bit. All gone. *Gone with the Wind*, the book I devoured in my early teens. Still a great title. (Margaret also *via col vento*.) What a sharp writer, *la* Margherita. What glinting eyes. I used to study her clean, clipped prose style. I like to use *and* because for me everything connects. She never used *and* because for her, nothing connected. In writing, you can't hide who you are.

Over the years her work simply evaporated from public view, even *Sun Raining on Blue Flowers*, which had impressive critical attention and despite that still managed to appear on best-seller lists. Most of my writer friends never have heard of her. I feel compelled to reawaken interest in her few books, not that I have the power to secure her a place in the canon, if *the canon* even still exists.

ARRIVALS. ALL POTENTIAL. I REMEMBER mine, the black iron key the real estate agent Pescecane (yes, Dogfish) handed over after I signed the last paper, me walking through the empty rooms—counting them: eleven, most of them small. Four below once housed farm animals and still had enormous, smooth stone floors and a rime of fluffy white mold from uric acid. Upstairs the ceilings soared because there had been attics (long since collapsed) for grain and chestnut storage. I'd forgotten the dank *cantina* tacked onto the long kitchen and dining room wing. I remember the creak of the latch, then pushing open the shutters, the view pouring in like grace received. Casa Fonte delle Foglie, fountain of leaves. Maybe that's why I fell for it, that poetic name scrawled on the oldest local maps. Apt for my leafy plot of olive, linden, ilex, and pine layered around a curve of hillside. I'd only seen the inside once and didn't even remember the two upstairs fireplaces, or the sagging beam in the kitchen. Not mouse skeletons in the pantry. My house from the outset seemed *mine*. I literally rolled up my sleeves and set to work.

What the three women are seeing now—will it imprint forever, or will it slowly fade once the vacation ends? Like that house I rented one July in the Mugello north of Florence—the vintage fridge formed such an igloo that the door wouldn't close. If you touched the handle you got an icy shock. I can't picture the bedrooms at all, but I remember decades-old Christmas cards and christening invitations in the sideboard drawer. Memory has shut the doors all the way down a long hall. Only one stands open at the end, an empty white room with white pigeon dung in a line on the floor under a rafter. Who snatches up their roots and roosts in a foreign country where they have no people? I did. Margaret— well, she was born to roam. "Now you can never go home," she used to threaten.

But you can go home; it's not drastic, that is until you're not sure where home is. How many hopefuls have I seen arrive and begin life here only to wake up one day—after the restoration, after the Italian class (*I thought Italian was supposed to be easy*), after the well gone dry, after the boozy lunch-after-lunch with others who speak little Italian, after stone-cold winter—and think, *What in hell am I doing here?*

Even so, powerful propulsions drive us. Drove Margaret, drove me. In the Florence train station, arrival signs flash right next to the enticing departures. *Treni in arrivi, treni in partenze*, one suggesting the other. (I still want to board every one.) Margaret abandoned her Casa Gelsomino, Jasmine House. Long her destiny, then not. Two summers she returned, staying with us. By that time, she was critical of Italy, and one night when her patience snapped she said to me, "You're like a child. Naïf. Perpetually astonished." I said nothing. She'd ripped into me once before.

Colin chided her. "Oh, Margaret, you know that's bullshit. Kit sees all." And he poured her a shot of grappa to end the evening.

"Italy's an old country. That, at least, you know. Babies are born old here. That you don't know." She threw back the grappa in a gulp, looked wide-eyed for a moment, and said, "*Buona notte.*"

And these three, just choosing their bedrooms and flinging their luggage on the bed, just noticing that these Tuscan manses have no closets, just a cavernous, creaky *armadio* in each room. What brings them to Luisa's stern villa? Is the end of their story already embedded in the beginning? Eliot's *in the beginning is my end* exasperated me as a college junior. How dreary, I thought then, but now, I do wonder, when and how will my time here come to an end? Fate, too propitious a word—but what red thread connects an unforeseeable end to the day I arrived in a white sundress, opened the door, threw up my arms, twirled around—to the surprise of the agent—and shouted, *I'm home.*

WALKING TO THE HOUSE, BASKET of sticks in hand, last rays of sun exploding in molten splotches on the lakes out in the valley, an armful of chard, sprigs of thyme and rosemary in my pocket, Colin waving from the front door, Fitzy springing after a copper leaf spiraling toward the grass, *Stairs to Palazzo del Drago* left on a lawn chair, Gianni beeping, mouthing *buona sera, Signora* as his van freed of passengers speeds by, a little music—Thelonious Monk?—drifting from my house, there, like that, the subject chose me.

CRAZY SALAD

COLIN'S VEAL CHOPS, A FIRE, a most excellent brunello from our stash, and an unexpected rain pelting the black windows—what could be better? Of the great experiences of my life there are many, but nothing exceeds the plain happiness of a fall night at home, Bach cello concerto on low, a couple of handfuls of chestnuts to roast over the coals. It's beyond luck that I sit here listening to Colin compare versions of Mozart operas he loves, talk about Walter Benjamin's *Arcades Project*, the messiest book ever written, and about how his corduroy pants pocket has ripped. Plus, he keeps our glasses filled halfway, toasts various absent friends, and, leaning in to poke the fire, looks warmed and handsome in the leaping light.

As I swirl my glass, the flames bounce glowing crescents onto the wall: broken moons, transparent and colliding. How shall I proceed? What can I observe that prefigures the fate awaiting me, awaiting these three women, who might have now discovered Tito's spider-haunted wine cellar and are opening some dusty, sure-to-be-sour vino nobile di Montepulciano? Sharply kept in my mind's eye, the ritual ancient Egyptians practiced. On the day of a pharaoh's birth, slaves began to build his tomb. When my note-book with good paper ends, when my computer files are jammed with notes and lists of words and questions, will these new arriv-als on the hill be gone, will Margaret be laid to rest at last, will I leave or stay?

I think I am a reliable narrator but I'm not sure. I'm the sort of writer who likes to have two projects going at once. Or three. My poetry is sporadic; I don't force it. On that, I'm with Keats, who thought poems must come to you as naturally as leaves on a tree. More mundanely, writing for me is like cooking—I like to have *all* the burners blazing when I'm in the kitchen. Though this sounds as though I'm a house afire as a writer, I've written only three books of poetry and two short prose works. The first of those was on Freya Stark, who set off in the 1920s for Arabia and Assyria, where no other western woman had traveled. She was a stellar writer. The second book—a short bio—focused on Maud Gonne. Yeats, my all-time favorite poet, loved her passionately and gave her face some immortal lines. Two of the oddest are food oriented. "Hollow of cheek as though it drank the wind / And took a mess of shadows for its meat." In another poem, she favored "a crazy salad with her meat." She was a crazy salad herself. Once she had sex inside the tomb of her dead two-year-old son. She hoped to capture his spirit for a new child. (I almost can under-stand a grief like hers.) Writing is a crazy salad, too. Crazy main course and dessert as well.

What gives me the confidence to begin a new book? Well—I won two major awards for my collection *Momentary Maps*. George Clooney riding through my adopted village of San Rocco on a mo-torcycle stirred far more local interest than my faraway awards. Tuscans are not much impressed by celebrity of any kind, even Clooney, though the *carabinieri* in their Valentino uniforms did es-cort the mayor to my house to present me with a bouquet of lilies. I went to New York, Boston, D.C., the West Coast. How glorious to be lauded and toasted but after that, nothing seemed to happen because of the two framed citations, except a few offers for visiting lectureships at universities, and why would I want to do that? Winter in Ithaca, summer in Arizona? The two foundations gave me substantial cash (substantial for a poet anyway), with which I gratefully replaced the septic and heating systems in my house.

Poetry, they say, makes nothing happen but truly it makes everything happen. The electric line, the pith of the language, the *nailed-it* figurative image, that's my home, my first love, and the thing that people perish for the lack of in their lives. (Someone else said that, but who?) I was honored. Many poets labor forever in a vacuum. I wish I could believe the awards were deserved, but I deeply suspect that living in Italy, well away from internecine literary wars, helped. Maybe I was only the one everyone could agree on.

If you know of me at all, which I doubt, it's probably for *Broken Borders*, my Freya book. Through Margaret's connection with a producer, the unthinkable happened and my concise tribute to a heroine of mine became a wide-release film. You've seen it, sure you have, but who knows the name of a writer behind a movie? Chaste Freya would not have appreciated the screenwriter's addition of sex scenes with Assyrian desert warlords. I consoled myself with the fact that many new readers found their way to Freya's actual books. She (though dead) and Hollywood and I made money. Again, not money like the digital whizzes or even like my cousin in real estate, but a benison for me. I finished the kitchen renovation. The rest I stashed away.

My Maud book, too, gave me egress into larger worlds. She simply called out to be written about and I heard her. The playwright Orla Kilgren adapted my *Swan of Coole* for the stage, wonderfully interweaving Yeats's poems with my text. Five years later, the curtain still rises four nights a week in Dublin. Colin and I make many friends through various productions and festivals, and god knows, enough of the actors and directors have found their ways to Tuscany for exhaustingly long visits.

Sometime expat that I am, in love with Europe since my Florida childhood, I've never taken on an American subject, certainly not five of them—the women, me, and Margaret, who's American only by birth, and from Washington, D.C., at that.

I'll fly on cultural memory, instinct, wax wings if I have to.

By Chance

AS COLIN PUTS DOWN THE fire, I step outside to see the black woolly sky punctured with diamantine stars. In other places they shine; here they blaze. You have to gasp. Best to fall on your knees. Through the trees, the Malpiedi house looks like a gray square smudge against the darker hill. Is one of the women looking out the window, amazed at the fiery constellations? Tonight, five stars form a connect-the-dots waterfall splashing onto a wedge of moon. Is another having her first dream in Italy? And the third, her little dog at her feet, perhaps sleeps the deep country sleep, darksome and silent, and will wake at four a.m. dazzled by the knowledge that she is waking up in Italy. *Italy!*

LOCAL ARTISANS STILL MAKE BLANK books with leather spines and pretty paper covers. Friends give them to me for birthdays. Visitors leave them with notes saying they hope I will be inspired. A writer must be in want of a blank book, right? In this lifetime or the next, I won't be able to fill all the daunting white pages, especially since I usually work on a legal pad or computer.

But tonight I take a special one off the shelf. A bone-colored vellum spine and abstracted yellow flowers bind a thick book that opens nicely. Will I find my way? A reviewer described my poetry as "sparse and harsh." My prose, instead, luxuriates in detail—what I think of as illuminations. (Why write prose unless you can go off on side trips, layer, and loop back to the subject at hand?) Here, I'll hope to start at the beginning of an odyssey, a hundred revelations and stories.

The ending? As in the last line of a poem, a novel (even this hybrid) may find that its own end feels like a beginning. Or a spinning—a dime tossed off a high bridge.

SAN ROCCO LIES JUST BEYOND two curves downhill. I zigzag over on a Roman road and I'm at the town gate in ten minutes. Doubtless, this is why the three women chose the Malpiedi place. I've seen the website. "Easy walking distance to town" jumps out as what everyone wants—an isolated house but near the piazza. When I walk in tomorrow morning, as is my habit, most likely I'll hear of the three women's arrival; probably an incident or two will have circulated via Gianni, the driver; and also Grazia's opinion, formed from maybe three emails, will be widely quoted.

Before I go to bed, I draw an orange leaf on the first page and write *New Leaf.*

What follows will accumulate slowly. Their stories will float around town. Many will come to me directly. (Oh, I'll invent no doubt.)

Even now, I intermittently forget about Margaret's book. (Failing her.)

Working title: *Margaret Merrill: Exile at the Window.* A short book, a tribute, really—something I feel obliged to accomplish, since in the end I fell down on my part of our rocky friendship. I'm bothered by that. *Plagued* may be an overstatement, but there it is, a nagging, unfinished feeling, like not making the doctor's appointment when you're so overdue for a mammogram that every time you undress you're imagining your x-rayed breasts pocked with calcified white dings like the surface of the moon.

May she find space here to breathe again.

I'LL PUZZLE OUT MY OWN story, mapping constellations. Wish I may, wish I might.

THE THREE AMERICAN WOMEN ARRIVED shortly before the first frost of October 2015. Their individual stories began in once-upon-a-time land, but their story together began by chance, as most stories do (and what if I had not sat next to Colin Davidson on the Florence airport bus). As I learned, they met in late April in Chapel Hill, North Carolina, USA.

When the bus arrived at the Florence train station ten years ago, Colin helped me with my lumpy bag. A stranger comes to town, that story. We intersected. Millions of atoms swarmed and re-formed in the air. I have an exaggerated sense of smell (not always a bonus). As he put down my bag on the curb, over the diesel fumes, I caught his scent of lime water and sun-dried linen, a scent from some idyllic tropical island I was yet to visit. I wanted to bury my face against his shoulder. You're here, I thought. He smiled and I remembered a quote from somewhere, *the poet with the big lips*. We looked at each other, I think with surprise. I'm reserved, I would never do this, but out of nowhere, I asked, "I'm Kit Raine. Do you have time for a drink?"

I DRAW A LARGE *X* on the second page and write *X in Flux*. I have no idea why.

All dark below. I latch the shutter.

Benvenute. Welcome.

II

Orientation

CHAPEL HILL, NORTH CAROLINA

"YOU'RE LATE, CHARLIE, WHICH IS fine with me. I don't want to go anyway."

"Ingrid had a loose wire cutting into her jaw and I had to run her by the orthodontist before school. Sorry. Those wires must have gone off track for half the kids in town. We were stuck for over an hour for a five-minute fix. It's always crazy when Lara is away. We'll be there in plenty of time, Mom—it doesn't start till eleven."

Camille slipped on a light sweater, lime green. Not an easy color to wear and with her pale skin and newly blond-streaked hair, she thought she looked sub-aqueous, or possibly jaundiced, in the hall mirror. She felt a moment of shame. Is every late-middle-aged woman in America blond-streaked? And what is late-middle-aged now? Surely she qualified as simply old. She saw Charlie over her shoulder, looking at her with a frown, a worried look she'd first seen on him in kindergarten when his sweet potato didn't sprout and everyone else's grew a dangling vine. "I think you'll love it," he said. Unconvincingly, she thought.

"Where is Lara this time? Someplace exotic?" Charlie's Danish wife works as an anonymous inspector of hotels and restaurants for an annual Scandinavian guidebook. She's traveling constantly, leaving Charlie to squeeze in his painting around hauling Ingrid here and there and—recently—driving his mother to physical therapy, Fresh Market, and, today, out to see Cornwallis Meadows. Usually Camille would drive herself, but three weeks after the replacement of her right knee, he thought the least he could do was take her.

"You know, I'm not sure. Maybe Vancouver." It's Lara who's encouraging Camille to move to Cornwallis Meadows, an idyllic over-fifty-five community. Since Charles Senior's death last year, Lara has been on the subject of the five bedrooms and the waste and how it must be lonely, not to mention the burden of mountains of stored stuff in the garage and attic. Charlie sees her point but can't imagine his mom out of the sprawling clapboard house with the deck built around a live oak. How many birthdays have been celebrated under that canopy of branches? Camille has her long borders, yes, a responsibility, but she loves knocking about among the phlox and wormwood, adding a couple of hundred daffodils every fall, and gathering joyful peonies in late spring. Charlie remembers his practice, how ants shook down from the white and pink peonies onto the black lacquered piano as he pounded out "Ol' Man River" and "Clair de Lune." White ones had a rosy smear in the middle, and he thought his mother had kissed each one.

"Vancouver sounds super. A great dinner and a fancy hotel. I'll take it over this jaunt." Camille sent out only this quick jab. She'd agreed to visit Cornwallis Meadows. Her daughter-in-law, she knew, was not just trying to manipulate her. She was genuinely concerned about Camille starting to figure out what Lara called "the next stage" of her life. But Camille suspected, too, that she had her eye on the house Charlie grew up in—its spacious glass-walled living room overlooking Spit Creek and the kitchen with miles of travertine counters. Who could blame her? Charlie's painting career might never move them out of flimsy Karlswood Valley starter homes. Lara actually dreaded the airports, room service, kitchen visits, the inspecting of shower doors, turndown service that knocked just as you were dressing for dinner, and even looking under the hotel beds. A glamorous job that isn't.

Maybe Charlie was childish. He didn't want to think of the house gone, strangers stuffing their golf clubs and Christmas decorations in the attic where he still stores his old snorkeling gear, tennis rackets, college textbooks, and early paintings. His mother's paintings are up there, too, facing against the dormer. Lara had mentioned that maybe if his mother liked Cornwallis Meadows, they could move out of the brick ranch with three shoebox bedrooms and yellowed hardwood floors. Charlie didn't see how that would be possible, unless his mother continued the upkeep and steep taxes. He didn't know how much money his dad had left. He assumed plenty for the rest of his mom's life, and he hoped a nice windfall for him afterward. He knew about the enormous life insurance policy because his mother had given him a big birthday check. "Mom, just give it a chance. Just a look. Be fair. You might really like ol' Cornwallis. All the art classes. You never should have stopped painting. You know everything about it—you've memorized every painting after 1500. And they say the restaurant is good—grilled halibut, pot roast, garlic chicken—I saw the menu online—really great choices at lunch and every night—no dreary cooking for one. There would always be someone to do things with, you know, you and Dad were so . . . so together. And you'd have your own apartment and car."

"I know, sweetie. I'll keep an open mind, but, really, my knee is going to be fine and I . . ." She waved her arm around the living room, including the brimming bookcases, the piano, the two blue velvet sofas and the rug brought back from Turkey on one of their expeditions, as they always called their trips. "You know, Charlie. Home, all this"—she gestured again—"for a long time."

Charlie saw her perplexed look change to a frown. "Mom, you do exactly what you want to do. You will anyway."

Nice that he thinks so. Since the afternoon last spring when Charles came home from work, she has no idea what she *wants* to do.

"I'm home," he called from the front door. His last words.

"I'm in the kitchen."

He tossed his briefcase on the floor by the hall table and ducked into the bathroom to freshen up. Rinsing lettuces at the sink, water running, she didn't hear the thud as he hit the floor, felled by a massive heart attack as swift as it was fatal.

CORNWALLIS MEADOWS, FORMERLY A VAST dairy farm bordered, the sign said, by an Indian trading path (later a mule track) that the British general and his soldiers were reputed to have trod during the Revolutionary War. The community managed a Chapel Hill address, though it was, Charlie now realized, near Hillsborough, way the fuck out of town. His mother put it more succinctly when after about fifteen minutes of speeding out old Highway 86, she observed, "This place is in East Jesus." They both laughed and Charlie buzzed open the sunroof and all the windows for the brown earth smell of plowed fields, the tender spring green auras around the trees, and the sluicing water in roadside ditches running from the April rains. Soon the honeysuckle would be rampant, sending out shoots of heavy perfume. A local restaurant makes honeysuckle sorbet every spring, and Charlie always takes his mother for dinner during that brief season. He relishes her responsiveness to simple treats, how she smiles with her whole face over a handful of grocery-store tulips or a basket of plums from his yard. Then he gets to feel personally responsible for her pleasure.

• • •

AT THE WIDE-OPEN WHITE CORNWALLIS Meadows gates, Charlie turned in behind three other cars winding up the drive to the columned antebellum house that now served as the dining room and presentation rooms for the complex. The house had belonged to the Dalton family for donkey's years, the family that a century ago funded half the university buildings in the area, as well as more recently the medical research center that still draws droves of people to retire nearby.

Later Dalton generations raised Tennessee walking horses, made bad marriages, and lost much of the solid fortune the first Tanner Dalton made, who remembered how by now? They'd died off and the last of them, Tanner IV, in his dotage sold the land and the house, married his nurse, and moved to Sarasota. The notable house and serene acreage that extended to the Eno River was snapped up by a Charlotte developer backed by serious venture capitalists. Therefore: Cornwallis Meadows.

WHITE, SQUARE OUTBUILDINGS LIE SCATTERED behind the house—four discreet retail businesses. Camille already knew of the locavore café; a shop selling expensive table linens, candles, and soaps; a hair salon, and Ink, a bookstore with the gravitas to attract top writers for events. The streets ranging on either side of the big house are lined with connected cottage-style condos, each with a small front garden and picket fence. In the distance looms a large, more institutional building, U-shaped, with one wing for assisted living studios, the other for terminal/hospice care. She had seen C Meadows, as the residents call it, when she visited Karen, a teaching colleague who sought help for blurred vision, only to be told she had a dinosaur brain tumor and two months to live. She'd lingered quietly for eight months, cared for gently by the hospice staff. After a visit with her toward the end, Camille stopped to pick up something to read at the bookstore and spotted on the used shelf—unopened—the books she'd bought for

Karen. She bought again *Guests on Earth*, thinking, Yes, aren't we? That's about right.

CHARLIE STOPPED IN FRONT AND hopped out to open her door. Camille placed her right foot—the bad side—on the gravel, then swung out her other leg and let Charlie hoist her up. Once standing, she was fine, but getting out of bed, a car, or a deep armchair sent hot nails of pain down her leg. Sometimes, in sympathy, the other leg hurt. "You look great, Mama. I like your hair like this." Camille did look great. The extra fifteen pounds she'd accepted as her lot melted away over the months, and her skinny, tennis-player body moved with its normal grace again. One of her friends said recently and crudely, "Grief agrees with you."

"Bye, sweetie. You don't need to come back. They run a shuttle to town. A little walk home would be all to the good."

A WOMAN IN RED PANTS and a swirly red and turquoise sweater paused at the beginning of the brick walk up to the house. She stared at the rows of begonias, pink-white-pink-white, bordering either side. As Camille passed, the woman said, "I would have preferred *groups* of pink, *groups* of white, and not in regiment rows." Camille smiled.

"I'm Susan Ware. Are you going to the freshman mixer in there?" Her hand felt solid and dry. Camille's was the opposite. She liked Susan's wide-open gray eyes, darker than her spiky silver hair.

"Yes. I'm Camille Trowbridge. I hate straight rows of anything, too. Especially tulips because they're bad enough!"

Susan laughed, startlingly loud. "Yes! Someone who agrees with me. They look 3D printed! Can't you see this bed interspersed with clumps of dusty miller, parsley, and lavender campanula?"

"That would be very pretty. Oh well, at least the begonias will fill out and last into fall."

She followed Susan inside, where they were given name tags and introduced to the residential manager, Blair Griffin, a dead ringer for Hillary Clinton down to the neon blue pantsuit. She shook hands firmly and welcomed them. "We know you'll love the lifestyle at C Meadows, ladies. Everyone does. You'll hear all about it. Walk around the house, get acquainted, and have some coffee while we wait for late arrivals." Her assistant handed them brochures and pointed them toward the coffee and pastries.

"Don't you hate to be called 'ladies'? Oh, there's Bitsy Sanford! Is she retired? I used to carpool with her a hundred years ago." Susan walked over to the wing chair where a big-boned woman in a striped blouse with a bow sat slumped over her coffee cup. Camille wandered to the dining room and surveyed the croissants and bear claws.

"Hey, good morning, those are as delicious as they look. I'm Julia Hadley but I shouldn't shake hands—my fingers are all buttery." They were. And she hadn't noticed that her croissant had flaked over her navy suit jacket and onto the rug.

Camille smiled and introduced herself, then reached for one of the croissants. "If we move here, I suppose we can have these every morning. Do you think they'll deliver them to your door?"

"Doubtful. And if they did, we'd have to double up on those dawn exercise classes."

"I'm just checking out the place. Are you moving here?" Camille asked.

Julia paused. "I have no idea what I'm doing." Then she shrugged.

Camille thought, I don't either. But I don't *have* to do anything. I *won't* do anything. Then Julia burst out, "I really do have to make a change . . ." She broke off and took a large last bite of the croissant.

Other women and two men met over their china cups and

talked in quiet voices. As though we are at a funeral, Camille thought. An image of her husband rose. His habit of running his fingers through the swatch of dark blond hair cutting across his forehead. Charles. Whose hands were sculpted from marble, whose earlobe she liked to bite. Charles, coming home, tossing his keys on the counter, shedding his jacket, heaving his bulging briefcase into the coat closet. Charles, his faint smell of rain and spicy cologne. No funeral. Memorial in the garden. After, after, he, after he was fire. Totally. He was fire and then consumed by fire. Wasn't there a gauge, like an oven thermometer, or did she imagine that? Unimaginable, Charles a resin urn of ashes, chunks of bone. All of him, whose shoulders shook when he laughed. She and Charlie never scattered him. He's still at home. A year and she still disbelieves her life is taken from her. Her mainstay. You are with someone. You plus him. Suddenly he is a minus sign. Disappeared. Not only him, but that third thing created, the marriage, broken as simply and loudly as a plate shattering on a tile floor. That greater-than-the-sum entity of plans, past, ambitions, sorrows, ecstasy, on and on. Everything *we* were. Dust unto dust. Elementary, but she can't grasp the fact. She rotated her foot to shake loose the pain stabbing her knee. Maybe that's why I lost my knee, she thought. One-legged me.

Breathe in, breathe in.

Her attention swung back to the high-ceilinged dining room with the large window onto a knot garden and a thin white wedge of the hospice unit. Is it just the formal décor, the Williamsburg style that keeps everyone stilled? Corner cabinets filled with silver compotes and crystal water glasses, the worn-thin Oriental rug, and the needlepoint bottoms on repro Chippendale chairs. Were the patterns on the chair bottoms all local flora? Someone's wife put her eyes out over those. Ah, Camille decided, all this says old, enduring, family. And most everyone here is a woman alone.

• • •

"SEVENTEEN, WE'RE ALL HERE, AND I welcome you heartily to C Meadows." Folding chairs supplemented the armchairs and sofas in the great living room, where Blair Griffin stood in front of the fireplace looking down on those gathered this morning to hear about life at the Meadows, to take a little tour, have lunch, and to decide whether to purchase units. The lunch would be special, a frisée salad and crab cakes, with a respectable chardonnay and an almond tart for dessert. Some would buy today. It was in her court. She smiled at the faces looking up at her. All were white except for an elegant woman in a purple sari shot with metallic thread, a Japanese woman with a walker, and an African American man leaning on a cane topped with an ivory horse head. "There's a chair," she said, motioning to him. One couple appeared to be just at the age fifty-five entry point. "Everyone comfortable? Let's get started. If it's time to turn a page, we hope you will love what you see here today."

Susan focused on the screen over the fireplace as appealing photographs seamlessly replaced each other, Ken Burns style. Exercise class in an indoor pool, then flowered chaise longues around an outdoor pool. Art class, a woman spinning clay into a pot. Two elderly women tottering down a garden path, dining room scenes with everyone raising a toast, the big house in snow lighted for Christmas, four youngish residents playing cards on a terrace: the active lifestyle beautifully curated.

A small movement along the baseboard caught Susan's eye and a black roach catapulted into the heat vent. "Seasonal menus," Hillary Clinton was saying. What was her name? Blair. "Chef Amos invites everyone to help take care of the vegetable garden. It's early yet, but by June, the garden is humming!" Susan's interest quickened. Up came photos of four women on yellow foam kneelers pulling weeds. Two others tying up beans on a wire pyramid. Susan looked around the room. Well-dressed women, mostly, with easy-to-care-for haircuts and little makeup. What would the world look like without hair coloring? She guessed everyone was fifty-five to eighty. Divorced? Mostly widowed? They wore casual sweaters and loose pants (Eileen Fisher?), or flattering wrap dresses, with a few wearing the die-hard Chapel Hill anti-style denim jumpers or shapeless long skirts with Birkenstocks, letting their gone-gray hair just hang and their faces show what the weather had done to them.

She remembered when one of the new young salesmen at Ware Properties mistook her for a colleague. "I'm not Katie," she corrected him. "I'm Susan." He laughed. "All you middle-aged agents look alike." It was then that she got the edgy haircut, revamped her wardrobe, started wearing bright colors with blingy costume jewelry and higher heels. She was the only person in the room in red, except for the vest of the man nodding off (narcolepsy?) three seats down from her.

"That's a glimpse," Blair concluded. "Let's each introduce ourselves and then visit the units. After that, we'll go see what Chef Amos has for us. Just say a few words to let us know who you are, and your interests. Thank you for coming, and I look forward to talking with everyone. Any questions, just ask. Let's start with you." She gestured at Camille, who rose and glanced around the room.

"I'm Camille Trowbridge. I taught—part time—in the art history department at the university until five years ago. I was married to Charles Trowbridge and . . . He. I lost him last year. We have a son who's married and I have one grandchild. I like gardening, travel, and I'd be interested in the art classes. I used to paint a long time ago and still think of myself as a painter. Oh, I love reading and have been in the same book club for twenty-five years." She shrugged, smiled, and sat down. God, she thought. That's it. She hadn't even said she liked to walk on the beach for miles, play tennis, watch Netflix with Charles after a good dinner and a bottle of wine, go to consignment and antique shops, fly up to Washington for exhibits. Liked to straighten closets and bookshelves, take baths, spend hours in the library, make soup, place bulb orders every late summer, write long emails to friends, water the grass on summer evenings, read *Pippi Longstocking* to Ingrid. The book club? It hasn't met in over a year. And the painting? She'd quit teaching to try again, and is still putting off even buying supplies. She felt exhausted. The knee thing has been going on too long. And it's not healing as fast as the doctor said. He made it sound routine. Well, maybe for him it was but it wasn't for her, and it was scary, too. She'd read over and over about that first fall, harbinger of all to come. For a year, when she climbed stairs her knee had crunched like Velcro pulling apart, and then one day it buckled as she loaded groceries into the trunk. Eventually, inevitably: surgery. Next, she foresaw, the step-in shower and the downstairs bedroom. Ha, next the retirement center.

She realized she hadn't heard the next few intros, but Susan stood up, her flashy red outfit a cardinal among wrens. "Hey, everyone. I'm Susan Ware, born and bred here in Chapel Hill. I'm single—my husband died three years ago. Some of you probably bought a house from him. I'm still selling real estate but am thinking of quitting to pursue other interests. Those interests? Gardening. Anything to do with flowers. If I had it to do over, I'd be a landscape designer. Also, please don't laugh, I'm into fishing on the coast, and I like trying all the new restaurants that are popping up in Durham. I have two grown daughters, both on the West Coast."

These weird summaries. Peepholes. Camille liked Susan right off. So, she's alone. No mention of a current partner. Maybe if she were my neighbor here, it would be fun. She and Julia Hadley, too. What about the elegant Indian woman? Or the one who just spoke, Catherine something. Willowy and sharp-featured in an interesting way, her nose like a quartz arrowhead. Catherines were usually solid and this one was moving down here from Connecticut. Almost surely, she said, she would be signing on for a cottage today. First impressions are mysterious, how they happen quickly and certainly.

Camille hadn't heard anyone else that she felt a pull toward. Crass, hearty, diffident, morose, oversharing, timid, sweet, earnest, condescending—everyone put forth one quality, it seemed, and within a moment a reaction quickly set. Or perhaps it was more primitive, as Charles always had insisted: all attraction is based on smell.

Now it was Julia's turn.

"I'm Julia Hadley. I'm from Savannah, and I've moved here only recently. I-I was married. I now mainly spend my free time reading because I'm deciding what to do next." Oh, no, how lame. A drop of sweat trickled down her backbone. She pressed on. "I love to cook and that's my passion—food. That's how I've spent my career. I worked as an acquisitions editor at Mulberry Press. They publish beautifully produced books on food, not only cookbooks but cultural history, too, like life on the rice plantations. I also still do their recipe testing." Oh, enough. Julia hurried on. "Ah, I like opera, photography, and sailing." She sat down abruptly, as if she didn't want to say another word. Sailing. She used to like sailing. Not now.

Camille listened. The Indian woman was a heart surgeon who had to quit working because of early Parkinson's. Another woman who looked like an older Audrey Hepburn was a psychologist who for years evaluated death-row inmates. Big-boned Bitsy ran a moving company for twenty years. Most everyone who spoke had worked; three claimed the title "homemaker." Two described themselves as cancer survivors, and one mentioned her heart transplant. Freshman orientation it's not, Camille thought. No one says they love Jack Kerouac, or that they'd spent the summer hiking the Appalachian Trail.

She walked out for the tour with Susan and Julia. Small signs showed the cottages' names: Vinca, Larkspur, Azalea, Marigold, Lantana, Zinnia. Unlike the first two units they saw, both rather generically furnished like a chain hotel suite, Morning Glory was an end unit, which allowed a view over the meadow and a side porch, along with the front garden. "Someone really likes narcissi," Camille noticed, "and several varieties of them."

A hummingbird buzzed the purple throat of a hanging fuchsia. "Look! Bring on the hummingbirds! They really know how to make this place appealing." Susan bent to smell one double narcissus that she knew to be fragrant. "Nicely done. Look at the hyacinths pushing up. Julia, can you see yourself on the porch, listening to 'Nessun Dorma' and rocking into old age?"

Julia nudged Camille as they toured the interior. "Who wouldn't like this little nest, huh?" If it were not lived in by someone off on vacation in Bermuda, she thought, she would plunk down her savings right now, run back to where she was housesitting for a suitcase, and be cooking by nightfall. "I love the colors she's used, that kind of icy melon with the sage—and that big comfy creamy white sofa." All the cottages had open plans—large living area, corner kitchen with a chopping block island and wine storage beneath, plenty of room for a table, a midsized bedroom, surprisingly luxe bath, good storage. "I'd like to be whipping egg whites in that big copper bowl. Look at that!" The walls above the workspace were entirely covered with copper pots.

"I'm smitten," Camille admitted. As soon as she said that, her lungs deflated with a deep breath. Actually, the place looked miniature, as though recognizing that when you're old you are to be reduced. Drink me, she thought, suddenly feeling too tall and ungainly.

The last unit they visited looked so dreary that she wondered why it was shown at all. An enormous TV dominated the living room, with an equally enormous recliner parked in front of it. Bare floors, nothing on taupe walls, stacks of newspapers by the fireplace unsmudged by any soot. "I guess we're seeing it because of the two-bedroom floor plan," Julia said, glancing at the bare kitchen. Blair rushed them through, saying something about the owner not settling in yet and directing them toward the view of a small pond where ducks glided about.

Everyone loved the vegetable garden behind a white fence with an electrical wire ringing the top to keep out raccoons and deer. Rows of frilly lettuces ready to harvest, asparagus fronds waving behind clumps of healthy herbs, and grapevines sprawling across a long arbor unfurling tender yellow-green leaves. Rich furrows looked ready to plant as soon as the soil warmed.

At lunch, Camille sat next to Blair. Everything was carefully, delicately seasoned and very tasty. "What's your impression, Mrs. Trowbridge, or may I call you Camille?"

"Oh, please! Of course. Everything seems perfect, just perfect. If this kind of situation is what you need."

"Can you see yourself living here, really thriving here?"

"It's fascinating to contemplate. I guess I'll pay attention to how I feel when I'm back home today—see what that's like."

This one obviously won't leap today, Blair surmised. She stirred her iced tea. No chardonnay for her with all the work left to be done. "Most everyone who moves here wishes they'd done it sooner."

Camille looked down the table for Susan and Julia. Susan was talking to the man in the red vest, happily awake now, and Julia at the end of the table seemed to be looking at her companions left and right but not speaking. Maybe she was savoring every bite of the succulent crab and the tender greens with buttermilk dressing.

CAMILLE, JULIA, AND SUSAN GOT off the shuttle at the same stop. The streets swarmed with students in T-shirts and shorts, as sure as daffodils a sign of spring. "My house is just a four-block walk from here," Susan said. "Is it too early for a glass of wine? I would love to talk! Then I can drive you home."

A Soft Duvet

CAMILLE DIDN'T KNOW WHY SHE left the clock on Charles's bedside table, or why she continued to sleep on the other side rather than in the middle. She had to roll over in the night and tap the face to see at what god-awful hour she'd awakened without the slightest chance of falling asleep again. She squinted at the luminous red 3:07, slid out of the covers, and lay on top of the cloud-soft duvet. She concentrated on floating on the downy pillows, arms out (plenty of room), fingers, toes, hair, every part floating (except that leaden right knee). She felt sublimely comfortable, raggedly awake.

If she moved the clock, that would mean Charles would not smack off the alarm at seven a.m. He would not anyway, that she knew, but did not know. She stared at the black squares of the window panes, watching one burning white planet traverse the middle glass and cross out of the frame. Like us, she thought. Brief passage of light. Speck. Then she sighed, tired of this stubborn default thought of death. Anything could set her off: flowers wilting in vases, the evening news of school shootings and terror, the crazy frizzy-headed woman who grabbed her sleeve at the grocery store and said, "I'm a survivor," when clearly she was not.

She willed herself to think of something positive. Today was good. She met Susan and Julia! Susan's house on Hillsborough Road was one that Camille, driving by, often had admired. A 1930s cottage expanded over time by several professors. Small rooms, intimate with southern folk art and Parisian taffeta draperies and thin kilims. Quirky girl, Susan, kneeling at the coffee table, pouring big glasses of New Zealand sauvignon.

Camille couldn't remember when she'd last made a new friend. For a couple of hours, they'd laughed together, big laughing, not just polite laughing.

"Why are those retirement places always called 'meadows'?" Susan had asked.

When Julia responded, "Because it's where you're put out to pasture," they all laughed.

"Do you think you're going to move there, sell this fantastic place?" Camille asked. She *could* imagine Susan in the Morning Glory unit with the appealing garden.

"I can and can't see it. Can you? It's like you're checking in where there's no checkout. Oh, sunny now, everyone going to water yoga, pottery class, and pulling up weeds for the chef."

"Yeah," Julia said, "I was always ready to go home after the second week of camp. I really didn't want another braided lariat or plaster ballerina. But maybe it would be like college without the classes."

"Or maybe like house arrest without the ankle monitor."

"Gawd! Would it be like that? There are many accomplished, intellectual people out there, mostly women. Vibrant, too. They must not think so." Camille held out her glass for another splash. "Or maybe they're immensely practical people. What was it Blair said? It sounded benign, 'ongoing care as we progress along the continuum of aging,' yes, that's what she said. Realistic people."

"Continuum of aging! That's just it, eeek, a mind-set. And

remember she jokingly, ha-ha, said residents call the place 'The Bubble.'" Susan emptied a bag of cashews into a bowl. "The place *is* pretty, but does it seem like the next big thing? Do you think you can breathe inside a bubble?"

Julia was ambivalent. "I love the place—and do I need sanctuary?—but do I want possibly thirty years of it? Hell, forty. I may live to be a hundred."

Camille agreed. "I think there's a lockstep set up and we're supposed to find ourselves marching along. However, the place proposes a pleasant answer to that ugly question, 'What if I am alone?'"

"When you put it like that—yes, it's feasible. But thirty years. Obviously, we may well have a huge hunk of time to invent. What if you're one of those at ninety-three who's still in a book club, getting your hair done, and shopping the online sales at Saks?"

Susan's Welsh terrier, Archie, barked to go out. "Maybe we've overreacted," Julia wondered. She picked up her jacket. "Let's do talk more. I'm stupid with confusion about many things! Can you come to my house for dinner tomorrow? I'm house-sitting while I figure out what to do. More on that later."

CAMILLE AND CHARLES'S WIDE CIRCLE of friends began to dissolve about five years back. A strange movement started happening that reminded her of her early twenties, when you *knew* you'd keep in touch forever, but everyone suddenly scattered and took up new places. Recently, a few friends had died early. Horrible that Bing fell down a flight of stairs, and ebullient Alice felt one hard pang in her side and was Stage IV with pancreatic cancer. Little rocks on the moon are examined minutely, but not the thin wall of Alice's sleek abdomen. Daisy was now far gone in dementia; best friends Frieda and Juan moved to a retirement community in Asheville, and almost at the same time Ellen and Vick—so many great trips together—bought a condo with a glass lanai overlooking Santa Rosa beach. *Come anytime. We miss you.* Colleagues fell away as the force of propinquity evaporated; after the job ends, gradually you're not invited and you don't invite.

Disappeared friends fill Camille's contact list. She needs to delete, delete, delete. Neighbors she and Charles often had drinks with turned weirdly extremist and thought schoolteachers should carry weapons and Muslims were taking over the country. At Charles's memorial, they suggested she get a gun to feel safe. "Well, you're sweet to think of me," she'd replied, though she wanted to say, *Get a gun to feel safe? That's an oxymoron, you idiots!* She avoids a few acquaintances, too: the overly solicitous Mindy Sampson, whose condolences always included a reminder of how fortunate she, Mindy, was to have her Bill still on the golf course every Saturday. "I know you're not thinking of anything now except for getting through the day, but you *will* find happiness again, maybe through web dating. I know someone even older than you who met her match that way. They're on a cruise right now."

Camille felt alarmed at Mindy's opaque blather. "I'd hate cruising," she'd replied, thinking, *Now if she mentions the seven stages of grief I will have to smack her.*

After Charles died, Camille was aware of her rising intolerance toward most of the living.

She always knew that anyone can be eliminated in an instant, but now she knew viscerally. She did not want to feel this way, knowing the root: her rage that Charles was gone while the rest of us are still standing. Some just get dreary, Camille thought, as they age. At this juncture, age sixty-nine, face it, she wanted to avoid people who'd previously slightly annoyed her. They now seemed irksome.

4:20. HER ROOM TURNS CHILLY and Camille slips back under the duvet. New smart thermostats with minds of their own seem capriciously to decide on no heat in the middle of the night. Usually she had to wait out an insomniac night, running through memories (*I'm home*, he called out), but she dozed, snapped awake, dozed again.

The clean resinous smell of fresh-cut pine wood invaded her dream, or was she sleeping? Boards, a pile of them, and she is nailing them together into a long box. She paints the box in joyous colors, bright aqua; images flit by, she will paint orange sea urchins, a Greek blue evil eye, many-rayed suns. The bright, sharp hits of the hammer thud along her backbone. She closes her eyes at each strike—no, I can't be sleeping, she thinks. Egyptian mummy lids with hieroglyphics, marble battles on sarcophagi—ah, yes, I am building my own coffin. She lacquers the boards a brilliant gold, with mauve mallow flowers and gloomy weeping willows always carved on old New England graves; she continues painting, a compass at the head, a ring of small keys, the box solid, rectangular, and, yes, smooth corners. Five feet, eight inches, just big enough. Am I sleeping, she wonders. That blue rubber beach ball I had when I was small, white rabbit, rattlesnake under the steps, swirled indigo marble of earth seen from the moon. She's painting quickly, precisely, freely. A lighter layer of thought imposes. Not yet. I can upend the box and use it for storage. Nail in pegs for shelves to store blankets and Mother's Wedgwood, and then, clever, am I not clever, later the four shelves can become the lid to close the box.

9:00. CHARLES HAS OVERSLEPT. THE windows glow with dewy April light. Late. But Camille's hand swipes the cold side of the bed. Empty. She is half a body, cleaved down the middle. Her left side is missing. She must get up; she has physical therapy for her damn knee. The dream returns, that magnificent, horrible painted box. Charles was good at interpreting dreams. He always made them even more absurd than they were. What would he have thought? Not today. Not any day, Camille thought. We won't know what he would have said, will we? She threw on her gym clothes and laced her shoes. Her knee felt better. No, Charles. I already know what the dream means.

Exile

JULIA DROVE EARLY TO THE Carrboro market because she especially wanted the olive bread from Chicken Scratch Farm, and a carton of their pale blue and malt and ivory eggs. From the minute Susan dropped her off at the professor's house late yesterday, she'd started planning the menu for dinner with her new friends.

The blank weeks of the past three months spiral behind her. She wakes up full of resolve. By the end of her second coffee, the day seems endless. She knows no one in town but wait staff—and now Susan and Camille—and has no idea how to change that. When she saw the double-page ad in *Chapel Hill Magazine* for Cornwallis Meadows, what drove her to sign up for the tour was the appeal of structured days alongside others living structured days. No one else's drama controlling the hours. Interesting things to do, friends, calm, a place to get her bearings. Who expected to be exiled from the life they'd made at age sixty? No, she'll be only fifty-nine this year but the rounded 6-0 facing her in 2016, that infancy of old age, already seems upon her. Sometimes she wakes up in the mornings feeling that she is being slung centrifugally on a carnival ride, pushed by g-force, and unable to counteract the backward gravity. Free-floating anxiety, that's all.

She walks early in the mornings and learns the streets lined with houses that look as though interesting lives take place inside. She bookmarks food blogs and reads the cheery banter of upbeat women who seem to spend half their days hovering over the stove, and the other half on social media posting stagy photos of plated food. A few inspire her. The stack of books from Mulberry Press, where she was an editor, keeps her company. She spends a couple of hours every day testing recipes for their history of southern relishes and pickles, the last project she acquired before she left. Paul and his son, also Paul, still send queries and share the designs for ongoing projects. They miss her and she misses them terribly.

At lunch, she tries lauded restaurants in Durham, food trucks, and Mexican dives, many so delicious. Some nights she has dinner at Crook's Corner, the friendly mecca of southern food, where she sits at the bar and orders shrimp and grits. She signed up for a spin class but quit. Cycling like that emphasized the obvious: I'm spinning my wheels.

JULIA IS IN CHAPEL HILL courtesy of Professor Hubert Ganyon, her sophomore year Humanities III teacher at UNC. He offered her his house while he travels in Turkey on a grant. She couldn't quite remember his project, something to do with Greeks exiled there, a study of an abandoned village where they eventually were driven out. She had attended a lecture he gave in Savannah, noticed by chance in the paper, and had ended up having coffee with him after his remarks.

When he inquired about her life, she'd somehow mentioned that her marriage was unraveling (understatement), and that she had such fond memories of her college years in Chapel Hill. He was tiny now, bony, with a great flare of white, stand-up hair and eyes still as blazing as when he lectured about the Roman expansion across wide swaths of the world. A knowing look, too, in those pewter, glittering eyes, as she told him something of her life since his memorable class.

"If you want to leave, or need to, this is serendipity. I'll be gone almost a year. The trip is my long-awaited retirement gift to myself. I'm going while I can maneuver those stony hillsides. My house is in walking distance of everything. There's not even a cat. Nothing to do but keep the lights on, sort the mail, and remind the gardener to weed."

Those unexpected gifts that come your way—best to take them. His offer was the impetus Julia needed to escape the excruciating, ludicrous situation her life had become.

She did not tell him about Lizzie, she could not speak of her Lizzie, just an abbreviated version about her husband, Wade, who'd flipped, who'd betrayed her, who'd lost his way, who was so far beyond her reach that she hardly could look at him. What confused her most was how foolish he seemed. In the face of what happened, *this* is how he reacted. Well, Julia thought, and I reacted by disappearing. Both of us a mess.

IN HIS EARLY EIGHTIES, HUGH lived alone in a book-filled, time-warped house just off campus. Two closed-off bedrooms of children long fled, still furnished with camp sailing flags and baseball trophies; a downstairs with high ceilings, old-world green brocade sofas to sink into, shutters letting in golden ladders of light, and only three photographs of the wife lost years ago to leukemia. Julia wondered if the high-necked lace wedding dress might still be wrapped in tissue in the attic. Hugh, young and vital, gazed at his bride in the photo, obviously mad about her. Taller, she looked out, head tossed back, into some confident future. A future confirmed every day by Hugh.

The house was neat, not dusty as she feared, thanks to the enthusiastic work of Belinda, who came twice a week and cleaned furiously for three hours. Julia spent hours browsing his books and moving on to the next one on the shelf. *Medea*, that rage certainly rang bells. Didn't the ancient Greeks know everything? She dipped into Jung and copied in her notebook his idea that when a change needs to occur, someone will appear on the other side of the abyss and offer a hand. She read *Broken Borders* by Kit Raine, a biography of the indomitable Freya Stark. Traveling alone way back when into Arabian lands that no woman at all and few men had entered, she seemed braver than any Hollywood superhero. The Freya quotes set her dreaming. *When Mehmet had given us our supper in the cabin of Elfin, we climbed into the dinghy and rowed about the southern harbor under the full moon. Three of the three hundred fishing caïques of Budrum were there beside us, the day's catch of sponges spread out on the cut stone quay-side of Triopium. The boats themselves squatted dark in the headland shadow, their rough and tattered sailors all asleep. A haunted, a magical remoteness lay on the sleeping town . . .*

I would like to be given my supper by Mehmet in the *Elfin* cabin, Julia dreamed, then to row at night, see the moon's beams crossing like swords underwater, and far below ancient foundation stones "gnawed by the sea for more than two thousand years."

She'd not read so much since college. This is why I'm here, she thought. I need a reading sabbatical. I need new ideas, stimulation, possibilities. When she fell asleep on the sofa, she dreamed she was rowing but not moving. She looked down and saw the anchor chain wrapped around her ankle.

She'd expected the rich trove of books, but the kitchen was a surprise, updated during Hugh's romance in his seventies with a younger woman who cooked. He'd said the romance hadn't lasted—she fell for a sous chef at the Carolina Inn—but Julia was grateful for a robust stove and the granite counters everyone preferred then. Had the girlfriend instigated the investment in All-Clad cookware not even scorched on the bottoms?

Julia brought with her from Savannah a box of Mulberry Press cookbooks and her own knives, her car a jumble of books, sweaters, an envelope of photos, letters, and her laptop flung on the backseat. She can hear Wade shouting as she backed out of the garage. "Julia, get back here right now. You are going nowhere!" He clutched a crowbar in his hand, taken up from the tool table. Raised it. Surely he would not hit her, though he might hit the car. He gripped the iron so tightly that veins bulged all up his arm as she jettisoned backward into the street. Savannah was quickly in the rearview mirror. She shook halfway through South Carolina. Now, she lived every day with the relief of emptiness in the lively university town where life went on with her invisible participation. She did not open Wade's emails or answer his calls. Someday she'd go back for the rest of her loved objects. She didn't care about the furniture or the house, even though she grew up there, but she did want her bowls and platters. And her mother's china, the rest of the photographs. The house legally belongs to her father. He turned it over to her and Wade not long after Julia's mother died. He always said they could live there forever, then pass it on to Lizzie. Lizzie, doyen of a stately piece of the Savannah patrimony. Bizarre in the extreme.

SHE UNLOADED THE BOUNTY FROM the market: a bunch of ranunculus and freesias, eggplant and peppers to stack with mozzarella and tomatoes, big knobby garlic, the good bread, eggs, and a plump chicken to roast with lemon. She will cook! She will spend the morning roasting garlic for her wonderful savory soup, thumbing through her cookbooks to find an inspiring dessert, setting the table with the dead wife's good coin silver and charming floral china.

In Dreams Begin Responsibilities

"SUSAN! THIS IS ODD! BOTH of us living here for decades without ever meeting. And one day after we do meet, we run into each other." They're at A Southern Season. Susan is bending over the purple and white nicotianas and the mixed spring bouquets in the flower section just as Camille pushes her cart toward the cash register with cheeses to take to Julia's dinner.

"You know, we've probably passed each other dozens of times. Do you think Julia would like these"—Susan raises a handful of the fragrant nicotianas out of the water—"or one of those orchids?" She tilts her head, considering.

Camille had seen Ware Properties signs on houses forever and had a vague memory of meeting Susan's husband, Aaron Ware, at a political fund-raiser. Tall, well-dressed; the image goes blank other than that. Memorable suit, though, well cut and fitted. Maybe Susan had shopped for him. She has no recollection of seeing Susan. If she had, she'd recall someone with such a flair. Camille admires Susan's hip gray jacket stamped with black medallions, urban and a little tough, short black skirt and strappy heels. "The delicate ones suit Julia. But maybe a long-lasting or-chid might be better."

"Kind of generic, but they *are* cheerful. I always touch them to see if they're fake."

"I've been looking forward to her dinner." Camille doesn't say that all day she'd been excited about seeing her new friends again. Sitting around with them at Susan's last night, just chatting, had been *fun*. She hadn't had fun in, how long?

"Me, too. See you there in a few." Susan feels a bolt of exhila-ration for the night ahead. The three of them, each on the verge of changes. And much to learn about each other. Susan senses Ju-lia's damage, and that Camille still feels sucker-punched by her husband's death. Is it easier for me? she wonders. Aaron has been gone three years. She lived in a vacuum for a year, and then one day she stepped outside and a small bird on a twig began to sing ferociously, a song far stronger than the tiny body reasonably could project. Susan listened, transfixed, and after that life quietly started to resume, not the life she had before, but a life that would continue. Susan then ran the company, but sold the building and the business last year. She stays on for a few clients. Neither of their girls, Eva and Caroline, was interested in selling houses. Adopted as infants from China, the girls had challenges growing up in the South. Susan always made sure they had the best birthday parties with ponies and clowns, wore the cutest clothes, and went to the best and most protected private schools. Her strategy—she made them enviable. Still, they fled to California for college and ever since, they've been happily launched in their IT careers in the multicultural Bay Area, where they feel less alien.

What she's looking for is the next big thing. Though the girls will object, she's actually considering a small nest at Cornwallis Meadows. She'd feel free to travel. Free from the sharp memories in every square inch. Married to a dynamo real estate broker, she was married also to some deal always pending. Most of the trips

they did take had business attached. They'd managed a few flying vacations with their daughters, but mainly their getaways took
place on Figure Eight Island, where Aaron had sold initial plots by
the dozens when the barrier island off the North Carolina coast
began to develop. He scored a beachfront lot for himself, where
they built an iconic gray shingle house with a long porch. Originally planned for a long-term investment, Sand Castle became
their haven only two hours from home. They could load the car
after work and be grilling burgers by dark.

AARON, SIX YEARS OLDER, STARTED showing signs of dementia at sixty-five. He worked to conceal lapses and lost words.
Eva and Caroline, home for holidays, insisted, "Everyone forgets
things, you've just stored a million more names and facts than
most people—your hard drive is overloaded." And, "Daddy, I'm
going to sign you up for these word challenge programs, KenKen
and Lumosity. They're fun and keep you agile."

Denial, denial, until Susan started finding notes and lists he
depended on. She became more and more despairing as smart,
smart Aaron stared at a milk bottle or an onion, casting about
for the noun. Early onset, the doctor said. They told no one.
They told each other, *This will be slow, there are good years left. New
drugs will help.* He took the prescriptions that made him sick. He
started washing them down with a couple of hits of bourbon.
Who could blame him? He had to have antidepressants, otherwise he couldn't stand to get out of bed. Count backward by
sevens? He wept. He used to add three-column numbers in his
head. After a couple of complicated years, they restructured the
company so he could retire. The crushing depression lifted as he
forgot he was succumbing to dementia. Then, the coup de grace.
Aaron's younger brother needed a bone marrow transplant and
Aaron offered to be the donor. What did he have to lose? He was

required to undergo an MRI to qualify. A symptomless tumor showed on his liver, a blot already the size of the onion Aaron couldn't name.

Susan was stunned: he diminished daily before her eyes. He was dead mercifully fast. Susan was sixty-one; Aaron sixty-seven. Too soon. The girls took Susan with them to California for three months and she went back and forth between their apartments in Berkeley and Mill Valley, blinded in the harsh light glancing off the Pacific Ocean. Inside the barbed pain lodged in her rib cage, secretly there was a burning votive of sad relief. Healthy Aaron could have lived for years, descending further and further into the no-man's-land of Alzheimer's, pulling her life down the well after him. Of the many fearful prospects of living with an erased Aaron, she had a recurring horror of sex if he had no idea who she was. Was sex ever forgotten? She didn't want to know.

At home again, she immediately donated all his real estate suits, all the dress shirts, jogging and golf clothes to the homeless rescue shelter. She began volunteering there two days a week. She processed the defeated or belligerent men who exited during the day. She made medical appointments, arranged transportation, and checked them in before curfew. Sometimes one of them would be wearing an Aaron suit, still with the jaunty silk square in the breast pocket.

SUSAN PLACED THE SPRING FLOWERS in her cart. Should she buy the nicotianas for Julia, too? She smiled as she remembered Aaron leaning across the table at the expensive New York restaurant, saying *Sweetheart, why not have the lobster* and *the cracked crab?* She remembered something else he said; she'll share it tonight for a laugh. She grabbed the nicotianas, then decided to dash to the back for a bottle of very good wine.

• • •

WHEN CAMILLE WALKED INTO JULIA'S house and heard the name Hubert Ganyon, she remembered him well. She'd loved auditing his seminar on Greek and Roman art when she first started teaching. She and Julia discovered they'd been on campus at the same time, Julia as a student, when Camille, newly married and holding her fresh MFA, began teaching art history. Hugh later moved on to Princeton but had kept his house for retirement. "I can still see him in the classroom, standing beside the slide of Hermes by Praxiteles. He was totally silent before such a beautiful thing, just let the class stare, take in that perfect form. Professor Ganyon was, of course, young and gorgeous himself. I had a crush on him."

"It was a coincidence that we met for coffee just when he was looking for a house sitter and I was looking for a speedy exit from Savannah."

Susan noticed that Julia never mentioned her husband, she always said she "left Savannah." He must still be there? "And what coincidences! We three meeting in an unlikely spot. We could have gone on different days and never met."

JULIA OPENED THE LONG SHUTTERS and lighted candles on the sills. Mellow light illuminated the spines of books, the draperies' faded rose colors, the faces of the three women: Julia, pale and attentive, all silky taupe and loose sable curls; Camille, every feature defined, and blue, blue eyes intense and focused, her long legs curled up on the sofa; Susan, girlish and angular, ready to laugh, sprung with energy. She launched right in. "This is totally spontaneous—just tell me if I'm crazy—we've known each other all of two days—but I would love for you two to come with me next weekend to Figure Eight. We—I've—got a house smack on the water. The beach is wide and usually quite empty on spring weekends. I'm not a great cook but I really can do breakfast, even ham biscuits. We can walk, cook or go out to this great fish place, talk about what we want to happen, not just what we think should happen."

"Or what someone else thinks should happen." Camille sighed, thinking of her daughter-in-law's grim little smile.

"I just remembered a few minutes ago something Aaron said once when a client wanted to be shown property in a retirement community. He teased her out of it by saying, 'You want to sign on for a luxury cruise down the River Styx?'" Everyone laughed.

"I would love to go to your beach house. My son and his wife, maybe mainly his wife, are convinced that I need to 'simplify,' as they put it. When Charlie called to see how I liked Cornwallis Meadows, he seemed disappointed that I didn't fall in love." A small pressure was building in her mind. Being older, being alone made those around you want to see you walk some walk they imagine appropriate. She didn't feel obsolete in the least and was not going to abide others' good, wrong intentions.

"Well, without doubt, the Meadows would simplify life enormously." Julia uncorked the pinot noir Susan brought. "Remember those croissants? And the decent chardonnay at lunch? Remember Morning Glory?"

"I also remember the dismal Barcalounger in that brown place with the newspapers stacked everywhere," Camille said. Her position was beginning to solidify.

They all laughed. "Do we want to simplify?" Susan wondered. "That is the question. What if we wanted *more* complication? Why this pressure to simplify now? I did love the kitchen at Morning Glory. But wasn't there a funny smell in there?"

"I would absolutely prefer a weekend at the beach to making any decision. I'll bring a big beef stew. That's the question, Susan—to simplify; that's kind of the crux. I'm thinking that's issue number one for me. I've escaped a big chaos in Savannah. A calm day to me seems a good day." Julia slipped into the kitchen.

She was attracted to the steady groove of the Meadows, even though she was the youngest of them and could conceivably start any complex life she wanted.

At Julia's table, they praised her garlic soup, the lemon chicken, smashed potatoes, and tiny green beans with tarragon and crumbled bacon.

Camille passed the platter of chicken around. "I had the weirdest dream last night. This came from nowhere, like most nutty dreams." As she described the coffin and the images, she had a flash of insight. Maybe the dream did come from somewhere. Was she even sleeping? "After I nailed together the box, I saw this palette of brilliant colors in front of me, and what I'm remembering now is how *happy* I was to paint designs all over the box. The sequence must have lasted hours. How long do dreams last—are they all instantaneous? I have no idea. But what a dismal task, building my own coffin. That's *too* negative. Why would I dream that? Then I upend the thing for shelves. Such a practical move— blankets and sheets, I think. Why? I'm puzzling this one out."

"At the tour, didn't you say you used to paint? Maybe these were symbols that meant something to you from paintings," Julia said, "but the coffin bit is a little chilling."

"I studied studio art in college, I even got an MFA at UVA. Then I thought I'd be a painter, but getting married, having a child, all that totally derailed me and I loved teaching my one or two courses a semester. We'd go up to New York. My artist friends were already showing. I'd come home feeling sick. Everything seemed trivial. One gallery exibited hotel notepad doodles, cross-dressed Barbie and Ken dolls; another prestigious gallery showed a room full of tires. Then at home, they were showing kitsch. Some good landscapes but mainly dreck. And life was, oh, full. I was happy with the house, the dinners, the whole thing. For a while, I had a little painting room off the garage. I was out there recently and found two boxes of desiccated art supplies. Finally tossed them! Truth is, I lost sight."

A silence. Then Julia breathed out a long sigh. "Well. There you have it, my friend. Obviously, *obviously*, painting is the big message of this. And the coffin, you readied it for burial out of despair, feeling that life's over, but then you're painting like crazy and standing that box up for *storage*—the housewife's obsession!"

"Well, Miss Freud!" But Camille was intrigued. "What did you dream?"

"I was in a cabin in the woods and a huge bear was trying to rip into the window. Somehow I know the frame would withstand only a hundred-and-twenty-five-pound force."

"Your exact weight, no doubt," Susan ventured. "Maybe you're the bear and also yourself inside." Julia served a salad of ephemeral greens with avocado and crisp slivers of cucumber and radish. Susan continued, "While you all were struggling with the forces, I was diving into a huge swimming pool and somersaulting way underwater. Just as I was about to burst, I kept breaking through for gulps of air."

"I like that—freedom and release," Camille observed.

"Who said that every part of the dream is yourself, like if you dream of a house, you're all the rooms?"

"That sounds hopelessly egotistical. I, I, I."

"Wasn't it Jung?" Julia had made some notes about that.

And the night proceeded. Camille and Susan shared their stories, though Julia did not. The lemon soufflé was devoured and the wine emptied to the last drop.

As Julia cleared the table after they left, she turned up the music. Etta James singing "At Last" filled the kitchen, and through the open door to the back garden, spring tree frogs seemed to pick up the beat, screeching into the night. My love has come along. Not a chance, Julia thought. She sang, too, her voice trembly but full of vibrato.

Muse

IT WOULD BE A PITY to quit Margaret, as Colin suggests. (Why does he come up with this idea? Because she made him edgy. Because she stared at him. Because she ridiculed others so he knew she ridiculed us? Because she flew in the face of any accepted idea.) If I did shred her pages, she would be bits of oblivion, she who was vivid. She who was driven. Also, damn it, she who left me the money to have this freedom to write, just as I was on the edge of returning to the U.S. for a teaching job. I would have kept the house, thanks to what's left of the poetry prizes and my inheritance. I could rent to colleagues and friends, still spending summers here. I don't like someone sleeping in my bed. A first-world problem, I know, but one's own creative life is important, too, and to give over two thirds of my life a year would dampen the spirit. I've taught before. Rewarding at times but you do walk into class, open the silver faucet in your throat, and the lifeblood pours out around your feet. Magically, the students do not notice.

For now, Margaret stays.

. . .

"WHAT KIND OF NAME IS that, Miss Kit Raines." Those were the first words Margaret ever spoke to me.

Soon after I bought my gone-to-ruin place in Tuscany in 2003, I was invited to dinner at the apartment of two expatriate Greek women, both translators, stylish in a vintage way and given to quoting poetry, which endeared them to me immediately. We'd met when they introduced themselves in line at the *porchetta* stand.

The Greek women, Ritsa and Vasiliki, lived in an apartment in a vast *palazzo*. The dining room walls and ceiling were covered with frescoes from the time of Napoleon's invasion. A bit funky— the formal table held a line of candles stuck in wine bottles, a taverna moment. Everything was set out on the sideboard and we served ourselves. A hearty vegetable stew and lamb chops. Cold salads with feta, other cheeses, and mounds of fruit. It was a hot night. A pitiful little fan put out a hint of breeze. I was introduced to the other guests: novelists (oh god, Muriel Spark and her partner); William Weaver, the translator; a nonfiction writer whose name I didn't get; a journalist from Torino; and Riccardo, now my friend and the only one left who knew Margaret. Suddenly, I realized that a colony of writers lived in these hills that I thought I'd discovered.

One guest was Margaret Merrill, a writer I had long admired. She'd moved to San Rocco about twenty years ago after living for years in Sicily and Rome. I knew she was in the vicinity and wondered if I'd ever meet her.

I was awed by the company, interested in the sapphic Greeks, and drawn to Margaret Merrill, who wrote about clandestine, convoluted political situations, the raucous lives of workers, women in black, children, and about the insidious infiltration of the Mafia into everyday life. I'd read only one of her political books, *In the Cold Shadow*. What those kinds of informative, investigative books cost the writer! They're published, make a splash or not, and inevitably they drop into an abyss. But her luminous fiction dazzled me. An original for sure, she reminded me of Marguerite Duras, Djuna Barnes, Jean Rhys. That elliptical style. The power of suggestion.

Here she was, taking delicate bites, sipping wine, the woman who chose to live in severest inland Sicily, driving the pen across page after page, recording the toughness, humor, and cunning of the dirt poor. When I read *Labranda*, the novel that percolated up from the ruined postwar South, I knew it was one of those blessed books that I would reread, teach from (when I had to), and pass around to friends. In it, she wrote about a love affair that never could work (married-man thing), but she intertwined the romance with the stories of three families. Their lives were desolate and hard, their humanity shining and strong. She exposed the almost-norm of incest. Little girls were fair game for fathers and uncles. Margaret wrote unsparingly, brutally of the push-pull of the foredoomed love affair and also the fatidic lives. I flashed on her as a great eagle staring down from an aerie. It struck me with the same power as James Agee's *Let Us Now Praise Famous Men*, a book it resembles in its penetration of a time and place. Her photographs matched her prose—reserved and stark. Come to think of it, she must have been influenced by Agee. Shall I ask her?

I always will associate the color blue with Margaret. She's wearing a gossamer voile shirt with a blue evil-eye medallion around her neck. She has the dead-level gaze that I associate with the words *steely intellect*. When she was young those lowered eyelids must have been considered smoldering. Now they looked slightly tortugan. I venture, "I just wondered, are you influenced by James Agee?"

"I certainly hope not," she snaps—do I see a hint of a smile? "He's a bit sincere for me." The way she said "sincere," it almost dripped. She quickly turns back to the famous translator beside her. *Damn.* I look down into my salad and cross my eyes.

By the time the pistachio gelato comes around, a dozen empty wine bottles stand on the table. I join in where I can but this is a lively group of old friends, almost like a family gathering. (I was often chosen in Red Rover, Red Rover for my ability to break into the linked arms.) Together they started migrating from Rome during the terrorist years of the Red Brigades and high Mafia years, and on into the 1980s. They settled in abandoned houses and *palazzo* flats they picked up for nothing and restored. The Greeks haven't restored much; bits of fresco sift down onto the table.

Margaret talks about her research trips to Bulgaria and Russia; she's followed, her room is bugged, a shadowy man on the midnight train to Sofia. A woman whose name I didn't catch talks about a family dispute over publication of her grandfather's correspondence with Winston Churchill. Oh, those papers left behind. What grenades they become. (Note to self: burn all diaries before rigor mortis sets in.)

As the party breaks up Margaret asks about my name. "Well, it's Catherine, of course. Catherine always was my grandmother, so I became Kit." Impulsively, I ask her to dinner on Sunday. Impulsively, because I have no furniture and few dishes, only a rudimentary kitchen with a couple of pots and pans. I do have my mother's silver.

I PICK UP A BLUE-CHECKED cloth at the market to cover a stained marble table the previous owners left behind in the garden. Let's hope the ground stays dry so the table won't sink. Best keep it simple: spinach crêpes (bought in town), chicken breasts rolled with prosciutto, roasted asparagus, and fruit.

Covered and set with the flowers, the table looks quite inviting. Anything would, really, under a pergola dripping with blooming jasmine. Margaret, I learn, completely restored a ruined tower attached to a small stone house. Her writing room at the top of the medieval lookout affords her three-hundred-sixty-degree views of primo Tuscan landscapes. From her early Italian years working with the postwar American Renewal Foundation in

Sicily, where she oversaw a team of teachers and ended up direct-ing the rebuilding of bombed schools (postwar lasted a long time in the South), she has solid technical knowledge of structures as well as the foibles and habits of workers. She was her own contrac-tor. My innocence (ignorance) must be alarming to her. Margaret slightly hesitates before she speaks, as though she might reconsider what she's about to say. But then she lunges in. Right away she starts correcting my Italian. "Please, you must not say *G-O-vannie.* Say *Jo-vannie.* Accent on *vannie.*" She makes you feel that you're being watched. Judged? Probably. But I can tell she likes me. You always read of a twinkle in the eye, but she's the first person I've met who has one. She borrows copies of my poems.

LONG DINNER UNDER THE JASMINE; Margaret blowing smoke rings at the moon, me wedging my knee against the table to keep it from sinking. She starts to sing "Blue Moon" in a moody voice. I sit very still. She goes somewhere. Where? I'm intrigued. She's a writer like me, single. Foreign country. My future? Well, my future does not include the CIA or whatever the Italian secret ser-vice is, as is whispered about her. At the get-go, washing up after she leaves, I know that my sorrow about my mother's fate lifted in Margaret's presence. Mother Muse.

WHERE'S COLIN AT THIS POINT? He's floating out in the ether where we don't know each other. It will be almost two years be-fore he'll pack for Florence, where his London architectural firm has landed an extensive restoration project. As he arrives there, I'll fly in from home, where I've finally settled my mother's es-tate. Colin and I board the same bus into town, and our futures reposition.

• • •

MARGARET REFUSES TO FALL INTO the straightforward narrative I intend. Oh, it's me. (Who can say "It's I"?) Just beyond my grasp is a link. And is there a connection to find with the three women who've lighted in the branches nearby? I expect her to remain stolidly Margaret. Unto herself.

Sand Castle

"UNBELIEVABLE! SUSAN, THIS IS SPECTACULAR!" Julia slid the huge pot of beef bourguignon onto the kitchen counter. Camille struggled with her roll-on and a sack of vegetables. At the door, Susan dropped grocery bags and began opening shutters, letting in the white spring sunlight and the tang of salt air. The kitchen, open to the dining and great rooms, had sweeping views of dunes, beach, and ocean.

"It's always such a big, big *relief* to be here," she said. "I love this place. My whole family does. Did." She opened double doors onto a porch with rockers and a swing. The sound of breaking waves filled the room. Archie, who'd slept the whole way over to the coast, began to bark. "It always seems impossible that you can be unhappy where tides lull you to sleep, and you open your eyes in the morning to those smeary purple sunrises over the ocean. Amazing—it happens every day!"

THEY MADE ANOTHER TRIP TO Susan's car, retrieving Julia's pot of vegetable soup that only sloshed a little in the trunk, various beach bags, the lemon cake Camille baked, and Susan's box of special teas and coffee beans. Camille wasn't surprised at the sloshing. Susan passed two or three cars at once, swerving back as an oncoming car loomed. Camille had noticed Julia, too, casting a glance at the speedometer as it wavered around eighty-five miles per hour. "Aren't there speed traps around here?" Camille finally asked. She wondered if perhaps Susan had a reckless streak.

"I know this road like the palm of my hand. The cops are only out on Sundays along here."

"I don't know the lifeline on your palm; I'm hoping it's not short," Julia joked.

"Okay! My girls always fuss at me." Susan got the message and slowed to seventy-five.

"We are not going to starve, are we?" Julia wiped up the mat in the trunk with paper towels. They'd stopped at Harris Teeter for crabs, wine, and cheeses.

After she settled Julia and Camille in their bedrooms—Eva and Caroline's rooms—just steps from the sand, Susan proposed a long beach walk, lunch, and a rest. Friday, Saturday, Sunday. Three days. Susan had a wild idea she wanted to bring up. She also planned to tackle Aaron's office and the storeroom if she felt motivated. She thought she could be quick with the two file cabinets stuffed with yellowed receipts for washing machine repair, trash pickup, and driveway paving. More onerous: storeroom shelves full of deflated beach rafts and mildewed duvets. Could she ever sell Sand Castle? Eva and Caroline hardly ever visit and when they do they might stay a long weekend. Her younger brother Mike sometimes brings his family up for a week in the summer. Sometimes her cousin Mary and her partner drive up from Atlanta. Has the life seeped out of the place? Occasionally, Susan drives over alone for a few days. Archie chases gulls and runs like mad on the beach. He has to be washed down after every outing, otherwise his hair turns stiff with salt.

A year ago, she brought lanky Willis Sherman, whose house

she sold when he divorced, to Sand Castle for Easter weekend. His wife at age sixty-five up and left him for the lawn maintenance contractor. The wife, Willis told Susan, said she'd been happy enough with him, until the contractor made her laugh. They'd had coffee, then more, and soon she was filing for what she jubilantly called "a silver divorce." Willis wasn't vitally wounded. After the sale of his house closed, he began to ask Susan out for dinner. She enjoyed his mild company, his flashy bow ties, and his thin-lipped self-sufficiency, which apparently had driven the wife crazy. Fine with Susan. She wanted no permanent appendage. Going out with him was a distraction, and then she brought him here, wondering if she wanted to get to know him better.

If she'd toyed with the idea of sleeping with him, she saw the minute he walked in her door that nothing of the sort was going to happen. He seemed like a looming, strange interloper in her sanctuary. His sharp, pointed nose made him look like a giant pelican. He picked up the family's shells in the big glass bowl and she squelched herself from saying, *Don't touch those.*

She showed him to the back guest room, not wanting him in the girls' quarters. He was fine. They had a quiet weekend playing Scrabble and watching movies. She overlooked his baggy shorts and ugly sandals that revealed yellow talon toenails. He liked the dog and the beach walks. Turned out, he made a delicious margarita. She never again answered when his name came up on her phone.

NOW SAND CASTLE FEELS INHABITED. Camille compliments her on the blue and white great room with its ikat-patterned chairs, sisal rug, and octagonal coffee table stacked with travel books and fashion magazines. Julia loves the long trestle table and the sleek kitchen with nothing on the counters. Susan sees through their eyes how fresh and inviting the house still is, not just a repository of memories.

. . .

JULIA UNPACKS HER FEW THINGS and for the first time in three days checks her messages. Automatically she deletes ones from Wade, only two this time, without opening them. Her friends tried to reach her for the first month after she sped out of town, but she never responded and finally they stopped writing, except for the occasional *hoping to see you soon.* She was a scandal but she doesn't care. She'll reach out to them later, she tells herself. One text from her dad. Only he knows the whole story. He's snug in his glass-walled condo on the Savannah River. His text, only a brief *Miss you.*

But here's a message from Alison, her next-door neighbor. Maybe there's something about Lizzie, who'd always loved Alison's menagerie of a house. Alison's kitchen smelled like orange marmalade and spice cake. She reads quickly: *Dear Julia, I am missing you today. We just got a new dog—shaggy unholy mix—who loves to slobber and jump all over you. I'm saying this, my friend, because I don't know what to say. Heaven knows you had reason to leave. I'm sure you know—people knew about him. Wade looks abashed and miserable. Bet you hope he is! I can understand that you want to cut everything off. Just hope it's not forever, Wade or no Wade. I wish I had something good to tell you but I've seen no sign of life at your house, except for W's coming and going. Miss you, Alison.*

Delete.

She misses her dad. At eighty-six, he loves to cook, play tennis, and collect two things, hot pepper sauces and paintings of boats. *Daddy,* she texts, *I'm at a NC beach with two new friends. It's great! Talk next week. Hugs.*

If I can muster the strength, she thinks, I'm going to tell Susan and Camille.

ARCHIE TAKES OFF AS SOON as Susan steps out the door. Fast as his legs can go, he runs toward the waves, plows in and tumbles, rolls in the sand, shakes, then scampers and yelps at sandpipers. Mindlessly elated, he darts and speeds back, barking at their heels. *What's wrong with you, why aren't you splashing and twirling?*

The three women walk to the end of the island, where four houses are sandbagged against erosion. "That must hurt," Camille says, "their investment down the drain. Who would buy these dangerous mansions?"

"It's really sad. Parts of the beach are washing away. Lots of people are planting grasses, hauling in big rocks, putting up those flimsy fences to hold in the sand, but the island still slips away more every year. We're lucky our house sits on a slight rise. I've toyed with the idea of selling Sand Castle—not because of the water level. We're safe for fifty years! It's just—it's not the invigorating place it used to be for me. I love being here with you, but normally I come alone. I eat a lot of ice cream out of the carton and watch stupid TV. Gardening in sand isn't fun. I do still adore the long walks. The peace." On those home-alone weekends, she felt sometimes that the house was breathing and she was not; the house held in all the past while she was fading into a nebulous future.

"You have plenty of time to decide," Camille says.

"Yes, we'll revive it with you—ask anytime." Julia laughs. The wide, empty beach—a boon and a gift. She feels like bounding into the surf herself and would if it were not sixty degrees with a sharp-edged breeze coming up.

Susan continues, "Good! Really, I can't imagine not having it. The house sits on my interior map of *me*. If I erased it, there'd be a big gap."

"If you need to, that's one thing; if you don't . . ." Camille trails off.

"You know I sold the business, and Aaron was smart enough to have a fat life insurance policy. Not that we ever saved that much. We spent everything, but I've been lucky that he was so responsible. If I let this house go, I could give the girls enough that they could afford two dinky places in California, where everything costs the earth. You can't imagine the rent they pay for dreary one-bedrooms."

She doesn't say that she awakened early this morning thinking of hammering a Ware Properties For Sale sign next to Sand Castle's mailbox. In that half-awake state, she'd happily banged the stake into the sand because she thought for a moment that she had someplace else she really wanted to go, though she wasn't sure *where*.

As they turn back, facing the wind, roiling clouds move across the sky. They step up their pace. By the time they reach Sand Castle, cold drops begin to splat on their heads. Julia can't find where she'd left her sandals, and then she spots Archie at the walkway, gnawing the delicate straps.

SUSAN TURNS ON THE GAS log to take the chill off the great room. Not one for hauling wood, she had it installed after Aaron died. Julia towel-dries her fine, springy hair, pushing it into curls. Susan brings over to the hearth a pot of bergamot tea and a plate of Camille's lemon cake slices. Camille's longer hair hangs in bedraggled strands, but Susan's good short cut just looks sharper, slicked and pointy. "Forty-five minutes," Julia says, stirring potatoes and carrots into the beef so they'll be done when she pulls her rich stew out of the oven.

They all put on sweaters. Slanted rain batters the windows. Out at sea branches of silver lightning fork and pierce the water. "Thanks for arranging this dramatic event." Julia smiles. Thunder rumbles the house all the way down to the foundation.

Susan tosses Julia a cloud-soft throw. "Are you freezing?"

"Rain at the beach always seems bone-chilling." She passes the cake and no one demurs or says anything about it being too close to dinner. In the lamplight on the bookcases, the big window reflecting the women around the fire, Camille luxuriates. For the first time in a year, she doesn't feel as though she would float off if she were not tethered. She catches the sudden mysterious sparkle on the ceiling as her engagement ring flashes light. For so long she's looked for signs of Charles's presence. Stupid, she knows.

Julia wraps herself into a blue mohair blanket. She sips slowly Susan's tea, with its hint of bitter orange. "I think this is the only moment I've felt no tension in my shoulders since I hightailed it out of Savannah." She smiles broadly. This easy happiness lifts her, illuminating her dark blue eyes that always look slightly surprised.

"You look beautiful right now," Susan says. "Your eyes are the color of the lapis lazuli ring my mother wore, that same depth of blue."

"Oh, thanks! I think we all look a bit redeemed by today. I'm happy to be here with you two." Julia puts down her cup. Suddenly emboldened, she says, "I'm not sure we're ready for this. You've both been forthright and I know I haven't. I'd like to try to tell you about what has been going on with me."

"Hey, don't worry. You are under *no* obligation to dig up the past for us!" Camille loves it that Archie has leapt onto her feet and begun to snooze.

Thunder pounds through the house. "Christ, it's going to shake the fillings out of our teeth," Susan cries out.

Camille is not sure she's up for Julia's story. She senses that it isn't going to be pretty and she is relishing this respite from gnawing grief.

But Julia continues, "It's hard. Hard. But I do want to say a few things. Not to burden you—my saga could sink the weekend." Julia smiles. "I know this will sound twisted, but I've almost envied the two of you. Your husbands died. Awful to say! But in these months I've been in Chapel Hill, I often have wished mine had. Oh, god, it would be so clean. I'd be left in a clear space, at least with him."

Susan's mouth drops slightly open; Camille rolls her lips in, as she does when speechless, but neither says anything.

Julia exhales a long whistling sigh. "Can I do this?"

"Julia, no, don't worry. Only if you want! We're having a fine time and no one thinks we need to rush things, right, Susan?" Camille pours more tea.

Susan brings over three glasses and a bottle of her usual sauvignon. "To hell with tea! I for one would love to get down to it, Julia. You often seem distraught, I'm sorry—so distracted, and oh, lovely. I would like to know your story ASAP. Maybe it actually would help."

So, Camille thinks, Susan is one to cut to the chase. She wasn't sure she liked that.

THEY ARE THREE IN FIRELIGHT, the storm waning, the beef bourguignon simmering in the oven. Later, Susan will toss the salad. Camille will prepare a cheese plate. Susan has set the table with her shell place mats and Aaron's generous breathe-in-the-aroma wineglasses.

And now, the fire and the wine and the tentative voice of Julia and the storm moving away.

"Maybe the first thing to say is that I have a daughter, Lizzie."

"Where is she?" Susan asked, thinking of her two sweet ones both far away in California.

"Well, that's the big horror. I don't know right now, I think in San Francisco. She's addicted to, well—cocaine and prescription drugs for sure, and probably heroin again—the worst. Let me back up. My husband is Wade, Wade Tyler. He's in Savannah. Oh, I never changed my name. I kept my name, Hadley. That became an issue later but Wade didn't mind at first. Later, he said part of me never married. I'm still thinking about that."

Both Susan and Camille frown, then smile encouragingly, not knowing what to expect next.

"Back to Lizzie. We had this hideous incident last fall. 'Opioid OD,' the hospital chart said. That's opiates, like what the dentist gives when your wisdom teeth are pulled. You feel nice and woozy."

"Oh, yes," Camille remarks. "I liked the Percocet after my knee surgery."

"When you're addicted, it's another story. Her meds were oxycodone and Xanax. She swallowed a full bottle. Her roommates, as addled as they usually are, got her to the emergency room. She survived.

"To go back to the beginning—Lizzie started on drugs when she was in high school. They say marijuana isn't a gateway drug, but for her it was. She told me once that she took to it right away. One boozy party with pot and she says *that's for me.*

"I hate talking of her this way—you'll only know her as this pathetic junkie. When she was small she was bright and curious. A little buttercup who loved clay and books and horses lined up on the windowsill. We had the best life. I'll never forget *that* anyway; I have fifteen pure gold years in a jewel box in my head. Wade is one of the chosen—if I believed in God, I'd say he was blessed. Every part of him is beautiful, down to his toes. I was the luckiest girl in Savannah, believe me. This sexy husband, this smart little girl who liked princess costumes and puzzles of the world. Now I don't even know if I still love her. I think I don't. I love the she before she became who she became, this inflated monster of my lovely daughter.

"But I can still glimpse Lizzie who's always there—when we were out walking today I thought of her at St. Simons, where we used to go in summer. She loved body surfing. Finding sand dollars. A little love. We always had such great times with her."

Camille shifts under her throw and Archie jumps down. She leans toward Julia. Susan puts her hand on Julia's foot. "Oh, honey."

"Flash forward, after the happy jewel box years to Lizzie's blossoming addiction. You can imagine how we thrashed over what caused her to slide into drugs. There's little to pin it on. Oh,

Wade opened the door to her room when we came in early one night and found her half naked with her boyfriend. She was fifteen. Wade had a flying hissy fit and threatened the poor scrawny boy jumping into his Jockeys. I was on the stairs, disbelieving that this adolescent was speeding by me holding his pants and crying, and Wade yelling, 'Dirty ass.'"

Susan and Camille can't help but laugh, and then Julia does, too.

"Wade shook Lizzie by the shoulders and shouted 'tawdry' and 'shameful.' He spotted the bong and called her a little idiot. Lizzie didn't speak to him for a week. That sort of thing. Not much. Not often. And we weren't that worried. Most people try pot, grow up, and move on. I know we were good parents. She was adored. I forgot to say, my father is my rock. He doted on Lizzie, as did Mom, who died when Lizzie was eight. He's always been generous to Lizzie. Of course now, we've made him stop giving her birthday and Christmas money. We stopped long ago. Wade got sick of his hard-earned going for her self-destruction. But then we felt guilty, thinking of her rent, her car insurance. She'd call, desperate. We gave in many times. I tell you, it's a lose-lose situation.

"By eleventh grade, she started staying out too late, acting surly. We thought it was a stage. Senior year, a respite—she sailed through the SATs, did well in school, and we thought she was fine. Then her freshman year at Emory—she said she wanted to be a doctor—when she came home for Christmas holidays, I thought she looked odd. Her fresh, peachy skin had turned sallow. Even the whites of her eyes looked dull as an eggshell, no shine at all. I suggested girls' lunch, then hair appointments, some shopping for gifts. She didn't want to go but begrudgingly agreed. I remember, we were getting our nails done together and I looked over at her—stringy, unkempt hair, circles under her eyes, a listless look, not even trying to make conversation with the nice Vietnamese woman, and I thought, if she weren't my daughter, I'd think she was a drug addict.

"Instinct? It just hit me. I talked to Wade and he agreed that she seemed out of it and alienated. She didn't want to string popcorn for the tree, or help decorate. I was worried that she was rundown or getting a cold because she was sniffling. Later, I learned that was a prescription drug sniffle. She didn't eat the holiday dinners she used to love. She didn't even buy gifts for anyone.

"Christmas Eve, we were getting ready to go to my dad's for dinner. She'd left her coat and her handbag downstairs. While she was in the shower, I opened it. Pills, envelope of pot, and a bottle of white powder. I told Wade and he went ballistic and banged on the bathroom door. 'What the hell is going on . . .' and so forth. Short version, we didn't see her even at spring break, until the summer when she arrived home, having flunked out.

"Therapy. Community college. Therapy. But she kept disappearing. A spiral. Wade was devastated; we both were, and he was really good, trying everything to help,"—she paused—"with only an occasional outburst of anger, which resulted in her going off with some of her seedy-looking friends for days. Wade has what I later learned to call an 'anger management problem.' I was just as mad at her as he was, but I took the helpful, tell-me-what-can-I-do-to-help, we're-so-concerned, walk-all-over-me-once-again approach, which didn't work any better."

"This is the worst, Julia." Camille feels again her own helpless rage when Charlie got his seventeen-year-old girlfriend pregnant their junior year. Charles had remained calmer than she, meeting the girl's parents, discussing abortion, adoption, all the impossible options. Then the girl miscarried and Charlie didn't date for the rest of high school. What a nothing incident in comparison.

Julia gets up to stir the beef, then plops back down on the sofa. "Well, it gets worse but I am not going to play this violin much longer. Lizzie quit community college and lost all her Emory friends and even her high school friends, who'd straightened up by then and joined sororities and majored in psychology and prelaw. Next, she went to a small experimental college in Arizona.

That didn't work out. She hated the 'fucking desert.' Next we heard she'd walked away from there and landed in New Orleans. She called saying she wanted to try Tulane and please send tuition money, she was fine now and realized what a mess she had been and she was coming home soon and could we go sailing? We sent the money. Well, guess what?

"Fast forward. We've got her in rehab three times, once without her consent, and that went nowhere. The other two times, she agreed but left the New Orleans place after two weeks of detox. Then it was California. Everything loose rolls West, my daddy says. She stuck with the super clinic outside San Francisco for only a month. She walked out all clean, we thought, insisting she was fine. Insisting on not staying another day in that hellhole. And no, she was not coming home. Within two weeks police stopped her as she drove away from a lowlife bar with some doofus. They were speeding in more ways than one. The police frisked them. He was arrested for possession of whatever he had; she was held overnight and let go. One more valentine ripped in half.

"By this time, we had no denial and little hope left in us. We rushed here and there to help when she hit various walls. Hit them she did. We were plowing the ocean.

"In San Francisco she waited tables and worked in a terminal care center and lived with a bunch of other dropouts in a storefront in the Tenderloin, the druggie haven. Now and then one of her friends would call us and say she was really worried about Lizzie, that she was going home with all kinds of men she met in bars, and AIDS was rampant. That she was having blackouts and didn't remember the night before.

"Lizzie didn't keep in touch. After all we meant to each other, she was living an alternate reality, totally swallowed by her stupid addiction. We'd had a big life, the three of us. A real life!" Julia bites her nail and stares into the fire.

"We tried tough love, tried being supportive, being nonjudgmental—you have no idea how hard that is. Yes, yes, it's the drugs talking. But she's listening! What part of her won't wake up? She's devious. Manipulates us. Lies. We all three landed in her vicious, vicious cycle.

"I feel like she's the center of a roundabout and I have to circle it no matter what direction I need to take. She likes drugs. She doesn't want to quit. Sometimes she does. She cries for hours. She blames everyone but herself. She has this ironic humor— everything for her happens with quotation marks around it. She maintains that she functions well and of course she doesn't. She's a smashup on the freeway.

"She's thirty-five now, so it's been an awfully long haul with all this. When she overdosed in San Francisco, we hardly could admit it to ourselves, but she meant to. She left a note. It said, I've never spoken this, not even to my father, the note said, *What's the point? There is no point.* We were broken in half and terrified. But something else broke, too. I just froze toward her. *What's the point?* My anger was gigantic and Wade was about to pop. We tried to act calm. Surely this would be the turnaround of all this madness. We brought her home. She was trembling on the plane and looked like a zombie. She spilled her water. She pressed her forehead to the window. Banged it a couple of times. I tried to anchor her with happy memories. 'Remember that time we flew to New York? It was your first flight and . . .' She stopped me right there. 'Do we have to go down memory lane?'

"We hoped she had hit the proverbial bottom they say you have to hit. We found the best help, once again, but she made fun of the doctor, who tried to get her to make a list of things that could inspire her to change. Something in me started to hold back; my illusions were stripped. The weirdest part: I became bored with it.

"She drank coffee by the gallon and sat by the back kitchen window rocking back and forth and looking out at the garden. She read self-help books Daddy brought over, then tossed them in the trash. One afternoon she went out for a walk and came home high and mean, totally unlike the vulnerable rag doll we brought home from the hospital. She'd sold the jewelry my mother left her. We found out later she'd ordered Xanax and Klonopin on the Internet. She used Wade's computer! She even took the kitchen money out of the sugar canister. Being at home was driving her crazy, she let us know. She was taking the first thing smoking on the runway back to San Francisco. That's the last we've seen or heard of her. I found a letter in her wastebasket. It was addressed to Honor Blackwell in San Francisco. I Googled the address—a purple slum house in a not-horrible neighborhood. The letter said, *I'm heading back. Turn down a bed for me,* then trailed off and she'd thrown it away. When I look at the sky and see contrails dissolving, I think, *that's Lizzie.*"

"No wonder you love Hugh's quiet, empty house," Camille says. "You're brave, really brave, to break away from what's tearing you apart."

"I guess. But the Wade part—I wasn't brave. When she left the last time, Wade and I were destroyed and wildly relieved and guilty about that. You might say we had our own toxic cocktail going. You'd think we'd cling together, but the opposite happened. We began to give up, maybe on each other as well? Every time I looked at his handsome mug, he reminded me of our failure, and his rants to me against Lizzie became unbearable. All the where-did-we-go-wrong discussions! I couldn't mouth the words anymore. I started working longer hours, loving my job even more than before.

"Lizzie *is* the victim of drugs, but you know what? We are *her* victims. She's about killed our spirits. Sometimes I think she's like someone running randomly, slinging around a sledgehammer. Let it fell whom it will. Did I use *whom* right then?"

Camille says yes.

"Please, pour me a big glass of that wine, Susan!"

. . .

THE OVEN DINGS. THEY LOOK at each other as if they've been jarred awake. "Your famous beef!" Camille says.

Julia shrugs out from under the mohair throw. "Let's have a long dinner. There's more to say but not at the table." She looks flushed and alert.

Okay, Camille thinks, we know the worst.

This will be good to get over with, Susan thinks.

Susan lights the candles as Camille slices bread. They serve themselves bowls of the rich stew as they talk about dogs, the farmers' market, politics, and cars. The bread is excellent for dipping into the warm broth.

SUSAN LEASHES ARCHIE AND TAKES him out while Julia and Camille clear up the dinner dishes. The stars are bright again, the moon gone.

"Before we go to bed, I want to get the shrimp into the marinade," Julia says. She's brought the prepped ingredients in a jar. "Delicious shrimp salad, grilled crab, and asparagus—that takes care of tomorrow night quite nicely."

"Julia, you're a girl after my heart, thinking during one meal of what's for the next. There's plenty of my lemon cake for dessert."

"We have fresh orange juice. I might make a sorbet."

Archie visits his favorite bushes, while Susan texts her daughters. *At Sand Castle. Thinking of selling. What do you advise?*

ARCHIE DASHES TO HIS BED by the fireplace and the three women decide to call it a day, too. Susan stays in the great room, searching the Internet for comps for her house. She's on another mission as well. Camille selects a Joanna Trollope novel off the shelves and heads to her bedroom. She opens the window to hear the receding tide scooching through shells. Julia just wants to sleep. A memory surfaces, her wedding. A police siren outside the church blaring throughout the entire ceremony. A portent? She has not cried since she left Savannah. Now she cries.

III

What Do Tourists Want?

THURSDAY—COLIN'S "ON" WEEK IN LONDON. After years of fierce commuting on Monday and Friday from Florence to London and home, he has enough Italian work to stay at home every other week and all weekends. Still, who likes to commute? I'm a stay-at-home. My life = my work, my work = my life. That's why I fit well here. The Italian way—work to live, not live to work.

With so much solitude, I'm bound to accomplish a lot, yes? Well, this is one of the most sociable places on planet earth. I have to fight for time. There's always something delectable cooking at my neighbors' and friends' houses. Always someone stopping in to drop off chestnuts and ricotta still warm and a bottle of home-made *vin santo*. When Colin's away, I linger longer in town, read more, go to movies, invite girlfriends over for lunch, sometimes join the monthly book group for lunch at Trattoria Danzetti if I've had time to read the Italian novel.

The only way I can walk as much as I do every day is by listening to books. I put up with the earbuds (that remind me of the plugs I had to wear in the heavily chlorinated pools of my childhood) because the kilometers race by when I'm involved with

Hilary Mantel, Edith Pearlman, Virginia Woolf, or those scratchy voices of the modernist poets reading their work at the dawn of recording.

The trouble is—I often meet people on the roads and must stop, press pause, chat, pet their dog. Today I met Grazia just as I closed my gate. She stopped her car, got out for the ritual kisses, and asked me to go to her house for advice on renting it. Grazia teaches violin at her aunt's house in town. She wears long crêpe skirts, scuffed boots, indeterminate tops, and she juts out an ample bosom. For the violin to rest on? Her black-bean eyes dart and sparkle. When she smiles, she flashes perfect teeth, refrigerator white. She smiles now.

"They will surely be Americans. I've put the website into English because the Americans will pay the most. What will they expect? You will know. Please come and tell me."

As we step into the foyer, the first thing I say is, "Air the place out for days!"

"I know all that. I hardly come here since . . . Two Romanian women will clean head-to-tail. What do I do to make the American *like* the house? So someone will want to buy it and I won't have to worry."

We walk from room to room. "You'd have to be tone deaf and oblivious not to love this place, Grazia. Don't worry. Your parents had lovely things. You might put away some of the china?"

"They're not pleasing to me, the dishes. I prefer my own plain white." She pulls out drawers full of table linens with monograms, oversized silver cutlery, thin platters decorated with fish, some with flowers. "All old." She looks bored. Since she grew up here, she doesn't even glance at the dining room fresco that delights me every time I get to see it. She didn't even photograph it on the website advertising the house for rent. Italians do take art for granted. (Another reason to love it here.)

Between the two windows some fanciful artist created a trompe l'oeil garden scene that must have replicated what you actually saw from the adjoining windows. He (maybe she) painted a balcony with a stone balustrade overlooking boxwood rows, tall topiary balls, and an arching rose arbor covered in white and pink blooms. (*Rampicante* is a word I love. The Italian word has more force than *rambling*. All those emphasized syllables impart vigor to climbing roses or wisteria or honeysuckle.) A path down the middle of the fresco leads the eye into the view of hills, layers of hills, blue going darker, the cones of the two extinct volcanos you see from the windows. A smart and fun painting. The view from the real windows is blear now, but the witty replica may inspire someone who finally buys this place to re-create the original garden. Most interesting is this: off to the right side two figures are seated, looking out at the view beyond a balustrade. You see the people only from behind and they are in shadow, only a suggestion of a woman wearing a rose-printed shawl, a man with his head tilted, contemplative. They must be the original owners (the *S* monogram) looking out at their splendid garden. On the other side, a black and white bird perches in the leaves of a potted orange tree. "Do you know who painted the fresco?" I ask.

"Mama always said it was a nun. Two or three hundred years ago. She left the convent in some disgrace and survived by painting scenes in villas. Someone should study this. A few other villas have what looks like the same hand. I prefer bare walls but would never paint over this because my mama would rise out of the grave. Oh, the black and white bird, Mama said, symbolizes the nun's habit."

Upstairs, we examine the beds and I have plenty to advise. "Get rid of these chicken-feather pillows. They stab you in the night. Some new sheets. These are pretty vintage ones but hard to dry." (I've been almost rope-burned on heavy linen sheets before.) "Your mother—grandmother?—crocheted the coverlet?" Starched snowflakes, a thousand of them.

"Grandmother. One of the treasures of the house but I will leave it on the bed."

"You know, Grazia, Americans like to read in bed. I'd get some lights with more wattage." More wattage than one candle, I think. Italians always say they don't read in bed, they make love. Even luxury hotels often have bedside lamps no brighter than night lights.

"I don't know about that. They seem fine to me."

In the downstairs bathroom, mildew rings the shower. It reeks like stagnant frog water. "All these towels—I'd replace them. Americans are used to soft towels. I know the Italians aren't, mainly because they dry theirs outside." I don't add that these thin antiques feel like emery boards.

Grazia is surprised, having never met a soft towel. "That's expensive. For the whole house?"

"Believe me."

A rank drain smell rises from the kitchen sink. The vintage vacuum cleaner with its deflated balloon bag must be from the '50s. "I'd say a new one is a priority. And also mops." Disgusting, the ragged gray mop and a broom with the straw half worn away.

We go through the drawers and shelves and make a list: a couple of nonstick frying pans, a sturdy pasta pot (Luisa's is dented aluminum), a good colander, wooden spoons—rancid— that didn't usher in the last century. New dish towels, mixing bowls, a large steamer. Grazia balks at the idea of a coffee maker or espresso machine, and vetoes any kind of food processor or mixer. Her mother made everything by hand. And a Moka pot is just fine.

"Should I tune the piano? Remove all the books. They're in Italian?"

"Leave them. These people are coming to Italy, after all. Who knows if anyone will play. You could wait on that if you want."

One room crammed with trunks and boxes and furniture will remain as is. Seven bedrooms is enough. Grazia still has to empty each *armadio* upstairs. Luisa left some prize evening dresses and tailored suits. A vintage shop in Florence would scoop them up, but Grazia will give them to her aunt who will someday leave them again for Grazia to dispose of.

WHOEVER LANDS HERE IS LUCKY. There's some funk but the villa has noble bones and gracious spaces. My own place is more intimate and suits us, but I think to wake up here would expand your mind every day. I visualize making love with Colin in every one of the bedrooms and on the *divano* in front of the living room fireplace.

Climbing up to the Roman road that leads to the monastery, I shift to remembering what's real. We have our spot beneath a stone wall high up on the land, a dip in the thick grasses where we take our green blanket on Sunday afternoons after our *pranzo* of salads and roast guinea hen. And on warm nights, for the stars. So far, no wild boar has nosed our bare bodies. Then I reposition my earbuds and turn on the voice of Nicole Kidman reading *To the Lighthouse*.

White Wisteria

BLISS TO WAKE UP TO the sound of waves rolling in. Julia is the first one up. When Camille and Susan wander into the kitchen in their robes around nine, she has waffle batter ready, juice poured, and a pan of bacon already made. "You accomplish everything effortlessly," Camille says. "I consider it a major event when Charlie brings his family over for quiche and salad for Sunday brunch. And how orderly the kitchen is."

"My secret weapon: clean up as you go."

After breakfast and a beach walk, they drive into Wilmington, where the gracious neighborhoods invite them to stroll and make up stories about the inhabitants of the white houses all surrounded by pink and white azaleas. They buy carnations and lavender soaps for Susan's house, and stop for ice cream cones in the old town. After lunch at a waterfront café, Susan finds new walking shoes, and Julia shows them some of Mulberry Press's publications in the bookstore. In the art section of the bookstore, Camille selects tubes of watercolor paint, six brushes, and paper. "I might as well paint a big clichéd sunset," she jokes. But she's excited to think of taking the paints down to the dunes. This is the first time she's bought paints in how many years? She cannot remember.

By three, they're back at Sand Castle and out on the beach with Archie. "Julia, tell us the rest, if you will," Susan says. "You know how the crime novels always have 'the hook' propelling you from chapter to chapter? I'm dying to know about Wade."

"That is, if you want to," Camille adds. She wonders if Susan is not being a bit pushy. That daughter, Lizzie. What a disaster.

"Yes, I'll try. I'm sure you've guessed what happened next. I hardly could blame him. We were both morose. I sort of wished I'd met some cute guy. But"—she laughs—"there's not an abundance of cute sixty-year-olds out there. Wade went way down the age scale. I think she was around thirty, thirty-three maybe."

"Is he still seeing her?" Susan asks.

"No idea. If we hadn't endured the long Lizzie ordeal, I think I would have been strong enough to weather a betrayal—though I doubt that would have happened—but after all the rocky years, it seemed non-negotiable to me. We'd always had each other. It was like the keystone fell out of the arch. Here's how it all came down.

"Wade always had a huge temper. I was silly enough to be thrilled with it at first. It showed he was passionate, and he was. He was jealous of anyone I looked at, or he imagined I looked at. He was one of those southern boys who go to Woodberry Forest and
· UGA then return home more southern than ever to work in the family business. His daddy owned a boating supply, marine paint company. Wade loves the water, loves sailing. Fitting in at Georgia Marine was easy. He's six-two, green eyes, deep, the color of malachite—I used to melt when he looked my way. Even though his father was black-haired and his mother, too—she was Jewish and warm-skinned—Wade's hair is blond as an angel's. Who knows how the gene pool twirls? When I met him I was so physically attracted to him that I never considered anything beyond his heavenly shoulders, racehorse legs, skin the color of honey with

the sun in it, and his great smile that promised and delivered the moon and stars. My parents were won over, too, even though he wasn't quite our social class. Things like that really mattered in Savannah. Not as much now.

"We were wildly happy. When Lizzie was born, she was our darling. *Those were the days, my friend* . . . Any chinks? Oh, Wade lost his temper at a slow waiter and turned over his chair getting out of the restaurant before we were served. And he might have invented road rage! He told off one of Lizzie's teachers when she said Lizzie needed to be more organized. And there was the incident in CVS when a prescription wasn't ready. Security escorted him out. Lizzie and I were exempt from his anger attacks. I told myself he was under stress, et cetera, and after Lizzie's problems started, he was.

"Okay, moving on to after Lizzie left the last time, when we started pulling away from each other. I couldn't bear the devastation. I threw myself into work. I learned later, he threw himself onto Rose Welton, his new marketing consultant and web designer. I only met her once at the company holiday party. She has puffy lips that must be pumped full of something. They look like two boiled shrimp. Oh, meow. She's pretty enough.

"He was coming home late—dinner meetings, an Atlanta trip, and he flew to Jacksonville for a boat show. I hardly noticed. I watched escape movies on Netflix and the endless series about the wimpy Scottish laird. Even if I barely could look at him, I assumed this stage would pass and that we'd eventually get back to a normal, or new-normal life.

"When he left one night, I caught a scent of the cologne I gave him for his birthday, verbena, woodsy and musky, eighty bucks! Very provocative. Ding, ding! Sherlock Holmes! 'Where are you going for dinner?' I asked him. 'Oh, we'll just go to the club. These reps will like that.'

"You already know I'm a snooper—I looked in Lizzie's bag and found drugs—but only when I'm desperate. He left. He'd been online and his computer hadn't shut down yet. I looked at his credit card bills, all paid automatically and I don't see them. There was plenty to make my blood boil, including some Jacksonville expenses at boutiques and the hotel spa, four restaurant charges in Atlanta, and more at places out from Savannah. Also really extravagant florist bills. I remembered that he'd brought me a small nosegay of daisies not long ago. I felt as if I had a grease fire in the brain pan. Those silly daisies must have assuaged his guilt over the French tulips or roses he splurged on, roses, now that I think back, because of her name.

"An hour after he left, I drove through the club parking lot. No black Range Rover. Obviously he was dining elsewhere. Where would he take someone after dinner, I wondered. Surely not to a local hotel. Maybe her place. Is she married?

"Then, I realized—the boat, of course. So, this little detective drives to the marina where my dad keeps *Suncatcher*, his sailboat. It's really our boat now. I parked at the shadowy far end of the lot. We keep the cabin key in a hatch under the cushions. I let myself in, then pocketed the key. I latched the door from inside without turning on any lights. As I sat there, I had to ask myself what I would do with the information I was about to acquire. I had no idea. I kept thinking, So this is how it feels. I thought, This is not going to happen.

"In about an hour, I saw lights swing into the lot. And, lo and behold, through the curtain I saw Wade, always the gentleman, opening the door for Sweet Thing. Arm in arm they walked to the boat and he helped her in. She sat down and—I couldn't see much out of the crack in the curtain—adjusted a scarf around her neck. He opened the hatch and then let it slam. He tried the door and I heard him sputter something, then stop short. There are no windows on the front of the cabin and I'd pulled the curtains along the side. 'I must have left the key at work,' he said. 'Damn, this is embarrassing.' She said something; they left. I waited, cold and revolted.

"On impulse, I looked in the galley fridge. Champagne. Good Champagne. I popped the cork and poured myself a glass. The bed in the bow was spread with the contour sheets my mother had someone make for the boat, and that enraged me again. I poured another glass, turned on the ship-to-shore, and listened to static communications out on the water. I sent Wade a message: *Spending the night at my dad's.* I wasn't ready to face the truth just yet. Instead of their having a sex fest in that bow bed, I slept there rather soundly."

THEY SIT DOWN ON A log. Camille wants to take out her paints from her bag. As she listens to Julia's story, she looks at clouds, the horizon, the wavy waterline, wondering what instant of these images she might capture, and if she could blend white with a speck of blue to capture the silvery edge of the foam as the wave retreated.

Julia continues. "I sat on the news. I avoid confrontation if possible, but it was not going to be possible. I arranged a leave of absence at work, with the proviso that I could freelance edit for them. That's when I saw the notice in the paper that Hugh was speaking. That's when he offered his house. I told my dad and Alison, my neighbor.

"I shredded papers, gave away a pile of my clothes and books I'd never reread. Some fanatical instinct took over. I completely cleaned and ordered the house except for Lizzie's room, which I left just as it was, down to a pile of sweatpants and T-shirts on her closet floor. I guess he found the flat Champagne on the boat. He never mentioned it. I remained cordial to Wade—small talk and dinner on the table—but he picked up on my smoldering anger and one morning called me 'cold as a cod.' That afternoon, can you imagine, I cleaned our bathroom's grout with a toothbrush and Q-tips! Then I loaded my car. He came home to change for sailing 'with clients' and I finally confronted him as I shoved my cookbooks into a box. He tried to get my keys and almost broke my finger. He was shouting and denying and blaming. And that's how I'm through with other people's lies and dramas."

"You must be PTSD. Or at least in deep shock. That's quite a pileup of bad," Susan responds, and Camille agrees. "Would it help to talk to someone? I have a friend who's very good."

"I'm talking to you! That's better. After all the shrinks and clinics with Lizzie, I'm done with that. I don't want to backslide into them anymore. When someone is hell-bent, all that talk, talk, talk is useless. I need space to figure out how to live, how to silence the voices that keep clamoring for my life. No, not *those* kinds of voices! Not hallucinations. Memories. Now I want forward motion. My feet out of quicksand."

Camille opens her bag and takes out her new sketch pad. "Yes, you need exactly that," she says. "Let's start with a watercolor of this spot right here. You can hang it as a reminder of a turning point. Every time the quicksand beckons, you look at this and listen to the waves and think about good friends." She stands up and hugs Julia.

"Let's go up, Julia. I'm famished." Susan whistles for Archie. "I'm going to run you a bath with mimosa salts. Candles around the tub. You need to chill, big-time." She rests her hand on Julia's shoulder and they head for the house. Camille opens the tube of blue. Other lives, she thinks, exhausting.

THE SPRING DAYS BEGINNING TO lengthen bring back sweet lingering twilights. Darkness, no longer plopping over the land like a velvet stage curtain, gives in to the light more every day, allowing a vast space to play at sunset with flamingo, mauve tending to gray, and azure with a glittering edge. As the friends prepare their feast of shrimp and crab, Susan opens the doors onto the back deck and calls them out. The western sky over the marsh behind the house is filled with cotton-boll clouds, the bottoms fluffy and rufous. Through layers of tints, the orb of sun wobbles gently down. "Fertilized egg yolk," Julia says. Camille says, "Fireball." Susan says, "Sun."

WHEN THEY GATHER AROUND THE fire after dinner, Susan brings out her laptop. "Just look." She indicates the screen. "You don't have to say anything." Before them appears a square stone house on a slope of olive trees. On one side a pergola droops with white wisteria. Behind the house lie distant hills and two conical peaks. "Extinct volcanos," Susan said. "We could lease this house. It's right outside San Rocco, Tuscany. It's an hour from the sea. And not far from Florence. Firenze, I should say."

Camille and Julia look at her quizzically and frown, then laugh. "A lease with an option to buy," Susan adds. "Isn't it beautiful? The wisteria is *white*, not purple. Most people plant purple. This is a sign. I've looked all over the Internet and at all my sources, even looked in France and Spain. This is the most appealing place I found. I think we would love it. And it does not simplify—it complicates." Susan, years ago, had fallen hard for Tuscany when she and Aaron celebrated their twentieth anniversary there. She always meant to get back but never has.

"Are you suggesting that we lease, you mean *move* there?" Julia marvels. "What an idea! Susan, you are one bold sister!"

Camille rotates the screen to see better. "Click on the inside shots!" Beamed rooms with high ceilings flash by: peach, cream, pale yellow, white, each with large stone-framed windows. The kitchen has a real butcher's chopping block on sturdy legs, a long shallow marble sink that reminds her of cloistered nuns chanting, worktables instead of counters, and all shapes of pots and pans around the biggest fireplace she's ever seen. "Julia, look at those pots. Little Morning Glory's copper fades into oblivion, right?"

"Yes! Is that a wood-burning stove? Is there a regular stove, too? Look at that marble-topped table. It must be for making pasta."

"Would you possibly consider this?" Susan asks.

Silence. Then Julia says, "I cannot imagine anything more phenomenal. But, really, this is fantasy."

Camille adds, "Well, worth looking into. I could so completely love this! Think of all the art!" She didn't remotely consider this possible.

Julia does. Some of life's best decisions are made irrationally. A fireplace. A window. A saffron-colored wall. A view of volcanos. The thought of a mythic sea just over the hills.

The out-of-nowhere idea stirs them. A house in Tuscany, where they know no one. Everything open to reinterpretation.

OTHER WEEKENDS FOLLOW AT SAND Castle. They talk into the wee hours. They reminisce about sororities and apartments with roommates after college. Camille had loved the communal closet at the Chi O house. She's never, before or since, had such wardrobe options. They talk about friends, mistakes they made, biopsies, trips, what it's like being alone. Why, they wonder, after family life ended, didn't more people banish loneliness and live together? Things, they conclude. People can't part with their stuff, their mother's stuff, attics and basements full of stuff. We must be afraid of sharing a kitchen or bath, they realize. "Are we like that?" Susan wonders. Camille thinks she is, but she becomes so infatuated with the idea of Italy that she back-burners the thought. Rising through her—the realization that she must break through. So much talk of women and glass ceilings. Hers presses right on her head. She begins to appreciate Susan's drive that she'd been wary of at first. She could learn from Susan. Julia is coiled to spring. She finds the whole concept enchanting. They talk about residency options, the Tuscan coastal towns, and Italy's system of fast trains. She pictures them stepping onto a sleek Italo and speeding through the countryside, eating sandwiches, the green hills flashing by the window. Alone in her room, however, she's sometimes engulfed by waves of fear that Lizzie would need her, waves of hope that Wade would repent, and random waves that wash over, lifting her feet from the sand and tumbling her roughly to shore.

Susan sticks to the bright notion *what do I have to lose?*

Camille backs out in late July. She can't. And Lara works to convince her that she shouldn't. She keeps mentioning Cornwallis Meadows. Charlie, skeptical, says little, although at breakfast one Sunday, he remarks that Dad would surely recommend Cornwallis if he could. "But he can't," replied Camille, "can he?" The idea truly takes root then. Her two friends inspire her more than her own hardwired timorousness holds her back. Yes. She's going.

They all decide.

Yes.

SUCH AN EMPRISE TAKES TIME but was accomplished: Susan opted to close her Chapel Hill house, not sell. At home alone one afternoon, she was reading in the sunroom and experienced an undeniable love for the bronze bars of sunlight hitting the heart pine floors, the design books on the coffee table, the two nails for stockings over the fireplace. Everything happened here, glorious, good, bad. Her miscarriages before they gave up and adopted, those sad days lying in bed, leaking out hope. The girls' projects, the kitchen messes from their cookie and fudge attempts. Aaron's golf bags and fishing gear on the back porch. Full, jammed life. Let the house go? Not yet. What if Eva or Caroline wants to come home? She threw a farewell party in her garden and invited all her friends and colleagues.

SHE HIRED A GRAD STUDENT to come twice a week to flush the toilets, air out the rooms, and pick up flyers on the porch. She trusts her gardener. Her hundred houseplants she put out on the street with a sign: FREE.

Camille offered her car and home to Charlie and his family, and they arranged to rent their little place to a visiting professor from China. She was pleased that Lara finally got over the shock and became excited for her. Charlie, she'd always known of her good boy, would take her side whatever she chose. She told him about the coffin dream and, as a painter, he understood intuitively what it meant. They planned a Christmas visit. How fabulous to introduce Ingrid to Italy. She left behind the urn of ashes.

Julia filed for divorce. She wrote Hugh that as of October, she'd find someone good to take care of his house. And could he come stay in Tuscany, because he might like to study the Etruscans? She'd heard nothing from Lizzie and made no contact with Wade, other than the wrenching business of serving him with papers. She made a quiet trip to visit her father, who thought Italy was a splendid idea and asked when he could visit. Her father agreed not to reveal her whereabouts except in emergency. She did not drive by her house.

They all made arrangements—gardens, bank accounts, insurance, good-byes to baffled friends, medical and dental checkups. All three began online courses in Italian. Hugh's housekeeper's daughter's divorce coincided with Julia's exit and she was thrilled to move in the day Julia left. Susan had an eye lift and was quite pleased to see her gray eyes widen again. She installed the FOR SALE sign at the beach. Her daughters agreed—it was the right time for their mom.

Camille practiced watercolors and loved her color studies, and experiments with transparency and opacity. Julia wrapped up her recipe testing. Susan sold two stellar properties, then closed her office at Ware Properties. To her surprise, her brother, Mike, bought Sand Castle.

In October, they will fly to Rome.

San Rocco

THE MORNING AFTER THE ARRIVAL of the three women, my neighbor Leo whistled under my study window. His three notes mock a certain bird (a blackbird?) that often sings nearby, leading me to the window because I think it's Leo. He knows I'm up early, usually working, but has no concept at all that he possibly could be disturbing an earthshaking line of poetry. Still in my nightgown, I looked out the window. He was holding a chicken.

"*Buon giorno.*"

"*Porca miseria,*" he replied. Pig misery, one of my favorites of the milder Tuscan curses. "We have the new neighbors. They have brought a dog. It got out and into my garden." The chicken's head, I noticed now, was drooped over and limp. "I chased, Candida was squawking to heaven, and it dropped her."

"Oh, awful. What are you going to do?"

"I went to the villa door and introduced myself. They started fluttering around like chickens when they saw Candida. Americans, like you. Three ladies. One of them raced out in her bathrobe and started chasing the dog."

"You must be angry."

"*Boh*, she was ready for the grill. And I have a three-month rabbit, too. I invited them for dinner tomorrow. You must come, too."

I'm always taken aback by the Tuscans' lack of sentiment for their food sources. Leo has petted that rabbit, carried it in his pocket, fed it tiny bits of lettuce, and now he's ready to skin it and enjoy every bite. Realism, I suppose. Like Margaret's. How much power she gained when describing children in the postwar south of Italy when she wrote that beatings for wives and boys happened routinely; incest was "not unexpected" in the lives of girls. Always the opposite of sensational, her understatement was devastating.

Though I cringe now, I probably won't think about the gray bunny when Leo's wife, Annetta, places her boned and stuffed *coniglio* on my plate. Especially if her sister has made those crisp rosemary potatoes.

TWELVE HOURS IN TUSCANY, AND the three women already have a dinner invitation. Happens all the time in Dallas and L.A., right? Someone rushing over and inviting you before you've even unpacked? Yes, especially right after you've run over their cat, or backed into their mailbox.

I MUST GET ON TO my projects. On my screen this morning: Margaret.

When Colin moved in, he'd ask me, "Will we need to buy a chain saw?"

"Do you think the shutters must be oiled every year?"

"Is that Roman painting of Janus in the museum a fake?"

"How will we get the well tested?"

I'd look up from my book. "Call Margaret—she would know."
Brief bio:

*Born in 1938 in Washington, D.C., Margaret Merrill graduated from
Georgetown University. Except for stays in the United States, she lived
in Italy from 1964 until a few months before her death in 2013. She
wrote three novels, three books of investigative nonfiction, and was on
staff at* Corriere della Sera. *She also was a frequent contributor to
major newspapers and periodicals in the United States and Great Brit-
ain.* Stairs to Palazzo del Drago *was published in 1968, followed
by* In the Cold Shadows *(1974),* The Taste of Terror *(1979),* Sun
Raining on Blue Flowers *(1988),* World Mafia World *(1994), and*
Labranda *(2009). Her photographs have appeared in her books and
have been exhibited in Italy. She was awarded the Rome Prize, a Guggenheim Fellowship, the Prima Donna Award, and was a finalist for the
National Book Award.*

I leave out the last spectacular act.

After writing for a couple of hours every morning, I follow
into town my special path that Colin keeps free of brambles. Between two ancient cypresses at the edge of my land, a gate opens
to a narrow *sentiero* that winds over the hump of hill, past chariot-
wide stone pavers of a Roman road, and down into the village. It's
always a slight shock to descend from solitude and views, to drop
into the waking-up streets where merchants sprinkle water from
plastic *acqua minerale* bottles and scrub around their thresholds,
trucks hurry in for morning delivery hours, the woman far gone
in dementia calls greetings from the door of her son's shoe shop—
buon dí, tutti—and the toasty fragrance of baking bread drifts out
the *forno* door across the street.

San Rocco is set like a brilliant medallion on the lower slopes
of Monte San Lorenzo. No other hill town charms me as much. If
you've ever read Italo Calvino's *Invisible Cities*, this could be one of
his dreamy fictional creations. What enchants? Maybe it's the via

Fulvio, ancient *decumanus*, the classical straight east/west Roman road dividing the town in half and laid to catch the sun. Maybe it's the fountain of diving nymphs and dolphins in the middle of the elliptical piazza; maybe it's the cluster of café umbrellas at one end, and along one long side, three rival restaurants with outdoor tables and menus resolutely posted, only in Italian. (I appreciate that.) The Duomo with frescoes of the Last Judgment anchors the opposite side, and worn marble steps provide locals with a place to sit and watch the inevitable repetition of each day.

The Friday market, small and boisterous, pulls me in every week. I visit the fish truck on Wednesday and the *porchetta* stand on Thursday. Always something tasty to eat. It's a wonder I'm not gargantuan. We have a pastry shop, a book/art supply shop, enough clothing stores, a dry cleaners, and three antique shops that draw people from Milan and Rome. Two excellent gelato places and other righteous trattorias scatter along the streets that radiate from the *decumanus*, along with two boutiques where chic young women lean in the doorways, managing not to look bored, and branching *vicoli*, tiny streets, lead to artisan jewelry, a shoe-store, and a knitwear designer. Five thousand souls, all particular. (And, naturally, a few creeps, fascists, and grumps.)

Though archaeologists flock here to study the Etruscans, the main piazza originally was a Roman circus for chariot races, hence the graceful ellipse. The Romans were grid-minded but I don't see how this town ever could have been conceived that rigidly, given that the steep terrain requires curves to get from A to B. I guess they gave up on the *cardo*, their usual north/south road that intersected the *decumanus*. By medieval times, the circus perimeter was built up with rabbity warrens of shops, stands, houses, and later the rambling noble *palazzi* you still can get lost in. Anytime sewers are repaired or gas lines installed (and most recently fiber optic cables laid), workers discover grain storage wells, vaults, cellars, and sections of Etruscan road. A few of the ancient stone arches still function as doorways and windows of shops. Layers of time happily coexist, one of the comforts of living here.

I go to all the cafés because baristas are among my favorite Italians. I love their efficiency and skill. This morning I'm at Violetta's Bar San Anselmo. She swirls into the foam of my cappuccino the design of a lyre because she knows I'm a poet. (That's another thing I love about Italy. The person making coffee knows a lyre symbolizes poetry.) "*Signora*," she tells me, "you have new neighbors. Gianni says they are *simpatiche, molto simpatiche*. Have you met them?"

"No, they only arrived last night."

"Yes, but already Leo has met them." Is that a rebuke?

News travels fast in this town. Violetta probably knew before I did what I would wear today.

MY OUT-EARLY-INTO-TOWN HABIT COMES FROM Margaret. When we first met, I'd see her on mornings when I walked in. I was trying to establish a writing rhythm but finding Tuscany too alluring—and I still love to see the town come alive. Walking over the hill I took my Italian verb book, memorizing conjugations, but when I got to the town gate, I put away my book and concentrated on seeing Anna arranging vegetables, the garbage collector sweeping the street with one of those witch brooms made of twigs, the barber lighting his first smoke, leaning back in his chair with a tabby sleeping on his lap. Often I'd run into Margaret at Bar Beato Angelico, where they should but don't have a plaque over her regular table. She'd put down her paper and cigarette and motion me to join her. Smoke, smoke, everyone smoked then. (Not I.)

Without plan, we began to meet a morning or two a week. She was just as happy without me. The bar soon filled with local people nipping a coffee before work and with tourists who, assuming no one there speaks English, have conversations novelists cannot resist tuning into. Not surprisingly, I soon saw in Margaret herself the same stunning quality of her writing—the observer with the archaic smile.

IN COMES GIANNI, OUR LOCAL taxi driver. "The women have no men," he tells me. "They are on solo trips. They have come from the South of America, bringing a little dog, naughty, who peed in the carrier and barked all the way from the Rome airport."

"They have no car?"

"No, but Grazia will sell them her mama's Cinquecento as soon as the brakes are repaired."

"Is that legal?" I know that it is not, unless they are registered residents. That Grazia. Maybe she has some scheme that gets around the law. I wouldn't be surprised.

"Why not?"

Why not is the local response to every preposterous proposition. Another thing I love.

"I told them about their famous neighbors, the poet and the architect. You will be friends as you are of the same country."

"Yes, we're all American. We'll love each other," I laughed. I'm still a foreigner. Always will be, one of the sharp hooks in my flesh when I think of staying forever in this place. If I went back to the shady neighborhood in Florida where I was born and raised, I'd blend like an alligator or mosquito into the landscape with never a thought of being the exile far from home. Colin scoffs at that. "We're the new people. Citizens of the world."

As the day is unseasonably warm, I take my coffee to an outside table on the piazza and open my vellum-bound book.

NOTES:

Will not yet say how she died. (Dire.) I'm saying now how she was as a friend. (Luminous.) What she wrote. (Janus!) She may or may not have

been a "courier" between Italy and the CIA. (She denied; I'm sure she
was.) She may or may not have been a lesbian. (If so, she was a lipstick
lesbian and now who cares anyway?) She once humiliated me publicly.
(Why? Jealousy?) She named me in her will. (Ferocious generosity.)
She was drawn to trouble spots. (Why? Pushed to the edge, she liked to
decide whether to jump.)

Margaret, maddeningly elusive but what a wicked, raucous sense of humor. I miss that. Those seven years I knew her in Tuscany, she was slippery even in answering basic questions that should not be difficult between friends. *Why did you never marry again? You were only in your twenties* . . . She'd pour into a glass a big splash of the martinis she brought over in a Mason jar to my house. We only drink wine but she was always a martini girl. No one could mix one the way she could, or so she believed. She'd laugh. "Tried marriage twice and after the second crash landing, I thought, This is just not going to work out," as though she were bad at piecrusts. And then she'd notice the white dahlias I'd planted and warn me that they must be dug out in autumn; they'd never survive the Tuscan winter. With Margaret, conversation was a series of detours. Muddy road ahead.

WHEN I START TO PAY, Violetta tells me that Gianni has bought my coffee. This is a charming San Rocco tradition and another reason to love this town.

A DOMANI:
See You Tomorrow

"WELCOME TO THE HOOD, ARCHIE!" Julia scans the open shelves for the Moka espresso pot she knows must be there—Grazia has left an obsessive inventory—then spots it on the windowsill. For their arrival Grazia stocked the kitchen with a few provisions—bread, cheese, prosciutto, coffee, oranges. "American canine invasion on the borders! Killing and mayhem!" Julia pauses and looks around the kitchen. "This is odd—I feel like I have cooked in this room all my life. How simple. And aren't these checked curtains across the lower shelves *so* characteristic? I've seen them in Italian cookbooks. Brick floors—what are they called, *cotto*? Cooked—how practical. Spill anything." Julia is already dressed in jeans and a red sweater but barefoot. She unrolls the felt pouch of chef's knives that she brought over in her luggage. At Mulberry Press, she was the chef for authors' events and occasionally she catered parties for friends.

"I can't believe that huge marble sink. You could bathe two babies in there. Archie! What a disaster. He never saw a chicken in his life. Now on our first morning he's murdered the neighbor's hen. Oh, what was his name? Leo! He was sweet about it and now we're going to have to eat the damn chicken."

Susan couldn't help but laugh. "I cannot believe little goofy Archie has the killer instinct."

"He's never been out of North Carolina. He is insanely confused. When we go in town, we'll buy Leo something nice. Wine?" Camille saws into the bread, prepares a platter with everything Grazia brought, and pours big glasses of blood orange juice. On the long kitchen table, the mound of cheese, rustic bread, and oranges forms a still life. The juice looks dark and powerful—a glass will speed you into the day. They are starving, not having eaten since the exceptionally good sandwiches at a highway grill en route from the airport.

Camille begins a list of what they need in town, but since what they need is everything, she starts to sketch the kitchen fireplace. She is already enamored with the house. Winter in this beamed room, she imagines, a fire popping, boiling pasta water steaming the windows . . . She has not thought of Charles since the plane touched down in Rome. Is he exiled from here?

"I let him out," Susan is saying. "I should have used the leash but I thought he'd just pop out and back in." She scoops up Archie and whispers in his ear, "You were very bad," and poor Archie whimpers. He so liked the feel of feathers in his mouth.

"HEY, YOU TWO. GIANNI IS coming at nine. I feel like I'm going to the prom. Archie, my friend, you are staying here. You'll be fine in the kitchen." Susan walks him again, surveying the property as they stroll. A short distance downhill, she finds a stone building with a glass front, a structure she knows to be a storage for lemon trees over the winter. She'd seen one at the famous garden La Gamberaia when she traveled with Aaron years ago. The long room is full of pots, those gorgeous green glass demijohns you pay a fortune for at Restoration Hardware, spiderwebs spanning two yards, gardening tools (some perfectly good), and rusty iron chairs. Bulbs, she thought. I could plant them now for spring. She has no way of knowing that naturalized daffodils cover the entire hillside in early April. Over many years, Luisa added irises and tulips. Wild orange-spotted lilies thrive in bright clusters.

She circles the house. Fruit trees, a couple of lichen-etched terra-cotta olive oil containers, some roses still sputtering out a few blooms, and many boxwood domes. Gianni must know a good nursery. She visualizes the rusty chairs under the linden tree, and lavender and santolina along the drive up to the road. Around the front door spilling catmint, dusty miller, and verbena. Pale pink verbena. Water falling somewhere. Archie scratches in the dirt and begins to root. He looks up, guilty and frantic. "What is wrong with you, little one?"

Camille hangs her clothes in the looming *armadio* that squawks when she opens it. Her chest of drawers is freshly lined in blue and white fleur-de-lis paper. Because of her knee, she has the downstairs bedroom at the back of the house. Julia's and Susan's bedrooms are in the vast upstairs, where there are three others, plus a large room that's used for storage. This house was built for a multigenerational family, not three lone foreigners.

Out the window, she sees Susan poking her head inside a stone building with arched glass doors. What a great studio, all that sunlight streaming in. She spreads her sweaters and tops around on the bed and begins rolling them, as her efficient daughter-in-law taught her to do. With only four drawers, she needs every centimeter of space. This must have been the dead couple's room. It's spare, the original minimalism, really, with walnut chest, *armadio*, and bed handsome against white walls. She runs her hand over the thick plaster, following the sweep of someone else's hand as he'd smoothed the surface. (Her mother wielding the spatula, spreading the boiled frosting on her birthday cake. Her mother would admire the crocheted bedspread of hand-sized snowflakes.) For Camille, though she loved the carved bed, that scratchy spread will have to go. She'd also like some good towels. The aqua ones in the bathroom look new but skimpy. She looks around her room. By the bed stands a rickety floor lamp in lieu of a bedside table, and on the chest on the other side, an iron relic with a twenty-watt bulb. Don't the Italians read in bed?

CLEANING SUPPLIES, JULIA NOTES. AMMONIA. Bleach. Ajax. Window cleaner. Scouring pads. The kitchen seems well scrubbed, but Julia has the urge to rub down every surface, especially the pantry where the shelves are slightly sticky under jars of honey and jams that will have to go. The fridge, closed since Tito died, smells like ozone. She looks up words and writes her list in Italian. Wonder if I could find a food processor? Or at least a stick blender? How to say that in Italian? She knows she is going to learn the language quickly. Susan has a feel for it, except for rolling *r*'s. When she reads passages aloud, she's taught herself to race through. Her instinct is right. Even if she mispronounces, she speeds on. *Tutor*, Julia writes at the top of her list. She wants to start immediately. Today she is going to buy a cookbook in Italian. Outside her front bedroom window, the land steps down and down, with a few dots of farmhouses far below. The other window looks east; the full frame of it is filled with a glorious tree, bare of leaves but gaily hung with burnished and glowing yellow persimmons. *Kaki*, she learns. The first thing she will cook in the kitchen of Villa Assunta.

AT NINE, GIANNI KNOCKS. HE will drop them at the town gate and all morning they can explore San Rocco. He recommends Trattoria Stefano for lunch, and then he will return them to Villa Assunta because of the jet lag. Tomorrow, he has suggested a trip to Ikea, near Florence, since they will need supplies for the house, with a stop afterward at his cousin's organic restaurant, Verde. By then, Grazia's mother's Cinquecento will be ready and they are on their own.

JUST INSIDE THE GATE—THEY MARVEL at the medieval arch and the vast doors—Julia spots the fresh pasta shop. "Let's get some on the way out—go all the way into town and start at the far point so we don't have to lug everything." That was hard. They want to stop at the *forno*, at the gelato shop with the tempting linen store next to it. They pause for cappuccino and meet Violetta, who offers the coffee at her bar. Small streets drop downhill off the main street. They wander in galleries and jewelry shops as wide as an arm span. At the end of the street, they find a cookware store and indulge themselves in a food processor and a good coffee machine with pods. Julia selects three spatulas and some ice trays. They don't yet know that Italians think iced drinks cause stomach problems, hence no trays in the home fridge. They buy a steam iron to replace the relic they'd seen in the pantry, and three hair dryers. Martino, the owner, introduces himself and offers to deliver. "Of course I know where you are living," he tells them. "*Una bella villa.* You honor us with your choice of San Rocco."

The second coffee they take at the smaller Piazza XX settembre, overlooking the public rose garden and a view of the agricultural valley below. This barista, Paolino, bows as they enter, smiling as though they are long-missing cousins. He, too, offers the coffee. "What is this?" Camille wonders. "Do they always do this?"

"Bizarre. I imagine it's because of Grazia's family, the house . . . I don't know but it's great." Umbrellas are put away for the season. At the outdoor tables, the women turn their faces to the midmorning sunlight. They forget about exposure and skin cancer and just bask in the warmth, consulting their lists and staring at windows, a balcony still dripping with pink geraniums, shiny paving stones, and people going about their daily lives. They feel they are walk-ons in a play and, of course, they are, the ongoing drama of life in a small town. Internet images of San Rocco occupied them over the months of planning, but they were in no way prepared for the limpid light bathing the renaissance façades of ochre, rose, sunflower yellow, and cream. The white marble steps leading up to the piazza's church have over centuries worn to the soft gleam of soap, and the tower bells ringing the quarter hour, the half hour, and the hour gong so resoundingly that their bones reverberate. "That's the nanny-goat bell." Paolino nods toward the bell tower as he gathers their cups. He's worked on cruise ships for years and speaks English. "Every church gives a different sound. Santa Catarina, the struck dishpan; San Fillipo, the goose honk; Sant'Anselmo, the leper's bell. You know, the lepers had to warn that they were approaching." Susan is transfixed by Paolino's thick hair—cut close on the sides, with a frothy top that makes her want to say *pompadour*. It sweeps up and back, a glistening tar-black surfer's wave about to break. Julia thinks the croissant, called a *cornetto*, is terrible, the dough all wet and wadded in the middle. Camille imagines a straggling leper ding-a-linging across the piazza followed by a cavorting goat and a goose. Jet lag, major jet lag.

Paolino waves as they gather their bags. *"A domani."* See you tomorrow.

"I'M GOING TO THE BOOKSTORE where they sell art supplies. Meet you in an hour on the church steps?" Camille has a large tote she intends to fill.

"Yes, I'll get groceries," Julia adds. "And the bread."

"I'm just going to wander around." Susan hoists her bag onto her shoulder. "Every street looks tempting." Susan, used to engaging with strangers, introduces herself at Anna and Pietro's *frutta e verdure*. The outrageous display of citrus lured her. How many kinds of tangerines are there? What's that? *Cedro*, huge and rippled. Lemons, some large and bumpy, some small and smooth. What's that? *Bergamotta*. The fragrance meets her as she leans over to see the labeled crates. Used in tea, she remembers. Whatever else it is, she thinks, it smells like lemon blossoms and oranges; something I'd like to spray on myself. What a beautiful word, *arancia*. We must have the blood oranges. Julia will be thrilled. Anna and Pietro pick out prime fruits for her, and Anna describes an *insalata*, Susan understands that, with oranges and fennel. Anna also gathers a bunch of beets. She looks equivocal but holds out the three together. Susan buys the beets, too. Usually indifferent to cooking, she wants to carry half the shop home—the enormous *funghi porcini*, shiny chestnuts, and huge leafy wings of something called *gobbi*. "*Dialetto*," Anna says. "*È il cardo.*" Well, I'll puzzle through that later, Susan thinks. Anna chooses a *cedro* as a gift to her. Julia will figure out what to do with it.

In the cheese shop, she buys a large wedge of sweet Gorgonzola, tiny black olives, and a jar of truffle butter.

At first Camille doesn't see the bookstore owner crouched in the back of the shop. She is reading in a low chair covered in a ragged Oriental rug. Signora Bevilacqua unfolds herself and rises. She is both stooped and tall, her hair clipped up in gray loops, and her ivory face gently wrinkled like crêpe paper. Her eyes are clear and dark amber.

Every Italian word she's memorized flies out of Camille's head and she's reduced to pointing to the tubes of oil and acrylic paint, the brushes, and rolled linen for canvases. The shop cat twirls around her ankles, then the ankles of the *signora*, who opens drawers and points to brushes with delicate sable tips, to watercolor sets that cost a fortune, and to rolls of tracing paper. Tape. Pencils, erasers. Tubes of raw sienna, raw umber, burnt sienna, and *terra verte*, a muddy green for this landscape. A color wheel. "*Sì*," Camille agrees over and over. Her bag loaded, she thanks the *signora* and remembers what Paolino said. "*A domani.*" See you tomorrow.

She runs into Julia, emerging from the grocery store. "Guess what? They deliver! This is the most civilized place. They stock all the local wines, too, and I bought a mixed case. The store is minute but everything you need is right there. Makes our giant stores at home seem a bit silly. And they were lovely people. There's Cinzia, her husband Quinto, and their son Tommaso."

Julia did not say that Cinzia's oval face and perfectly straight nose reminded her of Lizzie. Momentarily, she had the familiar nightmare feeling of being trapped in an unmoored bathysphere. Lizzy. Dizzy. But Quinto handed her a slice of San Daniele prosciutto and, concentrating on the buttery taste, she righted herself.

Early in the day for it, but Susan orders a hazelnut gelato. The girl seems surprised that she only chose one flavor. With a medium, she said, holding up the cone and raising three fingers, you can choose three. Susan smiles and holds up one finger. Down to basics, she thinks. Holding up my finger like a one-year-old. I've got to study *now*.

Susan sits on the lip of the fountain, enjoying one of the pleasures she almost always denies herself. A fabulously gorgeous young woman strolls by, wheeling twins, both smiling. "*Buon giorno, Signora,*" the young woman calls, as if they were neighbors. Her life, Susan thinks, her amazing, beautiful years of *life* in this place. She catches herself; the woman's life might be horrid. But the dreamy one tosses back her thousand ringlets and steps away, who knows, back into the pages of *Vogue*. Susan thinks she might cry.

Twelve fifteen. They are early for San Rocco trattorias. Lunch starts at one. But the door is open at Stefano's. "Okay. We're in a film. The waiter is too gorgeous." His shaved head shines like a polished pecan. He sports a soul patch and a pointed, highly styled beard. The fitted gray shirt and tight jeans leave no doubt about his lean and muscular body. He is Stefano, son of Maurizio, whose family flung open the doors sixty years ago and have been cooking pasta and mixed grill ever since. Stefano, thirty, insists on new ideas. Not just traditional Tuscan food but innovations, too, especially on the dessert list which previously had been only *panna cotta*, tiramisu (which he loathes as an American invention), and crème caramel. Now there are seasonal fruit roulades, *vin santo* cake, and in autumn, fig and walnut tarts. Maurizio is fine with this, as he's overheard local expatriates sigh over the "same old menu." Chief cook Zia Valentina, Maurizio's sister, feels fiercely partisan toward what her grandmother cooked. Good enough for the family for centuries, good enough for badly dressed tourists. Thus, eruptions of shouting and clattering pans in the kitchen, often causing diners to look at each other in alarm.

Today all's calm. Like everyone, Stefano knows they will live at Villa Assunta. He even knows that one is or wants to be an artist, as he has met signora Bevilacqua in line at the post office. He will hear later this morning of the extravagant purchase of the food processor, a two-year-old model that Martino was delighted to sell. He suggests the *pici*, the preferred pasta in San Rocco. Susan wants hers with big garlic, Julia chooses wild boar sauce, and Camille decides on spicy tomato sauce. They love the *pici*, rolled long and thin, like a thick spaghetti. After they decide not to have wine, Stefano brings over a liter anyway and they surprise themselves by finishing it with their second course, the mixed grill with roasted potatoes. The meats are lean, almost stringy, but richly flavorful. The local bread has a fine texture but since the cuisine is a salty one the dough is mixed without salt. This will take some getting used to.

They don't want it but Stefano brings them Mont Blanc, a swoon of a dessert made from puréed chestnuts and whipped cream. "Very special. For special guests."

LUCKILY, THE FRESH PASTA SHOP is still open. They'd decided on a long rest followed by an early night, with a simple dinner. Susan remembers the tagliatelle and the jar of truffle butter in her bag but picks up some ravioli as well.

Shop owners have locked up and headed home for *pranzo*. Smells of long-simmered sauces and roasts drift from upstairs windows. "I don't want to eat for days," Susan moans. Just outside the gate, they spot Gianni's van. "How do you like our San Rocco?" He slides open the door and they pile in with their packages.

"*Paradiso!*" Julia says.

"Ah, no, *Signora*, but maybe close."

"What does *gobbi* mean, Gianni? And *dialetto*?" Susan asks.

"Hunchback. Dialect. You have bought *gobbi*? It's like the artichoke but more difficult. You could call it *cardo*."

"And why hunchback?"

"*Non lo so.* Perhaps because the leaves curve?"

Julia gets it. "Must be cardoon. The most difficult vegetable on earth. I've never met one in person."

As Gianni turns down the drive the harmonious house fills the windshield. Camille rolls down the window and breathes deeply. She turns and looks at the others in the backseat. "We're home."

AS SUSAN CARRIES INTO THE dining room the bowl of truffle pasta redolent of loamy woods and parmigiano, she pauses in front of the fresco. It's dark in the garden now but she noticed earlier the conceit of the house's view reappearing on the wall—the garden foregrounded, rose arches, the two distant volcanos. She feels a prick of joy: she gets to look at this for many fabulous dinners. I'm going to check all the outbuildings, she thinks. I wonder if those iron arches in the painting might be rusting away somewhere.

Camille, bringing in a pitcher of water, joins her. "Isn't this just too much to bear?" She also has spent a half hour looking at the fresco. She found herself smiling the whole time. "There was a big spirit at large here, wielding the brushes! I wonder if she— surely it was she—was the owner, or the daughter. Look at that sharp little bird!"

The Good Word:

CENA

I ARRIVE A FEW MINUTES early at Leo and Annetta's for the dinner cooked in honor of the murdered hen. If he's home on time, Colin may join us. He does not like to miss a meal at Casa Bianchi. I'm bringing a pear tart, although I know that Annetta also will serve her apricot or plum crostata. My Italian friends instinctively distrust foreigners' cooking. They're always telling me how to do the simplest things, as though we in America have no idea how to stuff a tomato or chop an onion. When they like something I serve, they express genuine delight and surprise, as if they're witnessing a dog performing a smart trick.

As I unburden my tart and wine on the kitchen counter, Annetta and her sister Flavia are setting the table. At one end they've plopped a tall vase of autumn leaves and rose hips. Usually they don't bother with decoration. This is a special occasion. The chief of the *carabinieri*, his wife and baby have arrived, along with Flavia's husband, Roberto, who remains in the family although Flavia left him years ago and moved in with her sister and Leo. The hen and rabbit turn slowly in the fireplace, along with skewers of sausages and pork liver.

Enter the three women. Camille, Susan, Julia, they say, and I rush to introduce myself. They're flushed from the chilly walk. My first impression: very American. What is that giveaway that most cultures have? Why don't Americans look Swiss, or English, or Germans look American? Well, the one with cropped gray hair, Susan, could be French in her bias-cut skirt, stack-heeled boots—did she walk up the hill in those?—and asymmetrical red and gray sweater. She cocks her head slightly, letting me know that she is appraising us. Not in a bad way, just aware. All three look clean, scrubbed really, with shiny hair and open faces, all smiling with their great American teeth. Innocence? Is that the dead giveaway for American women? (But Margaret never looked innocent.) Just as baggy pants are the hallmark of American men?

Julia seems a bit shy. She's examining the roasting meats in the fireplace and the coals hissing and popping from drops of fat. She has a questioning look. Camille looks around at everything. Her first Tuscan farmhouse. She compliments Annetta and Leo on the open room with the long table dominating all. "I can see your priorities!" she laughs. (I'll be working double time tonight as interpreter.) She admires the casual comfort of six oversized armchairs arranged around a low round table heaped with magazines, books, yarn baskets, and fishing tackle. She says to me, "Hey, Ralph Lauren, heads up!" It's true—plaid blankets, taxidermy owl, an upright piano, mismatched dining chairs.

They have brought flowers and wine and at Ikea today they have found an olive wood cutting board for Leo. (Were they subconsciously thinking of him beheading the chicken?) He turns it over and over, examining the work. (They will learn later that he makes better ones himself, along with carved napkin rings, walking sticks, and birdhouses.) Though it's not our local custom, Annetta hands around glasses of prosecco because this is a special night. Usually we arrive at eight and sit down, with no preliminaries. *"Benvenute, cin-cin!"*

So here they are. Two days ago, they had their worlds. Now,

rashly and happily, they have this new one. Can't everyone envy them? Everything unfolding, everything new and shining. I like them immediately.

Annetta, sensitive to the language issue, seats the women together with me across from them. The men, as usual, are at one end of the table. Out comes the platter of antipasti: *salumi* olives, crostini, and pecorino. "You are in for a major treat," I tell the women. "Annetta may be the size of a ten-year-old girl but she is a mighty cook."

Leo asks about Villa Assunta. Are they comfortable? He volunteers to bring over fireplace wood. Annetta notices that they didn't close the shutters at night and tells them they'll be warmer in winter and cooler in summer if the shutters are closed. I rarely close mine and doubt if the women will either because the rooms become as black as inside a coffin, and it's hard to wake up in the gloom. A cultural thing.

The baby is extraordinarily large for six months. She placidly sucks on a piece of bread. The mother, Margherita, looks wan, exhausted from hauling around such a hefty girl. Eugenio, the *carabinieri* chief, assures the women that he will do anything possible to make their stay pleasant. Handsome as he is, I imagine the women are each flashing on just how pleasant he could make their stay. No, surely I exaggerate; is that what *I* think instead?

Flavia and Annetta bring in a bowl of penne in what looks to Julia like a plain tomato sauce. Instead, it's lively and complex. "This is delicious," Julia marvels. "How do you make it?"

Annetta shrugs. "It's simple." She always says that. "I add two handfuls of herbs and parsley chopped finely, and my own tomato sauce. Some *peperoncino*, spicy hot. We grow them and I will give you some. It helps most pastas." Julia notices that Roberto, husband of Flavia, is devouring his. And she does, too.

Everyone has advice. Where to buy electronics, gas, which vendors at the Thursday market have the best vegetables, what priest is the least boring. The women are asked where they plan to travel, if they've been to Sicily and Elba. They're warned against Naples (one of my favorite cities) and given numerous recommendations for places to eat in the countryside. What does not come up, as it hasn't ever come up for me either, is who they are, where they come from, what they do. I've never figured out whether my Italian friends are indifferent to my life away from here, or if, as written on early maps, a primitive *there be beasties* mentality exists beyond known territories. It's quite odd. When I leave it's as though I have dropped off the edge. When I return, everyone's thrilled I'm back, but no one, no one, asks a question. Live in the moment? Yes, they do.

Flavia helps Leo dismantle the rotisserie and carve. The platter is unceremoniously placed in the middle of the table and soon the women get the idea: you lean in with your fork and stab the piece you want. Flavia's rosemary potatoes, the bread, and wild salad greens similarly just arrive and casually travel around to everyone. The baby chews an olive. I see Camille staring. "Don't worry, she's loved them for weeks now. And she was born with three teeth," the mother says.

Roberto lunges for a sausage. "I don't think he's eaten for weeks," Camille laughs. Flavia compliments the wine the women brought, but to me it tastes strangely metallic. I may be coming down with something. I'm usually ravenous, especially at this table, but tonight I feel abstemious and unattracted to the savory meats. Susan reaches for seconds.

NOW THE APRICOT CROSTATA, MY own pear tart, the bitter little glasses of *digestivi*—Leo drinks only grappa—and the fire burned down to coals. "That is one of the best meals of my life," Camille says. She's had her back to the fire all night and is about to melt. Rather late for a hot flash.

Colin must be late. Poor babe, he'll be stuck with some leftover lasagne.

"*Una bella cena.*" I start the good-bye kissing rounds.

"That was a beautiful dinner?" Camille repeats. "*Una bella cena*, Leo, Annetta. Flavia."

THE FOUR OF US WALK out together. Annetta calls and runs to them with a jar of her hot pepper flakes. "We are lucky to have them as neighbors," Julia says. "Do they know that their food is better than any multi-starred restaurant in the U.S.?" I suddenly feel elated that the women are among us. Each one has the spark of curiosity. I remember well that heightened sense of arrival. In many ways, I still have it. They all three speak with southern accents, but Julia's is the melodious English-tinged coastal Georgia one. I would like for her to sit by my bed and read to me. Susan I recognize as a straightforward person. She'll get a lot done. Camille—my impression is that she's the most protean at this moment. Ready to change whatever needs changing. They're nothing like Margaret.

"Yes, the Bianchis. They're the best of the best. But you'll find that the everyday food here knocks you sideways all the time. The standard is impossible to grasp unless you live here."

"I didn't catch your last name, Kit," Camille says. "And do you work here? How long have you been here? Gianni says you are a writer?"

"Raine. I'm from Coral Gables but I've been here twelve years. Seems like forever."

Julia shines her flashlight in front of their feet. "Kit Raine! Oh, I read a book you wrote on Freya Stark!" she remembers. "It was on the shelf at Hugh's," she explains to Camille and Susan. "I loved it."

"I'm amazed." I'm always amazed when someone reads anything I write. "That's so cool to hear. No, I just work at my desk, nothing else, though I do some research for Colin. I think I fell for him because I always wanted to be an architect myself. Just in a nutshell, before I came here, I taught at UC Santa Cruz—catching waves, as I now think of that year. Then I got a full-time job at the University of Colorado but I had to quit. I spent four years taking care of my mother in Coral Gables. She had MS. Then melanoma. I taught part time and tried to convince myself to marry my high school love. After she died, way too young, I made my great Houdini escape to Italy. This place has given me the big blank space to write plus an exciting fallback when I'm looking for diversion." No car parked on the road. Colin must be delayed along the way. "You'll have to meet my partner, Colin." I explained that he works here at home and in London, always juggling luggage and plane tickets.

"What a life. And you're still young. And gorgeous, I might add."

"Susan, you're a *principessa* to say so! I'm forty-four. But I'm one of those old souls. I've always been forty-four."

Only a Week

JULIA. CAMILLE. SUSAN. ALL SETTLED in well and happily after a week. The three bought down duvets at Ikea and replaced Grazia's heirloom coverlets. They brought home wineglasses, new shower curtains, spatulas, bath mats, and a soft dog bed for Archie. They forgot to look for towels better than the skimpy new ones in their bathrooms. No one wanted to go back to Ikea's vast parking lot and endless aisles. Camille found it annoying to be there at all, though Gianni insisted it was the only place to stock up on practical items. Camille thought it was depressing that someone could furnish an entire apartment in an afternoon and have a pleasant place with absolutely no dimension at all.

At the Saturday antique market, Susan found romantic crystal sconces—twenty euros!—for her bedside. Camille spotted a brass library lamp with sufficient wattage. Julia moved a marble pedestal lamp from the back hall chest to her room. Julia chose place mats in town and Camille selected a couple of soft throws for reading by the fire. Susan began to keep flowers on the kitchen table and on the broad stone sill in a living room window. They equipped each bath with a small space heater to take off the morning chill. The villa's thermostat must be pre-programmed but they haven't yet figured out how to override the settings. Heat goes off totally at midnight and back on at six, not fast enough to warm up the house by the time they get up.

Wi-Fi works better than at home in North Carolina, but somehow the phones, with new chips Gianni bought, have low signals. Only messages marked TIM come through.

"Who is this Tim who keeps calling?" Camille wonders.

"We don't know any Tim," Julia agrees. When Gianni explains that TIM is not a strange man but Telecom Italia Mobile, they startle him as they whoop with laughter, get caught up with it, and can't stop. Uncontrolled laughter, the kind that hurts, catapults them to the next stage, the one where they fully realize how little they know and how much they want to find out.

The delivery of the blue Cinquecento feels like a milestone. Wheels. Grazia adds the car price and insurance to their lease and retains the ownership papers. "This way it's yours; I hold it for you until you are residents," she explains. The women don't fully understand but go with it. Though the backseat requires contortion, the front is roomy. Being the smallest, Julia isn't happy about her fate to fold into the rear. Susan already has admired the Italian driving skills and is anxious to practice. As soon as Gianni and his cousin deliver the car, she takes off. "Where are you going?" Camille calls out to her.

"I'll try to find that nursery we passed. Hyacinths and crocuses would look pretty along the drive. I wonder if anemones will grow. I've never had luck with them." She grinds the gears, backs into the turnaround, and shoots up the hill. She opens the ragtop just as Luisa did in all kinds of weather.

JULIA STUDIES HER NEW COOKBOOK, *The Science of Cooking and the Art of Eating Well*, a classic by Pellegrino Artusi. Since it was published in 1891, she thought it would be only a launching pad for her, the recipes antiquated and calling for many ingredients no longer available. From her publishing job, she's familiar with metric measures in the kitchen, but they by no means are second nature as are ounces and cups. He's casual anyway about measuring. *Pugno*, she reads, a handful. *Quanto basto*. Just enough. Nice! As she laboriously translates recipes for ragù, risotto, ravioli, she realizes how much of the traditional cuisine carries over intact. Except nowhere does she find a recipe for pasta; Artusi assumed everyone knows that. She bought a Lorenza de' Medici cookbook, too, and tags every other page. So simple, the ricotta crostini, even the osso bucco. Julia hits on the idea of keeping a good log of what she cooks. Then she wonders if she could tie her cooking adventures to her learning of Italian. She has a flash—a book published by Mulberry Press! *Learning Italian*. Oh, brilliant. This would double the fun of learning both. About everything served at the table, there must a story, an anecdote, something to learn, and obviously, new words.

THIS MORNING, CAMILLE SETS UP a place to paint in the room opposite hers. By rearranging the daybeds and cane chairs, she clears a spacious corner where she shoves a desk under the window. Gianni is bringing a rectangle of wood two feet longer than the desk. He'll help her cover it in canvas and place it over a layer of felt on top of the desk. This will protect the tooled leather insert as well as give her a good work surface. She longs for the light of the glass-fronted *limonaia*, but that will have to wait until spring. She plans to start with still lifes, maybe à la Giorgio Morandi. She's found a book on him in one of the bookcases, along with a two-volume set on the history of frescoes and a stack of paperback art books on Tiziano, Pontormo, Sassetta, and Bronzino. She could, she realizes, study just that bundle all year. Pontormo's favorite color, and hers, an icy apricot. He favored mauve, ash, washed-out blue, but also aqua and plum. Bronzino, such stark

clarity; Tiziano, those heartbreaking, immortal faces; Sassetta—
how he cleverly worked landscapes into the backgrounds of the
religious subject matter. She pores over the Morandi paintings.
Bottles, bowls, pitchers, essential shapes pared into abstraction.
Even his landscapes were all about volume. If she painted as many
repeats as he did of the same chalky-colored cylinders she'd go
crazy. Same with Cézanne and those endless Mont Sainte-Victoire
landscapes.

Start simply. Three kumquats on a blue plate. Even that isn't
simple, not if you want to capture in paint the essence of kumquats, something like that scented mist they emit from the skin
when zested. On a small table raided from the pantry, she arranges her supplies. When will she pick up a brush, uncap a tube
of zinc white, and begin?

Julia leaves a note on the kitchen table: *Walking into town and
will stay through lunch.* She tucks her camera and her thick five-
subject notebook into her bag. *Off to see the wizard,* she used to
say to Lizzie. *Alive somewhere, Lizzie. Probably fuzzy and sick and full
of blame. Wade.* Four in the morning in Savannah and where does
he lay his head? *No, no, not now,* she said to the surging memory
of his solid, comforting presence in the bed beside her, his even-
breathing self. She forced his silhouette onto a view of blue hills
whose undulations resembled the contours of a sleeping man
under rumpled sheets.

A STOOPED WOMAN IN ONE of those print housedresses, or
are they some kind of wraparound apron, straddles a ditch and
parts the weeds. Julia looks at the weedy plants piled on newspaper at her feet. *"Buon giorno,"* she calls, startling the woman.
"Mangia questa insalata?" You eat this salad? she manages.

"Sì, la nostra insalata del campo." Our field lettuces, but Julia
understands nothing after that. The woman holds up a curly handful she's just cut, then tosses it onto the paper. From her basket,

she takes a porcini mushroom as large as a fried egg and offers it to Julia. *Crudo* is part of what she says. Raw. Only parmigiano and oil. Julia gets this. She's exhilarated to have her first conversation in Italian.

"*Sono* Julia," I'm Julia. She extends her hand. "*Abito . . .*" She couldn't think of what to say after "I live" so she pointed behind her. "Villa Assunta."

"*La casa di Luisa,*" the woman says. Her smile reveals gaps where incisors should be. "*Sono* Patrizia." She points to a square smudge of house down below in the valley. Julia assumes she's saying that they're neighbors.

"*Grazie, Patrizia, ciao.*" She does not yet know that one doesn't just say *ciao* to someone you've just met.

"*Arriverderla,*" Patrizia responds formally.

Julia folds a tissue around the prize porcini and carefully places it in her bag. A raw salad of shaved porcini sprinkled with olive oil and parmigiano. How simple can food get?

In town, she stares at stone crests above doors, slashes of light down the alleyway streets, the row of slender marble columns on a long balcony, a glimpse of a frescoed ceiling in an upstairs apartment, a boy who stepped out of a Piero della Francesca painting. (If she stays a dozen years, she still will see something new every time she enters San Rocco.) She reads all the posted menus and takes a few notes—*ribollita, pollo al diavolo, stinco di manzo, zolfini.* The Trattoria Danzetti's door flies open and she sees a chef eating his early lunch with the staff. She would like to join them. A waiter steps outside to smoke. At the pastry shop she admires the woven tops of the fruit crostatas, like Annetta's. What a skill with dough, although she didn't like them very much. Such a difference—American pies are piled with sweetened fruit whereas these favorites are just a rather thin layer of fruit jam. She selects some raisin pastries for tomorrow's breakfast, then at Anna's buys artichokes just arrived from Sicily.

Macelleria. Butcher shop. She steps in and gasps. An enormous cow stripped of hide hangs from a chain in the ceiling. A paper towel on the floor catches the last drops of blood. A small crowd seems to be admiring the haunches. Covering her mouth and nose, discreetly she hopes, she turns to the glass cases. As she catches the butcher's eye he laughs and winks, recognizing immediately the American's squeamish reaction to his prize from the Chianina beef auction. Julia bites her lip and tries not to turn away from the lolling head of a rooster and his flopping red comb. She manages to order three thick veal chops. At the doll-house-sized grocery, she stocks up on supplies and asks for delivery. They can take home her veal, her prized porcini, and pastries, too. Dinner is shaping up nicely. But it's time for lunch now and she returns to Stefano's trattoria.

An American man stands by a table of six women. Stefano pours wine as the American explains the varietal to upturned faces. Everyone tastes. Stefano seats Julia at the next table and recommends the *ribollita* his aunt is serving forth today. "A soup that gives you the energy to climb Mount Amiata. And let me introduce your fellow countryman. He is Chris Burns and these are his ladies on the tour of food and wine. He brings them always to my crazy father's trattoria to taste *la cucina casalinga*, the home cooking. Chris, this *signora* is La Julia. She has come to live here." They begin to chat, everyone half turned in their seats. They're from Northern California, traveling for two weeks with Chris, a winemaker who takes special clients on in-depth tasting trips twice a year. San Rocco is one of their stops because of the local syrah and because Chris and Stefano struck up a friendship at a wine fair a couple of years ago.

"I don't want to interrupt your tasting. Great to meet you!" She reaches for her notebook, ready for a lovely solitary lunch.

"Don't eat alone, pull your chair over here," Chris says. "Stefano can shift us over." She does. She sits between Lucy, who owns pizza restaurants in Marin, and Alicia, who, with her husband, owns a chain of San Francisco wine stores. Stefano brings out chicken liver crostini and a platter of fried porcini. Chris pours her a glass of what they're tasting. "This is juicy." He holds a big gulp in his mouth and rotates his head in circles. "Only one year in oak." Julia thinks he'll go on about how the wine was produced, but he says instead, "Reminds me of the purple velvet dress my high school girlfriend wore to the prom. Just luscious. Nothing has ever been more luscious than that dress until now." The women laugh.

Julia takes a long taste and says, "Well! It reminds me of a bowl of hot grapes in the sun when I first kissed my college boyfriend!" They all touch glasses just as the one o'clock bell strikes. She tells them what Paolino taught her about the nanny-goat bell. Her soup arrives with their potato and speck ravioli that Chris has paired with the wine. He spears one of his onto her bread plate.

They talk food. Just in from Florence, they have many recommendations, so many that Julia grabs her notebook. "I am dying to get to Florence," she tells them. Then she shares the story, in brief, of how she and two friends upturned their lives and came here to learn Italian, eat, explore, and figure out what shape the future should take. Chris listens intently.

Julia thinks, He's cute. Cute? Is she reverting to the high school proms? But he is attractive, not in an obvious tall-golden-god way like Wade, but full of life.

He insists that she share their braised quail with juniper berries. He hops up to open his second offering, a one hundred percent sangiovese. "Blood of Jove, that's what *sangiovese* means. The Roman god. Yes, that old. Back down to the most ancient roots. The Tuscans have preferred this wine since then." She notices his hands, too. Well formed, nails cut straight, and a firm grip on the bottle.

He pauses every other bite to say, "Oh, this is good. This is *so* good." His blunt-cut tawny brown hair keeps falling across his forehead. His face seems sculpted, all angles that complement each other. Ears—why am I noticing his ears? Usually they're ugly and primitive—but he has such neat ones, small cockle shells against his head.

"I'm a southern girl," she says, "and I know quail. I was raised on smothered quail. And this is the best I've ever tasted."

Stefano is passing around the platter. "Three hours in the slow oven. Until they are almost but not quite falling apart. And you have the juniper, olives, thyme, and for goodness, the *vin santo*."

Chris is delighted that he mentions *vin santo*. One of the great ones is made nearby and he plans to offer it with the fig and walnut tart for dessert. Just a taste. There is much to do this afternoon.

A FEW KILOMETERS OUT IN the country, Susan sees a sign for Borgo Santa Caterina. Since all roads are intriguing, she turns down a stone-wall-lined lane barely wide enough for the Cinquecento. If she meets a car, someone must back up. She follows a sign pointing down an unpaved road. Soon she curves into a pebble drive lined with massive lemon trees in pots. Surely one of the Medicis lived here. Flat and unadorned, the peachy stucco façade of the immense villa must be half a city block long. A discreet sign: HOTEL SANTA CATERINA. Curious to see inside, she stops for lunch.

This has to be the seat of an aristocratic family from the 1300s—massive chestnut *madie* and *armadi* line a vast room whose windows are swagged and draped in crimson brocade, the walls hung with tapestries and brooding paintings of robust half-naked women, *putti*, and horses. A slender Italian—what a *shiny* gray suit—leads her into a dining room with arched glass doors along one side of a former *limonaia*. The place could be nowhere but Italy. Shiny suit comes over and offers a glass of prosecco. Luca, he introduces himself. Susan sees that the suit isn't really mafioso; it's beautifully cut and topstitched, obviously bespoke. She likes the pocket handkerchief of orange silk.

One bite of the pasta with duck sauce and even a novice knows an Italian is in the kitchen. She declines a *secondo* and asks for a salad. Susan looks out at the garden, where roses trained on iron hoops along a wall frame views of distant volcanos and the broad valley. A few yellow buds still bloom. Is that Mermaid? Such a vigorous climber, thorns sharp enough for Christ's crown, with flat flowers the color of lemon juice. She's fascinated by the lack of grass in Italian gardens; it's such a staple in southern yards. And there are no foundation plants; the building firmly meets the ground where a narrow sidewalk rings the house. *Marciapiedi*, Luca explains. March of feet? Drainage away from the building, she supposes.

After lunch, Luca opens a door and gestures to the garden, pool, and spa. "The hotel is my domain; all this belongs to the inspiration of my wife, Gilda. You may find her in the spa or the cooking school right beyond."

"You're the owner? My compliments! It's a fantasy of Italy here. Do I have to wake up?" He comments that tourist season is ending and is she traveling alone? Susan tells him about Villa Assunta, which he knows, having gone to school with Grazia.

"Please, bring your friends. You are always welcome. Take a look around. My family has been here from many centuries. We would like to escape and go to Brazil or some islands but we must stay always."

Susan laughs. "You know the grass is always greener," she says, but he looks puzzled. Maybe because there's no grass.

Eva and Caroline will love this when they visit, especially the thermal pool paved with shiny tessellated mosaic. They'd be sparkling all over. She could pass on the red-wine bath in a copper tub and the hot gel massage tables, but even in late October, the outdoor pool that you wade into gradually, as into a pond, looks inviting. She almost sees Eva in her raspberry bikini and Caroline in a bright cover-up, hiding her extra ten, well maybe twenty, pounds, as they step into the water.

· · ·

SHE BUTTONS HER JACKET AGAINST a wicked wind shooting through the olive grove. Sprung from everything known, she thought. How shocking to be out in the world on my own. Even sprung from the dragging heaviness of Aaron, who seemed not as dead now. More of a companionable memory. She could think now of how Aaron would love the duck. He'd use the word *unctuous*. He'd want to buy the girls bracelets and shoes in San Rocco. He'd want to walk all the labyrinthine streets at night. He was no longer the confused face looking at her with accusing eyes. He was all his ages again, from the long-haired protester against Vietnam to the terrified new father leaning over Eva as she was bundled up and taken from the orphanage to the taxi, to the suave business owner cinching a contract.

How strange that we are feeling this comfortable, she muses. As though we just stepped in a boat and found the current moving us gently along.

"*CIAO*, I'M JUST SAYING HELLO." Susan steps inside the stone building marked La Cucina Santa Caterina. Luca's wife, Gilda, and an assistant scrub a marble worktable. Broth simmers on the back hob of an eight-burner blue stove. She introduces herself. "I just had a delicious lunch and Luca said I should take a tour." Gilda, small and slender like Luca, has a narrow face and russet hair combed straight back, giving her the look of a benign fox in a storybook.

"We are just preparing for an American group coming in today." She gestures to the stack of lamb chops and a mound of tough-looking greens. The assistant slides a tray of focaccia out of the oven. Gilda offers an espresso and Susan is tempted to stay, but surely it would be an imposition. Instead, she asks if the school is open to nonguests.

"We can always arrange something." Gilda smiles. Yes, Susan thinks, it's Italy. I'm beginning to understand. That's the motto.

• • •

AS SUSAN SEARCHES FOR HER keys, a Mercedes minibus pulls into the parking area and a group of women tumbles out. Julia! She jumps down smiling. "Julia, hey! What on earth?"

"What are *you* doing here? Susan, these are friends I met at Stefano's and they invited me to join their cooking class with a superb chef. This is Chris. He's guiding them to all the best places in Tuscany. This is my friend Susan. We ran away together."

"You'll love that cooking school. I met Gilda. It already smells good in there. Shall I come back for you?"

"No, no," Chris said. "I have to run back into town anyway. Dinner will be later, whatever we cook this afternoon reappears with a lot of good wines to taste. You're all welcome."

"Another time, I'd love to but I'll head home now. My dog, Archie, has been locked inside all day. Bye! Have fun."

CAMILLE FINDS THE DELIVERED GROCERIES by the door. Julia and Susan are still out exploring while she's spent the day in her new studio reading art books. Archie looks in, his head tilted. She lets him out twice, but otherwise how luxurious, having a silent day to herself. They've been wildly busy making the place theirs, now finally, time just to be there. She's never lived in a house that has a history longer than her own life multiplied by ten. All the weddings, funerals, tears, orgasms, baptisms, secret encounters, all the churned emotions and cooking smells, private triumphs, and birth cries seeped into the walls. (She hopes Grazia's father didn't choke at the kitchen table where she will have her dinner tonight.) The house must rest on bedrock reaching down to water and fire.

In a box under the stairs, she's found sepia images going back to the beginning of photography. Small men wearing the rough suits they were married and buried in, holding their hats and staring blankly into the future. Brides with drooping bouquets:

myopic, pious, dour, but one quite lyrically beautiful leaning on a balustrade. From her spirited look, she must have been in love with the person aiming the camera, but maybe she was just one of those people who looks back at the world with zest. A couple of dead babies, propped up on pillows but with closed eyes, cotton stuffed in their nostrils, and nosegays in their little folded hands. One of a beach party. Must have been World War II era—a long table, men in wife-beater undershirts and women in heavy one-piece bathing suits. Rubberized? All raising their glasses. Smoking cigarettes. One hefty guy in suspenders makes a V with his fingers—horns, the cuckold sign—over another's head. Grazia's grandparents must be among them but this party is long over and who remembers? The photograph Camille loves most is of the front door of Villa Assunta. No one interferes with the image. Just the heavy, carved door. Who took it? Half open, and a crack of sunlight angles in like, she mused, a spirit. She toyed with painting something from the photos. She loved seeing them and imagining the life in each. The cracked-open door? How to paint a door? Carefully she packs the box and replaces it on the shelf under the stairs. I don't want to paint the past. She knows that.

"JULIA WILL BE LATE," SUSAN announces, setting down a bag of groceries. "Much to tell. I saw a heaven of a garden. The countryside around here is sublime. You've got to turn into a landscape painter! Ha, I may. Not those sappy sunflower fields you see in every gallery. But, you know, the heart of this place. And they're everywhere— paintings waiting to happen." She tells Camille about meeting Julia, Chris's group, the cooking school, and the duck pasta.

"Let's surprise her and have dinner ready. Not that she'll be hungry."

"Maybe she'll go out with Chris. He's about her age, maybe younger. You know, it hardly registered, he's quite attractive, but I think he has one blue eye and one kind of hazel."

The X in Flux

WHAT COLIN TRIES TO GLOSS over but can't is how much he'd prefer working only from home. In London twice a month, five days each, he lives at the office. He keeps meaning to look for a studio but puts it off. He's not sleeping on the reception-room sofa, it's not that bad, but in a corner of the former warehouse in the revived East End. When his firm, Arkas/Wright, developed a hotel for a Saudi sheik, the client demanded that he see a completed sample room before he signed the contract. The architect on the project, Colin's friend Patrick, designed a luxury room at the end of their office building, complete with a swirly brown and white marble bath the sheik liked. So Colin has a handsome hotel room, a bit spooky, I think, and spa bath to use, with the most comfortable bed I've ever touched. There's a love seat at the end of the bed and a corner window looking out at the Thames. The drag is no kitchen, though he's tucked a microwave into the minibar alcove. When he's in residence, he stays crouched over his drawing table and computers in his office at the other end of the building. He steps out for dinner, usually with colleagues, then works late, a light hanging over him in the cavernous gloom. We text several times a day, talk after dinner until he falls asleep in the artificial room.

On the Fridays he returns, we celebrate. When two people work at home all day every day, the other person begins to seem like a version of you, or you of him. With the London interruptions, we stay separate (I must) and charged. But I'm not the one doing the flight delays and the trip into the city and the haggard nights in the closed offices. A bit of solitude I revel in, but I feel terrible for him.

Last night he was due home by nine but arrived at two a.m. The Florence airport runway is short. In strong winds, planes can't maneuver between the hills. He had to land in Bologna, take a train to Florence and then a taxi out to the airport where he'd left his car. Then home.

I was asleep when he got in. He fell into bed, not even showering. He smelled like jet fuel, as if he'd flown home clutching an engine. "What happened?" I'd already read his text about rerouting to Bologna. Even though I'd been roused from deep sleep, the smell turned my stomach. Metal. Fumes.

"You don't even want to know." Then he was sacked out. I was awake, curled around him, until the sky began to lighten and I fell asleep. The next moment, Colin was poking my foot, leaning over the bed with a cappuccino.

"I'm the one who should sleep in. Damn, this was bad, Kit, because the pilot almost landed in Florence. Then abruptly, and I mean abruptly, he pulled up again. Jerked up, lumbering like a giant turtle trying to fly. Several people screamed. The guy next to me roared. Like a sound in a nightmare. I was holding up the arm rests to raise the plane. We could feel the Gs dragging us down. Then the ass pilot said, *Sorry, folks,* in English though half the people on the plane didn't speak it. *Wind shear,* he said, *these things happen, folks.* I hate being called *folks.* I was terrified. Wobbly for two hours."

"You must have been absolutely petrified." When planes fall, the people on them have longer to experience what's happening than we're led to think. Anyone with a shred of imagination has to have flashes of fear when floating along at thirty-five thousand feet. I really hate coffee in bed. But the gesture is so sweet that I plump the pillows, scooch up, trying to look awake. Colin seems dazed, imagining (I would be) the plane soaring up over and over. He takes my hand and covers his eyes with it. Damp boy. Colin-face. You. Whiskery.

"Maybe I should open a local office and restore farmhouses for foreigners. Forget this pie-in-the-sky London firm. What do you think?"

"I think no. No way." Restoring houses for foreigners may be Colin's worst nightmare. Occasionally the houses become jewels, but usually the owners either ruin noble buildings with bad contemporary ideas or drive the architect to drink because they've studied and want historic restorations, down to the bent handmade nails. Worst may be the client who sends a hundred images of kitchens. *Can we discuss these?*

The cappuccino has the same metallic taste that I noticed last night. And a couple of other times recently. I swirl around the foam and don't drink. I didn't drink much at all last night. No hangover—I'm coming down with something. Or was something off? No, not at Annetta's table. Bronchitis season cometh. Colin is saying that Rick, his boss, wants him in London all of November and after that *we'll reevaluate assignments.* "Do we have any zinc? And is that ominous, what Rick said?"

"Could be. He may need me back full time. Christ." Colin flops backward on the bed and tells me about his week: the work for the firm pouring in from Ireland, Dubai, Majorca; the friends he met for drinks; the dream he had that he was lifted in the claws of an eagle and flown over Tuscany. He has wonderful success at his firm, but we both know what eludes him. He agonizes over all the shared projects—the hospital, the university theater, the private residences of the super-rich. I've seen his notebooks teeming with solo designs—severe classical but super-modern museums, stadiums based on ancient amphitheaters, fantasy racetracks, bookstores, even an ideal library that I would give anything to see built. I can put my fantasies on paper. My poems, though few read them, are full realizations of my vision. His is the real world of bricks and cranes and compromise and quirky clients, an unholy marriage of art and commerce. He must get his chance.

I run my fingers through his matted hair. He imitates a tech client who wants an upper-class British club atmosphere in his flat. "Can you tell me," the client said, "what is considered good taste?" Colin, to his credit, liked the client and they spent two mornings looking at books and shelter magazines, with Colin putting tabs on good-taste pages and X-marked ones on the worst-taste pages.

He dozes for a few minutes and I ease the cup onto my bedside table. Wind cutting around the edges of the house screeches like lost souls at large. In the distance, Leo's two horses neigh, long whinnyings that blend into the wind and carry it onward. When he sleeps, something in Colin that's wound up relaxes and he looks like he must have at fourteen when the openness of childhood still graces the face with innocence but the coming changes into manhood already are forming. His beautiful lips slightly parted, fringe of eyelashes fluttering once, balled fist unfurling those long fingers drawn by da Vinci.

In the shower, I wash my hair and slather myself with body wash. I sing "Somewhere over the Rainbow." My breasts feel tender. I stand under the hot water uncomprehending, then comprehending.

I'm not myself. I'm not right.

I'm not pregnant. I couldn't be.

WORKING ACROSS THE MORNING WHILE Colin heads out to the olive grove, I run through my Margaret papers. Her book *World Mafia World* gathers dust on my desk. I take it down to the living room, where Fitzy has commandeered my favorite chair. He accommodates me and insinuates himself across the pages. This is risky Margaret, getting to know the young wives of Mafia dons, functionaries, sons, and those affected by them. She set herself up as an English teacher in Catania, stronghold of crime fiefdoms. Through the children, she's invited to celebrations, ceremonies, Sunday dinners. A whole year teaching six-to-twelve-year-olds. I'm sure a good teacher. She's popular. The dons, store owners, even one priest have to be fought off politely. She overhears, she subtly questions, she teaches *Winnie the Pooh* to the youngest, *Charlotte's Web* to the middle group, and *Romeo and Juliet*, other victims of warring clans, to the oldest. She is said to have lost her husband in the Vietnam War. She's chaste, living under the name of Mary Merritt. Dark skirt and white blouse. Only the pearls to show her class. Writing furiously at night, hiding her notebook in a locked suitcase under the bed. *Brava*, Margaret. Here's where I envy her. The crusader giving over a chunk of life for a cause. (Not the only one either. *The Taste of Terror*, an analysis of the tense Red Brigades years, serves as a preview for the terrorism we're now having to accept as the new normal.)

The Mafia book, scathing and incriminating, placed "Mary Merritt" on a watch list so dangerous that she had to return to the U.S. for two years. A lucky return, as that's when she wrote her classic *Sun Raining on Blue Flowers*. The crusading books give me insight into her trap-mind, her toughness; the novels reveal lyric tenderness, love of the natural world, her sadness and rapier humor.

Hands to my breasts, yes, definitely tender.

AFTER LUNCH AT STEFANO'S (I pushed around my pasta), I tell Colin I need to pick up a couple of things in the pharmacy. He joins Leo for a coffee in the piazza. Two other guys sit down and out come the cards.

. . .

I AM STUNNED. HIT WITH a Taser. The swab is a live fire-cracker in my hand. Pink. Pretty in pink. Stripes. Pink bubble gum. As my mind shuts down, I rub my hand over my flat middle. A someone in there, kick-starting. Impossible. Twenty-four years of sex and now, now . . . So, when? I know. After Sunday lunch that mellow September afternoon, we took our green blanket to our hidden lair under the ilex tree, that sweet grassy dip that hides us from the world. Colin had recovered from one of his London weeks and was joyous and loving and wild. A brown leaf stuck to his back.

Pregnant! Never an option. When I was twenty and went in for birth control advice, my doctor told me that I could not get pregnant with such a tipped uterus. "At such an angle," he said, "no determined sperm could cascade over that ledge." I pictured an openmouthed salmon trying to leap upstream and forever fall-ing back. Not having to deal with pills and implants and foams and goo was fine with me.

I will keep this to myself until I can think. Never say never. This changes everything. The X plus Y, or X now in flux. A small boy with a toy sailboat. And Colin . . . He likes our friends' chil-dren and even has offered for us to keep them so the parents can have a getaway weekend. But he has always maintained that he doesn't want his own. He adored his younger sister when they were small, but she became a social-climbing, shallow, manipula-tive jerk. (Kittens become cats.) Our work would be sliced to bits. We'd be tied down.

A slender girl in plaid skipping rope, a willful girl she is. She flashes my mother's smile. My childless friends have much easier lives and more fun. How late am I? I didn't even notice but it must be ten days. No period. (Now a comma.) No "falling off the roof," as my mother used to say. Where did that come from?

A quiet abortion in Rome? That would be hideous. Like the moles Fitzy mutilates, tangled bloody rags. Emerging from some desperate room into winter light. Scraped clean. No one to know. D & C, dusting and cleaning, my mother called the procedure. Colin is forty, a mighty age; I am forty-four. Last gasp, aging eggs. (How unappetizing the sulfur smell when the dipped pastel Easter eggs were found weeks later in the bushes.) Remember Margaret saying Italian babies are born old? And children don't always turn out well, no matter what you do. The jeweler's son—porky little kid. He looks like a sausage about to burst out of its casing. I've seen him trip his sister, blame her, and get away with it. What if you had Grazia? Always stuffing tissues in her pockets, and her obnoxious laugh. That's not nice. Grazia is . . . Oh, why the hell am I thinking negatively? *Our child.* A slice of me, a slice of Colin. Oh, babycakes. The needle on the gauge keeps falling to empty. I'm stalled. Lose a tooth with every child, my mother said. Annunciation? No way. This late miracle—as though this being *always* floated out there, holding a sparkler in the sky, waiting for her moment. Her?

LA RACCOLTA:

The Harvest

SUSAN LOOKS DOWN FROM HER upstairs window. Why is Grazia banging on the door at seven a.m.? It's barely light. Four men behind her unload nets and ladders from a three-wheeled truck. "*Buon giorno*, Grazia."

"So sorry. I am forgetting to tell you that today we start *la raccolta*, how do you say it in English, for the olives?"

"Oh—the harvest. How exciting! May we help?"

"Of course. And Zia Maria and I will be back at one with the pasta. The table is over near Leo's. If you want, join in for *pranzo*." The men spread a net around a tree on the upper terrace and lean two ladders into the limbs.

By midmorning, they've picked an entire terrace. The crates brim with shiny black and green olives. They pause against the hillside for their break—robust *panini* of mortadella stacked between thick hunks of bread. Julia climbs a ladder; Susan picks from the ground, while Camille draws in ink on blue paper from the terrace above. She's walked the groves marveling at the character of the twisty trees and the ambiguous leaves shifting silver to sage in the slightest wind. Up close, she's not sure she likes them.

Some look like tortured blackened skeletons writhing out of the earth and trying to turn into trees. Some resemble crazed head-less dancers. She wonders why what symbolizes peace looks so tortured. The oldest man, Pierino, must be eighty-five. He leans over her shoulder and as if reading her mind says, "A thousand years in the wind and rain." Only he speaks in Italian and she has no idea what he's said. "It is good," he says in English. It's *not* good, Camille knows, but maybe inking in a million lancet leaves will make it so. Thin as an olive limb himself, he blends with the tree as he straps his picking basket around his waist. If she could cap-ture that. His whole life present at the yearly harvest, his body at one with the ritual of harvest. Probably the same gray sweater and rough pants for a half a century. At least I can *know* this bond, even if I can't experience it as he does. What in my life is as primordial? Only Charles, that early sense when we were together that we were one person halved. *Cleft for me*, the hymn goes, *let me halve myself in thee*. Though the right word was *hide*, not *halve*. Charles would be all over this. But no, he is not because he is powder in a resin urn in the back of the hall closet where I stored clothes I left behind. Old windbreaker. What I can do, she realizes, is help with lunch. She folds her materials into her bag and calls out, "Back in a bit."

Susan likes the rhythm, the string nets studded with fallen olives, a piercingly blue sky with scudding clouds. Archie gets his paws caught in the netting and is shooed away by Paolo, a jolly giant who doesn't need a ladder. One of the other men, Lucio, sings songs she's never heard. His high, plaintive falsetto voice comes from another era. This has been going on forever, and with-out our help at all, Susan thinks. "Hey, Julia, is this what we came for? Did you ever imagine? Aren't our arms going to be sore!" A flush of happiness suffuses her body. Here I am at the beginning of Mediterranean life. We join this stylized dance. Adrenaline? Whatever the rush, this wash of certainty is real. I'm on the verge, she thought, of finding fresh fields. I'm catapulting toward them.

Julia leans onto the ladder, hoping the scraggly branches hold. "Grazia says it will take four or five days. There are lots of olives! I want to pick every one, then I want to make the most gorgeous salad on earth with new oil." Chris is meeting her in town after the pause. Last night when he dropped her off, he said he had a good idea he'd like to talk about. "Do you think Grazia would mind if we brought Chris and his group to the harvest? I think they would be fascinated."

"Let's ask at lunch. We could pour some wine late in the day. That would be fun."

Reaching for a high branch, Julia suddenly remembers Lizzie roaring back into her dream, wearing the chenille bathrobe Julia took to the suicide attempt. Soft yellow, supposed to be comforting. Pitiful. She banged on the door of Villa Assunta shouting, *Let me in. I'm back.* Of course you'd appear after yesterday, when I was so happy, Julia thought. That must have been when Grazia knocked early this morning. She climbed down the ladder and emptied her basket in the crate. What do they taste like raw? she wondered. She bit into a ripe one. Wretched, bitter.

When everyone gathers at one, Camille brings a tray of cheeses and fruit from the house, plus a lettuce, cucumber, and radish salad and a plate of cookies. Grazia and her aunt haul out *salumi*, lasagne, bread, wine, and more fruit. Everyone draws up benches to the weathered table laden with food. The women let the Italian stream over them. Next year, Julia thinks, next year I will be joking with them. Camille thinks, I'll never understand Italian. Susan pieces together snatches.

AFTER EVERY MORSEL OF PASTA is scraped from the dish, the men rest under a tree. They pass around grappa and swig from the bottle. A few sips, some talk, and then they're quiet. Julia hears a snort from Pierino. Camille, Grazia, and her aunt Maria stack the dishes. Maria brews espresso in a Moka pot over a butane burner. She takes small plastic cups over to the men as Susan and Julia, ever ardent, begin picking again.

AS THEY DRIVE TO TOWN late in the afternoon, they realize, like a light switched on, that every man, woman, and child is in the groves. In the piazza, the conversation revolves around olives. The usually *bella figura* Italians wear rubber boots and shapeless wool that smells of closed trunks and mothballs. Men are two deep at every bar, nipping back espresso or red wine. This phenomenon lasts three weeks, until everyone is sick of hearing about yields and even sick of themselves bragging over their own oil, which is, of course, the best. Already, new unfiltered oil is for sale at several shops. Julia buys half-liter bottles at three places.

Chris is waiting for her at Bar San Anselmo, which is rowdy with olive pickers. She spots him in a corner and waves her bottles of new oil. "Let's get some bread. I can't wait to taste." Chris admires the brilliant green color. He admires, too, the excited flush on Julia's face and her exuberance over the olive oil. From the counter, Violetta sees what they have and brings over a basket of bread. They linger for two hours with a bottle of the house red, slightly sour. Each oil tastes a little different. All over-the-top excellent. Neither of them can choose a favorite. Chris tried some of his fanciful descriptions—fresh grass and spring wind, a melting emerald at the bottom of a well (Julia laughs at that), Irish moss. They give up trying. He tells Julia about the group's trip to Montalcino this morning. "The monks at this ancient abbey still sing the hours, what, eight times a day—lauds, compline, all the times you're supposed to pray. There was no one there but us, and they do this every day." He covered her hand with his. "The abbey is just spectacular. Pure, austere, and holy." They both look down at their hands. Something shifts. He lifts her fingers and turns them around. "You have nice paws. We should go there sometime, the abbey of Sant'Antimo."

Julia tips her head and looks at him. His eyes, ever so subtly different colors. "What is your idea that you wanted to talk about?" Move this back on track; I can't fall for him. Wade could walk in right now and say *let's go home* and would I go? Chris's cool hand over hers is the first touch she's felt in months.

He pours more wine. "I'd like to see if you'd be at all interested in helping me expand the tours I bring here. Tuscany is second nature to me. I'll always come here but I'm thinking of moving into Friuli as well."

"Is that near Venice?"

"Right. A great area. Great. I know the wines and some of the makers but I need a man on the ground, that would be you, to search out the best places to stay and eat. Then I might add Sicily, if I can get it together to leave my home business for that much time. I like the travel."

"*Mamma mia*—or do they really say that? I'm flabbergasted. It sounds fantastically interesting to me. A dream. You know, I'm all about reinventing my life here, but this moves beyond anything I've imagined." They talk details and times.

"Can I just get this out of the way? I divorced five years ago. I have a son, Carter, who's studying enology at UC Davis. My former wife kept the house and I live in a remodeled bunkhouse for workers in the vineyard."

Julia says, "Oh, okay, you don't have to . . ."

"It's all cool. Just one of those growing-in-different-directions things. Italy became more and more important to me, and she always wanted to go to Hawaii. Of course, that's not it by a long shot. I was across the room from her at a party one night, and I looked at her as though she were a stranger. Buffed, tan, big smile. Big hair. I had this wave of sadness smack me because I thought, I don't love her the way she deserves. It was odd. I'd felt politely blank for a long time, kind of neutralized." He doesn't say that sex with her depressed him; she felt like an inflatable doll. "I didn't want to feel that way; I wanted to throw myself into my life again. That's when I expanded my business and started these wine-in-context trips. I got a tutor and worked like a dog learning Italian. I missed Carter, my boy, when I traveled, but I didn't miss Megan. We split when he went to college. I guess I was as lost to her as she was to me. Yoga, cardio, tennis. She keeps busy. Fit. Oh, yes, fit. Met some pilot online. Carter's okay. He's with me a lot. I even have dinner with Megan now and then. California civilized."

"I wish my divorce—it's still pending—were that way. I won't even email with Wade—that's my former husband. I'm okay now." She tells him in bare outline about Lizzie's addiction, how it wrecked them inside and out. "Our good life upheaved and fell apart." What has consumed her for years, for this moment anyway, seems to take place as through the far view in a telescope. Speaking of her family, she is, if not relaxed, then at least calm. She feels a small burst of sympathy for Wade, a highway flare at the scene of an accident. "Work saved me. I've learned everything at Mulberry Press. The books are solid and aesthetic. I'll show you some I brought with me. They're not just *here it is, recipe and anecdote*, but cultural links, too, or history or why the recipe exists. Now I am thinking of doing a project with Mulberry myself. The work with you would be such a bonus." She smiles. "It would be exhilarating! I'm really excited."

Chris loves the idea of her *Learning Italian*. "I can be your wine consultant." Funny she chose those words—*solid* and *aesthetic*. That's what she seems to him.

JULIA ARRIVES AT HOME LATE, just as Susan and Camille sit down for dinner. She serves herself a bowl of risotto that Susan made with lemon and pistachios. Camille, salad queen, washed extra lettuces this morning when she prepared lunch in the grove. "We eat unbelievably well," Julia says. "Even the simplest thing is incredibly tasty. Why is everything good?"

"I think they leave it alone." Susan dribbles fresh olive oil over the salad.

Julia immediately shares her news about possibly researching Friuli for Chris. "Can we go on trips? Susan, you could visit gardens; Camille could search out the museums and architecture and ruins. I'll find the great places to eat. It will all be good adventure."

Camille proposes starting in Venice before Friuli. "Venice out of season. Snow—does it snow?—in Piazza San Marco? Imagine. Hot chocolate at that *caffè* where they play the schmaltzy music, gondolas . . ."

Susan, always up front, interrupts. "What about Chris? He's quite cool. And he seems completely at home in the world. Are you liking him a lot?"

Julia laughs. "A faint tingling in the long-dead extremities? I think so. What an odd sensation. Sitting in the bar with him, I had an image of us walking down a street together in some Italian city. Just walking, shoulder to shoulder. And it seemed right.

"Would I have an affair at this point? Why not? But probably we'll be friends." She found herself hoping instead for the affair. A romantic villa hotel with fine linens, a view over a stubbly winter vineyard, and . . . She tried to envision Chris in a hotel terry robe running a bath in a big marble tub, but she laughs instead. "I lived with this grinding pain, like a dentist's drill constantly in my head. You can't think of anything else with a drill running. That's gone. The relief is hard to describe. The *noise* has stopped, for now anyway. Today, I even felt a slight forgiving toward Wade. Still a *there stands Jackson like a stone wall* toward Lizzie, though." She ripped her life and ours, Julia thinks. No words can get at the pity and betrayal and violence. And if my head is a handful of shards, hers must be ground to dust.

"You're moving forward now. It's all good." Susan clears the table.

Camille pauses with the last of her wine, and Julia looks at their reflections shimmering in the window. "Yes, all good. Thanks to you two."

SUSAN BROUGHT HOME FROM TOWN three new garden books. Camille builds a fire in the living room. After Susan brews a pot of orange-scented tea, the three of them settle for the evening with their books. Camille is reading Elena Ferrante in English, with the original Italian version beside her. Every now and then she reads a few sentences in Italian, her lips forming the difficult sentence constructions. Julia goes upstairs to give herself a manicure, though olive picking surely will stain her coral nails again tomorrow. Chris will bring his group for a couple of hours. He offered to provide good prosecco. Soon, new oil will anoint everything.

Julia thinks, The years, the years of not looking forward. Now, what luck.

Susan tosses another log on the fire and passes a book to Camille. "Look at this garden—La Foce. Let's go there. They're open on Wednesdays."

Camille thumbs through the pages. "That's the home of Iris Origo. She wrote a strong memoir, *War in the Val d'Orcia*. I'm ready."

GREEN

COLIN IS UP EARLY, AT his desk, facing a thousand items to verify on the hotel project in Florence. From the design vantage, he's finished, but he must check on the builder's progress tomorrow. We'll go together and I'll walk around town and visit the Strozzi museum while he works, and then we'll have a free evening for a dinner along the Arno and our favorite hotel. Time for the big reveal. I feel that I have two heads and no one notices. How can he not know? Well, I didn't know either.

Strange that Camille noticed something. Yesterday, we walked over to Villa Assunta to see how the olive harvest was going. We have only fifty trees so we were done, thank god, the olives already taken to the mill by Fabio, who helps us. Tomorrow we'll pick up our fifty liters, more or less, and be set for the year.

Julia's new friends were imbibing and toasting. Chris seemed smitten with Julia, following her movements with doglike attention. She spread her glory around all of us but I did notice her hand linger on his sleeve when she handed him a glass. She's a bright light and obviously he's into her. I wonder if she is surprised.

Colin met everyone for the first time. I'm not sure he knew which women were at the villa and which were with Chris. Camille was next to me at the table and as everyone toasted she leaned close and said, "You all right? Would you like some prosecco?"

"Yes, I'm great. I'm fine with water."

"You look pale. I don't know you well, of course, but you look, um, not yourself."

"I'm absolutely fine, maybe a bit bushed from the olive picking. Thank you for the concern, though." I wanted to grab her arm and say, *What the hell should I do?* Or lean into her shoulder and weep. But she doesn't know me or Colin. Instead, I told everyone about what happens at the mill and how healthy the new oil is when it's fresh.

A whole murmuration of women, enthusiastic about Italy. Overflowing with a zeal I recognize and still feel in quick flares, although not for the olive harvest. It's fun to dabble for a couple of mornings and to enjoy the camaraderie, but if you're responsible, it's damned hard work hour after hour with your arms up, your face sometimes whipped by wind. Even with our quick *raccolta*, my fingers are stiff. I was very careful on the ladder. (Baby on board.)

Unlike most visitors, Susan has fallen hard for this late October ritual. She stayed out all day and will go with the men to the mill to watch the whole process. Grazia has given her a giant plastic container for a supply of house oil, and Julia bought glass bottles to transfer the oil into as soon as they have it. Camille wonders if she possibly can capture that particular green on paper. "It's limpid. Not really the color of anything else. Not celery, kale, not asparagus. It's not like a green light or a Coca-Cola bottle or moss. Oh, maybe close to a dollar bill?"

Because I *know* that everyone loves poetry, even if they don't think so, I raised a toast with my cup of water and misquoted a bit of García Lorca, who knew something about the virescent color:

Green, how I want you green.
Green wind, green branches.
Big hoarfrost stars
come with the fish of shadow
that opens the road of dawn.
The olive tree rubs its wind
with the sandpaper of its branches,
My friend, where is she—tell me
where is your bitter girl?
Who will come? And from where?
Green, how I want you green . . .

Colin looked at me with a frown; he knows the poem I've mangled. Lorca didn't even write "olive tree." His tree was fig. He smiled, shaking his head. "That's my girl. Now we know what green is." Everyone clapped and the prosecco went around again.

AS WE WALKED UPHILL, COLIN threw his arm around me and nuzzled my neck. What solace, his natural-born tropical scent. "What's up, poetry girl? Something bothering you? You seemed emotional when you were holding forth with the green poem."

"There's something to talk about, yes."

How did he pick up some trouble ion from my quote? "I should know your sharp radar by now. Later, we'll talk, okay?"

"Whatever you want to say, I'm always listening."

I couldn't say, *Oh, nothing to stress about,* since I don't know that. He may totally freak. I'm worried, but then I always am. *Don't be a worrywart,* my mother used to admonish me. How can you not? Many awful things happen. Will he be stony and accepting? I know him perfectly, down to his curved-in little toe that looks like a tiny shrimp. (*Worry:* from the Old English *wyrgan,* strangle. It's not *that* serious, is it?)

Whatever he says, whatever he wants, whatever he doesn't say, he always will remember this breaking news. In Florence, leaning on the Santa Trìnita bridge watching the jagged *palazzo* reflections in the Arno at dawn? Over dessert at our favorite trattoria where we ordered fried calamari the first night we met? Knee-to-knee on the train with the autumn countryside speeding by?

The Unexpected Garden

"WE HAVE A YEAR. MORE if we want! Are you just flabbergasted, as I am, that we get to do this?" Susan speeds into the dips and curves toward La Foce, overtaking tractors on the narrow road with a friendly wave of her hand. They have an appointment at eleven, confirmed by the daughter of Iris Origo, to see the writer's garden. Susan, if they get there, will lap up every square inch of the elegant plan. Italian gardens, based on pots and geometry and pergolas and water features, are a new concept for her, totally upending her English-oriented ideas of garden rooms and high-maintenance perennial borders—so casual in appearance but beastly to maintain. They're driving into the barren Val d'Orcia, a vast expanse of undulating hills relieved by cypress-lined roads, strips of feathery poplar windbreaks, fields of plowed brown earth patchworked with other fields of crushed brown sunflower stalks and cover crops of clover—a landscape of subtraction, but still inviting. She swerves off the road. "Let's get out. Camille, you should have an easel. Look at this!"

"I'm not up to painting a landscape this grand; I should stick with my still lifes. Maybe I could manage that white road down there, the one bordered by cypresses."

"Tuscany is beginning to seem like one big garden," Julia says.

SUSAN IS ENCHANTED WITH THE bones of the autumn garden. Formal boxwood hedges and borders are planted extensively, but the garden is not rigid. The young English guide points out what's *not* here right now—the peonies, allium, roses, and, of course, the wisteria the garden is famous for. "What I like best in gardens," Susan says, "is all over this place—the element of surprise! Step through the opening in the hedge and there's a fountain or a statue. Look, campanula creeping into the cracks of a stone wall and little sedums popping up on porous stone steps. Low stone basins tucked in the beds hold tiny water lilies—homes for frogs."

"That's the way you dress," Camille observed, "very cropped or angular but with unusual patterns or accessories, like right now." They paused to notice Susan's long mustard sweater over tan tights, a red, gold, and green scarf knotted just so, and her slouchy red shoulder bag. "I'd never think of that acid yellow with red, and it looks fabulous." At first, Camille had feared Susan might be too aggressive for her. She's come to see that quality instead as verve. And Susan always pushes them into the new.

Susan gives Camille a quick hug. "You're a darling." She takes out her new notebook, scrawling *The Unexpected Garden* on the cover. "I'm glad I brought my good camera."

A hundred photos later, before they leave, she asks the young guide, Nella, to take a picture of the three of them under a pomegranate tree. They pose with the ancient fruit of Persephone dangling around them, ruddy orange globes, mythic and luscious. A shaft of sunlight through the tree turns Susan's spiky hair into an iridescent halo. In the photo, she will look electrified, if not holy. Julia is caught about to speak, her mouth half open. Camille's face is shadowed but she smiles widely and her eyes catch the light. "Are you sisters?" Nella asks.

"Almost," Camille answers.

"What's the Italian word for pomegranate?" Julia asks.

"*Melograna.* A word I love," Nella says. "Pick a couple to take with you. If you open them underwater, you can get the seeds out easily. They look pretty scattered over desserts."

Julia nods yes. "You must be a cook. Where should we eat?" Nella mentions several nearby favorites.

"We'll be back in the spring. I can't wait." She's already thinking of Chris. He should add this detour to his days in the brunello vineyards.

They find Nella's favorite restaurant in a stand of oak trees. Just inside, a woman is making gnocchi. Julia asks if it's okay to take a video. The woman then exaggerates all her gestures as she forms thin ropes of dough. Italians are born actors. She arranges the small knuckles of pasta on a sheet pan, wipes her hands on her apron, and gestures to the finished pasta. *"Ecco!"* Here it is! Julia shows them the video at lunch. "Food Network, come crying!" she says. As she reviews Susan's still photos, she realizes that all those real estate years gave Susan a lot of experience. "Your pictures are better than mine," she exclaims. "I have a great idea! Would you work with me on styling and photographing the food for my book?"

"That would be wonderful! I'd love that." In a few minutes they are eating the lightest gnocchi ever made. It can be like rubber bands, but this is paradigm, served with a savory tomato sauce. Simple, yes, as is the salad of small greens with only a drizzle of new oil. "Ever get the feeling that we overcomplicate our lives?" Susan asks.

CAMILLE OFFERS TO DRIVE HOME, insists really. Susan sits in the backseat, looking at her photos and writing down ideas. A path along the terrace behind the house, a path so narrow that your legs will brush through catmint, lavender, run-wild spearmint, and cosmos. Where the terrace turns, a bench. We need secret places in the garden. Plans fly faster than her pen. Camille is humming and Julia has fallen asleep, her head cranked hard to the right. She's going to feel that later.

GROWING TRANSPARENT

NEW LEAF, INDEED. WHEN I printed those words on the frontispiece of my notebook, what did I know? I'm in town early because, well—can I sleep? I look through the pages, searching for inspiration for the coming-up day. Violetta brings over a *ciambella*, a doughnut, with my cappuccino. A sugar rush might be just the thing.

Colin snoozes away through anything, otherwise he would have been kept awake all night by my churning. Scared and shocked am I. In the night I was thinking of my mother—those four years I stayed home to take care of her. Her decline, her long death, seasons and years slipping by. I was lovingly caught, wanting to help, but wanting my life. And Ger—Gerald Hopkinson—standing by always. He was dear to me, the family friend who stepped forward after her diagnosis, when I came home from Boulder to stay. Our parents were close and he was my first date, first kiss. We were on and off during high school and college. Now we were both in our late twenties, neither having forged relationships. He was, still is, in banking. I never knew exactly what he did—money markets, stock analysis, investments, often calming people on the phone. I lived in limbo.

Ger lined up the care while I commuted and finished the semester, and then I was home from Boulder (my first full-time job teaching writing) for the duration. For relief, I taught one class a semester at the University of Miami. Mother came back from the melanoma surgery, but with a partially frozen left leg and her MS to boot, the struggle with her care was real and constant. Steroids puffed her body until she looked blown up and moony. The sheer labor became harder. I remember her anger flashing out, her swollen leg and the small white feet, delicate as a porcelain doll's.

I wanted her at home, not in some facility. She quite desperately wanted me with Ger and she didn't hold back on saying that she wanted a grandchild. I never told her I was fated to be "barren," as she would have called it. Ger and I just fell into each other again and it seemed we were on track to marry and live forever in Coral Gables. Why, I wonder now, why I didn't get pregnant— prime fertility time—during that mini-marriage. As Mother failed, I began to have attacks of claustrophobia when I was at Ger's bungalow. Even sitting on the front porch with a lemonade after tennis, I'd feel a rising panic. *Not my life.* Not that I couldn't have practiced my art with him. He encouraged me, he just didn't meet me in my zone. And I couldn't cozy up to banking. But our circles overlapped, and in that gray zone of commonality we had a shared history: powerful juju. He liked to travel and cook and all that—but who doesn't? I was not going back to Boulder. Though I loved the town, it was not my place in the universe. Ger's slobbering boxer turned around and around before he flopped into a comfortable spot. That's what I did, too.

When my mother died (the melanoma came raging back), I applied for a residency at a writers' retreat on the Tuscan coast. I got in. Ger knew without my telling him that I'd drawn a line, but I told him anyway. I *was* sorry and said so. Ever the gentleman, but he was ticked and made it clear that he wouldn't wait again.

In Italy, weeks of healing and solitude and blissful writing. Most of the poems that got me the awards were conceived (there's that word) in a spare room overlooking the Tyrrhenian Sea. When I read them now, they seem dark blue with the mourning I carried. My mother's death brought back my father's (slammed from behind by a semi on the Miami expressway, his vintage TR3 flew into the shallow bay, a trajectory I have rewound a million times). I was thirty-one. Both parents lost. I'd expected at the least another twenty years with them.

With a couple of other writers at the retreat, I traveled on weekends. San Rocco is off the tourist loop. We happened upon it. The grace, the dignity, the encompassed time—I walked around town and imagined a long recuperation here, a big project, something entirely mine.

After the writers' residency ended, I went home and packed up the house, leaving bare furnishings, putting too many plastic bins in a storage unit. What to do with thousands of family photos, my parents' college yearbooks, my grandmother's Spode. Things. More things. A woman named Stacy Jackson and her two daughters rented the house and within six months she and Ger were a couple. How could he have moved in and taken over the rent checks? Creepy, I think.

With my parents' money, I bought my house, Fonte delle Foglie, my heart's needle, outside San Rocco. Now I must thank Ger for inadvertently spurring me into a larger mental space. What I sensed was dead right. He and I lacked that mysterious quality I wanted and without which a relationship is in peril. The poet Rilke's definition of intimacy—that two solitudes protect and greet and touch each other—never sounded right to me. Too bleak and otherworldly. Spooky stuff. I had a better guide. From Robert Dessaix's *Corfu*, I copied this quote: "Intimacy is more, though, than just a burst of loving recognition between two people. But what is it? It is, perhaps, the experience we have sometimes—rarely, but we do have it—of growing transparent, softly penetrated to every corner by another's knowing gaze? And of his or her being pierced and known in turn by our inner eye." Guided by that and a million other things, I wrote furiously for a year.

My mother, would she be pleased, if she had lived? Probably she'd have worn out her hope by now. My mother was Idella Parkman Raine. If I have a girl, if I have a baby at all, maybe I'll name her Della Raine. Colin's last name: Davidson. Not bad. Della Raine-Davidson. Della is lovely. Idella, no.

New Leaf. Maybe Leaf would be a good name for a boy. Worked for Leif Erikson.

Thinking of my mother's things in storage reminds me—a wheel of Colin's roll-on broke, and he went out to the barn to rummage around for another bag. He came across a suitcase belonging to Margaret that she left when she took off for Washington that last time. He opened it and brought in a wild dress. "What else is in there? It's probably full of mildew."

"Looks like musty sweaters."

I shook out the dress. I remember her at a New Year's party in this spangled thing, off-shoulder crimson velvet as liquid as wine pouring. She was smoking a big cigar, which she liked to do for effect. I watched. She didn't inhale. Line in notebook: get rid of the junk she left. Clean out shed. Someone should wear that dress, but how intimate someone else's dress. Intimacy—she was off and on. She could wall herself off, too.

Is it because I'm female that I proceed in my notebook from "clean out shed" to a new poem?

OFF SPRING

We lit the so-called fuse,
drops of semen like glue we use
to wallpaper the nursery.
Smudge-pot in the belly, ballooned
and far-fetched. We were all once encased:

roly-poly skulls and crossbones, fat
little pirates not knowing we were holding
ourselves hostage. The brain plates slowly
push toward the center, and the whirl of water
in the funnel has nothing else to do but swirl down.
What keeps us on this earth sometimes
but blunder or an off-secret or
an opposite to stillness or a wandering
from this past pasture to the next
present pasture. Birth—an acquired taste,
a lump sum inheritance, an oxytocic surprise
visit by someone we weren't expecting to be
so funny, so open and unsutured, so brilliantly
nomadic and ragtag. For this we have all come out
to see you, lawless, see everything, to witness
the biggest explosion, finally sprung free.

This appeared whole cloth from words I listed in the back of my notebook: nimble, anomie (without law), funnel (*imbuto*), fontanelle, offspring, haruspex, font flow, offspring, ragtag, oxytocic: hastening childbirth, nomad: wandering in search of pasture. Words engender feelings as much as feelings are expressed in words.

Ever since lightning struck me, I've been writing poems nonstop. Where do they come from? Ether, ichor. Or a poet is a haruspex, in Etruscan times the one who divined meaning and future by the markings on the exposed liver of a sacrificed animal.

VIOLETTA BRINGS MY SECOND CAPPUCCINO over just as Camille comes in the door.

"I am not going to interrupt—you look enthralled." She waves from the counter.

I'll have to reread the poem later. "Oh, join me. I'm leaving in a few. We're going to Florence for a couple of days. What are you up to this early?"

"I think I'm picking up your habit. I just love the town as it starts all over. I *see* better when there are few people out. I even like that teeny street-sweeper truck that whooshes down the street. And the barista who delivers espresso to offices; he holds up a tray and walks along whistling. He's straight out of a Balthus painting. Where's he going anyway?"

"I think he's taking the mayor and his staff their wake-up shots. I love the electric street-sweeper, too. The driver is a friend's son. He sometimes stops and gives me a hug. Where else is that going to happen?"

Camille talks about her frightening attempts to "become a painter again at this late date," the Italian tutor she sees, and what she calls her "discovery walks." "I have eureka moments when I see an embedded column in a wall, or a stone coat-of-arms with carved deer antlers or pears or oak trees. Nothing subtle about those Medici ones—six balls. Or are they oranges? There's one street with the medieval overhang supported by flimsy-looking timbers. It's a stage set from Shakespeare, not that he was medieval, but it looks like the Globe Theatre." She adds, "My husband and I used to love going to London. We always tried to see a Shakespeare production."

"Have you come across the two painters' restoration *bottega* down vicolo delle Notte?" She has not.

"You'll love it. Matilde, she's the one with the wild copper hair, and her assistant Serena, who *is* quite serene, are top art restorers. They've worked on many fresco cycles in Siena, Montefalco, and Arezzo—all over Tuscany. Their workshop is crammed with paintings that have been gouged or spilled on, or are just obscured by layers of grime. They do what they must to bring them back."

"Okay. That sounds beyond fascinating. I'll find them."

"You have Archie with you!" As she opens the door, I see him, his leash looped around an outdoor table leg.

"Oh, yes. Archie wants to become like the white terrier that's everywhere—a town dog. Full citizen rights to sleep in the middle of the street!"

I like Camille. Of the three, she's further back in herself. Friendly and quick, yes, but some quality of, um, of waiting? Is that it? She's attractive now and must have been a raving beauty once. If she had flowing silver hair instead of blond, she would look like an oracle. A Roman second-century sculptor would have rendered that face as goddess of the hunt. We'd look at her now in the Borghese museum. I like thinking of marble Camille pulling back the string of her bow. Actually, she's paused in front of the ceramics shop, eyeing a pretty platter. I'm sure she's finding that when you start to cook in Italy, you need more platters than you ever considered. Then she walks on, talking to Archie, smiling at passersby. No idea at all that within the hour, her life will begin to change in a way she never considered.

Happiness belongs to the self-sufficient, so said Aristotle.

Now I have to hustle home and hope Colin is ready. We need to catch the ten o'clock train.

Discovery Walk

CAMILLE ESPECIALLY LOVES THE TOWN'S *vicoli*, the streets that climb or descend off the main street. Two donkeys barely could pass each other. Vicolo delle Notte falls sharply off the via Gramsci, then twists behind buildings to face the valley. The *bottega*, which she's never passed before, is flooded with morning light. In the window, Matilde of the blazing curls and Serena, stark as a Quaker, stand before a commanding Madonna in blue holding out her skirts where a miniature town nestles under her protection. Serena aims a hair dryer at the side of the Madonna's head, as though she's drying her hair. How clever, apply quick heat to a repaired patch, and then they can proceed.

Camille, peering in the window, gets a smile and wave from Matilde, who turns and shouts to another woman in the back. Camille hears a clatter, and then a young girl comes to the door. "*Buon giorno.* Can we help you with something?" she asks in English. Camille explains that she's new in town, trying to paint, and that Kit sent her. The assistant invites her in. She's Katie, an art student from Boston, spending an independent semester studying with Matilde and Serena.

Matilde leans over her box of tints and paints, brushes and powders, selecting a brush with two or three stiff hairs, and begins to retouch the earlobe of the Madonna. She speaks in Italian, forming a circle the size of an orange with her hands. Katie translates: "I don't know how this was damaged. Hard to say, but a section this big was at some time scraped by something. I'm perpetually astounded by how much survives plague and war and everything else, but just as astounded by the odd damages that occur. How? Who would do this?"

"Those paints, the hair dryer—looks like a Hollywood makeup artist's wares," Camille says. The women laugh. Katie shows her some works in progress—a large crucifixion punctured right in the middle, a faded landscape not so old, a lunette of a serious man's face, and a table filled with large broken fresco pieces like a child's jigsaw puzzle.

The women are gracious, but Camille sees that she's interrupting important work. "Katie, please tell them how I am in awe of what they do. Sorry my Italian isn't up to much."

"I will—they understand a lot of English from all the students they've had. Thanks for stopping by. And there are some workshops if you're interested. We're doing a papermaking one this weekend. The *bottega* specializes also in illuminated manuscript repair." She gestures to a glass cabinet stacked with thick, creamy paper. "Come. It's really fun and you go home with a beautiful packet of gorgeous pastel papers." She hands Camille a flyer.

"Let me check. My friends are planning a trip to Venice but I'm not sure when we'll leave. I would love to do this." Camille unties Archie and heads back up to the piazza, where she spends an hour at Beato Angelico furiously studying Italian pronouns. She wants to speak to Matilde and Serena. If I'm doomed to be only a Sunday painter, she thinks, maybe I could work in a different way. The waiter brings out a biscotto for Archie, a perfect distraction since it's as hard as a bone.

• • •

BY LATE MORNING, SUSAN AND Julia make their rounds in town: wine store, fruit and vegetable stand, butcher. Julia stops at the bookstore for a Venice guidebook. Susan will say everything's online, no need for a book to lug, but Julia doesn't cozy up to electronics and prefers style and sense of place over facts. She picks up a map, too, and a copy of Jan Morris's *Venice*.

They all meet for lunch at Stefano's, which is becoming home base, and map out a plan to travel north the following week. Chris is due back from an excursion with his group to the Maremma wine district near the coast. He will see his guests off at the Florence airport on Wednesday and Julia says he'll join them for the Friuli excursion. She already has put in hours of research.

"Let's take the fast train up and spend a couple of nights in Venice first," Susan suggests. "I've located a hotel right on the Grand Canal."

Good. Camille can take Matilde's papermaking workshop. She steps outside for a signal and shoots off a message to the *bottega* before Stefano brings the crème brûlée. "This is just a suggestion. I wonder if Kit would like to go with us. She speaks perfect Italian and I think she'd be up for adventures. Oh, this is so smooth. What's the flavor I'm tasting?"

"I think it's lavender. I'd love to have her. I think next week Colin is scheduled for London. Would she travel with us novices?" Julia has a fleeting thought of Chris but, she reminds herself, this is research. Business. Lucky he's used to traveling with women.

"After Venice, we'll rent a big car at the airport. Let's plan the Friuli part now . . ." Susan flips open her laptop.

"Are you going to eat the last bites?" Julia leans over with her spoon poised.

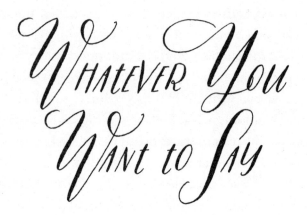

Whatever You Want to Say

COLIN AND I SPENT AN ideal day in Florence. We dropped our overnight bags at the hotel where we always stay. We like the old-world feeling—massive leather guest books on the trestle tables in the hall, baronial chairs, blue watered-silk draperies, views of domes. There are many new hotels where you could be anywhere; here, you only could be in Italy.

Running late, we took the eleven o'clock train and had lunch at a new place on the Oltrarno, the other side of the river. When we travel in Italy, afternoon is always a time for love. Gino gave us our favorite room that overlooks Piazza Tornabuoni and a slice of the Arno. Late in the day, Colin stopped by his project. As I walked in the San Lorenzo neighborhood to my favorite paper store, I rehearsed what I will say to him at dinner tonight. I can't just blurt out that our lives are forever changed. The best I come up with is to present a hypothetical: *How at this point in our lives would you feel if we had a baby?* That way we have a chance to start a conversation.

Maybe I should first ask if he wants to get married. Oh, we've discussed and discussed it, and I don't know why I hold off. If we were in America, I probably would have by now, but living here and not being married just seems part of cutting ties that bind. I like the idea of being able to walk without legal consequences, even though I love Colin unconditionally. But now, if I am to have a child, I would like to want her on my own as equally as I want her *with* Colin. Her, little Della. Ha! Big strapping lout of a boy. Leaf. Jamie, my father's name. Lionel, Colin's father's name. No way.

BEFORE DINNER WE GO UP to the hotel's small bar where Gino always remembers our favorite drinks. "Not the Campari Soda—the Campari only with a twist," he offers me.

"Gino, *grazie*, for me a ginger ale."

Colin orders Campari.

Then, bang. I sit there as Colin leans forward and puts his hand over my knee. "Kit, sweetheart. I have to say something and forgive me if I'm stark crazy. You've just been a little weird. Could you be pregnant?"

I snuffle a mouthful of ginger ale and it comes spewing out my nose. Sputtering, openmouthed, shocked, I nod. Then I begin to cry. Gino rushes over and I wave him back, trying to smile but turning over the ginger ale in my lap.

Colin slides his chair closer and puts his arm around me. "Kit, Kit, how long have you known? Angel brains, why didn't you tell me? This is . . ." He trails off, kissing my hair, starting to laugh. I'm hiccupping now. The two tables of other guests fix on us.

We stagger out into the cold Florentine night, a swollen moon wobbling in the river. I don't know how he feels—maybe he doesn't either. Until I calm down, we lean against the bridge wall. I urp only a little. "*Madre di Dio,*" Colin says. Then we walk on silently to the trattoria we always favor, tonight displaying in the window a tangled brown octopus that sickens me again.

We're settled at a table looking out at Piazza del Carmine. I'm weirdly hungry and order a plate of fried *funghi porcini* to start. Colin considers the wine list. For sure, he can use a glass or two. He leans across the table and cups my hands in his. He twirls the sapphire set up on tiny cat's teeth that my mother left me, then takes my ring finger and rubs it. "I know a gold worker here. I would love to design something for us."

Reflexively I say, "We don't have to . . ."

"Look, you, hey, we're in this together. I know when it happened, yes? Six weeks? Seven? We've made love since, but not like that Sunday, that memorable time together, well, two times, right? But why then? We've had endless times like that before. Or maybe not, maybe I went"—he lowers his voice—"deeper, maybe you arched in a new way. *Gesù*, why then?"

I don't want to think salmon-thrusting-upstream. Instead, I imagine someone pouring new green olive oil into a slim amphora, but what my body remembers is the gold rush of passion we felt together.

"Okay, my Kitty"—he knows I hate that—"not to worry. Seriously, all will be well because we will make it so."

Back in our silk-draped bed, tender is the night.

White Paper

CAMILLE AND THE OTHER STUDENTS follow Matilde up a cramped staircase at the back of the *bottega* and into a beamed mansard room. Rows of snowy paper clipped on strings hang to dry. The windows in the sloping room end at thigh height and you must lean down for a view of San Rocco's roofs and bell towers. Camille looks around at the assembly of vats, wooden screw presses, neat stacks of felt in different sizes, frames, bins of cotton and linen, and long tables. All texture, monochrome, light and grain, the workroom looks like a woodcut from another century, except for the motorized pulp-grinding vat. Camille's scalp tingles; excitement shoots through her. She felt the same in her own classes when the slides of work by Matisse, Sargent, and the Expressionists flashed by.

Matilde begins, "The workshop was founded in 1710, not that long ago in Italian terms." The faintly stirring papers seem to have active life in them; Camille wants to reach up and feel the surfaces. "Like the olive harvest," she later will tell Susan and Julia, "you're entering rituals longer than you can imagine. It's hard to say, but you're—well, stepping into a dance long in progress, and

later you'll step to the sidelines and someone takes your place."
A dance seems the right metaphor, as she sees the rhythm of the
work, the precise steps, and where you can go too far, not far
enough.

As a southerner, Camille thinks she should have known about
cotton linter, the tiny silky fibers that cling to the seeds in a cotton boll after the ginning process removes large fibers. Mountains
of the seeds are processed a second time to harvest these delicate
filaments, which then are formed into blocks. Matilde purchases
them from a specialist in Arezzo. Serena stirs some linter into a
stockpot of water, then pours this into the vat that pulverizes everything into a sloshy mess.

Matilde explains the goals of fine papermaking and Katie, the
intern, interprets for the group: Camille, an American fine press
printer, an English art historian on her sabbatical, and two young
Italian men who impatiently wait when the process keeps slowing
for the foreigners' questions. Katie does not translate when she
hears one say, "Why must they ask too many questions? Let's just
get on with it."

Camille knew of deckle-edge paper but had no idea that the
term comes from the frame that determines the size of the finished sheet. She wants to ask where the word *deckle* comes from
but since the boys look annoyed, she's trying not to interrupt;
she'll read up on the history of papermaking back at the house.
Vellum, she knows: thin calf skin. Parchment: isn't that more
generic—skin of goats and sheep and maybe others? Papyrus, she
knows, and who doesn't from the elementary school Egypt unit?
While the linter churns, Serena shows the types of paper they
make and explains how to fashion a watermark from fine wires
sewn onto the paper mold. They get to see repairs made on a trea-
sured illuminated manuscript page and on a letter from Cosimo
de' Medici to his son.

Camille feels a visceral desire to own a stack of this thick
paper.

Matilde fixes the deckle over a rectangle of screen and scoops up some of the slurry mixture from the vat. "Shake it to even the fibers, smooth it out." She hands the tray to the art historian. Everyone leans in to see the goopy, drippy slush flatten out.

After water oozes off, Matilde shows Camille how to press on a piece of felt to absorb moisture, when to pull off the deckle. Matilde carefully lifts the paper onto another felt and presses again. The students take over, Matilde and Serena guiding.

During the lunch break, Camille buys a *panino* at the bar with Rowan Volk, the fine press printer from Berkeley. He's planning a limited edition of poems on mourning and hopes to go home with enough paper. Camille does not say that's the last thing she wants to read. He shows her a Bologna artist's border of cypress trees for his cover. "You see them at every cemetery in the Mediterranean world," he says, "and I've fallen for the way they punctuate the landscape here." He pulls books out of his bag. She admires the line drawings and the way crisp type bites into the creamy pages. She recognizes the names of only a couple of his poets—C. D. Wright, Jane Miller. How lucky they are to be immortalized in these fine books. "You need to meet my neighbor. Kit Raines. She's a famous poet, too."

"She lives here?" A small piece of cheese falls into his beard.

"Yes, for years. She and Matilde are good friends." Camille made a mental note: order Kit's books. She gestures a flick away from her chin and smiles. He gets it. She wants to hear more about his press. She's just understood that the paper isn't at all passive but plays an active role in how what's printed on it is experienced. He goes first to wash his hands, then pages through the books with her. He's engrossed. She loves that. He shows her the hand-sewn folios, how the cover boards are papered, and how the finished book can be the balance point for the text. She takes out her pen and draws a lean cypress tree on her napkin.

"I'm going up to Bologna tomorrow to meet my artist and to a book arts exhibit. Want to come? It's just a day trip on the train."

He cocks his head and pushes back his chair to stretch his long legs. He's quite attractive, she notices.

"That would be splendid. I'm going to Venice on Monday, but tomorrow I'm totally free. I've seen fine press exhibits but I think I didn't understand that you're after a *concept* for the words, or would you say an extension for words?"

"Yes, both. Camille—Venice. That's a place for paper. There's this monastery out in the lagoon that prints books in dozens of languages. You must go. Lord Byron used to study Armenian there . . ." He seems to know everything about paper but never has made it himself. His eyes, black as obsidian, dart and dart, intense, tracking both of hers. They talk, talk all the way back to the *bottega*.

LATE IN THE AFTERNOON, SERENA shows them how to stack the paper they've made according to size and to squeeze each bundle under the ancient wooden press. Like handkerchiefs and scarves, they're hung to dry. Camille's favorite shape is the tall rectangle with roughly the proportions of a door.

Walking home, Camille casts about for the right design of her own watermark. *3C*, she thinks, Charles, Camille, Charlie. Then no, this is for me. An arch with a keystone lettered *VA* for Villa Assunta? Where my work will take place. *VA*, Virginia, where I learned and first met artists.

THE TOASTY AROMA OF BAKING fills the kitchen. Susan and Julia are making a flat cracker. "I saw the recipe," Julia says. They roll out a second batch, pulling the first out of the hot, hot oven. "*Carta di musica*—sheet music. The simplest recipe on earth—it's from the south of Italy. See, it's a flatbread as tactile and thin as old sheets of music. This batch is flavored with rosemary; the next with fennel. It's nothing but semolina flour and water—look how it puffs, then settles. The Italian miracle—something great can emerge from very little."

She breaks off a piece and hands it to Camille, who gives them both a hug. "This is just like the paper we made today! It seemed edible, too!" They gather by the fire with red wine and the savory crackers. Camille tells them about the day, mentioning that she's going on the early train to Bologna with Rowan. Can she explain the supercharge she got from the papermaking and the conversation about art books? "Let's go out for dinner. It's too late to cook. There's much to say."

North to Venice

WHEN JULIA INVITED ME ON the trip to Venice, I said yes immediately. "I love Venice. I've loved Venice since I was seven, when my parents took me there," I told her. "I was dressed in a dirndl dress from our previous stop in Austria. A little Heidi. I adored the sprigged floral pinafore over the ruffled white blouse. The first day, I left my handbag with felt cutouts on the gondola. It held coins from all the countries we visited, and my red diary, forever locked, the key on a ribbon around my neck. I was inconsolable. Daddy did his best with gelato stops, and my mother took me to a store for a new diary with nice paper."

"Camille may search for that shop. She's fallen in love with handmade paper. She's in Bologna today with this Rowan guy she met at the workshop. He's a fine press printer from Berkeley."

"Not Rowan Volk? He publishes the famous Volk Editions. They're works of art. In rare-book libraries everywhere."

"I don't know. Maybe. Anyway, they bonded. All I know is he's skinny and has a beard. She wants to ask him to dinner when we get home. Will you and Colin come?"

"Yes. Love to. You don't know how perfect an escape is for

me this week." I realized that I rested my hand across my middle. "I know Fitzy will be happy at Leo's. Annetta gives him scraps."

"Susan's boarding Archie at a farm outside town. She's worried that he doesn't 'speak' Italian and won't understand what he's told."

"Oh, I know the Bruni family—they're wonderful. Archie may not want to come home."

ORGANIZED SUSAN HAS MADE ALL the reservations. Oddly, though they've all been to Europe, none of the women has been to Venice. How will they react to that watery world? I go stony when someone says, "It's too crowded," or "Venice smells bad," or "I don't like Venice." When I hear that I think, *Well, I don't like you.* You have to be tone deaf and blind not to respond to the beauty of Venice.

Coming up—a chance to walk over narrow bridges, look up through Gothic windows at frescoed ceilings, look over the Grand Canal at Santa Maria della Salute's massive volumes rising out of the lagoon, look down at the colors of the *palazzi* swirling over the water's surface. Look, look, look. That's all I want to do.

THE TRAIN INTO VENICE ARRIVES conventionally but that's the end of normal. Out of the teeming terminal we enter a chaos of *vaporetti* disgorging passengers with too much luggage, a crush of tourists waiting to board, elegant water taxis for those who can't face the crowded ferries, and on the Grand Canal, the first sight of gondolas, those graphic black silhouettes drifting by as though in an etching of Venice.

Susan has reserved a water taxi, all gleaming wood and leather. Our driver performs a fast U out of there, sending spray over the people boarding the adjacent boat. He quickly slows—if everyone hot-dogged down the canal, the combined wake would further damage the buildings. Already, and for centuries, doors are worn or boarded up at the bottom, the embarking steps long since submerged.

Having made his gesture, he's in no hurry at all. We pile our carry-ons in the cabin, jackets, too, since it's warm, even humid. So that we miss nothing, we move to the open stern.

Leaning on top of the cabin, Julia props her chin on her hands and gazes. Susan has brought her good camera from her real estate days. She zooms in on the gardens we glimpse. "You all, this is *too* much," she keeps repeating. And it is. What a slide show— intricate façades of peach, ochre, the carmine shades, and gilt; cupped domes against sun-splotched, mottled sky; candy-striped poles; working barges loaded with trash, bottled water, and crates of vegetables. A long boat loaded with roof tiles lists precipitously, but one thing is for sure: Venetians know how to ply these canals. We glide by a row of particularly gorgeous *palazzi* throwing down their colors upon the water, and I see Camille turn away her face, her cheeks streaked with tears. They're dazzled—each with eyes wide open, mouths, too. Innocents abroad, as Henry James would have it. Maybe we all become innocent when we travel. Down stream, Palladio's severe church Il Redentore, plucked out of the air by a giant hand and placed on the quay. It's an offering to us, a building this perfect. I remember the chilling light inside, white as an icicle. Every color of Venice drained off. To stand in the coldness of that light you are purified. (I will go there tomorrow.)

I'm a bit queasy. I duck into the cabin and take out my notebook. What words fit this place? Impossible. I jot down: *shimmy, glimmer, shimmer, labyrinthine, a thousand mirrors, stippling, mercurial,* elegantissima, *gnarls of water, spumes like angel wings, water, water everywhere.*

We're here. Hand it to Susan. She scored a major scoop on some last-minute app. This hotel is a palace, almost a museum— those are Tintoretto frescoes in the grand hall. We're shown to a two-bedroom suite (four sumptuous beds, all draped), a living room between rooms, and a terrace smack on the Grand Canal. Enormous paintings, brocade, and tassel-and-swag everything, marble baths fit for princesses. "You are getting stars in your crown," I tell Susan. "Colin and I usually stay at this tiny inn on a tiny canal. It's sweet. But holy *madre*, this is incredible. We could be visiting the doge! Clearly, Susan, you have a killer instinct for real estate in all forms."

"True. I do. I can't help it."

Julia waves at boats passing below. "Don't ever stop!" she tells Susan. "This is genius. I've never stayed anywhere remotely like this."

"What did you tell them?" Camille asks. "That we are wives of sheiks—I'm floored. They've left flowers." She gestures toward a vase of pink roses on a painted chest.

I'VE LEARNED NOT TO INTRUDE with first-time visitors. If you know a place well, you tend to natter on, blocking the fresh impressions people have on their own. Susan will get them from A to B. I plan to soak in the grand tub, then take a long walk. We agree to meet on our terrace for drinks at six. Drinks! Well, little parachutist the size of my thumb: Shirley Temple with a cherry, here I come.

"FIRST TO SAN MARCO," JULIA instructs. She's in the lead over bridges and down narrow *calli*. They step into a portico at the end of the grandiose piazza. Stunned, they see at the opposite end San Marco looming like a fairyland caravansary in a mirage of the east. Familiar from books and movies, long arcades line the piazza, and the tilting tower anchors the whole scene to earth. They follow the strains of, could that be, "Cherry Pink and Apple Blossom

White" over to Florian's Café. The late November sun feels warm as they arrange themselves to face the raucous façade of the basilica. Susan looks up the history on her phone, Julia reaches into her bag for her guidebook, and Camille just stares at the winged lion and the powerful prancing horses that look about to leap into the piazza. "Our trouble must be that we come from a place with no winged lions," she observes.

"Symbol of Saint Mark. The place was built to house his bones. Much ado about saints' bones back then," Susan says. Julia shows them the photo in her book of the horses. "What we're seeing are copies—bronze. The real ones are copper. We'll find them in the museum." The waiter brings their lunch of pasta with clams and salads. "Their history goes way back, maybe to second-century Greece, then they somehow migrated to Constantinople where they were above the race course, the Hippodrome. The crusaders looted them and shipped them to Venice. Big war booty."

"So not the four horsemen of the apocalypse?" Camille asked.

"No, preceded that. You dig back and almost everything Christian has a pagan explanation," Julia said. She reads on. "Listen to this—Napoleon stole them and took them to Paris. They've traveled. He installed them over the Arc de Triomphe and after Waterloo they somehow got home again. *But*, in World War I they were sent to Rome and in World War II they were hidden in a convent in Padova."

"I think that's going to be the story of Venice," Susan said. "Layers upon layers upon layers. All floating."

AT DINNER I HEARD ABOUT their basilica visit. It was interesting. I haven't been inside for years because of tourist mobs but today they breezed right in. Early winter is best. Maybe I will go tomorrow now that they've described the circles of patterned marble floor tiles repeating the circles of gold glass tesserae on the ceiling, and the curves everywhere. "Our own architecture is quite square," Susan observed. I wonder if Colin has noticed this, how round the internal architecture is. Camille has an especially good eye; she made these circle connections.

We're in Venezia: we order all four courses. Julia takes out her notebook. "*Risotto all'onda,*" she says, "to the wave; perfect for my *Learning Italian*. And perfect for Venice—a stage of cooking compared to water movement. Look at this—black rice. You know what that's from?"

I don't say.

"Squid ink."

Susan frowns. "Wavy squid ink. Wow. Tastes better than it sounds."

Next comes an *orata* baked in salt crust. The waiter attacks the fish with a small saw, deftly skins and bones it, lifting off flaky slices and serving them with simple boiled potatoes on each plate. Julia has ordered, just to taste, *moeche,* tiny male crabs of the lagoon, crunchy and succulent. Outside the window, night boats ply the black-as-squid-ink canal. I have a few sips of the most excellent Friuli wine so I don't call attention to my abstinence. (Most pregnant Italian women I know don't give up a glass of red wine with dinner.) Heaven, a hint of apple, and an astringent mineral bite. Ordinarily, Colin and I split a bottle. Susan orders a second bottle and toasts travel around the table.

Camille has been preoccupied all evening, but suddenly she asks, "Did you notice the entrance to the Doge's Palace, that Gothic door right by San Marco? It's called Porta della Carta. Paper door. I love the name. Paper door! That resonates. Doors you can push through, doors that are impermanent, doors impossible to lock, transparent doors between two states of being, or doors you thought were closed to you, doors that are not doors."

"Beautiful metaphor," I say. "You could work with that." (I could work with that.)

"Why's such a substantial door called that?" Susan asks. When no one knows, she looks it up. "Maybe because it's near an archive.

Maybe because people petitioning the council stood outside with pieces of paper."

"That works, too," Camille says. Paper, she thinks. Tomorrow I will find good paper. Some for Rowan, too. Umm, Rowan. She bites her lip. What have I done?

Susan puts down her fork. "That was one fine dinner and I am so finished. If anyone wants dessert, I might manage one bite. But back to the horses—they look alive. I was stunned that someone, some maker, back in the second, maybe third century saw exactly as we see. I'm not even sure what I'm saying, but it's like he could walk in right now and we could pick up a conversation we'd left off yesterday. Did you notice on the real copper horses that the artist half cut a little gash on the eyeballs so they catch the light? He wanted the glint of life on those horses. He's telling us so."

I am thrilled to hear this. "Yes! The crescent cut is called *la lunula*. Little moon in Latin—it's on your fingernails." I hold up my forefinger to show the rising moon at the base of the nail.

"And someone knew to describe the cut on the horse's eyes like that. I've lived so long without knowing all these incredible things," Julia laments.

"You know what you need to know, my friend." Susan takes a bite of the ginger crème brûlée and slides it over to Julia. "Ginger. Write that in your book. Must be one of the spices the Venetians brought back from their saints' relic raids."

They are catching at the heartstrings of Venice quite well.

WIND COMES UP OVER THE water. A wind blowing from Constantinople, across centuries, blowing a puff of dust from the races in the Hippodrome? Pulling our jackets tight, hoods up, we retrace our steps to the hotel. In our own living room, we do what women through the ages have done. We put on our robes and curl up on the sofas to talk. This is when I learn much of their pasts and they learn some of mine. Around two, Julia nods off, then jerks awake. "*Seppioline*," she says, "little cuttlefish. I like the word. Also *branzino*, sea bass, *orata*, bream. They sound bronze and golden. *Buona notte*," she says, "I'm fading fast."

We all head to bed.

AT FOUR, CAMILLE FEELS AFRAID that her tossing could disturb Susan. She slips out of bed into her robe and tiptoes into the living room. She eats two chocolates left at turndown and pages through the hotel's fashion magazines until water reflections swirling on the ceiling draw her out to the balcony. The city is still alive. The wind has blown elsewhere, and it seems that the stars jangle, but it's only metal clanging in the moorings of boats along the quay. What was the word she'd just read in one of the magazines? *Gibigianna*. She says it out loud. The flashes of reflected light on water, how evocative. Rowan would like that word. Rowan. Charles, gone eighteen months and she's saying *Rowan*. Well, that's the least of it after yesterday. Sex was the last thing on my mind, she thinks. Since Charles died, sex is the subject I shove aside. That's over. And I'm *old* so that's okay. I had my share and more, all those years of freedom and easy connection with love and fire. She tries to envision Charles above her, looking intently into her eyes, Charles afterward at the bathroom sink, his broad back and nonexistent bottom, his quick wash of his "gear" as he called it, his glance at himself in the mirror and the smiling surprise she could see on his face. One thing she loved best about him was that he never lost his wonder that such a thing as making love was allowed. He was perpetually the eighteen-year-old who scored with the prom queen. Now this. *Betrayal* came to mind. *Disloyal.*

She sits down on the damp chaise longue. I deserve to be cold, she thinks. In Bologna, Rowan had taken her hand when they crossed a busy street. She'd looked down as though she were holding a fish. As soon as they got to the curb, she pretended to shift her bag and took her hand away. In the museum, he'd guided her twice by her elbow. She'd not been touched in eighteen months. A surge of current ran through his hand. Rowan is nothing like big Charles. He's bony, with a Roman nose and unruly eyebrows. And the beard. She doesn't know what she thinks of the beard.

After the fine press exhibit, where Rowan lingered over every cover design and layout, they stopped for lunch and looked over the books he'd bought. She loved learning about the typefaces and inks. Don't the most powerful friendships start when a person opens a new world for you? Rowan hardly ate. He had much to say about various printers, how many missed the crucial tie between form and content while others got it, got it. She loved his intensity. Her own ignited as they talked books, talked art. She has been reading about old pigments, how they were made from burned peach pits, berries, cochineal bugs, and charred bones. Can they learn to make them together?

After lunch, at the Morandi museum, she was the one who held forth. To her surprise, as she noticed the relationship to architecture of the boxy and cylindrical shapes in one painting, she put her hand on Rowan's shoulder as she gestured. "It looks like the abstracted skyline of some small angle of Bologna," she mused.

Rowan pointed out the wavy edges of Morandi's boxes, bottles, and teapots. He smiled. "They look deckled." With Charles, she'd never really discussed art, only in passing, never linked to him on that level of herself.

Charles wasn't indifferent to art but his interest, she realized, was perfunctory rather than passionate. She suddenly wondered if that was part of why she quit painting. She wanted Charles's full interest, and art was not the conduit.

She became so invested in their life together, all the vigor and fun and challenge of it, that she locked herself out. She never noticed when the marriage she loved began to dull her craving for making art. And, well, there was that trip to New York. She didn't want to think of that. Marriage kept me in a cozy cocoon, she thinks. Wings furled. That's harsh. I was happy. Admit it—happy but bound. Honey-soaked wings.

When they'd arrived back in San Rocco, Rowan offered her a ride home. As they drove from the lower hill toward town, he said, "I live right down the next road. I have the place for my sabbatical. Why don't I make us a quick pasta *arrabbiata*, my specialty—well, the extent of my culinary expertise. That and pesto."

"Sounds good to me. I told Julia, she's our resident chef, that I might be late."

ROWAN PUSHED HER CHAIR IN at the table and sliced the bread. "Are you married?" she asked.

"No. I was once. In my twenties, I fell for a doctor with two kids, six and seven. She was nine years older than I, and, man, she had an obnoxious ex. He was an emergency room doc at the hospital where she practiced. Briefly, we were married ten years and I helped raise her boy and girl. They were tossed back and forth with the ex and nothing ever seemed settled. Lot of problems, especially with the girl. I'm not proud of this but I couldn't love them as much as I should. Tess worked long hours. She was smart. Vivacious. My work didn't remotely interest her. A drift set in. I couldn't hack it with the kids when they became teenagers. Lorie, always a drama queen, flipped on Christmas morning when she was sixteen because I didn't get her the right computer. She stalked out of the living room shouting that she hated everyone. And Jack. Trouble. That same holiday, he turned up with a case of gonorrhea. Seventeen. This shit was constant. The final episode was the big New Year's Eve reveal. The ex called me and said he was having an affair with Tess, and had been for two years. That was it. Sick story from two healers."

"It was true?"

"And more, yes. They've lived together ever since. The kids, I don't want to go there. Walking disasters."

"No one since? That's a long time ago."

"Yes, you know, casual hookups. Two other involved relation-ships with former students, eager to hear about every *r* and *k* I set in type. Both flared and faded. Both young, eventually wanting that baby." He served us seconds.

She replays after dinner when he built a fire and in the middle of more talk of Morandi, perhaps more Morandi than he wanted to hear, he pulled her close and firmly kissed her. The next thing she remembers is his beard on her bare full breasts, and then she lies back on the sofa as he stands up and strips off his shirt and pants. She pulls off her sweater. At least the light is dim, she thought. "I don't know . . ." she begins, but he is on her and his hands are everywhere. Those white-as-porcelain hands that manipulate the tiniest type, those hands. She's dry but his mouth is not. Every-thing works. She laughs and he does as well. They're moving hard enough that she fears for the sofa.

"Where did *that* come from?" She has her arms still around him and can feel the standing knots of his spine. Did he orches-trate this? California free spirit beds down another hippie chick?

"From when you sketched a cypress tree on the napkin yes-terday. From when you introduced yourself: Camille. I've always loved camellias. And you were so wide-eyed at the papermaking class." No, he's passionate. He's who he seems to be. Obviously, skilled at more than typesetting.

So. That happened.

IT MUST BE FIVE IN the morning. I'll be a wreck for my full day in Venice, she thinks. I don't have to solve anything. Am I, un-derneath all the agonizing, glad? Charles. And Charlie! Wouldn't they be stunned?

Camille went back to her bed. Susan appeared not to have moved. She ruffed her pillow and determined to sleep. She had no eloquence like Rowan's—she'd merely thought him an interesting-looking person when she met him—nothing to explain why she'd had sex, really fine sex considering they were on a rickety sofa, with someone she barely knew. Such a grieving widow, she thought. But, am I full of regret, or do I feel that I should be? I'm not accustomed to being a free agent. What's the downside? I'm used to considering everyone. I don't have to. Maybe the surprising thing should be not that I had a one-night stand but that someone desires me, at my age. (And his age, too, as a matter of fact.) I didn't even worry about my thighs or my biopsy scar or if I'd sweated in Bologna. I felt aggressive. What I let myself flow into was a big rush of freedom. I thought that was over.

She slept.

I AM THE FIRST ONE up. I walk up the *calle* to a bar already crowded with locals on their way to work. At a quiet table with my cappuccino and pastry, I miss Colin and "our" inn with small rooms painted with scenes from commedia dell'arte. On our days in Venice, we walk for miles every morning, taking in current exhibits, spend leisurely afternoons in our room, then go out for *ombre*, drinks named for the small shadowy bars that plunk down a tumbler of simple red on the counters. Long dinners beside some canal ensue.

Good, I have a signal. It's an hour earlier in London but Colin already is poring over the plans for the Saudi hotel. He picks up immediately. "Still knocked off my perch," he admits, "but I'm feeling something I've never even considered—this more profound kind of intimacy. We couldn't be closer. But now we are. And it strikes me that—you know, the intertwining of DNA, this new person—implicates us in a new way."

"Implicates. Interesting word. What you say is true, but does it make you feel *sure* you want to go forward as somebody's *daddy*?

I've never understood the basics that other people seem to take for granted. Birth. Death. Seeds knowing how to be chard or sunflowers. The sun reliably shines. Seeing—the optic nerve, for god's sake. Miracle! An elderly person looks back at the child she was and that child seems still to exist. Now I'm caught up in one of those mysteries. I don't even know how my phone is calling you from this Italian bar." I pause. "And sleep. Who understands why we fall unconscious and start up a thousand stories on some internal screen?"

"Kit, stay calm. You're wigging out but you're right. Last night I dreamed I was riding on the back of a whale. Where does that originate?"

I laugh. "Well, that one seems obvious. But, yes, why does your brain present you with that image?"

"I've got a meeting, love. That image is why you love poetry."

"Hey, we'll talk later. I imagine everyone's up and ready by now. We're going to the Rialto, then the market. Julia is on a mission to learn all the names of fish in the Adriatic, quite the feat. She's going to flip when she sees the Latin names on the iced counters of fish, and even the name of the boat the fish came from. Then, a couple of museums, maybe just wandering about. Camille wants to go to art supply shops and Susan wants to get some books on Venetian gardens, oh, the Peggy Guggenheim garden. She'll most likely be looking for sculptures for Villa Assunta after that."

"They sound great. But think of me. Think of our favorite room with all the masked actors painted on the walls." On our first trip we succumbed to buying masks and both of us became totally spooked when we wore them while making love.

Masks scared me as a child on Halloween, even the papier-mâché Raggedy Ann my mother made for me. You put on the mask and *you* are gone. All the touristy masks for sale around Venice repulse me. I hope I don't get the "mask of pregnancy." Note to self: sunscreen, #50, even in winter.

. . .

BY EVENING, WE'D ALL COMBED Venice—back canals with
lines of sheets and shirts strung across overhead, stray cats slink-
ing down narrow passageways with bright lights shining at the end,
sudden piazzas where children kick soccer balls, and water, the
common denominator: everything bounded by water. At Julia's
suggestion, for dinner we traveled over the waters to Mazzorbo,
a lagoon island where adventurous winemakers brought back an
ancient vine, started a small inn and a restaurant. Susan arranges
a water taxi to take us over. I love this little island just beside lively
Burano, the most colorful village on earth. It's a living paint sale.
Mazzorbo is opposite, quiet, weedy, sparsely populated. (I started
to write *backwater* but wrote *timewash*. Nice word for these lagoon
islands: timewash.)

The restaurant is sleek, glassy, and subdued. Julia confers with
the waiter. Even I don't know some of the words on the menu.
Everything's local and they're using algaes and other plants that
grow in brackish water. *Salicornia*, Julia decides, is pickleweed
that grows on dunes at home. Camille misreads *squab* on the English translation, thinking she's ordering something with squash.
Half through, it comes out that she's vastly enjoying pigeon, which
she never could imagine ordering. "So much tastier than turkey,"
she says. "Remember it's Thanksgiving week at home." They talk
about their traditions, the rushing to the football game, the walks
in the woods. Julia remembers making pumpkin soup in a pumpkin and the bottom falling out as she took it into the dining room.
"Thanks, Julia Child! A mess!"

Susan said that after the girls decided they were vegetarians,
they always went to an Indian restaurant for Thanksgiving. Camille usually invited a table of students and cousins and Charlie's
friends. "My overwhelming memory is exhaustion—the endless
preparation, the cleanup, with the actual meal seeming to be over
too fast. I always threw out the cranberry sauce that no one ate."

But lovely. Charles at the end of the table, clashing the knives and asking who wants dark, who wants white. The late afternoon nap, the house quiet.

The winemaker has produced an extraordinary white from an almost extinct varietal. Golden and unctuous, the wine seems to sing. They hardly dare order a bottle because it's wildly expensive but they do. Sliced four ways, much is affordable. Camille shocks the bejesus out of us when she suddenly offers a toast to "uninhibited sex on sofas." Madonna! I take a sip of the wine. The Venetian sun has melted into the glass.

ONE OF THE MAGIC EXPERIENCES on planet earth: zooming in an open boat across dark waters toward Venice.

Yellow Vespas

CHRIS ARRIVED IN CORMÒNS LAST night. As Susan pulls into the parking lot beside the hotel, he is just starting up a retro-style yellow Vespa. He jumps off, hugs them all, and helps take in their bags. "How was Venice? Look." He gestures toward a row of Vespas. "The hotel lets guests use them. Ever ridden one?"

Julia had a moped in high school. Camille has ridden a few times on the back of the motorcycle Charles had in law school. Susan hasn't ever been on one but is ready for instruction. (I bet she is! Watch out, Friuli.) I've hopped on a few during my years here but I won't risk weaving along hilly roads now. Since wine tasting is out of bounds for me anyway, I'll plead work to do and pay attention to my Margaret project for a few hours. The countryside looks enticing, what we could see of it as Susan burned up the road. I'm getting cautious and if I were religious I would have uttered a few supplicating prayers on the way. Julia and Camille seem used to surging speeds and aggressive passing. Susan is a natural Italian driver; she gets that it's a blood sport.

· · ·

WHILE THE OTHERS SETTLE IN, Chris and Julia sit in the bar. She opens her files and he sees why she was a top editor. She has researched and prioritized the Friuli area; she's organized hotels, restaurants, towns, and points of interest, keeping variety in mind. "We can visit my choices and then choose what works best for the groups," she says. "I've left the wine to you, and that's top focus."

"Yes, but it's food, people, and fascinating places that make trips exceptional."

"Chris, *you* are what makes your trips exceptional. I saw that from the beginning. You have a natural ebullience that's infectious. You have a good time, so everyone does." He's quick to smile, quick to praise, Julia thought. No dark streak of rage.

"You're sweet to say so. You haven't seen me delayed for six hours in the Frankfurt airport, about to melt into a pool of butter. Or trying to find the emergency room at night when someone has projectile vomiting!"

Julia already has studied the regional food. At lunch in the hotel, she suggests *frico*. "Perfect for a chilly day, though we should have been tending vines to work up an appetite. *Frico* is local. One of the basic food groups here! It's like something fantastic happened to hash browns—a fried cheese and potato crisp, crunchy on the outside and creamy inside."

"I already can taste it," Chris says.

"They use Montasio cheese. I never heard of it but it's from local cows who've munched on something good." Already anticipating dinner, Julia scans the menu. She's stumped by many words: *guazzeto, abbrusolita, scalognato.* The food has absolutely nothing to do with the Tuscan dishes she'd come to know well.

Venison appeared in various preparations, deer liver in one.

CHRIS GOES BLESSEDLY SLOW AS they get their bearings on the Vespas. "We're in a Fellini movie," Susan shouts, but no one hears.

"This must be heaven in summer," Julia shouts, but no one

hears. They all catch snatches of Chris belting out, is he crazy, "America the Beautiful," followed by "Roxanne."

Rough-clad men with weather-tanned faces and hard handshakes open the doors to cask rooms. Tasting takes place on an upturned barrel. No T-shirts, as in California; no flavored olive oils, no mugs, no shopping hype. The wines come out one by one, always poured into proper glasses. Turns out, the men are the owners. They have dogs thumping their tails. They have work to do. The tractor waits beside the door; they're in briefly from the fields. Chris buys cases, and the owners also give the women bottles. Chris stacks everything outside to pick up later.

THREE VINEYARDS DOWN, TWO MORE to visit, but those are too far for novice Vespa drivers. In the late afternoon, Chris and Julia take the van. The others stay at the hotel with their books bought in Venice. Camille, probably the least obsessed with food and wine, writes on her laptop. She was too enamored of Venice to leave. *When I stood in front of the Porta della Carta,* she writes to Charlie, *a project came into focus. After weeks (decades?) of casting about, gazing at art, sketching, pondering, dreaming, I knew that I wanted my own paper doors. The workshop with Matilde was fortuitous because it gave me the idea of working with paper in a new way. I'm impatient to get to work now and I'm considering skipping the rest of the Friuli trip. But everything is fascinating me.* She thought of her canvases from art school and beyond, wedged under an eave at her house in Chapel Hill. Was there a smidgen of talent there? She had been given a fellowship. She recalled life models from classes, a still life of roses in a green bowl, a few landscapes. *PS,* she added to Charlie, *Look at my paintings in the attic. Is there anything to admire?*

I FIND A CHAIR BY the fireplace downstairs and write a few pages about Margaret.

These are easy memories from when we were close in those two years before I met Colin. We read aloud to each other, traveled Italy in her Alfa, sat at a table with a bottle of wine, poring over Anna Akhmatova, Cesare Pavese, and Nâzim Hikmet poems, analyzing sentence types in Italo Calvino and Katherine Mansfield. She constantly gave me presents—pillows from Turkey, lotions from the English pharmacy in Florence, maps, Italian guidebooks from the 1920s, other books, books, books. She didn't cook but loved to bring over the best white peaches or a white truffle when I invited her. If she didn't love what she ordered in a restaurant, she pushed it aside and selected something else because life is too short to be disappointed with things you can control. I was fascinated with her and I think she was a little in love with me. Perhaps in love with the life I had before me. She was already sixty-eight when we met, but like my three new friends, she didn't pay attention to her age. I didn't either. She said she was "born with the energy of two people." We often hiked stretches of the San Francesco trail from La Verna to Assisi, and the Rilke walk from Sistiana to Duino castle where the poet wrote the great elegies. Besides her Casa Gelsomino here, she kept an apartment in Rome that she'd had when she lived for many years with a woman whose name never came up and who was brushed aside when anecdotes from Margaret's era there were mentioned. We'd go down for weekends to see exhibits and stay there, a fifth-floor walkup with a terrace overlooking the Tiber. One bedroom. Twin beds. Don't ask. I didn't. As I said, she remains herself, a cypher. She was annoyed when I fell in love, but seemed riveted when she met Colin and praised his offhand wit and his passion for architecture. She came to prefer him to me.

Would she be amused with all this chasing around of wine, and plotting trips for women to be engaged, entertained, stimulated? I like to think she would. She was always quick to spot the ways women are put down. A girls' getaway might easily be condescended to, whereas a men's hunting trip would not. Not that either promotes the general good. *That* always preoccupied Margaret, though she would occasionally take sybaritic trips herself, especially after a punishing journalistic mission in a dangerous or rough area. The injustices of the world fueled her. I also feel weighted by the immense crises in the world, but what can I do, other than donate and vote for reasonable candidates, about the immigrant problems, about global warming, about terrorism? Compost my vegetables?

I'm sure Margaret would be on site with refugees, chronicling what she saw and thought, pinning people (in her frosty way) to the wall with questions. I can see her mind working on the context of world immigrations throughout history, the long-range effects of diaspora, the individual stories we cannot even imagine. That might be the book she was meant to write, and one that would last—unlike her writings on the attempted assassination of a prime minister or the wrongdoings of some forgotten politician. Burning topics inspire journalists, and those books written in a zealous fever disappear as soon as the fickle news shifts. She did write about southern Italians migrating to Germany for work; this massive migration from the Middle East would be a natural for her.

There should be a word for what I'm thinking—to imagine the book someone should write, even if the someone is dead. (German has numerous precise words for emotions not named in other languages. *Sehnsucht:* nostalgia for someone else's past or for something felt but not personally lost.) (I have this *Sehnsucht* for Margaret.)

At heart I believe that poetry has crucial work to do, all art does. What news remains from the cave dwellers? Not who killed the most game or ruled over the bush. Soot and blood handprints on the cave walls remain, and the sketchy stick figures and animals they drew. Art lasts. Still, the inexorable grind of world events keeps me anxious. Margaret, that's part of her immortality: she's that other voice in my head. She challenges. She pins me to the wall. (Oh, what's that German word for the unrest birds feel the days before their migrations?)

CHRIS WANTS TO GO TO the *enoteca* before dinner in town. Here are gathered many of the Collio region winemakers, freshly shaven, hair slicked back, wearing nice shirts and sweaters. Wine talk, nothing but wine talk. Chris and Julia shake hands with the men they've visited and introduce themselves to others. They don't look like Tuscans. They're sturdier, many have light hair and eyes, and they seem to hold themselves in more. Generations of living near Slovenia, of mixing with the Austrians, produced a different breed up here. "How great that these guys are friendly with each other," Chris observes. "Among top vintners like these, you'd think they might be snarky toward their competitors—I certainly see that in Tuscany and California—but there's a brotherhood here, a lot of leaning into the glass, heads nodding, wine swirling."

"Don't you love it that men kiss and hug?" Julia whispers.

The waiter sets down a board of cheeses for the group. He nudges Julia and points to thinly sliced pink ham. "*Il migliore,*" he says, "*il prosciutto della famiglia D'Osvaldo.*" The best—prosciutto made by the D'Osvaldo family. And it is. Julia resists the impulse to tear off the broad rim of fat edging each slice. The almost-transparent slice tastes pink and gently cured.

She rolls a piece and hands it to Chris. "We should see if we, you, can take the tour to the place that makes this. It's spectacular. The fat tastes like salted butter." Julia widens her perception of prosciutto, which previously she could easily pass on when the antipasti platters came around. She quickly notes the name.

At the bar, Camille and Susan order tastes of the friulano, then the odd ribolla gialla. Susan tries a sip. "Tastes like something the Roman gods might drink at their orgies." She purses her lips.

"Honey, toasted bread, cane syrup, melon," Camille jokes.

"That sounds like breakfast." The waiter pours them a lemonade-colored pinot grigio. "Now that sparkles. It's nothing like a usual house pinot." Susan holds her glass to the light and the wine sends off coppery glints. "White pepper, mineral, oh, what about stone-ground stone." She raises her glass. In a forest green tunic sweater, with her wind-burned cheeks, and her hair even more on end than usual, she looks elfin. Susan's laugh lights up the room and she finds a lot to laugh about, a quality that must have served her well with grumpy clients looking for crown molding in suburban tracts. "Let's run back and pick up Kit. You've noticed that she's not drinking—and she did that night at Leo's. Do you think she could be preggers? Let's ask her."

"I was wondering, too! But we cannot ask. Maybe she's just off her feed a bit. You go for her. I'll have another taste of, what?" Camille signals the waiter. "What else must I taste?"

He pours a sauvignon, Ronco delle Mele. "Hill of the apples," he says.

But no apple ever tasted as good. A hint of crisp citrus but not like the heavily grapefruit note of the New Zealand sauvignons they quaffed all summer at Sand Castle. "I like this. May I have three bottles to take home?" She hopes she's found a discovery for Chris and Julia.

She's loving the cross-pollination among her friends: how she's developing a more particular interest in food and wine—for sure won't ever go back to frozen quiche. She's become more interested in renaissance garden design, as is Julia. Being with Susan makes her want to be determined and ambitious. Susan and Julia are responding more to art. Susan came home from the last antique market with a well-done still life of cherries, which now hangs in the kitchen. They must all delve into Kit's poetry.

Learning the language, they've found differences in aptitude. Julia is picking it up with alacrity; Susan is diligent with verb lists and pronoun practice. She's not too shy to talk with the people she encounters in San Rocco, Venice, or wherever. She can laugh at her mistakes, whereas Julia apologizes, then speeds on. When she sits down to study, Camille finds herself quickly distracted. She's wondering if she's too old to learn conjugations or if she's swamped by sensory overload and just can't concentrate. What did Rowan call it? The Stendhal syndrome, named after the author, whose character almost collapsed from too much beauty in Florence. Camille keeps learning the same past participles over and over. When someone speaks rapidly, a veil falls down and she wants to doze.

Julia and Chris look so connected that the winemakers assume she is his wife. They've been invited to dinner. Camille sees Chris turn toward her and gesture. She hears the man he's talking to shout "*Certo. Tutti!*" Certainly. Everyone.

Julia comes over to the bar. "We're all invited to dinner at this man's brother's restaurant. Where's Susan?" Julia looks flushed, buoyant, like the ends of her hair might spark.

"She'll be right back. She went to get Kit. Aren't these wines amazing? You know, Kit seems to be avoiding wine, and we're wondering if she might be pregnant."

"Oh, no. She's too smart for that." Burned into Julia: the enormous risk of having a child. "I'm loving these whites; they're as complex as good reds. I'm not used to that."

THEY'D ALL AGREED NOT EVER to say again, *We're not in Kansas anymore.* At dinner, Julia wants to say it. She's overwhelmed by the surprise of the food what's-his-name's brother brought forth. Snails cooked in tomato sauce with pork. Not like refined French escargot but a hearty, bountiful dish. They don't get to order. Plum gnocchi arrives. They are seated with about twenty men and a scattering of women in an arched room lined with iron wine racks. Julia never did know the occasion, or maybe there is no occasion, but simply daily life in Cormòns. Woodcock from

over the border in Slovenia. *Capriolo:* roebuck, thigh of, she sur-
reptitiously translates on her phone. She notices that Kit's glass remains empty. In this company, you'd have to be a raging alcoholic
or, yes, pregnant to resist the superb wines. If she is, Julia thinks,
I hope she was trying for this, a last gasp before the egg basket
emptied. She catches Kit's eye down the table, raises her glass, and
sees Kit lift her water glass with a little back-and-forth movement
of her head and eyebrows raised. From this silent gesture, Julia
understands that Camille is right.

Chris puts his hand on her knee and she does not flinch. "This
is over-the-moon good. It's surpassing anything I expected. This
is the kind of town you could live in. I saw a quirky brick house off
the road to the hotel. Maybe I should chuck Napa and move here."

"Now you're influenced by us! You're going crazy, too." She's
thinking, what a great idea. Maybe once you've broken through
one absolute, the next one is easier. Suddenly she wonders if Wade
has moved on to another woman after Rose, and a sharp twist
catches in her stomach. The winemaker's brother—Mikal, he
is—comes over to ask if they're enjoying themselves, the lovely
Americans. "*Squisita,*" Julia manages. Exquisite.

"*Mille grazie.*"

Chris launches them into a discussion of local wines and explains that he will be back in spring with more lovely Americans.

CAMILLE, SUSAN, AND I EXITED early, well, it was almost
eleven, and Chris and Julia moved to a small table after the party
broke up. Julia thought they should try a couple of desserts for research's sake. A few of the men sat at one end of the table drinking
grappa. Gentlemen all, they stood as we left, making curt bows
and saying *buona notte*. Everyone's tired but me. All that unaccustomed red meat, and I mean red, jazzed my synapses. Two kinds
of deer, the big one that looks like a reindeer and the small *cervo* I
sometimes see on my land. I even had some of the goulash Mikal

passed around at the end. What a hearty chef, hulking, corvine Mikal, and what a generous table. As long as I've been in Italy, I've not met such a various cuisine as Friuli's, such a happy blend of all those unhappy warring states that captured this area. No wonder Julia wanted dessert. I, too, saw that Sachertorte on the menu.

WHILE THEY WERE GONE ALL afternoon, I wrote a poem, which always invigorates me. I rested and then took a slow walk along a stream. In my work, I try to include something I see and something that happens. A secret tic. I'm convinced this keeps me grounded. I'm sure Julia knows about the baby. She looked at my glass and then at me quizzically. I'll wait and tell them when we're all together. Since I haven't been to the doctor yet (because after that it's real), I don't think I should tell, but Julia I'm sure has guessed. Susan is driving slowly after such a boozy evening. When she starts singing "Blue Moon," I join in. Camille's head is bobbing awake, then sinking down again. Too late to call Colin. Three days and he's home.

I PRETENDED TO SLEEP WHEN Julia came in. She had not been eating Sachertorte all night. She crawled in her bed around five and didn't stir until Susan knocked at eight thirty. I was re-reading *Austerlitz* by W. G. Sebald because I remembered that he wrote about star forts and we are seeing one today. Julia's choice, along with Udine and Aquileia for Chris's tour. "Arise, arise!" Susan called. "They're serving fluffy pancakes with some kind of thick cream inside. A thousand calories per bite. Van is warming up because it is freezing."

ON WE GO TO AQUILEIA and Palmanova. To Maniago and Udine, back to Cormòns, then home. This rounds out Julia's research on interesting places for Chris's groups to visit in Friuli. En route, Camille says, "I hate to do this but I am dying to get back to Venice. I have this idea that's like red coal in my brain and something tells me that I need to explore right now. I'm loving this, too, and I want to see the mosaics in Aquileia—how *do* you pronounce a word with six vowels—but after that, I thought I'd catch a bus or train, then spend the next two nights back in Venice. Kit, what's the hotel where you and Colin stay?"

We discuss logistics, with Susan looking up train and bus schedules, Chris driving, Julia taking landscape photos out the window. I'm trying to read about Aquileia, named for an eagle who flew over while some Roman outlined city parameters with a plow. Or so they say. It's decided. Chris will turn in his car, we will drive back to San Rocco, and we arrange to pick up Camille at the Padova train station en route home. I say mildly that Padova might not be easy to navigate, but these are Americans and they have utter faith in navigation systems on their watches and phones, systems that are ignorant of Italian drivers. Susan secures my (formerly) favorite hotel for Camille for two nights. Travel with others (herding cats) can drive you mad. Whims, logistics, misconceptions, and perhaps one pregnant woman who wants solitude.

AQUILEIA FASCINATES ME. LIKE MANY Roman settlements this was strategic, a river port and headquarters for launching raids up into the Danube. It had peaked by AD 14. Will the town fascinate Chris's group? We stop first at the basilica, built in AD 313. Yes! It's worth a flight to Italy just to see this: the oldest and largest floor mosaic of the Christian world. Why haven't I been here? Italy can always astonish you. I'm wishing for Colin. We are used to exploring together, falling into our own world of associations and reactions. I'm missing a limb that isn't missing. "What's your favorite part?" I'd ask him. Mine is the three fishermen (are two of them angels?) lowering their net formed with tiny black pebbles

into a striated sea where all kinds of fish swim. A feeling of exhila-
ration sweeps through me; I can't stop smiling as I wander around
these fantasia expanses of mosaic.

WHY TRAVEL? THIS! ACROSS EONS, the hand of the artist
reaches for small mosaic bits. A riot of animals, fish, and birds
spreads across the floor. A peacock—that must have been fun to
fit the blue stones into the tail fan. A deer as big as the roebuck
they served us last night. Donkey, lobster, heron, partridge, ram,
a rooster pecking at a tortoise—the makers reveled in the natural world. There's an allegorical and biblical context—Jonah and
whale, angels, maybe other stories I don't recognize, and pagan
images, too, a winged horse and a languorous man sacked out
under a pergola. Camille leans down to photograph a realistic
group of snails. "What's your favorite part so far?" I ask.

"I love this group of snails. But did you see the fishermen? I
suppose they're apostles. That net—completely transparent but
made of stones—in the sea just knocks me sideways. And the
swirly octopus!" (Okay, Colin—I can travel without you!)

"So many fish everywhere. It shows their world, I guess. This
was a port, the sea nearby, water everywhere. Some of the fish I'm
sure can be identified. We may see them on our plates at lunch."

"How did this survive? I read earlier that the town was destroyed by Huns and once or twice by earthquakes."

"It just got filled in and covered over somehow. Mud, straw,
dirt, then some flooring went down. The Austrians took over at
some point and discovered it. The town goes back to 181 BC. Just
think of all the hordes that have overrun it."

THERE'S A LOT LEFT TO see but it's quick. A row of fluted
columns used to be the forum. In the archaeological museums—
funerary marble busts and statues that used to line memorial roads;

urns; and monumental tomb markers with Latin inscriptions. A profound cache of vivid mementos. That most of the town is still unexcavated makes me want to be an archaeologist with a ton of money.

There's confusion getting Camille to a train, as there always is confusion in a travel group when someone breaks trail. She never elaborated on the "sex on the sofa" episode. Is she meeting this Rowan in Venice? She said she wants to explore an idea. Anyway, she's off on her jaunt.

Onward. We drive to Palmanova. This is where I think most of Colin because the Venetians devised this nine-star-shaped fortress also as a utopian place to live. Palmanova, built as a moated fortress, was as an ideal city. This would intrigue Colin. I read in W. G. Sebald that forts designed like this almost inevitably were outmoded by the time they were built because of interim advances in armature. This ties into Sebald's whole philosophy of a constantly dissolving world, that everything falls away as obsolete in the moment it appears. We are perpetually in arrears. Such a melancholy, well, tragic world view. (Margaret would agree with him.)

Palmanova, built in 1593, was meant to protect residents against raging Turks, Austrians, whoever tried to scale or batter the walls. The Venetians conceived the idea: beauty reinforces the good of society. What a lofty utopia. Everyone was to have the same amount of land. The plan was idealistic, the *centro* a hexagon, with eighteen concentric streets radiating from the center, and four ring streets intersecting the radials, a beautiful design. The trouble was—no one came. Finally, in 1622, Venetian prisoners were released to occupy an otherwise empty town. I think it's true, as Sebald observed, "The more you entrench yourself the more you must remain on the defensive." I would not like to live in a fort, no matter how ideal the hexagonal central piazza.

Interesting as it is theoretically, we wonder about a tour stop here. Julia is madly taking notes. Chris thinks not, though the history is compelling. Susan stops us at a café for coffee. "I'd bring them here," I say. We're standing at the bar. "There are many things to think about." Susan reaches across me for the sugar. Like the Italians, she's taken to copious amounts in her coffee.

I've read a bit. "What I immediately think of is three paintings on the ideal city by unknown artists around 1480 (one used to be attributed to Piero della Francesca). Palmanova must have been influenced by that prior century's obsession with mathematical cities. They were laid out with specific proportions, perspectives, and vanishing points (all without the mess of actual humans, markets, animals)."

"I agree," Julia says. "Chris would just have to prepare the background—everyone would be fascinated."

(For my notebook: I wonder if these paintings of groups of buildings had anything to do with mnemonic memory palaces I've read about. The layout of this town could be one. So many windows and doors to store words. I can imagine locating information in each quadrant created by the web of streets; then each becomes a memory prompt. I've tried the method myself, using the rooms of my childhood home as repositories for stanzas of a long poem I wanted to memorize, Keats's "The Eve of St. Agnes." It worked, though the poem is forever tied to the blue bedroom of my parents, the breezeway with bamboo furniture and ceiling fans.)

Like an Italian, Chris stirs in two sugars. "You are right, Julia, Kit. Walking around here makes me want to study the plan. From above it must look like an angular mandala."

"You *are* a California boy!" I say.

Julia laughs. "Well, I'm entranced."

"So am I. Maybe that's what we all have in common—easy enchantment." Damn, I'm missing Colin. He should be here. I want to talk about all this with him. We grab a quick pasta for lunch—mine with veal cheeks—and drive to die-and-go-to-heaven Udine.

· · ·

JULIA HAS LOCATED A HOTEL in the center, adequate but not up to Chris's guests' expectations. Who can blame them; they're paying *un sacco di soldi* for their grand tour. Many of them will not come this way again—why not splurge? Julia apologizes—it didn't look dated in the photos—but the place is fine, a bit tired but with large rooms and bathrooms fitted with old marble sinks.

Susan and I take off for a long walk around town. Julia and Chris are entering info notes and researching possible atmospheric *agriturismi* (farms open to guests) nearby. (They're in his room, I note.) "Take notes and photos, please." Julia waves good-bye. Susan is great with directions; I tend to get happily lost. We search out the museum, the lofty Tiepolo ceiling in the Oratorio della Purità, and the dusty-looking Caravaggio portrait of Saint Francis in the Galleria d'Arte Antica, which turns out to be a good copy.

"Couldn't you buy that house with the vines? Couldn't you move in your books and set up immediately?" Susan gets Udine. It's a livable, dignified town. "One thing learned, since I have been living here," she continues, "*the good life* is available for the asking. Why settle? It's incomprehensible to me that we earnestly entertained the idea of moving into a nice, oh, yes, retirement community. What we did not know!" We pass well-dressed matrons with their dogs on leashes, kids on bicycles, men playing cards and taking in the afternoon sun at a café. We pass a shop for baby clothes. I barely glance at it.

"All true," I agree. "But not close to a major airport. Impossible for me."

"Oh, right."

HAVING FOUND A COUNTRY INN at a vineyard for the tour, Julia goes back to her room. She needs a shampoo and to organize her clothes for tomorrow. She wants to chat with her father. It's late morning his time. He's probably taken his coffee out on his balcony overlooking the river. How she would like to slide open the door and join him. She looks quickly at her calendar. Just over three weeks until he arrives for the holidays. She hasn't spoken to him for a week. He would love to see the little towns of Friuli. She needs privacy to think through what has transpired on this trip and what she wants to happen. Last night after the three desserts, after a strong *digestivo*, she and Chris drove back alone from the restaurant to the hotel. "Come up for a moment," he'd said. "We can go over the rest of the trip. Seems like there are some choices to make." Inside his room, he closed the door and they kissed. The kiss was sweet, then ignited. I don't want this, she remembers thinking, to be like one of those clichéd movie scenes where they start backing toward the bed, flinging off clothes, ravenous, and placed in impossible positions, impossible for the woman's pleasure anyway—backed up, standing against a wall and battered. But he held her, kissing her throat, her ears.

"You are marvelous," he said.

"No, you are." She writes on a piece of hotel stationery, telling herself the story. We kissed. Finally, we sat on the edge of the bed and he flopped backward, his hands over his head. "I never expected to feel this way. You are someone I know, have known all my life. I've never known anyone as easily. Are you sure we didn't meet in another life?" I am both thrown by and drawn to his eyes, one tawny like a tiger's-eye bead, the other the faded blue of an old chambray shirt.

"I know. I know." I laid my head on his chest, listening to the solid thud of his heart. We talked about the vintners, the evening, the shock of roebuck on our tongues, about whether Kit is pregnant. He loves Susan and Camille. He says, with all of us, he feels released. I know that feeling as well. My friends multiply my life.

After those umpteen tastings of wine, I simply drifted, fell asleep. I said, *We're all right*. Silence. I remember saying, *Your eyes excite me*, then hearing a low honking snore. Later I woke up and found that we'd stretched out side by side on the bed, Chris curled around me, holding my hand, his even breath behind my ear. I disentangled and crept out to my room. Kit was turned away, though I suspected that she'd awakened. I crawled under the blanket, still in my clothes.

(MY COMPOSING METHODS MAY SOMETIMES be suspect. How do I know about this scene? Her pages were folded into our guide-book.)

SUSAN WENT TO THE ROOM to call her daughters in California. Morning there; evening already falling here by five in the afternoon. We're swinging toward the darkest day of the year. Does my little sugar spoon of protoplasm feel the earth moving on its axis? I walk back by the baby shop and examine the onesies, the minute yellow sweater, fragile embroidered dresses only grandmothers would buy (my mother will miss everything), lace-trimmed socks, impossibly tiny lambskin shoes—this is Italy, after all. The other window displays folding strollers, room monitors, bouncy chairs, and high-and-mighty navy blue and white carriages that look constructed for royal bairns. I'm stunned, not having thought until now of all the paraphernalia in my/our future. I share the Italians' fearful superstitions. I wouldn't think of buying anything until I'm practically on the way to the hospital. But I snap a photo of the shoes and send it to Colin.

It seems like longer than yesterday that we were in Aquileia. That's travel: time expands and compresses in unexpected ways. Just to take in one of the most pleasing piazzas I've ever seen, I order a hazelnut gelato at a café on Piazza della Libertà, and spend half an hour looking at passersby and patterns of shifting shadows. The great poet Czeslaw Milosz was right. The tragedy of living is to have only one life when there are many possibilities laid before us. Shouldn't one spend a life, or at least part of it, in Udine?

• • •

CAMILLE HAS COVERED A LOT of ground during her after-noon in Venice. She's sent home vials and packets of pigments from a miracle of an art supply store. Her project is coming clear to her now and she hasn't even picked up a brush. She stocked up on handmade paper and will work with Matilde and Serena as she needs more.

Browsing in venerable bookstores, she's spent almost a thousand euros on decaying leather books with pages of drawings and etchings of Venetian buildings and country villas, a few tomes of renaissance poetry, and in a regular bookstore, she's splurged on art books—Giorgione, Palladio, Veronese. How she feels, she only can liken to falling in love, when every sense is heightened and intensified, when extraneous emotions fall away. She feels like a lens in the sun. After two trains, a *vaporetto*, and miles of walk-ing, her new knee throbs. Her calf muscle wants to cramp with every step back to the hotel. Even so, you just should not have room service in Venice.

After a rest, she hauls herself up and slowly walks back to a six-table trattoria she passed earlier. Without the others to hear, her Italian improves. She orders with no hitch. Over a bowl of mussels and a grilled fish, she meets Americans at the next table, a young couple from Baltimore traveling to Europe for the first time. After the usual where-are-you-from conversation and ob-servations about Venice, the woman asks Camille, "Are you re-tired? Or do you work?"

Camille answers, "I used to teach, now I'm a full-time artist."

SHE HAS THE WHOLE NEXT day to play. The buoyant excite-ment gives her bolts of energy slightly tamped by her irritated knee. She frequently stops for coffee or water. They didn't get to see the Carpaccios when they were here before. She adores the painting of Saint Ursula sleeping in her bedroom while the angel pauses at the door bringing her palm frond of martyrdom. Why is she martyred? She fled her father's marriage plan for her, taking along with her on several ships eleven thousand other virgins. He'd betrothed her to the barbarian Conan. She's about to suffer her fate. She's peaceful now in her lovely room with the little dog by her bed.

By chance, Camille discovers the hidden-in-plain-sight Carlo Scarpa museum, actually his office design for Olivetti typewriters, right on Piazza Grande but inconspicuous. A place to fall deeper into whatever she's falling into. She lingers on the details, the brass cylinders supporting the marble stairs, adamantly modern lines so quietly executed that they seem timeless, the sculpture on a square of water, always water, reminding you that you're in Venice. Here I am, she thinks, with Scarpa, the amazing architect. I'm beginning a long romance with him. She returns to the bookstore and buys a detailed and illustrated Scarpa book, then rushes to the Querini Stampalia palace and garden for a quick look at the Scarpa revisions. Susan should be here for the garden. Camille raises her arms over her head and shakes back her hair. Now I'm on fire, she thinks. Timorous to tensile. She limps a little on the way back to the hotel but hums as she goes "I Set Fire to the Rain." We must have a dinner with Colin and talk Venetian architecture. Scarpa loved Roman lettering; I'll tell Rowan all about that.

After dinner, she falls asleep with Scarpa, savoring what he loved: Japanese design, polished stucco, base materials used with precious ones, water, always for this son of Venice, water. Water, lapping doors, seeping under doors, doors opening to water, back doors opening to narrow streets, damp, water, the mind soaked, the body soaked and drifting.

SEVEN HOURS LATER SHE WAKES up with Charles in her vision from a dream of walking along Spit Creek in their backyard. No narrative: there he is, Saturday clothes, tennis shoes, just walking as he did a million times along the path to the bridge he built himself over to a short woodland walk. He's going to see if the white cyclamen are blooming, Camille thinks as she hauls out of sleep. Then she is awake. She parts the drapery just as the prow of a gondola passes her window. From the canals of Venice to Spit Creek. Charles, good for you. I'm glad you're checking on the garden.

WE SPENT OUR LAST DAY wrapping up their research. From Udine, we chased a lead up to Maniago, a town famous for the production of knives. Chris wanted to find one place his clients could find unique items to buy or import for their retail stores.

The artisan knives could inspire elegant murders. Slim and sculptural, the stiletto points make you want to pick up one and perhaps pierce someone's heart. They look way too refined to gut or skin something. I bought a jade green one for Colin. The handles are horn, antler, or the pretty colors of Perlex, whatever that is. Maybe he will cut the string on packages. (Oh, cut the umbilical cord.) After a brief visit to the cutlery museum, we knew all we wanted to know about knife making and drove back to Cormòns for our last dinner.

UP EARLY AND ON THE road, Chris ramps up the sound of k. d. lang, all of us belting out "Hallelujah" and then her incomparable hookup with Roy Orbison, "Crying," bare poplars on the roadside whizzing by, everyone happy with having seen new sights, Chris weaving around tractors, beating out time with the heel of his hand on the steering wheel, until we hit traffic and the van subdues, everyone in a travel trance. I fall asleep.

CAMILLE MADE HER TRAIN EASILY, arriving in Padova station in time to wait and wait for the others. Their trusted navigating systems neglected to know about road construction. She'd been standing in front of the station for an hour before she sees the van swing into the taxi-stand lane, Susan leaning out the window, waving.

"There's Camille, look at her—she looks sort of disheveled but vibrant." Susan threw jackets into the back so she could get in. "Do you suppose she met that Rowan in Venice?"

Camille piles in. She's picked up a sack of *panini* in the station. We fall upon them and Chris turns up the music again. Sam Cooke. All of them know the words to "You Send Me," and "Change Is Gonna Come."

$\mathscr{I}$NVASION

OUTSIDE SAN ROCCO, THE GANG needs to organize. Chris stops at a supermarket and they gather supplies for the evening. He is coming to dinner and Camille has invited Rowan. Kit demurs, wanting an evening alone with Colin. They pick up Archie, who seems reluctant to rejoin his family after the tasty lamb bones, after being allowed to sleep on the foot of the bed and to run wild chasing dumb guinea hens around the farm. They drop off Chris at his hotel, and then Kit, who leaps out as Colin jogs down the driveway to meet her, his arms flung open and a big smile lighting his face.

Susan turns into their drive and the three of them breathe a collective sigh. Great trip, but great to be home. As they slow to descend the driveway, Julia leans forward. "Oh, no. We left the front door open. Wait. We wouldn't leave the door open." A packing crate stands off to the right. A panel of light falls from the doorway into the garden. "The lights are on."

Susan stops in front rather than driving around back as they usually do.

"The door is open," Camille repeats. "Damn! Someone has broken in."

"Maybe Grazia is here. But her car isn't." Julia slides open the van door. Archie leaps out and runs inside.

"Archie," Susan shouts, "come here!" She's afraid that someone possibly is still inside. "Archie!" She irrationally leans on the horn. Silence. Julia and Camille get out cautiously and walk to the side of the house, to the kitchen door they always use, since they have only the big iron key to the front. Silence.

Susan keeps leaning on the horn. If thieves remain inside, she wants their attention. The entrance looks normal. But Julia and Camille find the window by the kitchen shattered. A garden table pulled up underneath allowed someone to climb in. Julia points to two clear footprints. They walk back to the front and the three decide to enter together. Suddenly they hear someone from behind the house shouting their names. Here comes Leo, asking what's wrong, uttering Madonna curses with every breath, what's the matter, oh, *Dio*, and Annetta running up behind him almost squawking.

Together they cautiously enter the house. The hallway looks normal. The first thing they see in the kitchen is Archie, transfixed and rigid in his best pointer mode, glaring at the kitchen fireplace. Three white kittens curl in a bread basket lined with a towel. Ample food and water surround them and their donor has taken the time to spread newspapers for their convenience. In the sink, plates and forks, two wineglasses. Julia recognizes the leftover pasta with ragù she'd left in the freezer. "Christ on a cracker, they had dinner."

"Can you believe the wineglasses? What wine did they open? Oh, where's my cherry still life?" Susan notices.

"Where's our new food processor?" Julia surveys the kitchen but finds nothing else missing.

"What the hell?" Camille asks. "We've been robbed. But

they've left cats! This is insane. Dinner? They had dinner? They knew without doubt that we were gone."

Then Julia finds the drawers in the dining room dumped out, napkins and place mats scattered, silverware everywhere on the floor, the thieves apparently not interested. The sofa and chair cushions lie scattered in the middle of the floor. As Leo points out, as all is swimming into focus for the women, every mirror, print, and painting has been taken down. All are lined up along the walls, rather carefully. "They were looking for a safe," Leo says. "They were interested in money." He called his friend Eugenio, the head of the police, whose six-month-old daughter at the dinner had munched olives.

Camille crosses the room and turns down the hall to her bedroom. She spots a bracelet on the floor at the threshold and, inside, mounds of upturned clothes, the mattress skewed on the bed. This can't be; she closes her eyes. They took my jewelry. Because the police have not arrived, she doesn't want to touch anything. The white-gold links on the brick give her hope that she has not lost all the touching mementos Charles had given her throughout their marriage—the gold rope necklace with a sapphire clasp bought in Charleston when he turned fifty and he'd said, *Because of our happiness, all the years we've shared.* The pearls with a strand of amethyst woven in, and the romantic cascade of four-diamond earrings. Twenty-fifth anniversary. She never owned a lot of jewelry, but what she has is good. Really good. She wore one piece every day and thought of the occasion that brought it to her, a moment of meditation on the good luck of her love. Her wedding present, a teardrop emerald with tiny diamonds along the chain. Please don't let that be gone, she whispers out loud. Before her, the emerald had been Charlie's darling mother's gift from his father when they married. No other objects she owns have half the emotional meaning.

Annetta sets to work putting the dining room in order until

Susan stops her. "Fingerprints," she says. "Tampering with a crime scene," she says, forgetting that Annetta speaks no English. She gestures to her fingertips and Annetta shouts, "*Certo, cara!*" Certainly, my dear.

Camille loops her hand through Susan's arm. "I'm afraid all my jewelry is gone. I'm an idiot. I left my drawstring pouches in my bottom drawer."

"Oh, my friend. I'm afraid." She and Julia have already looked upstairs where, mysteriously, nothing seems disturbed except the upended mattresses.

"At home, I'm always hiding my stash of jewelry—in plastic bags under the sugar, in the toy chest under Charlie's drums, in a tampon box. I never slid them between sheets in the linen closet, under my lingerie—the obvious places—nowhere near the mattress, or pillows, or bookcases, or handbags, or fake shaving cream or tomato soup cans. Certainly not hollowed-out books. And now, my god, stupid. I could have left them in the dryer under a pile of T-shirts. I've had many ingenious places before. So good that I often forget *where* I stashed them. Charlie always teases me about my places to hide my treasures. Once, one pouch was lost for six months, then found in Charles's toolbox in the garage."

Susan had much experience with clients' houses robbed while listed for sale. She'd heard of every hiding place imaginable but before this trip to Venice, she'd found the ultimate one for her own jewelry. "I just looked. My stuff is still in its hiding place. I wish I'd mentioned it. You know the brush by the toilet? Standing in that stainless-steel container? I've noticed that every Italian bathroom has one—it's because of poor toilet design. I put the things I wasn't traveling with in a plastic bag and stored it under the brush in the container."

Camille manages a laugh.

The *carabinieri* arrive. Eugenio, the *maresciallo*, the marshal, sweeps Camille into a huge hug. The three men in their spiffy uniforms look as if they could handle major crime. One speaks excellent English, having lived in New Jersey for several years. They comb the house. One takes photos. No use to look for fingerprints, they assert, the thieves are not dumb; they wear gloves. They ascertain, as we already had from the way the glass scattered, that they entered by the back hall window and exited through the front door. Susan thinks, *Sherlock Holmes*. When Julia triumphantly points out the footprints, they collectively shrug. Everyone wears athletic shoes like that.

We enter the bedroom. Gone. Everything. The *ladri* took the time to untie the jewelry roll, open the blue satin pouch, remove the contents, and leave the holders on the pile of underwear and turned-over drawers. The red pouch holding the emerald, gone. The one piece of costume jewelry, a string of glass beads, was rejected and remains on the floor, but one of the guys accidentally grinds it under his boot. Camille picks up the white-gold bracelet in the doorway. They probably thought it was junk.

More hugs all around from the police, who are especially moved and keep repeating to each other that the pearls came from Camille's mother, a mother's jewelry being most resonant to them. Then there erupts a discussion of hiding places. A safe? Absolutely not. They maintain again that thieves are not stupid; they have tools to rip that wall safe right out and buzz into it. Should we have video surveillance? No—you think they don't wear masks? Julia doubts that they ate her ragù and drank the Chianti *reserva* in masks and gloves.

The handsome chief advises, "Choose a flowerpot in the garden and dig a hole under it." Or, there, the tall, muscular one demonstrates, wedged on top of a beam in the kitchen. "They can't look on top of all the beams in the house," he reasons, "just as they can't dig under *all* the flowerpots."

"This is getting surreal," Susan mutters.

Camille didn't say that every time she wants her earrings, she does not want to unearth them from the garden. Besides, scorpions love living under pots. It's getting late. Anyway, she now has nothing to hide from any jewel thief.

Susan questions the *carabinieri* about searching at gold dealers for the jewelry. "Useless." They put on their coats. "The gold will be melted down by morning."

"Gypsies," they conclude. "They're camped outside Florence and are raiding the country towns. It's mostly women for these small jobs. If they're noticed, they claim to be house cleaners. The kittens, though, that's a new touch." They depart. Nothing to offer. No lead to follow.

Annetta and Leo make the rounds of hugs, too, and go home. We stare at the three frisky kittens Archie is circling, obviously enamored. Julia starts the washer. No one wants to touch the garments handled by the smart women thieves, who somehow had known their schedule. Too bad they had not ransacked Julia's room instead of Camille's. That Susan. Smart. When Julia left Wade, she'd stored every piece of jewelry she owned, except for one gold necklace from her father, good to wear with anything, in a safe-deposit box in Savannah. Of course, Lizzie had long ago sold Julia's mother's treasures.

Leo stops by and tells Colin and me. We rush right over, just as Chris arrives by taxi, totally unaware of what happened. Rowan drives up, too, alighting with an armful of lilies.

"YOU ALL WERE GREAT TO help us clean up this chaos," Susan said. She opens a bottle of cold prosecco and raises a toast. "It could have been worse!" A man sent by the police arrives to board up the window and Susan hands him a glass, too.

"Unfortunately not," Camille has answered multiple times. No, she never had gotten around to insuring her jewelry beyond the household policy. (Beat on head again.) "We've been told a million times how safe it is here," Camille said.

Everyone laments with her, but Susan remarks, "Everyone

keeps saying how sad the loss of such sentimental gifts, and yes, that's true, but I'm also thinking, yeah, and how sad the loss of all that gold at two thousand dollars an ounce."

"What was that about not looking for the jewelry because it would be melted down by morning? Emeralds don't melt. Sapphires don't melt." Susan stands behind Camille's chair, her hands protectively on Camille's shoulders.

"I AM GOING TO COOK," Julia says. "Let's move into the kitchen and I'll give everyone a job. Chris, if you'll put on the pasta water. Susan, salad. Rowan, please set the table. Kit, you and Colin must stay. We need moral support. Would you two open the wine and find the big glasses? Several bottles, I'd say. I make a killer carbonara. Camille, you just stay where you are."

"I know it's shallow," Camille continues, "to be so upset over material things. I know it's a first, first-world problem."

"Don't be silly," Julia answers. "You'll never get over this."

"I'll buy you a diamond as big as the Ritz," Rowan jokes. "By the way, what's that big crate outside? Did the robbers leave you a gift?"

Susan laughs. "That's the start of my new business. More on that later. We've had quite a day."

NOT THE FESTIVE EVENING THEY'D planned. But not the worst. Everyone told their stories of losses. A truck backed up to a house in Napa while the owners were away and took everything, even the refrigerator. A stolen car, a bicycle, a friend who had her bag snatched. Camille is not consoled. Julia serves a mound of *spaghetti alla carbonara* to each and they eat every morsel. Colin keeps his arm around me.

Chris and Rowan insist on sleeping over. They help make up beds in two upstairs bedrooms. The *carabinieri* guaranteed that the Gypsies would not be back, and also pledged to patrol the road every hour, but everyone feels safer with a full house and they're able to say *buona notte* with more calm than they anticipated. Archie falls asleep beside the fireplace with three kittens curled against him, as though he were the mother. "Oh, *Madonna serpente*," Susan says. Her first Tuscan curse (overheard in the olive grove) and it's a big one. Snake Madonna.

IN THE NIGHT, ROWAN WORRIES. He stealthily pads barefoot down the stairs and slowly opens Camille's door. She is still awake, drowsing over a book. "Just checking on you." He sits down on the side of the bed. "What a blow. I am so sorry. What can I do? Can I just hold you until you fall asleep?" Camille slides down under the covers.

"Yes. Please." After all the words, plain human warmth comforts her.

Upstairs, Susan sleeps. She was up late, too wired to relax, firing off emails.

Julia crosses the hall to Chris's room. He is out for the count but sits up immediately, thinking the robbers are back. "Julia! Shit! What a nightmare for you. But, whoa! You are a vision."

She peels off her nightgown over her head and tosses back the covers. "You're leaving tomorrow. When will we have a chance to be together again?"

Clasps and Chains

I KNEW THE STORY OF the robbery at Villa Assunta would be all over town by the time Colin and I walked in for coffee. We're settled at Bar Beato Angelico, with cappuccinos and pastries, but we hardly can take a bite or sip for people coming over to our table to discuss the terrible event.

We are taking a train late this morning to Florence. Colin has made an appointment for us with an obstetrician, someone recommended by one of the architects on his project. I'm nervous, always nervous at the prospect of feet in stirrups and someone saying *just relax*. I have been avoiding the ordeal.

In San Rocco, when something bad happens, people take it personally. Everyone here is sorry and embarrassed that the nice American women were robbed, and everyone has a theory. A certain disreputable guy who does odd jobs comes in for a lot of blame. Gypsies, yes. Anytime something happens, the Gypsies are blamed. (Not that much happens.) A tourist got all upset because her wallet was lifted, and then it was spotted in the chair next to where she had coffee earlier. Drunk teenagers vandalized a house under construction. A dog ate poisoned meat, but many thought he had it coming after a solid month of all-night moon barking. Of course an older woman has a lot of jewelry. She should have known better than to leave it under clothing. Her hiding place was bad. Because of wide distrust of banks, and a tendency to avoid revealing income that will be taxed, many Italians keep cash at home. Just look under the flowerpots! Most have a foolproof place to conceal valuables, and it's not behind books or in the toe of a shoe. A pity, the consensus goes, some of the jewelry came from her mother.

I speculate to Colin, "What comes after all this? The thief's wife may at this moment have hidden inside a sock the handful of pearl earrings, the emerald, and the pearl necklace that couldn't be melted. Maybe her ugly husband yanked off the gold parts, but maybe he left them intact for her, love of his life, and in a few months she may lift out the creamy pearls and fasten the gold clasp around her neck. She may look in the mirror and try to imagine where they came from. Maybe she will dare to wear the dangling lustrous pearls. On that same day, Camille may be at the market and see a woman lean over to buy apples, her pearls swinging out."

"Not one of the great losses of the world, not important in the face of the poor struggling to survive, dead-end wars and terrorists, or people not respecting the earth enough to take care of it, on and on," Colin says.

"But, yes, the world is private, too, and when your home is invaded and a lifetime's collection of intensely personal belongings is ripped away, a lingering sadness starts up. Camille felt stripped. Mentally assaulted. Really angry. Thing is, losing jewelry isn't at all like losing money. It's romance, heritage, an inner concept of beauty. That's why those fragile earrings found in Etruscan tombs move us with their sense of the ancient wearer. She's touching her earlobes twenty-six hundred years ago and you feel it. I love my mother's ring"—her bluest of eyes, her generosity—"and my mean aunt's ring"—did she love, ever?—"sparkles on my little finger. I'd much rather lose the money they're worth."

"Right. You're always right. If you compare importance to world events, your own life always will seem frivolous. You start where I leave off, my love."

"Don't be ridiculous. By the way, I rolled up a lot of cash and shoved it into an empty wine bottle. It's corked and standing with my vinegars."

"The bills unfurl. How will we get it out of a bottle?"

"Easy. Break the bottle." Now, off to the game-changing appointment.

BY MY CALCULATIONS I AM ten weeks along and overdue for this exam. I did start prenatal vitamins as soon as I knew for sure. The embryo soon turns into a fetus (etymology: off-spring). The creature right now weighs only ¼ ounce but has lungs, heart, all the vital organs, already working. This makes my knees want to buckle. Something three centimeters long already has a stomach and fingernails. As Sylvia Plath put it, I've "boarded the train there's no getting off." As you already know, I am perpetually surprised at life's basic functions. How a spider knows how to construct an intricate web, how stars wheel across the sky, how the heart keeps on thudding. I'm naturally going to be struck with wonder over the creation of another human for the planet.

IV

What's More Precious?

AS THE STORY CIRCULATED AROUND town, *everyone* told the three women a story of their own losses or the losses of friends and family. Like labor sagas for the pregnant woman, these stories don't help; they inspire further fear. But cumulatively, Camille had to see that she was not unique, at least, and for those who had lost life savings they'd jammed in a milk carton in the fridge, she was among the lucky who'd lost only jewelry. (She rejected that.)

Over lunch at Stefano's, she confessed to Rowan that some primordial part of her deep in the medulla wondered if making love with him incited the gods to take away Charles's gifts to her. He laughed her out of that one. But something primitive in her feared retribution. Rowan countered, "This is a different take: you just came home from Venice fired up over your own life, this project you haven't told me much about. You've come home with supplies and art books, pigments and poetry and architecture. Laden with riches. Odd, that the mementos, all clasps and chains when you think about it, of your former life disappear at the same moment these new stimuli appear. Do you possibly agree?"

Stefano sets down a platter of crostini. "What is so serious?" he asked. "Everything's better with these and a glass of vino."

Camille is silent. Rowan's is a mysterious interpretation, something to contemplate. But then she says, "No, I can't leap to that mystical level. I don't like the eye-for-an-eye idea—so mean. Look at all the people who are horrendously rich and nothing is taken away from them in order for them to move forward with purchasing a helicopter for their yacht. Why should I—part-time art teacher with a frugal husband—have to lose to gain?"

Rowan laughs. "Touché. But I'm still struck with this timing. If you take it as a symbol, it might help." After lunch they go to his place for the afternoon. She wakes late in the day, languorous and sated but with a twinge of sadness. She thinks of how many times in her life she's turned to sex instead of what she might have otherwise pursued. Why hasn't she begun the work she now knows she wants to do?

THE GIFTS BEGIN TO ARRIVE. Leo brings over wooden salt and pepper grinders he made out of fruit woods. He even leaves packets of coarse salt and whole peppercorns to grind. The owner of the linen shop where they've bought tablecloths invites Susan in and gives her three hand-woven cotton dish towels, almost too nice to use. Stefano discounts their lunch by half. In the wine store, Giampaolo gives them a bottle of grappa. Four lovely notes are left stuck in the gate. Patrizia, the woman gathering greens whom Julia met on the road, appears at the door with a pan of lasagne. All these spontaneous gifts leave the women with nights to ponder their meaning—the loving spirit of what is given, the grand subtraction of what is taken away.

CAMILLE HOPES FOR A SILVER lining. The jewelry will be returned in a paper sack by the front door. The police will turn in to the driveway, siren jubilantly blaring. They've recovered everything! The thieves are in jail! Every time she gets dressed she wishes for the necklace with the crystal box of happy diamonds that Charles gave her for a big birthday, or the dangly amethyst earrings the color of Tuscan grapes. She thinks of when her old (Mother!) pearls once broke in a restaurant, sending waiters and Charles to scurry under tables. I won't replace the jewelry, she thinks, not even if I could. I'm sorry I won't be passing it on to my granddaughter, but so be it. Now that I know what it's like to lose it, I won't experience that again. Charles—lost. All his gifts—lost; this loss attaching to the loss of him, loss on loss falling through me, a cement-filled box thrown into the ocean. She remembers something from the dream of him on the woodland walk. "Cyclamen." He'd turned, and, smiling, said, "More precious than jewels."

AT FIRST HE DID NOT come to Italy. Now he again can walk around in her mind. She had not expected this roaming ghost. When her parents, her older sister, cousins, friends died, and there have been many by now, they all retreated after the period of fresh grief, surfacing when she was reminded that *Sophie adored anemones* or *Mother's house smelled like this pine oil and brownies* or *Billie Holliday was singing that night when Ralph* . . . Her parents, much loved, never visited her dreams. Her mother comes closest to her when Camille searches her yellowed and brittle recipes for cornmeal fried okra and caramel cake or brown sugar muffins and grits soufflé. Her father comes back when she hears someone whistle as clear as a bird, or she passes a golf course, or sees someone nip back a bourbon in one gulp. Her sister, Sophie, whose breast cancer metastasized radically, appears only in quick images: skipping rope, falling off her horse, fainting in a soft heap at her wedding. Immortality, she'd always thought, is how you live on in the memories of those left. She's saddened to find that so little

remains on a day-to-day basis. But she's beginning to feel heart-
ened that the force to *move it* pushes strongly through her.

If she'd stayed home, she muses, she would have revived her
book club, picked up Ingrid at school, kept up with colleagues,
attended art department lectures, maybe opted for Cornwallis
Meadows—a lucky end unit with hummingbird feeder and swing
on the porch. That nice Catherine at the orientation, moving
down from the north, would come over for tea in the afternoons.
Nothing wrong with that. But. What if I'd missed Villa Assunta?
A thousand images rush in: Venice, her studio, the paper workshop, Rowan's beard rough on her breasts, Julia laughing in the
kitchen, everyone toasting and sharing all the new experiences
at dinner, Susan's joyous and maniacal maneuvering in their blue
Fiat, countless explosions of taste, amazement at markets, sweet
San Rocco, and the light crossing the piazza like a sundial at all
times of day, the three damn thieves' cats cavorting about the
house and weaseling into their hearts. Oh, yes, they have names:
Bimba, Ragazzo, and Vino, the latter bestowed after dinner when
the minx jumped on the table from Susan's lap and licked her glass.

Susan's Sphere

TO UNPACK THE CRATE THAT might have arrived during the robbers' dinner and ransacking, Susan asks Leo for help. Maybe one
of the thieves ambled to the door, wineglass in hand, and signed
for it. Cheeky bitches. Nailed and constructed as though it con-
tains the _Mona Lisa_, the crate holds instead an astrolabe and a stone
statue heavy as the rock of Gibraltar.

AS SUSAN WAS LEAVING THE Peggy Guggenheim sculpture
garden in Venice, she passed an antique shop filled with things
you wouldn't think mortals could own for mere money. Amid
immense baroque paintings, complicated reliquaries with marble
angels, and ornately gilded, carved, and brocaded furniture, she
spotted a rusty astrolabe—she wasn't then sure of the name but
knew it was some sky-charting instrument—mounted on a curli-
cued iron base. Beside it, a stone garden statue, a pedestal sur-
mounted by the slim figure of Mercury with a tight smile, almost a
smirk. Small, maybe in total four feet tall. She thought, That's the

size gods should be. Quick and nimble moving among the clouds, earth, and the underworld. Didn't Mercury go to the underworld? Seduce someone on the way down? She loved his pointed helmet with wings that looked blown back, and the winged heels of his sandals. It would be marvelous to have such clip-on wings, just lift off and cross the Grand Canal. The shop owner opened the door. "May I be of assistance, Signora? You are admiring my Mercury? He is the god of travelers like you, you must know."

"I did not," Susan answered, "but he could be the god of a beautiful garden." She shook his hand and stepped inside.

"*Sono* Renzo Sciavonni," he said, introducing himself. His tight suit shone like sterling silver and his waxy slicked-back hair required such ample products that Susan found herself trying to imagine peering into his bathroom cabinet. She told him her name and that she has a garden in Tuscany that needs a god. "Obviously your garden already has its goddess." He smiled. Always the polite flirtation in Italy, even in overrun Venice.

"*Grazie, Signore.*" Susan laughed very loudly. The globular bronze instrument intrigued her. "Tell me about this, I know it's not a sundial. I know it somehow plots the heavens." She leaned to examine the intersecting spheres pierced through by a long arrow, the angle of earth's inclination, she assumes.

"*Brava.* You're admiring a spherical astrolabe, also called an armillary sphere. See how good my English is! The ancients were smart. This device gave them the ability to calculate altitudes of stars, positions of the moon and earth, positions of themselves."

They were hers. Susan mentally placed them in the garden at Villa Assunta. A garden thrives on punctuation marks and a place to be drawn to. She imagined Mercury greeting her and her friends as they alight from the car. How mysterious the astrolabe would look in a bed of artemisia and yarrow. Are those two plants as ancient as the Roman gods? Did the astronomers calculate and cavort amid patches of lambs' ears and dianthus?

The prices were astronomical, too. Renzo was ready to negotiate politely up to ten percent off, but he had not reckoned on dealing with the top-selling real estate agent from Chapel Hill, North Carolina, who combined inquisitiveness, charm, and plain savvy to bring him down thirty percent including shipping. He couldn't help but admire her.

LEO PRIES OPEN THE BOARDS but calls for Colin and a dolly to haul Mercury out of the box. There he stands, sentinel of the front garden. The astrolabe Susan places in front of a stone terrace wall near the iron benches she'd dragged out of the *limonaia* when they first arrived. What a perfect place to sit and contemplate those brilliant ancients who invented such an instrument. Nerds, they must have been, like her daughters and their associates in Silicon Valley.

Susan is thinking of the garden in spring and summer, but her thinking is like this astrolabe—in intersecting rings. She's projecting: that moment when a single thought stretches out into an arc that lands in the future. (*Ah, you're spinning out, how marvelous,* Aaron used to say.) On impulse, she'd given Signor Sciavonni her card. "Please email me when you acquire other garden antiques," she said. "I love sundials and iron trellises and stone lions raised up on their haunches. Even those—I know they're common—four seasons statues." She left the shop with lights strobing in her head. She'd seen iron fanlights, lion-face fountains, and fanciful gates at the Arezzo antique market and had paused to look without seeing beyond each.

Now she connects the dots.

Walking back to the hotel, avoiding tourists' elbows and shopping bags, she dialed Molly Dodge in Chapel Hill. On houses that Susan had listed for sale, they'd worked together many times staging the properties by taking portraits, sideboards, and lamps from Molly's barny antique store and giving character to lackluster interiors, or even completely furnishing a house whose owners had moved out. She'd especially loved setting tables for imagined guests and creating serene bedrooms in pale teal toiles.

"*Ciao, bella*," Susan almost shouted over the din of tourists. "I'm calling you from Venice!"

"You are kidding," Molly shouted back. "I am so envious I can't even speak." They talked about home news, with Susan's eyes welling up, a fierce attack of homesickness right in the middle of Campo Santo Stefano. Then she remembered the bleakness of her office after Aaron died, how the company felt like a deflated blimp. How she felt like a deflated blimp as well.

"I'm extra good. My friends are just incredible. It's like a college apartment but no one's messy or drunk or failing out. We're having one adventure after another. But I'm calling because I have a super idea. I just bought two special garden antiques for the house we're leasing in Tuscany. You just cannot find anything remotely like these things anywhere else."

Molly knew. She has a furniture and bricolage picker in France, and less and less for more and more seems to be the rule.

They decide that Susan will buy half a container to ship back to Artful Dodge Antiques. Fountains, fanlights, gates, garden furniture, statues, railings, convent sinks, table bases—endless! They'll see how it goes.

"Then you come home, girl! We miss you. Wasn't it terrific when we played house—and we got all those babies sold for top dollar, too!"

"We did. Now southern gardens will be transformed. This will be fun!"

JULIA POURS RED WINE INTO her braising pan, and the comforting smell of sizzling onions draws everyone over to see what's cooking. "Time to start celebrating again," Susan tells them, "and I have news to share." She finishes setting places for six, then takes out prosecco glasses and pours. She guides them out into the cold, shining light on her treasures. "They're now guarding our house, and the astrolabe will help in case we lose our bearings in the universe."

JUST THEN, COLIN AND I walk down the hill toward them swinging our flashlight. Susan beams light on the archaic smile of Mercury and the mathematical markings on the astrolabe's bands. "These are for us but they've sparked an idea that I am now in hot pursuit of. More later!"

Rowan arrives and we all move inside around the fire. He has brought over a few of his publications and he, Camille, and I pore over them before dinner. Rowan has his fame, if not fortune. Rare-book librarians buy his books, from Berkeley to Oxford, as do collectors of first and rare editions.

I'm beguiled by his offer to publish a limited edition of my work; he's tops. I'm thrilled that he follows my latest poems in literary magazines, difficult poems—quick moments from my unconscious. (Impossible for the conscious, writing mind, to truly represent the unconscious. Built-in failure, but I try.)

He also brought some Sardinian pecorino called Fiore di Monte that Julia raves about and keeps slicing and piling onto a board with slivers of focaccia, olives she baked with hot peppers, and lemon peel. They're in no rush for dinner. Rowan keeps the kitchen fire stoked and the music of Ennio Morricone playing. When the track from *The Mission* comes on, Julia says, "Oh, please play that at my next wedding, funeral, whatever."

At the table, Susan tells them about calling Molly from Venice and their agreement to try their luck as importers. "This business works well for me because I can find stunning garden antiques and ship them home. Molly pays my bank in North Carolina when she sells them, so I am not earning Italian money. I do not want to get mixed up in Italian taxes. I can't ever earn money here but I can import from here—totally legal."

"You are amazing! Always coming up with the unexpected. Ha, you got us here with two flicks of your computer screen." Susan pours and Camille's glass catches a tilting convex reflection of a kitchen full of warmth.

"Yes, and you're right," Julia says. "Chris has explained that as his consultant, I am paid in the U.S." Chris! Now he's gone. Julia took him to the train for Rome this morning. He's called from his hotel, already missing San Rocco and Julia. Tomorrow, he's back in Napa, back to business, to his son home for holidays, and to planning for the next trip.

"Not likely to be a problem for me," Camille observes.

Julia has made a beet salad with burrata, followed by *stracotto*, which just seems like good beef stew to Susan.

IN SAN ROCCO'S FOUR ANTIQUE shops, Susan finds two vintage terra-cotta sphinxes; a stone *trogolo*, a trough for animals and charming as a planter; a Liberty (art nouveau) gazebo that unhooks its parts and lies flat; a wrought-iron trellis small enough to fit in a pot of climbing clematis. This is too much fun. Villa Assunta becomes a temporary exhibition garden for Susan's trove. She realizes she will have to rent a storage room as her collection grows, otherwise the property will begin to look like a bizarre junkyard.

A *fondo* is what she needs. On side streets, she's seen a couple of FOR RENT signs on the stone storage rooms at the bottoms of houses, usually too small for a car. Laden with iron locks, handwrought through successive ages, their wide doors open to the street. Inside, the heaviest beams support the house above. The dank rooms look as though green demijohns of wine and amphorae of olive oil still should line the walls. She walks all over town but now sees no sign saying *AFFITTASI*.

At the end of San Rocco's elliptical piazza, tucked into a storefront no wider than two arm spans, she's passed a real estate office with beveled and wavy oval glass in the paired walnut doors. Along the side of one door, a case displays notices of houses for sale. Naturally, Susan has perused the mansard apartments and the noble farmhouses marred by garish turquoise swimming pools. (What she could do with a pool at Villa Assunta!) She stares at one seemingly Olympic monster, imagining a stone surround, various sizes of boxwood balls at the end and, umm, how should some falling water be incorporated?

Before she inquires about a *fondo*, she pauses for a coffee and to look up several words that explain what she's looking for. Best not to appear totally unprepared. Recently all three women have been studying with a tutor Grazia recommended. Signora Perruzi comes after lunch for two hours twice a week. And there's homework. The language seems daunting, endless.

When Susan orders a coffee, Violetta suggests instead *una cioccolata calda*, a hot chocolate. *Sì*, Susan nods, and soon her idea of hot chocolate explodes—this is dense; her spoon could stand up. What a revelation. She'll surprise Julia with this tomorrow.

SUSAN RINGS THE BELL. INSIDE the office, she meets Nicolà Bertolli. She's at the front desk but is not, as Susan first assumes, the receptionist. She's it. Petite, all voluminous curls, chic Prada-ish suit and red lips that only slightly stain her big smile. "I've heard of the three American women. It is lovely to meet you," she says in perfect English. She gestures toward the cushy pecan-colored linen sofa and chairs squeezed into the back of the office, and they sit down. She tells Susan that her husband, Brian Henderson, is English. They have the office in San Rocco together, but he also has an office in Florence as the Tuscan representative of Lloyd Bingham Estate Sales and Rentals. Brian fell in love with Nicolà and Tuscany when he was in study abroad and found at the end of his term that he couldn't leave. "He's still very English," Nicolà says, "but he has an Italian soul and four Italian children, all grown now and living in Tuscany. We still spend a lot of time in England. I love London and he has family in Sussex."

Susan knows the famous British company but had no idea there was a branch nearby. Nicolà may be her age. They appraise each other, both fashionistas who could be competitive, but decide that they are friends. "I love your hair," Nicolà says, tossing her own loose locks. "It's a statement, saying, I think, *Don't mess with me.*"

"Well, I would kill for those shoes!" Susan replies. How does she even get them on, all those gladiator straps and the long expanse of leg up to the English-looking tweed skirt. At our age, in an almost-mini! Maybe I'll get one, Susan thinks. My legs are just fine except for that small explosion of broken veins behind my knee.

Nicolà talks about local villas for sale, about property listings for rent all over Italy. About how hard it is to manage houses that people rent to foreigners. She knows about the robbery and asks if Susan is the one who lost her jewelry.

"Mine was hidden under the toilet scrubber," Susan says. "I tried to give Camille a necklace of mine but she said she doesn't want jewelry ever again. Thanks for asking. Back to the backstory, my husband Aaron and I owned a pretty large real estate firm in North Carolina. Not at all in the league of Lloyd Bingham, but, yes, we did amazingly well. Aaron died three and a half years ago, and I've eased out of the company. We loved it. I'm house obsessed. One of my favorite parts was staging the houses. You must come to Villa Assunta. We've had a good time bringing it back to life. My two friends and I are in love with it."

"I know the property. Quite undervalued. It has a superb perspective out on that flat extension of land. Do you expect to buy it?"

"We just arrived in October. We three are at crossroads, so we're just taking it day by day. Who knows!"

"Are you here to look at other houses, to compare?"

"Ah! No. Oh, now I'm embarrassed. I'm only looking right now for a *fondo*. A lowly storage unit! Probably not at all what you represent." She glances at the sleekly produced brochures on the coffee table.

Nicolà laughs. "As you must know, we represent everything. And I will find you a *fondo*. What is it for?"

Susan explains her new scheme and Nicolà is fascinated. "And Susan, the 'staging' you mention. That's not done here and it should be. Often these venerable properties are pretty dour. I tell the owners to buy new lampshades and linens and to spruce up the kitchen, paint walls that haven't been touched in thirty years. They don't want to get rid of their grandmother's *madia* or buy a high-end stove. They don't realize that buyers have changed. The rustic charm doesn't charm as it used to. Especially the bone-hard living room furniture. We must talk about this. And the gardens of magnificent places can look weedy and bedraggled as you drive in with Russian bajillionaires, or Americans, excuse me, who expect to *buy* what's taken centuries to make, but require a sanitized vision of what that is. The clients now are not like previous waves, when they wanted adventures in restoration. Now people want everything perfect when they deposit their suitcases all filled with electronic devices and spa cosmetics. I had a woman weep when she saw a villa's huge array of aluminum cookware—a hundred pots of all sizes. She said it gives the Alzheimer's. Flowers— bloom on demand. Pizza oven, yes, though they almost never use it. No power outage! Instant Internet. And yet they long for the mellow ambiance that drew them here in the first place. I can't imagine who buys those big corporate makeovers of castles and huge farm complexes, those soulless pseudo-Tuscany re-creations. Some decorator swoops down from London and wrenches everything into Scandinavian Gustavian gray. Those places are deadly dull. We—Brian and I—are after the authentic experience. But without anything dreary." She's talking a mile a minute. Ranting.

"I get that. Not easy. Walk the line," Susan responds. "Truth be told, we're maybe a bit like those picky renters ourselves. We aren't too thrilled when the iron pipes send up a rank, dank smell from the bowels of the earth. And what do Italians have against insulation around doorways? But you are right, it's disappointing to be in a denuded place. There's that perfect point between tradition and the present. By the way, what's a *madia*?"

"Every house had one—a chestnut bin where bread rose. Usually drawers under the bin part and what do you say, cupboard. The awkward thing is, because you must raise the top to use it, you can't put anything on top when it's not in use."

"Oh, that's what it is! We have one in the kitchen. It's beautiful but in the way. Julia stores bowls in it. I'll have to tell her she should be kneading bread. I didn't know what I was looking at, but I've seen one left open and used as a bar at a restaurant. Clever."

Susan likes Nicolà. She could talk all morning. "Listen, will you and Brian come to our house for dinner? I know this seems quick, but I'd love for you to meet my friends and I promise a great dinner—not that I will cook!"

THE THREE WOMEN HAVE DECIDED that all winter they will invite friends on Friday nights. Julia will use those dinners as primary research for her *Learning Italian*. They've agreed that by Thursday, the guest list must be set so that everyone can do their bit. Susan, the flowers and table, Julia the food, Camille the shopping and sous-chef duties.

Susan describes Julia's writing/cooking project to Nicolà, and Camille's blooming interest in making art after putting it off for decades. "She's revving up. It's like she's orbiting the moon looking for the right place to land." Susan puts on her coat and holds out her hand to Nicolà. "I was nervous to come in with my awful Italian." She pulls out of her pocket the piece of paper where she'd written *Vorrei affittare un fondo*. I would like to rent a *fondo*.

Nicolà laughs and takes the scrap of paper from her. "When you are fluent, I'll frame this for you."

Susan heads toward the cobbled Roman road for home. She walked into town with a list of past participles in hand, as Kit suggested. All the way back she practices.

Holy Days

WINTER. COLIN AND I RISE to a white sea of frothy fog in the valley below us. It's thrilling to throw open the shutters and lean out into the *aria fresca*. All morning, the sea rises, finally enveloping the house, and then the vapors burn off in the midday sun. I shake three scorpions out of my boots stored in the barn. Our wool socks smell of the sheep they came from. Colin tightens the shutter fittings so northern winds won't fling them about in the night.

"You must have a mind of winter," poet Wallace Stevens said. I do: I am planning major accomplishments over the closed-in months. Not that winter ever gets Minnesota-serious here. But stone houses hold a chill. We're pretty snug with radiators that lightly clang four musical notes when they start up, and with a *scaldaletto*, a fuzzy kind of mattress pad that all Italians I know use from November until April. It's electric. With warm down above and the plushy thing below, you feel like a humid, snoring bear in a cave.

First—I'm having a party. The holidays are coming and before my new neighbors scatter with their visiting families, it's time I introduced them to my best Italian friends and some of the foreigners. And I want to celebrate. I have wild holly on the land, and mistletoe in the crotches of almond trees. My house will be filled with roses.

I can flat lay down a feast though I'm not inspired in the pastry/ cake department. From a woman in town I can order a brilliant hazelnut roulade. I love winter food—short ribs, my mother's potatoes dauphinois, pork with red cabbage and chestnuts, mushrooms over polenta—all odes to winter.

WHEN I WAS GROWING UP in Coral Gables, Minnie, our housekeeper, used to tell me that fate happens in threes; whether bad or good or bad, she believed our Lord sends things in bundles of three.

I'm going for three good.

One: After the visit to Dr. Caprini (meaning goats, how wild), I felt exultant. Who could ever expect a mystical experience while lying on an examining table? When I was gelled and connected to the sonar (stomach still concave), and the aqueous image of that tiny splotch of gray and black smaller than a bay shrimp (head apparent) appeared, I almost crushed Colin's hand. I wanted to shout! And then I wanted to cry and did. Dr. Caprini seemed excited, too, and didn't make me feel worried at all about being as they term it an "elderly primigravida," meaning someone over thirty-five pregnant for the first time. She was, instead, marveling that I am pregnant, given my age (eighty-five percent of women are sterile by forty-four) and the inclination of my uterus. "This is one determined little creature," was her opinion. She has capable cool hands, iron-gray hair pulled into a tight bun, and a wedge of a chin. No little whippersnapper is going to pull anything on her watch. I liked her. She said, "You'll be fine. You have a young body. You are not having twins and for that I'm grateful. One is enough." I laughed. I got chills. "The sex isn't visible quite yet," she said, squinting at the blurry squiggle.

"That's fine—we're not sure we want to know anyway." More tests later, books to read, a vitamin to take, a diet high in protein and vegetables—it's all easy for now. My breasts are like Eden rosebuds about to bloom, pressing to open, explosive. (Spindly roses along the side of the house in Coral Gables. I'm missing my mother every day.)

Two: Colin's team won an award for innovative design and a commendation for excellence in adaptation to site. The work was a university student center in Manchester. Next, we learned that Colin's London firm will expand early in the next year. They're opening offices in Dubai and Miami. Dubai because it's Dubai, Miami because three major commissions came through—a museum, a municipal complex, and a destination pier with shops and restaurants. He found out on the last trip that he has a choice of staying in London, with more flex time to be working on Italian designs, or the chance to spend part time in the Miami office, if he wants, on a project-based schedule. This means life here becomes easier; the brutal London commute can lessen. And Florida—if there had been a job available after my mother died, I'd probably be there yet. The place I always crave is far inside the idea most people have of Florida. You have to dig for my Florida, but it's there, a primitive landscape of hot sand and rioting foliage and alligators with comical wide jaws and trees dripping with moss, and coasts as you imagine them. Should Little Miss X draw her first breath there? Or should Young Master X draw his in Florence, the air of the Medicis, intrigue of the renaissance, the opposite of primitive? Colin sees all this as excitement and possibility, not as stress, so I am seeing it that way, too, only occasionally seizing up with uncertainty and, well, stress. (No Italian word exists for stress—it's imported from English: *lo stress*.)

We are looking at remodeling my small stone barn. If Colin outfits it with a large-scale printer and other equipment he needs, he can work more from here. Right now, he has his drawing boards set up in a spare room. An architect in town lets him print at his office. Not the best.

There's little light in the stone barn, only that coming in from the arched door built wide enough for a cart, but he can embed a skylight on the back side that doesn't show, if we can obtain permission. The cart door can be all glass, as there's a side door. To stand beside the entrance, an astrolabe. I will surprise him, if I can get Susan to find another one. When I looked up the function of the astrolabe, I came across a reference to Heloise and Abelard, those philosophical star-crossed lovers who were passionately romantic in the early eleven hundreds. Teacher/pupil affairs rarely come to good ends. Heloise's furious uncle had Abelard castrated for his dalliance with his niece but not before a son was conceived. He was called Astralabe. I think they felt that their love was as dimensional as the heavens and bambino Astralabe symbolized their astronomical love. But when I talk this out to Colin, he only says, "Hmm. We should name ours Sonogram?"

"Well, what about Abelard. That is a nice name."

"You're kidding. Richard is a nice name. James. Placido. Alessandro. But Abelard? He'd be Abe or Lard." He pushes me back on the bed, kissing my neck, blowing in my ear, tickling me until I'm kicking my legs in the air. "But I *am* partial to Balthazar."

Three: We're getting married. *Gesù!* I'm unaccountably thrilled. As is Colin. We did not care before that we were arrested in boyfriend-girlfriend mode. Now, every night at dinner we talk about when and where and how. We're listening to music in the kitchen, dancing between checking on the green beans and the chicken twirling on the rotisserie in the oven. I toss out the idea of marrying in Coral Gables, in the same chapel where my parents married and I took first communion. (I was intensely religious for about six months.) I suggest our garden this spring with the jasmine dangling over the pergola and the profligate Lady Banksia rose arching over the door. But really, do I want to bulge in an ephemeral wedding dress? It should be sooner. He imagines Greece. Just us on an island. On New Year's Day? Since neither of us has been married before, the documentation required for foreigners is less baroque.

Actually, there are more than three fates right now. In my own realm, lines are coming to me as I fall asleep, as I wake up, and I'm remembering them whole.

By day, I'm writing poems that surprise me. I'm allowing in fragments of emotions, bits of esoteric knowledge I pick up in my reading, and a looser form, the lines broken more casually. When each poem is done, I turn back to my three women's adventures or to my Margaret project, which took a jolting turn when we were examining the barn and I came upon her suitcase she left during her back-and-forth travels to the U.S. after she sold her Casa Gelsomino.

I dread opening the barn, since two *barbagianni* live there. Last time I went out to store the summer fans, I opened the door and the two owls, tall as one-year-old children, stared down from a beam and flapped their wings—a three-foot wingspan at least. Their eyes drilled into me. They croaked otherworldly sounds and I spooked, dropped the fans, and ran, waving my arms and screaming.

Today they are not in residence. We have an archive of luggage stored on the back shelves, from backpacks to duffels, an array of roll-ons and giant folding monsters I hope never to travel with again. Hers is stacked with those. "Can you hoist it into the house?" I ask Colin. "I'll go through it later."

We find a friend's battered calfskin bag filled with dried-up tubes of oil paints, stiff brushes, rags, his painting slippers, and on a rolled canvas a quite decent still life of blue plums in a pewter bowl. (The rime of light on the fruit worked its way into a poem.)

"Oh, here's Jeremy!" Colin says. "He's got work at the Tate now. Wonder if he wants this back." Jeremy lingered too long one summer.

"You could ask. I think he abandoned it. Such juicy-looking plums—we could hang them in here as a memorial to all the nights he kept us up talking about sight lines and Emil Nolde's work, and the grad student he was poking."

COLIN HIRES A MAN WITH a truck to haul off Jeremy's ruined art supplies plus tons of accumulated nonsense that piles up so slowly that you don't realize what a nasty burden you have—mildewed suitcases, split hoses, a table with a broken leg, paint cans, plant fertilizers turned to cement, junk, junk. Emptied, the barn suddenly looked spacious enough to imagine white plaster walls, cleaned-up stone floors smoothed for a couple of centuries by hooves, and a long worktable with some cool industrial lighting over it.

After lunch, I open Margaret's suitcase. She's tucked sachets of potpourri in the side pockets. The heap of clothes gives off a scent of ferny woods, mildew, and spice, maybe curry. The suitcase must have been stored for five years. I don't find the stack of paper immediately, a thick pile of pages tied up with a thin yellow ribbon stuffed inside a handbag. The title reads *Incendiary Remarks*, with *Margaret Merrill* handwritten beneath. I thumb through the pages of single-spaced type, some scarred with cross-outs and amendments in the purple ink she favored in her Mont Blanc pen. "Colin," I shout down the stairs, "I can't believe this—Margaret has left a manuscript!" I empty the suitcase out on the bed: a jacquard silk bathrobe that looks like a man's, three sweaters, those orange suede boots I always admired, a bottle of Dior perfume gone sour, cotton nightgown, black skirt, then at the bottom a box holding a string of pearls and the Murano glass beads I once gave her but never saw her wear. Now I think she found them tacky.

Colin bounds in, riffles through the pile of clothes, and picks up a blue sweater shot through with grosgrain ribbons. "That's pretty. We're finding treasure today. Would you wear that? Or that dress I brought in the house before, the one that looks like it emerged whole from the Grand Bazaar?"

"So flashy. Oh, maybe I will. But, look. This is definitely a manuscript. I don't recognize it as anything in print. It has to be an unpublished book that has moldered in our barn for years. Can you realize what this means? A lost Margaret Merrill?"

"Well, yes, to you. I doubt if the world will tilt on its axis." We push back the clothes, sit down on the bed, and start reading. A novel? The epigraph says: *I prefer a drop of blood to a glass of ink. (George Seferis.)*

"Rings true. Margaret despised theory." We turn to the first page, which begins: *Rain fell in great gray slats across the valley. I was newly home, still relishing home, my cantilevered stone steps to the dining room that to my satisfaction always give guests a moment of vertigo, the mustard velvet chairs around the fireplace, windows that open to the view of a gigantic tower in the adjacent* palazzo. "Hmm, that's Casa Gelsomino. Is this autobiographical?" I flip forward and read randomly. "Has she written a memoir?"

"I'll leave it to you. I want to get some work done." Colin picks up the blue sweater again and smells it. "You remember, she always had a scent. Not fresh like you, sheets drying in the sun. More like incense that priests flick around a coffin, sort of smoky and forbidden. Or worse, like she just walked out of a hashish den where someone was murdered." He laughed.

"She did have a noir quality."

MARGARET. MAUD AND FREYA WERE easy to investigate and easy to bring to life on paper. I loved Margaret well and then later not as much. When I read my San Rocco poems in a Washington bookstore—I was thrilled to be invited—she happened to be in town. I'd known her several years by then, my witty, so-worldly friend, well known across a spectrum of writing. My early years—when I wondered if I would surpass *A Glass of Morning Rain*, my first book that got me the position at Boulder. I was the case-study "struggling" writer, dealing with rejections and dismissals, trying to get another book published, hell, trying to get poems published. Then I did. Things broke open for me when I sent out my work based on Italy. (Maybe I'd just learned to write after seasons of solitude at my desk.) (How I miss that concentration I could achieve then.) One sequence was an abecedarius, based on the letters of the Italian alphabet; another was inspired by Italian words I liked. I tried to fit each word—*cipresso, mirtillo, girasole, luna, chiacchierone, sera, cielo*—into landscape or event. I think there were thirty in that series. Most popular, if I can even use that word in regard to poetry, were the prose poems about daily life in San Rocco. I worked to make them authentic, wishing I could glue onto the pages the yellow broom blooming on the hillsides, the worn-out ropes of the dwarf who carries wood on his back to the pizza ovens, the walking sticks Leo carves, the navy-blue print housedress aprons older women wear at home— all the tactile sensations that constantly pour on me in this wondrous place. That work was my first book, *A Glass of Morning Rain*. Okay, pun on my name, sorry.

The Washington reading went well. You can tell when an audience is with you. I began to enjoy the experience and I felt braced by Margaret in the back. Team Kit, I thought. During the Q&A after I finished, someone waved a hand and asked, "What is the reaction of local people to your book? Do they like the poems?" I didn't know that anyone local would ever read them and was just forming that answer when out of nowhere, Margaret, looking like a thirties movie star in a white linen suit, stood up and said, "No! They won't. They'll think foreigners should mind their own business. They'll invent ways they're condescended to, and besides they don't like contemporary forms. To them, poems need to rhyme." She sat down.

What? I was stunned and simply said, "There you have it. I honestly don't know, but Margaret Merrill has lived in Italy a long time. Maybe she knows. I wrote the poems with love. I would hope that survives translation, if that even happens. Is there another question?" What possessed her to interrupt *my* event? Recognizing her name, many turned to look at the possessed woman, now examining a notepad but with her chin raised. She appeared to look down to those of us far below. The mood broke and it was over.

Why didn't I confront her? Why didn't I? A character flaw, no doubt. My family just let things simmer until some burst of heat caused a sudden explosion. That's me. That's what I do. I was subdued at dinner after the reading. She took me out to a buzzy place full of politicos (ugh) where six men came over to say how they admired her exposé of the Mafia. She ordered oysters (ugh) and Champagne "to celebrate the beginning of a grand career." Not a word about her jab.

Late, back at my hotel, I emailed Colin. *Weird, weird. I think Margaret is jealous of ME. Don't laugh!*

The Seven-Thousand-Mile Conversation

THE FRIDAY NIGHT DINNERS HAVE added four chapters to Julia's *Learning Italian*. While she cooks all afternoon, she sets her laptop on the counter and chats with Chris. She chops, scoops onions and garlic into the pan to sauté, thinking he's so close he can smell them sizzling. He tells her about the progress of this year's pinot noir. The barrel tastings promise a super product. A few splats of olive oil pop out and she swabs off the screen. There— the big smile of Chris at his office in Napa. She likes his desk, two wine barrels topped with an irregular slab of redwood. He sits in a twirly bar chair of cowhide and horns. In a denim shirt, unlike the fitted clothes he wears in Italy, he looks western. His smile transmits across cyberspace the energy she knows well. He's cooking with her as she tells him about the semolina gnocchi with parmigiano she's sliding into the oven, about the duck breasts with balsamic reduction and orange peel she has ready to serve.

TWELVE AT TABLE TONIGHT. SUSAN has arranged small pots of white cyclamen down the middle, white plates, and a green cloth. She's excited that Nicolà and Brian are coming. Camille has invited Chiara Bevilacqua, the bookstore owner, and her female partner, name yet unknown, plus Rowan, Annetta and Leo, Colin and Kit. Camille has been closed away all day, emerging at lunch to warm up a serving of leftover lasagne, which she took back to her room, promising she'd be on hand to open the wines and arrange the antipasti platter. Julia and Susan are excited for Camille. She's working! After weeks of wheeling around in the air, dipping and circling and flying higher and swooping again, the silence in her room sounds like music to them.

"It's full winter," Julia tells Chris. "Fall was still hanging on when you left, but there's been a distinct turn. We hear owls all night." Julia pauses to look for a hot pad. "You should be here. Come back!" The just-braised broccolini mixed with the onions, garlic, and a couple of anchovies smells bitter, good bitter. Chris watches as she starts prepping, for tomorrow, a rolled turkey breast that Gilda at Hotel Santa Caterina demonstrated in the cooking class Julia attends two mornings a week. She slices the big breast almost through on opposite sides and flattens it out. "Gilda says stuff it with anything you want and I'm going to try various combinations but right now, I'm copying what she did, spreading a layer of ground veal, a layer of coarse bread crumbs, and some chopped pistachios." She rolls it the long way and ties it with string in four places.

"You're killing me, you know that." Chris leans in close. "I'll have pasta with jarred tomato sauce for dinner tonight. How will you write about this rolled thing for your book?"

"There's a lot to say about turkey here. *Tacchino.* They are huge, if you buy a whole one. Twice the normal size. This breast alone looks like a whole turkey! And—I promise, you would not know you are eating turkey. It's juicy and savory. I thought it was veal. Turkey sandwiches? Forget that! This is the best. And pistachios. I didn't know they are used a lot in Tuscan recipes. I'm researching that. Why pistachios?"

"I don't know. I thought they were just for breaking your fingernail on when they bring out a bowl with a Campari Soda. I'm missing you. You're the only one I could discuss pistachios with for hours." He hesitates. "Julia, I was wondering. Say no right away if I'm off base. Would you like for me to look up Lizzie in San Francisco, if she's still there? I know you haven't heard anything in months and I know you want to have time to get your life back, but you must ache about this."

Julia put down her spoon. She didn't answer.

"Hey, you there? Just an idea. I could go to her last address—didn't you ask me if I knew the Scott and Sutter Street area?—and as quietly as possible see if I can find out anything."

"Chris, Chris. Thank you. I do push back my worry, I have to, but I'm afraid of *choosing* to fall on my sword again."

"Think about it."

"Thank you. It's wonderful that you offer. She'd think we sent a spy. You're too sweet to think of it. But don't . . ."

"What if I just case the hood?" How to read this? He heard her hesitate. "You've been through too many wringers. I don't want to meddle."

"Oh, here are the kittens. Can you see Ragazzo? Look how they've grown so fast."

"Ah, subject over. Cue the kittens! Cute!"

Julia laughed. "Right. Let's get back to *our* subjects. When I talk to you, when I'm *with* you, I'm just me, not a part of a zombie squad in Savannah! Speaking of, you know my daddy is coming for Christmas. We decided to stay here a few days, then go to Rome. Rome! I can't wait. He wants to go to Naples, too."

"You're killing me again. What I'd give to spend the holidays in Rome with you. Does he know how lucky he is?"

"He does! Lizzie was the light of his life but now it's back to me. You'll meet him. He's special, not just that he's my father either. You'll be with your boy for Christmas?" Lizzie at Christmas, salt packed in the gaping wound. Ghosts of Christmas past, indeed.

"Part of the time. He's going up to Tahoe afterward, and I'm going to catch up on work so when I get to Italy in late March, I won't have to worry." They've finished their final polishing of the Friuli tour, which happens in April. It's already fully booked.

"I've got to get moving on the dessert. Talk tomorrow?"

"I'm already waiting."

ℐCATTERING

'TIS THE SEASON OF MUCH to savor, beginning with San Rocco. Swags of lights, with bulbs that look saved from the 1940s, hang over the streets. The town government erected a decidedly pitiful and scraggly pine in the middle of the main piazza. School children decorated it with garlands of dried bow tie pasta sprayed gold and a few pine cones they'd gathered in the town park. The three women find it charming, such a counter to Christmas as they know it. No mall shops play carols on loop, no "O Holy Night" bringing tears to their eyes in the aisles of toys to be forgotten within twenty-four hours after Christmas. The pastry shop window glistens with rosy, purple, and apricot marzipan fruits, coils of almond pastry, puffs of cream-filled meringues, and glacéed kumquats and chestnuts. The weekly market features buckets of mistletoe and holly, a few fir trees (even more scraggly than the town tree), their roots wrapped in burlap and ready to plant after a brief season indoors. They'll be adorned with small notes to Babbo Natale, chocolates, paper snowflakes, and a strand of blinking colored lights that might cause a fire at any minute. Churches display scenes of the nativity; some are elaborate renditions of renaissance paintings, some are formed from homey materials such as a matchbox for the manger and a shoebox for the plastic donkeys' stalls. Camille is especially touched by wise men made of pipe cleaners and sheep made from steel wool and toothpicks.

The three friends love the early winter evenings in town, the bars crowded with merry people toasting, the mornings with shops full of women hunting and gathering for feasts, the charged air of *festa*. Susan meets Nicolà for hot chocolate. Camille takes Serena and Matilde to lunch at Hotel Santa Caterina. At Christmas, Julia never has not shopped for Wade and Lizzie (well, last year Lizzie was MIA); now she shops for her friends. No comforting yellow bathrobes. No dizzying cologne to dab under his delicious earlobes. At least she can buy lambskin gloves for her father, and pearl gray cashmere socks. Several books will be delivered to Chris, including a giant tome on Sicily. For Susan, a measuring tape in centimeters and inches, and a coral soft wool scarf that Julia can see flapping out the sunroof of the speeding Fiat. For Camille, sexy perfume she'd never buy for herself, musk and gardenia, and a glass quill with some bottles of artisan inks in violet, deep blue, and amber.

COLIN BRINGS IN LOADS OF wood for tonight. I'm through arranging cypress boughs along the mantel. He's kept a fire going all day while we've transformed the downstairs for our party.

Colin cleared space in the living and dining rooms and set up borrowed folding tables on either end of our usual table for twelve. Now we can squeeze in twenty-two at our Christmas Eve-Eve splash. For music, my Irish expat friends, Brendan and Sally. He brings his guitar and she sings like an angel. He's good at stirring everyone to participate. Leo and Annetta will help me roast big pork loins in their fireplace, and this afternoon, I picked up the historic, epic hazelnut roulade, sure to be for Julia the highlight of the party. This many for dinner is normal in Tuscany but a big effort for me. Oh, wait, I forgot Riccardo, our translator friend who works for the Vatican and comes up only on weekends. That's twenty-three. I'll have to squeeze in one more place setting.

GIANNI PICKS UP CLEVE HADLEY outside customs at Fiumicino and heads right back to Villa Assunta, where Julia paces, alternating waiting at the front window and dashing back to the oven where she's baking her father's favorite lemon pound cake. He'll be exhausted, she thinks, and turns down his bed. The same bed Chris . . . She puts a pot of fragrant mint, sage, and thyme on his bedside table with a carafe of water, and even small chocolates, like at a fine hotel.

Cleve will stay through Christmas, and then he and Julia will travel for a week. He wants to visit the Italian Geographic Society Library and to wander in the Vatican corridors where he loved the globes and early maps when he was a young man on his first trip. He plans to have tea at the Galleria Doria Pamphilj and to have a Negroni overlooking the Piazza Navona rain or shine.

Susan will train it to Milano tomorrow to meet her daughters. They'll rent a car and drive straight to San Cassiano, a mountain village in the Dolomites, for Christmas. After a couple of days, they're planning to explore the Trentino-Alto Adige area. I can only imagine Susan in a rented car careening over the Falzarego Pass, which has got to be close to seven thousand feet. She'll bring them to San Rocco only for a weekend, starting a round of musical chairs, overlapping with Camille but not Julia. The daughters will get to meet Julia for dinner when Susan takes them to Rome on their way home.

Camille's Charlie, with daughter Ingrid, will arrive late Christmas Day from his wife's family in Copenhagen, Charlie taking the room across from Julia's father, and Ingrid sleeping in the never-used back bedroom. Charlie's wife, Lara, will join them after a couple of days. Camille plans to take them to Venice for New Year's Eve.

Susan has arranged hotels and pickups and even someone to come clean Villa Assunta twice a week during the onslaught. No one can keep the others' crazy schedules straight. They'll be home by Little Christmas. That they know.

We leave for Florida tomorrow, as soon as we clear up the chaos after our party.

CAMILLE AND SUSAN ARE READY to deck the halls. They've already dropped off white roses for the party tonight. Susan pulls into Villa Assunta with the car packed and one of the puny local Christmas trees tied to the Fiat roof. At the special Christmas market, they've picked out painted ceramic balls, tinsel, strings of tiny bells the kittens will go wild for, and sparklers. For Julia, they have a box of marrons glacés, a pair of pink quartz earrings made by a local designer, and a contraption that squeezes juice from the bones of fowl. Not likely to become a household favorite, but the novelty appealed to them and that's what Christmas presents are about, right, the *Oh lord, what* is *that?* moment. Susan lugs in a crate of clementines just up from Sicily, and Camille stands the tree in a terra-cotta pot and drags it into the living room. Julia already has placed around the downstairs three vases of rose hips and holly laden with red berries. Susan gathers more holly from the slope toward Leo's house and arranges wands of it with the long-stemmed white roses for the dining room. The fir draped with tinsel and a string of lights makes Susan want to sing "Silent Night," so she does. Camille and Julia laugh in the kitchen. The villa sparkles.

It sparkles more with the entrance of Cleve Hadley. Julia whoo-hoos and throws her arms around him, dancing him up and down the entrance hall, while Susan and Camille help Gianni with Cleve's coat and bag. He looks like Julia's father should.

Fine-boned like her, hair in shocks the color of ice, a neat pointed beard. Fit and tanned, he's small and precise but gives the definite impression that he is just right.

After a tour of the house, Julia takes him into the kitchen, where she has soup and bruschetta ready. He's enchanted. "In all my years, I've never seen a dining room this completely charming, even in Savannah where there are some spectacular dining rooms. You could step into the garden fresco, go traipsing through the rose arbor. Imagine how many people have had the same thought over the decades they've dined in there. Oh, this soup is just what the doctor ordered."

Though the flight was smooth, he's rattled by traveling for seventeen hours. The chickpea and pasta soup sends them all into a nap mode. "This olive oil, what makes it green?" Julia tells him more than he ever imagined about olive oil, the qualities and history and milling. "Tastes good, too." He smiles.

"We should squeeze in a rest," Susan says. "We have to be ready to party tonight." Cleve raises his eyebrows but nods. Julia settles her father into his room. She and Susan are off to town for hair appointments. Cleve showers, then flops on the bed and falls into a delicious jet-lag sleep.

PAPER DOORS

CAMILLE HAS NO INTENTION OF resting for more than fifteen minutes. Finally, finally, only this week her project broke open and she's reveling in the experience of intense focus, a heady sensation of catapulting forward. Maybe it was the email she received from Charlie: *Mom, I looked at the paintings in the attic. What a shame that you stored your talent up there. I've had waves of guilt. All that care you lavished on me! The paintings were dusty but luminous and moving. I've taken them downstairs and cleaned them. I'm having a great time hanging them in the hall, in the dining room, and one over the bed in your—now our—bedroom. That would be my favorite—a mirror on a weathered wall reflecting a lighted open doorway with mysterious objects that are not quite identifiable.*

Ah, a beckoning or foreboding doorway even back then. She hung on to that for days, still circling, still fearful. She could toss off a small watercolor of Susan's single pom-pom yellow chrysanthemum leaning in a tall glass, or an architectural detail of the stone surround of the living room fireplace. Rowan admired those, encouraged her, and still she waited. But the end of the year is coming, another year rolling toward her, its undertow already felt in her shoulders, the emptiness of her stomach, the small of her back. Too many year-ends hurtling off into oblivion. Now she feels an impatience with herself. A needle poking.

Three nights ago, she woke up at four and crept into her studio. All the materials neatly organized. Too neatly? She surveyed stacks of paper, tubes and brushes and pencils and canvases. My arsenal, she mused. She pulled her robe tight and sat down. "Time to begin." She spoke aloud. A legendary nun once painted in the house, Grazia had told them. On close examination, Camille had found that the claws and feet of the black and white bird on the fresco formed the initials *NM*. Clever nun. Nameless, but how many lives she touched.

In the night, Camille paints a door frame on a piece of her handmade paper. She pauses for a long time, then animates the door with private symbols, writing that looks chipped through instead of painted, and some writing that goes backward. The shawl on the woman in the dining room fresco becomes an abstract pattern reminiscent of the mosaics in Aquileia in Friuli: along the edge, tile-shaped squares like Scarpa's. Ink. Watercolor. Oil. On impulse, she glues a page on top of another, then another, fifteen, a stack. Now the door is thick. An object, not a painting. Light, though. Tears spill as she works. This is beyond where she thought she could go. She loves the look. She has made a strange artifact. A paper door, a mysterious new entity, not sculpture, not book, not painting. She recognizes that she has made something entirely her. *Flesh of my flesh.* New.

The creature from the black lagoon, she laughs, cools off from the white heat of her worktop. She inspects the rough deckle edges all around, thinking of a sealed scrapbook, a ship's log at the bottom of a trunk, the diary she kept at nine, its lost key. She dips her finest brush into burnt umber and adds a thin border at the bottom. Where to stop? When is enough enough? She blends the smallest dab of blue into white to make a washed-out tint like the thin light of the sky when the sun is blazing. That faint shade surrounds the rest of the door. *CT* she inks in at the bottom, and then she adds *#1*.

Thank you, NM.

Doors that push open, transparent doors, translucent doors, studded bastion doors, but not the flat images of Tuscan doors on posters. My doorways are entrances to, what, life, what life mostly is, the unconscious. And didn't Kit say that about her poems, she's mapping the unconscious.

As she'd added her crabbed cuneiform writing, backward writing, mirror writing, the mosaic-inspired patterns, she felt herself slide into what she'd call an altered state, if that didn't sound new agey. But it *is* a different kind of awareness, almost a suspension. She couldn't explain it to herself and decided not to try but to pick up a heavy sheet of paper again and see what swung open next.

This one began with a door within the door, as you see on some medieval gates for people to pass through while the huge outer fortress door remains locked. On only her second effort, she picks up the fine scissors and cuts out a shape for the light to appear from the next sheet of paper. The sun burns through above the small door and the writing above is crosshatched and illegible. What does it mean? It means color. Interaction of shapes. A ring of crimson around the sun, a shaft of letters. Another shaft of letters. Rays of writing in a private language whose meaning she might receive in dreams. The key to a desk; the iron key to the villa. A horse-head knocker from her house in North Carolina. She's knocking there, knocking and knocking and wondering why she does not answer her own door. Yes, altered state.

ROWAN ARRIVES LATE IN THE afternoon. They're all gathering before the party to exchange gifts, since both he and Susan will take off tomorrow. "May I show you something? Actually it's your present. I hope you like it." He follows Camille into the studio where the lamp on the worktop shines down on #1 and the scattered materials for #2. "You were with me when I discovered paper, then we had that day in Bologna looking at artists' books and more paper. You told me where to go in Venice. I can't thank you enough."

Rowan slips his arm around her waist and leans over the paper door. He's quiet for too long. What if he's trying desperately to think of some tactful encouraging words to cover his embarrassment for her. But she looks sideways at him and sees the sweet tinge of a smile, how he looked when he was too pleased to speak. She's seen that look three times, now four. He shakes his head slowly and pulls her close. "Brilliant. Brilliant. Let me say, I recognized you." He lets her go and lifts the paper door, his arms outstretched. "Camille. Trust me. This is a one-off, there's nothing like it. You've got to go with this all the way. You've nailed it. My Christmas gift! Ha! This is due for better walls than my yellowed office. Right now, let's hang it over your worktop to inspire you. This is where you began the great work of your next decade! Honey, you've got it in spades."

"Wait, are you sure? I . . ." She starts laughing and stops.

Rowan examines the new one she started this afternoon. "These have a quality of mystery but they're also direct, strong. It's like your dreaming mind is throwing out images for you to catch."

"That's close to what I'm after. But some of this comes just from snatches of every day, phrases that seemed to require being written backward. And the bird. See his feet? The letters *NM*, that's the nun I told you about. The mosaic, the shawl in the fresco. Things the day tosses out for me to catch."

"Just stay open. You are. That's how the North Carolina clay formed you."

"What?"

"Oh, you know, the creation myth that the gods slapped us into shape from local clay."

"True enough." Camille feels alarmed by his extravagant appreciation. "Don't go back! I need you here to cheer me on."

"You will be fine. More than fine. And I'll be back with the swallows."

"So long from now. Will we forget each other? The last thing I expected was to find a *boyfriend* on this trip!"

"Okay, girlfriend, give me some credit. We'll stay in touch. I write actual letters. I'll be back in late May."

By Candlelight

EVERYONE BRINGS GIFTS TO THE living room, where Susan has started a sputtering fire. Julia lights candles on both windowsills. "I've brought a special wine," Rowan announces. "It's a 2001 amarone. Chris would be proud. Let's find the big-ass glasses." Cleve winces at that. From his satchel, Rowan takes out his gifts, carefully wrapped in brown paper, tied with string and sprigs of rosemary. "Just *pensieri*," he says, "little thoughts."

"Ever the fine press publisher," Camille said. "Lucky I have another something for you, since my first gift was rejected." She hands him a red box.

He holds up a burly heather green V-neck sweater. "For the coldest day in Berkeley," he says.

Everyone toasts, unties ribbons, and exclaims. Julia has never seen a bone press but appears to be delighted. She passes a plate of walnut and Gorgonzola crostini. "Just a bite because Kit is throwing a huge dinner. I know the menu."

At Matilde's *bottega*, Rowan designed and made blank books—perfect travel journals—he has brought for them. He used ochre handmade paper covers, each stamped with a vintage design of sailboat, bicycle, or biplane. Julia gives him a bag of her lemon biscotti for the flight back to California tomorrow. Susan has two small pillows stuffed with herbs for him. "They help you sleep," she explains.

Everything's unwrapped and exclaimed over. The glasses of inky amarone catch firelight, the little tree shines with a bit of bravura, the crostini disappear. Cleve exclaims over gloves and socks: just what he needs. "Truly!" he says. "It's a comfort to have just the right gloves and socks." He sits down at the piano, which has yet to be touched. Oddly, he plays "Summertime," the three almost-dead keys plunking. They gather around him and belt it out, the southern women all remembering the Janis Joplin version, the Ella version, and Rowan, whose cultural memory would be more the Beach Boys' "California Girls," can only watch. Cleve pauses to take out three small boxes from his jacket pocket. "You girls, excuse the *girls* but you are to me. I don't want you to forget where you came from. I had a feeling that might be easy from what Julia reports." In the boxes each finds a thin silver chain with a white enameled *Magnolia grandiflora* pendant.

Still sensitive to the jewelry heist, Camille holds hers in the palm of her hand as the others immediately clasp theirs around their necks. "Very pretty, Daddy. Someone in Savannah made them?"

"Yes, that daughter of Alison. She's teaching at the art college now."

Alison, Julia's plump and lucky next-door neighbor. Julia feels a pang of anguish that Cheryl, a good ten years younger than Lizzie, is designing delicate jewelry while Lizzie falters . . . But no. She looks hard at the meticulous design, the waxy petals outlined in gold filament. "Oh, *brava* for Cheryl. Here, Camille, let me fasten it for you."

"You are too sweet!" Susan says. "This is so nostalgic—I have a giant magnolia in my front yard at home." What a mess they make, she thought, with their leathery leaves falling constantly.

But, oh, those few weeks of bloom when the scent blows through raised windows into the house at night and you know it's the breath of the South. You breathe in that fragrance and think, *Why live anywhere else, ever.* She walks over to the window and stares out at small lights down the hills in the distance. Everyone's at home. Everyone gathering. Not Aaron. Not barreling in with arms full of polka-dot wrapped gifts. At Christmas, his red silk bow tie, outrageous, his square college-fullback shoulders, how big and right he stands, building a fire. When the girls were little and excited. Now they're soon boarding planes that will take them forty thousand feet in the air over the ocean to meet her in a foreign country. Where there are no family julep cups on the table. No carolers from the Methodist church. No annual open house, the cinnamon and clove scent of mulled wine, with toasted pecans and cheese straws on the coffee table, the fragrant long-leaf pine that touched the ceiling, had to touch the ceiling, the obscene piles of gifts and the windows fogged.

She regroups and turns back to the different life, Cleve now thumping out "Angels we have heard on high . . ."

Camille calls everyone into the kitchen. On the table sits a fancy new food processor. "Advance gift from Charlie! He couldn't replace the jewelry but he could order this for us."

Friends

THEY SCALE THE HILL, TURN at the top of their driveway, and then suddenly, they see Fonte, lighted candles flickering in every window. "This is your life, Susan Ware," Julia whispers. She holds her daddy's arm.

Camille and Rowan bring up the rear. "Will you go back to my place after dinner?" he asks. "I've stashed another bottle of that amarone. We need to celebrate *Paper Doors, #1*. Celebrate in the best way possible."

"Sweep me off my feet," Camille says. "Yes! I would love to spend a cozy night with you. No, not a cozy night but a scandalous night. I don't want to think, but it's the last for a long time."

"Ha. Too bad we're too old to cause scandals."

Camille feels sad and excited. Tomorrow Rowan will be back in Berkeley for Christmas with his older sister and his ancient mother, while she will be delirious with excitement over seeing Charlie and Ingrid. "I know you hate leaving but are you also glad to go home?" I'll have a whole day to recover myself, she thinks, erase all traces and put on my mother-face.

"Yes. I adore my mother. My sister and I share the care. It's not a burden." Camille remembers her own mother saying, *Any man who doesn't like his mother has got to be damaged.* Charles loved his mother. She knows Charlie does.

What a good friend I found, she thinks. But you don't have sex with a friend, at least not in my realm. So, what is he to me? Lover! She laughs out loud.

"What's funny?" he asks.

"Life in general." They step up the pace; it's beginning to sleet.

CAN ANYTHING LOOK MORE WELCOMING and warm than a rustic stone house in the country, all lit for Christmas? I've bought out the entire candle supply in San Rocco. In the whole house, even the bathrooms, no electric lights are on except in the kitchen. Stefano has let two of his kitchen staff help me tonight. ("My Christmas gift to you.") Colin and I are not constantly getting up to clear plates. The table is set—snowy white cloth with huge linen napkins I've collected from the antique market, all with various monograms of long-lost women who set their tables for guests. My place cards I've pierced with twigs of holly, the only touch of red. Enough people are bilingual that I'm assured no dead conversation zones bog down the table dynamic. White roses (thank you, Susan), white hydrangeas (out of season) everywhere, giving their own light to the rooms. The closet-sized flower shop in town overflows with blooms someone trucks down from Holland greenhouses. No wreaths or sprays. Only cut flowers. Why? Because most are meant for the cemetery, which is heavily adorned for the entire holiday. Thanks to the dead, we have such abundance.

Everyone arrives. *Buona sera,* hello, *ciao,* hello. They bear gifts and wine. Lovely to kiss cold cheeks. I especially wanted the Americans Wally and Debra to meet the three women. They retired here from Chicago and have thrown themselves into practicing stone wall building and helping, financially and hands on, with *scuola materna*, elementary school, cultural trips. (Those who really learn to live here.) Debra writes a bilingual newsletter that we all look at to find out what's going on. Ah, the Villa Assunta contingent. Rowan's last night. Tomorrow he returns to Berkeley for his last semester of teaching book arts at Mills College. I give them all big hugs. "All good sabbaticals must come to an end, *amico*," I whisper. He hands me three of his publications, treasures. Susan looks terrific in a red velvet fitted jacket with a white satin shell. And this must be Cleve Hadley, what a southern name. I already feel protective toward him, sensing how he must have suffered with Julia over the slacker granddaughter. Our good friends Guido (oh, devastatingly good-looking in the manner your mother would advise you against) and Amalia, Nicolà and Brian, Stefano, and then witty Canadian expat Belinda and her German diplomat (retired) husband, Karl, also stamp in shaking off rain and sleet. (How to make it rain: plan a party.) Karl has scraped his fender on a stone wall when parking and steam seems to emanate from his ears. I hand him a to-the-top glass of prosecco. Belinda is wearing what looks like a Scottish kilt ("unfortunate," my mother would say) and I see her eye my outlandish garb skeptically. I catch myself in the mirror and quite like this surprise version of me.

Everyone heads toward the fire. Colin has created quite a blaze and seems proud of it, or of something. He is beautiful, my man. Lucky, he is. Colin looks, how to say it, he looks kind. You see his fringy long lashes (didn't Elizabeth Taylor have a double row?), how his gaze lingers as his lips form an archaic upturn. You know he's *there*, all present and accounted for. He doesn't appear, as many men do, to hold back, reserve judgment. His vibe is *You're just fine, my honey*. During dessert, he's going to announce our late little straggler. I didn't want to say anything early on because I thought the conversation would be baby, baby all night. I touch my middle to feel the slight, hard mounding, as when at the beach as a child I covered my feet with wet sand.

Stefano's waiters pass my antipasti platters: various *salumi* crostini of chicken livers (*crostini neri*, the one item no Tuscan party exists without), crostini of peas and mascarpone, bowls of baked spicy olives, prosciutto wrapped around bread sticks, cheeses, endive leaves stuffed with farro salad, mushroom pastries, and fried vegetable slivers.

For dinner, I have scattered the three women among the guests so everyone meets new friends. For my right side, I've claimed the charming father of Julia, an old-school gentleman. He is wearing a paisley ascot, a camel blazer with horn buttons, and his polished wingtips look bespoke. Everything about him is neat and just so. (Heartbreaking what that family endures.)

Fitzy leaps to the mantel. He's snowy white, his plume of tail waving among the flowers. Imperial and impartial, he surveys all with startled citrine eyes, a *lar familiaris*, a family god crucial to the Roman household. He does blink at me, the one who feeds him, looks down at my dress, Margaret's dress rescued from the suitcase, hung in the sun to air. When I tried it on, Colin insisted that I wear it. "You look exotic, like the favorite in a Turkish harem," he claimed. Gold silk with drooping sleeves (watch out for sauces at the table), a sash of amethyst brocade, and a wide swath of ruched crimson velvet hem trailing the floor (she was even taller). I feel glamorous, like a woman in a D. H. Lawrence novel, or a Bloomsbury *literata* looking forward to a louche weekend in the country. I hope I don't look like I'm wearing a thrift store bathrobe.

Everyone here? No, not Riccardo. Late train? Luca and Gilda are coming, though it's hard for them to escape their hotel and they usually dash in just as we sit down. We'll wait. What's the hurry?

Many of the people I love most in San Rocco gather at our table. Julia, Camille, and Susan, only here for a season, have so naturally become a part of my days that I can't imagine this hillside without them. Since they're older, you'd think I might be responding to their maternal auras but, mothers all, they don't seem to have them. Or perhaps they've shed them. Still, I feel a benevolence will fall on my baby by their presence. If I'm weepy and exhausted with a newborn, I'll find solace at their kitchen table. I know I could call in the night, that we'll sit in the piazza on late summer afternoons drinking lemonade and passing the baby around. Friends, I guess, but because they have had their big losses, they're freed in some way that makes them vulnerable and open. We laugh. We're bonded, too, by sharing this small patch of Tuscany.

Guido is on my left. We always flirt. Amalia and Colin don't care at all, knowing us well. Guido is a little younger than I, slim as a skewer, with tar-pot-black eyes. His family, settlers in the 1200s, owns the biggest villa in the province. They're great wine-makers and their castle is the attraction that makes San Rocco prosper more than other small villages. Amalia also comes from those tottering aristocrats who once minted their own money and never knew the extent of their land. Both are late and exquisite flowers on thorny old stalks. You wouldn't think Amalia beauti-ful unless you know the Leonardo da Vinci painting of Ginevra de' Benci. She's a dead ringer for that enigmatic and remote portrait—but Amalia has better hair. Ginevra's mien is somber but Amalia's face often breaks into an electric smile. (Ginevra was said to be a poet. From her whole life, her only remaining lines: *I beg your forgiveness. / I am a mountain tiger.*)

The bell jangles and Colin opens the door to Riccardo, Luca, and Gilda, who're given a quick glass of prosecco and brought to the table. It's nine, it's time for the potato ravioli and the Collio wines Chris gave us. (*Cin-cin*, Chris, all alone in California. Come back soon.) Not that she ever cooked, but Margaret taught me this lobster pasta (a brief lover/chef gave her the recipe), easy and rich beyond belief. It occurs to me: Margaret is a household god.

Leo and Annetta, my Italian family and always hospitable, help pass the platters and fill glasses.

Riccardo, man of words and terrific translator of my poems

and many others far greater than I, starts the toasts. I seated him beside Susan, garden maven, because he is a rosarian and also because he has a crocus field. He hand-gathers the stamens and dries them, augmenting his meager income with local sales of his saffron. (I have a vial for Julia.) I'm sure they'll find common topics. That he is at the Vatican all week provides him with amusing or horrifying anecdotes. He rises to toast the pope, whether truly or ironically we can't tell. He mentions the good future, then ends with some joke about America's current politics, not all of which I get, as I'm overseeing the serving of the stuffed pork roasts, smashed potatoes, and vegetable bundles tied with chives. Cleve, I knew he was one to recognize a situation, rises and thanks all for receiving his daughter and her friends with such warmth. He responds to Riccardo's digs about crazy American politics with a funny reference to Berlusconi's *bunga bunga* parties, pretending that was what he hoped for tonight (a slight barb from Savannah, but smooth), and then, softly (sweet cane syrup, tupelo honey) toasting Colin and me, he says he would like to welcome all of us to Savannah, Georgia, whenever we can come. I see Julia's eyebrows fly up at that, but she then stands and in a tremulous voice thanks us in Italian. *Brava!* She simply says how lucky she and her two friends are to have picked Villa Assunta, as it were, out of a hat. "Makes you believe in fate," she concluded. "We are so happy to have this fate and to be here tonight." Camille and Susan clamber up and clink glasses all around.

"To Kit and Colin, our marvelous hosts," Camille adds. Waves of conversation ensue. More politics. "At least we Italians recognize fascists when we see one," says Stefano.

"Ah, now you do," Susan laughs. Sally mentions the coming exhibit at the Strozzi gallery; Brian is talking about immigrants washing up on the southern islands, so many, he claims, that the islands are about to sink.

"They want the same things we want," Debra insists.

"They should have stayed home and fought for their country,"

Karl counters. Gilda announces that she will start a meat carving course at her school. Students will each have a whole pig, learn knife skills, and how to use every part except the squeal. This makes my stomach flip. I raise my water glass to Leo and mouth *Grazie!* The roasted pork—sublime. I crunch into the crisp and crackling skin.

Riccardo quotes an ode by Horace. (Yet another reason to love the life here.) The whole world is where we live, not a narrow place. When I moved here I felt as if those blinders that keep horses oriented in one direction were removed. Stefano's men clear the plates and present the wild salad with local goat cheese and yellow beets.

BEFORE DESSERT, BRENDAN REACHES BEHIND him for his guitar and starts in with "Per Te," a favorite from the Italian singer Jovanotti over in Cortona. From down the table Colin toasts me. Does anyone notice my glass of blood orange juice? (Maybe only Wally, a teetotaler who had issues long ago.)

Rowan rises and says thanks to the Italians at the table for welcoming yet another stranger. He looks handsome in his craggy, bohemian way. Gilda raises her glass in praise of Julia and her cooking talents. "She is more adept than we are. We are jealous of her abilities!" Julia shakes her head no, and leans over to give Gilda and Luca a hug. Dessert. I must say, a hush falls as Annetta and I bring out the magnificent roulade. At the same time, Colin scrapes back his chair and it turns over with a loud crack.

"Dearly beloved," he begins. The English speakers laugh and the Italians look at each other with shrugs. "To Kit! You know her as a committed writer. Someone who came here to give her work a new focus, which she did. Someone who did not want to follow an expected path. She didn't count on falling in love with someone still flailing around in his career." He pauses, looking at me. "She has been my lodestar. We love living among you. We love all of you. As you know, I'm forty. Kit is forty-four. Our future is laid out, right? We're free to travel, to work like demons. Free. Well, raise your glasses, please, because we want to toast the interrupted future." The waiters fill everyone's glasses with fine Champagne. "We want to tell you of our unexpected fortune. We're expecting a baby. In June, we will be parents."

Brendan starts a drum roll on the guitar as everyone stands, draining glasses, calling *Hear, hear*, all astonished except that I see the knowing smiles of the three women. Everyone rushes to embrace us. The Italians begin singing the victory song of the soccer teams. Amalia crying, the three women nodding *We knew, we knew*, Riccardo (maybe appalled) retreating to the corner to light a cigar, Nicolà starting to dance near the fire, joined by Belinda in her ridiculous kilt skirt. Wally and Debra grab the bottles and keep everyone topped off. In the midst of all, no one forgets the hazelnut roulade. Julia seems astonished. Out come the limoncello, grappa, and Averna bottles, a cheese board and walnuts to crack.

A bowl of clementines. We linger long. No need to go. We have the rest of our lives. A magnificent evening for us at Fonte delle Foglie. *I am a mountain tiger.*

V

In Touch

Ciao, Kit—Stupendous party! Stupendous news! Of course we knew, ever since the dinner in Cormòns. Just a quick thank-you from here in the Dolomites, where the word cozy must have been invented, but contemporary, not cuckoo-clock cozy. Our lodge is all soft, sleek bleached timber, steaming hot tubs, velvety robes, and views into the far yonder. But—no snow! My girls are skiing down a piste made from snow guns. I hope neither breaks a leg. On either side of the run the hillsides are stubby and brown. No crowds or queues for the lifts. I use them for sightseeing. We can hike through pastures up to a rifugio. Oh! Potato and apple soup, venison with truffles. Julia would be blissful! I am sitting out on the broad terrace in the pale sun. We ordered fondue for breakfast! The air feels intoxicating, as though we've lost cabin pressure and a mask blowing oxygen has descended on us. The apples—amazing. Ruddy and sweet/sour. We've munched the whole basket left in our room. Ciao from San Cassiano. Hope you're enjoying Florida. A presto, Susan

PS I'm cc'ing this to J and C, as I am almost out of battery.

Hey, Susan, hey, Camille,

You all were sweet to Daddy. He loved you both! Wasn't Kit and Colin's party fabulous? We found many new friends. We'd better watch out—we may ensconce ourselves in San Rocco so thoroughly that we'll never leave. Christmas was strange but peaceful. We had an afternoon stroll around the Spanish Steps area, prosecco sitting outside, then dinner, excellent, in our hotel. Afterward we watched Three Coins in a Fountain, *earlier female explorers of Italy. Younger—and more romantic. Silly, but I cried. Neither of us mentioned Lizzie or Wade. I'm becoming a master of living in the moment. After grand days in Rome—warm—we came to Naples on the fast train yesterday. A different world. I'll be a long time absorbing the dizzying differences in Italian towns—Atlanta and Charlotte and Raleigh are not profoundly different, right? Well, the quick trip from Rome to Naples lands you in a warp. Racist, I guess, but I've heard that Italians say "After Rome begins Africa." Well, it does seem stupefyingly different. Just from the taxi to the hotel, Daddy and I were gripping each other's hands, and I cried out a couple of times but the driver just laughed. Finally, I relaxed when I realized that other drivers expected ours to cut and swerve and careen, and that they even expected to drive behind a Vespa with three on it carrying a bicycle horizontally. One smoked, one pulled in the front wheel when necessary, and another manipulated the back wheel, all laughing and calling to friends. No one seemed perturbed but us. Susan, you'd fit in just fine! Today we wandered along Spaccanapoli, the straight street (the Roman* decumanus) *that splits Naples, up little lanes where it looked like murder could occur, and off it on a cramped little lane where they sell all the paraphernalia—much of it battery operated so the figures move— for the* presepio *setups we saw all over San Rocco. These are incredibly elaborated. Wonder why that craft became quintessential to Naples. Kitschy as hell, of course, but I found myself leaning down and exclaiming over the tiny woman ironing, the man shoving bread*

into a forno, *the vegetable seller, the manger animals shaking their
heads, plaster angels (I bought a few), on and on. Daddy thought
a little bit went a long way. We proceeded to one of the celebrated
pizza places for lunch and I know it's heretical but I thought the
pizza wasn't that great—chewy, bready dough and thin tomato and
cheese—though the mozzarella is the buffalo milk type. I like the
thin Tuscan crust much more! Back at the hotel before we venture out
for the afternoon—a handsome* palazzo *with a dignified courtyard.
Below my window, someone is going through the trash with a stick.
Actually, the contrasts get to me in an exciting way. A place where
you don't know what to expect. Haven't we become up for that? Let
me know how your trips are going. Miss you! Julia*

  Dear dear friends,

  *San Rocco seems even more intimate at Christmas. Charlie and
Ingrid are falling hard for the place. Ingrid, almost fifteen and
just out of braces, asked her parents to move here. She's enamored,
hearing of a high school called a* liceo, *where she would study Latin
and Greek. (She hasn't excelled at Spanish, however!) She's loving
the pudding-thick hot chocolate and the melt-in-mouth cream-filled
meringues. Most of all, she loves the villa. I think it conjures* The
Secret Garden. *Charlie and Lara, too, are stunned by every room
and also by the way of life. Even Lara, who always finds fault,
as my mother would say, is silenced. She walks from room to room
kind of nodding her head and smiling. This is good. Of course,
she does take exception to the cats, and keeps shooing them off the
furniture. "What were you thinking, keeping three cats?" she asked
incredulously.*
  "We weren't thinking," I answered sweetly.
  *The four of us grilled one of those giant local steaks and cooked
potatoes in the fireplace. We had a big salad of wild greens that
Patrizia dropped off. Annetta brought a blackberry crostata. Julia,
we did well! Tomorrow night, we're invited by Gilda and Luca to a*

feast at the hotel. My family will be awed and thrilled. I am having great fun seeing our town through their eyes. Charlie, dreamboat boy, is attuned to everything he's seeing. Lara wants to rest, as she travels all the time. But she is making an effort.

Susan, thanks again for finding us the apartment in Venice. I can't wait to see their faces when we arrive! Charlie researched all the art—he may swoop to heaven in a cloud like the Virgin. He's reserved a table for us for New Year's Eve. Right on the Grand Canal. Hoping for snow. Want me to visit your antique shop, Susan? Can't wait to be there. I have a soul connection to that mirage on the waters. After they fly out of Venice, I'm giving myself a day alone. It will be sad to see them go but as you know, that city speaks to me. And—I am looking forward to taking up where we left off at Villa Assunta. Travel well. Have many epiphanies before Epiphany when we again raise our glasses together. Xxxooo, Camille.

CROSSING THE BRIDGE

RIDE BY, LOOK AT THE neighborhood. Chris wouldn't recognize Lizzie if he saw her naked in the street. He needed to drive down to San Francisco to have the design of his vineyard labels adjusted. Now that his son, Carter, is finishing his master's at Davis, Chris wants to add his name on Magnitude Vineyards' back label. Carter will be an astute winemaker; his palate is discerning, especially during periodic barrel sampling, when you have to know, while the wine is evolving, what the wine *will* be. A fourth-generation winemaker, Carter is wed to the sere California hills and can't wait to come home and start updating—he says it nicely, "innovating around what already works." Chris gets the message. Move over, Dad. Fine with him. The girlfriend, also graduating in enology, will come, too. Waka, delicate, slender as a soda straw, Japanese American. Her grandparents, born in Sacramento, were rounded up and put in a camp to wait out World War II. Her hair hangs straight down to her waist and she's always fiddling with it, tossing her head, swooping it up in her hands and letting it fall, often while delivering a confident opinion. Could be useful.

Could be irritating. Carter wants her there and Chris has a phi-losophy about allowing his boy what he wants whenever it seems reasonable. He's sure that's why Carter grew into a generous man.

In late February, the green Marin hills glow. As Chris speeds down 101 slightly faster than the flow, traffic moves smoothly. Emerging from the tunnel, he bursts onto the full view of the white city floating on choppy cobalt waters, the bridges like glim-mering Erector sets, and pristine triangles of sails cutting toward Alcatraz. Chris fell hard when he first moved here and even now, he feels a billowing excitement. What's happening on the West Coast *now* sends out ripples that the rest of the country feels a de-cade later. He knows that.

He turns in to the Marina neighborhood, imagining living in one of the Spanish Colonial houses from the thirties, a small courtyard where Julia is setting the table for friends. He finds himself humming, then stops. Do I always have to think *city by the bay*, Tony Bennett crooning at the Fairmont? A bit embarrassing, his throat tightening with emotion anytime *I left my heart* starts up. *Oh, Dad, cornball!* Carter would say.

September, the pretty girl—Lauren?—leaning on her elbows at the bar, *high on a hill*, first job, the end of his summers in the unlovely, dusty fields of his parents' farm in Modesto—crops and heartbreak and a prevailing feeling of exile—the shock of arrival in the chilly city *halfway to the stars*. He swerves right as a motor-cyclist almost clips his front fender. San Francisco, like no other, even Rome. Even now, rife with techies. At least they buy wine when they're not drinking livid green juices. Or *sourcing* those leafy greens.

A few weeks in San Fran, and he'd known that his desire to escape all through his teens was right. He grew up an exile—from this sharp air and the undulating hills with heart-stopping views, where everyone is young and rapacious for what's to come. The last edge, razor edge of the country. He loves it, loves the grandest ocean, the cold, cold waves along Point Reyes's sweeping beaches, invigorating foggy walks. California is overpopulated, but the land itself remains primitive and lonely. Opposite of his more intimate love, Italy, with its humanly shaped landscapes and towns. What luck, to have both places, like Julia and friends, falling hard for a way of life so diverse from their southern heritage. Julia, what if they'd met twenty years ago? The children they could have had, the trips, the building of Magnitude Vineyards, her publishing books, the bi-country life. But instead he has Carter. He can only be happy for that.

Speeding toward the city, he's elated. Not here, that's over. A plane must soar over the pole and land in an ancient, mellow place bordered by a bluer sea.

BELOW LOWER PACIFIC HEIGHTS THE ambiance gets pretty low although now it's dotted with spiffy cafés. He's looking for the last known address of one Lizzie Hadley. No, she'd probably have the husband's last name. The jerk. Tyler, Wade Tyler it is.

He tries to think of what Julia said about Lizzie, other than the chronicle of her downward spiral, her crash and burn. Does not suffer fools gladly. Used to have a pet turtle named George. Collected shells. No clue what she looks like. Wait, Julia mentioned her small teeth when they saw a barista smile in Friuli. *Lizzie has teeth like that, little pearls.* Not much to go on. Doubt if she smiles much. Especially if she has a meth smile.

A row of dingy Victorians, three of them fixed up by optimistic remodelers. A few spindly trees surrounded by dog shit. Other houses at least painted, with pots of agave or grasses on the porch and Roman shades on the windows. Down and out in San Francisco is not quite as down and out as in other cities. Real estate is too valuable for landlords to let property go too far into shambles. He can tell at a glance; this neighborhood is gentrifying. Crackheads soon to amble on to the last fringes. He slows at her intersection. Second house in, worst house on the block, purple and peeling, looks like a possible drug habitat. Julia mentioned purple, and not all the way derelict. A lank-haired woman smokes on the steps and a skinny guy leans against the railing, checking his phone. Chris parks farther down the street and walks back to the corner store cattycornered from the house. Another lavender Queen Anne Victorian looks possible, but an ancient black woman exits and begins sweeping her porch. Next door to her, painters in hazmat under tarps are scraping off decades of lead paint. Another house about to flip.

He buys a bag of chips, mints, and a bottle of water. The Pakistani owner hardly looks away from his computer as he rings up the purchase.

"You know of any houses for rent around here, or any for sale?" Chris asks.

"Everything for sale," is the clipped reply. He squints at his screen. He's wearing a limp T-shirt printed with a skeleton image.

"Good for investment, I'm sure."

"You know what these suckers sell for now? Fix it up, triple your money."

"What about that purple three-story?"

"Nah. That's sort of a halfway place. Halfway to what, I'd like to know."

Bingo. "They're recovering?"

"Seems like some of them are."

"Not for sale or rent then?"

"Owned by the city. They all get paid. Nice work."

"I guess I've heard about that." He gestured to the woman smoking on the steps. "They come in here to shop, I guess."

"That one does. The guy lifts himself a free beer now and then. I just let it go. Poor sucker. He can't even talk. Just stutters." He blows through his lips and flips them with his finger, blubbering.

"The house next door—someone's gussied it up all right." He didn't want to appear too inquiring.

"Paid three hundred thousand. Put that much into it, now it's worth over a million."

"All that and you get to live next to a halfway house."

"You got it. And you get your car window smashed."

"How many live there?"

"There were eight. I haven't see two of them in months. A guy tattooed, even around his eyes. And a southern girl, all hoity-toity but when I got mugged last year she heard the glass breaking, came running over and got me an ambulance and stayed with the shop until my brother-in-law got here."

"Oh, man. Mugged?"

He turns his profile, showing his bent nose and a rippled scar running up his cheek and back into his hair. "Baseball bat. They got a whopping seventy-two bucks. Me, I got a month of hell."

"Very bad. Sorry to hear that." He decides to come clean. "Hey, I'm actually looking for a southern woman. About thirty-five. Her family hasn't heard from her in a while. This is confidential but I'm wondering if this woman who came to your rescue might be the one. How many southern belles are there in halfway houses? This cross street is her last known address."

The Pakistani looks wary. "I couldn't say. Go across the street and ask those losers."

"Oh, that's okay. Probably a mistake anyway. Thanks, man."

"Ah, well. What the fuck. The woman is called Liz. Is that the name you're looking for? She's long gone. Ambulance took her away. She's probably overdosed."

CHRIS DRIVES ON TO THE super-cool graphic design studio on a leafy section of Pacific Avenue and orders the slight redesign of his label. The front image, a simple pen and ink of a vine at bud break, remains but he's revised the back. The young woman working with him wears a flared black skirt in stiff panels and a white blouse with winged sleeves, Comme des Garçons, or

maybe something even more hip, black ankle boots, her hair—
structured to the max—falling like a raven wing across half her
face. Chris flashes on the woman smoking on the steps at Lizzie's
halfway house. Her mouse-colored hair in ropy strands. Eyes lost
in space. Her legs askew so that if anyone wanted to, he could see
her crotch. Chris didn't want to. Hell, no. But her doleful look,
glazed, sad, barely registering him as he passed, sends a frisson of
sympathy through him for her, for Lizzie's lost potential, for Julia's
sorrow, even for the ass Wade, what he'd endured with the two
women he loved.

CARA *JULIA,* HE WRITES, *I tried to call but got the unavailable
message. I know you said no to me looking for Lizzie. I overrode that because you hesitated, and I'm sure you want news. I didn't plan to encounter
her, just to see if she's still there. I did go to the intersection. The mom-
and-pop owner knew her. He said that she isn't there anymore. An ambulance took her away.*

He told her about the mugging and Lizzie getting the man to
the hospital and continues: *There are others at the house who might
know where she is. Do you want me to go back and ask? This sounds seriously bad.*

He went on, writing about his day, pausing to pour a stony
white from his neighbor down the road, to slice into the roast
chicken he picked up at Whole Foods.

*Wondering what you are up to, where you are. Sometime, I want to
show you San Francisco . . .* Un abbraccio forte!

A strong hug. Now, wondering, tonight, where is that Lizzie?

Almonds: The First Flower

IN LATE WINTER, A BLISSFUL day arrives. Soft air descends. Mild enough to open a window. Margaret always maintained that pressure systems become blocked at Gibraltar, allowing the warm Mediterranean on our side to work its magic. True or not, I always imagine massive storms held back by a big rock. The almond tree just outside my study blooms, albeit tentatively, the unostentatious flowers sending out a faint scent, not of almonds but of the white paste one of my friends used to eat in kindergarten. Such a mild winter that I never uprooted the white geraniums in pots along the stone wall. Now I'll only have to trim the dead away and they'll reboot for summer.

What winter there was, we missed while in sunny Florida. We came back here to days of long walks up the mountains, our boots slushing through damp leaves, to a skittish pair of *caprioli* leaping among our olive trees, and to the grunts of wild boars searching for acorns in the night. All our friends were ready to serve forth *ribollita* and sausages and beef stews, especially Julia, who completed a study of Tuscan pork with Gilda over the winter. They sliced and parsed local pigs, especially the boars that are hunted assiduously but still manage to double their population every couple of years. (Margaret said she wanted to write *Wild Bores I Have Known*.) Julia is making her own fennel-flavored sausages and grilling the big liver, which I've managed to avoid. Her first fricassee tasted gamey but after she got the soaking-in-vinegar part down, her daubes have been succulent and fall-off-the-bone tender.

With Colin away in London, I have the day and I need it. Since we returned, I still haven't completely unpacked. The work I did there lies on my desk, a stack of notes, and one folder with six poems. Margaret's manuscript, too, is part of the pile, her work and mine now hopelessly entwined. Instead of diving into that wreck, I step outside to clip almond branches and stand them in a jar on the kitchen counter. Spring. Coming.

At five months, I have a lunar curve. The little moonwalker baby-steps around once or twice a day. Late at night I feel her, weightless, somersaulting. Or him, undocked and floating in the mother ship. We elected not to be told the sex. I don't know why, except that it gives us more room to imagine the mystery of this mystery being.

Never, since playing with dolls, have I thought of myself as a mother. I aligned with the many women writers who never had children and who knew that motherhood strikes the death knell for creativity. (*Knell*. Old English: *cnyllen*. Old Norse *knylla*, to beat, to strike.) Imagine Virginia Woolf with a passel of brats. Jane Austen. Eudora Welty. Colette. Simone de Beauvoir. Edith Wharton. Elizabeth Bishop. Willa Cather. Well, Margaret, too, so I thought.

Now I'm scurrying around to find counterexamples for new role models. Sylvia Plath—we know how that ended. Joan Didion, not ideal. Jhumpa Lahiri. Zadie Smith. She's a strong one. No others come to mind but I'll keep thinking. My mother maintained she double-doted on me because pregnancy and birth were horrible enough that she never had the nerve to try again. Mine has been sweet, but coming up are the months when my body billows outward, and I'm left just holding up a flapping flag on this ship that has set sail. Who knows, if Virginia Woolf had birthed sweet sons, maybe she wouldn't have loaded her pockets with rocks and waded into the River Ouse.

Our family doctor in Miami was happy to be proven wrong. He gave me good news, too: if you have a child after forty, you're four times more likely to live to be one hundred. That takes away some of the anxiety about leaving a motherless college student. Miss X may be in her midfifties when I am swooped into the beyond.

The most surprised person I encountered on our Florida trip was my first love, now friend, Ger. I had to meet with him and Stacy, the woman who rented my parents' house, because of the screen porch wood rot. (Plus I wanted to see the house.) Two window frames in my mother's room need replacing. I agreed also to paint the kitchen and put in a new dishwasher. (Their rent is so low that I thought they could just do these things themselves, but no.)

Ger didn't notice. I was wearing a bulky cardigan and leggings. It was only when Stacy stepped out to make coffee that he asked in a pinched voice, "What's new with you?"

I doubtlessly beamed, and said, "I am expecting a baby in June." He almost swallowed his teeth as he restrained from asking how that could be. I answered for him. "I was shocked, too. Accident! I'm thrilled. I was blown sideways at first. As you know, I could never . . ."

His partner's girls prance in, sweet, all ponytails and flounce and mouthfuls of braces. I'm happy for him. If we come back, either they'll have to move, or maybe I'll sell them the house, which is hard to imagine. It's my only major asset; what money my parents left (dwindled by my mother's long illness) I used to buy Fonte delle Foglie. My parents loved every wall and footpath

and keyhole of our sprawling stucco house set back from the street
and surrounded by palms and moss-hung live oaks. I told Ger that
Colin has a chance to work out of Miami and that we might be
spending time here. I asked him his plans.

"I think we'll marry. She makes me happy and I hope I do the
same. Who wouldn't love those girls? They light up any room. You
know, this house still reeks of you and your family. Sometimes I
think I'm going to see you flying down the stairs with an armful of
books, or your mother lying on the chaise longue in the sunroom.
That pink silk throw over her legs, her head in a cloud of smoke.
Your dad's workshop still has his tools all lined up on the peg-
board. Anyway, I'm thinking we'll move soon. Start fresh in one
of those waterfront spec houses. Hot tub and Weber, the works."
He grinned, knowing my disdain for spec and tract housing.

Reeks offended a bit, but I knew what he meant.

I saw friends who shrieked and jumped up and down. A couple
of writers from the University of Miami writing program invited
me out for Cuban food. (Garlic chicken = soul food.) The chair,
also a poet, asked me to teach as an adjunct anytime. Good to
know.

LAST, BEST, SURPRISINGLY, OH *MADRE di Dio*, we married.
Why not now, we thought. I arranged everything in two days, and
let me say that's the best way—no stress, no huge expense, and
the element of spontaneity intact. The ceremony took place in the
clapboard chapel where I was baptized and where my parents married. In the end, we only had Ger and Stacy, a colleague of Colin's
and his partner, three of my high school friends (all divorced!),
and six of my parents' close friends who'd helped raise me. The
Episcopal priest looked rheumy and bored but delivered the vows
in a strong voice. Gladys, my mother's best friend, read a poem
I requested by Jaime Sabines. Melanie, who went off to college
with me and was my roommate until she dropped out to travel

with a band, merely said she'd sing a surprise song. I thought the priest would go into nuclear meltdown when she started belting out Al Green's "Let's Stay Together." After, we took everyone to dinner and that was that. Everyone toasted, reminisced, and then Melanie became the DJ and everyone danced to "I'll Be There." Colin's parents couldn't come but sent a nice check and a set of sheets that will not fit an Italian bed. I asked Ger to store them at my mother's house.

Wed, we are. I wanted to keep my mother's sapphire and diamonds wedding ring, and Colin wanted me to have his grandmother's wide gold band with a single emerald. I'm laden and sparkling. I gave him my father's wedding ring, not mentioning that it had been cut off his water-swollen fingers and repaired. We had the word *forever* engraved inside the rings. A fearfully big word.

ON PLANES, IN THE CONDO we rented, on sleepless nights—this man I married sometimes sings in his sleep, which may be the single most endearing thing about him—I wrote, read, took notes. After absorbing Margaret's manuscript, I know that I'll not find out anything else. What I have is plenty for the book I want to write so that her work is not forgotten. The rest, the secrets I found, the complexity of her character, the sorrows and surprises I will leave alone except for judicious gleanings. I always thought she fell for Colin. I found out why. I thought she was jealous of me—what on earth have I done that she hasn't done better—and I found out why. Other things. She's still a cipher and will remain so. But I think maybe I've come closer to her than to anyone I've known, Colin included. And she left a paradigm novella.

When I wonder what I should do, what I should write, when a moral issue arises, or even when political candidates debate (she had a clear bullshit radar), it's the Margaret-in-my-head that I consult. *What would Margaret think? Margaret would be all over that.* Often there's a clear answer for me to contemplate, maybe not agree with, but there she is, compass rose, keeping me on course. Maybe everyone needs a mentor like that.

NOTEBOOK:

The start of a poem, after reading Margaret's manuscript:

I know what I know. You don't know.
How can you be and not be me? But that poem of Ovid's
I read during siesta about the same siesta in 8 BC.
Easier than calling on a telefonino
while whizzing down the autostrada, I touched
old Publius Ovidius Naso.
I've touched the river merchant's wife
and a white rooster killed
by a fox thirteen hundred years ago. But you're Not Me.
And I only work here. The owner is out, no one is
here to take your call. Your settings
have been changed by a remote host.
And if everyone lit just one little what,
we could take back the light. At least.
Eat more, weigh less. Lean on me.
I'd know your hand in a bucket of hands.

(Ovid's siesta poem—or as we say, *riposa*—could have been written today. "The River Merchant's Wife": Ezra Pound. The rooster, an anonymous ancient Chinese poem, I think. I've lost the reference.)

IN THE FOUND STASH FROM Margaret's suitcase:

I became pregnant [Margaret writing, 2008? Not exactly sure of the year] in January of my senior year at Georgetown. Since

I was living at home, it was easy to keep my changing shape
a secret, even from my father. My mother had left him two
years ago. I elected to move home from the dorm to keep him
company, to try to fill the house with activity. He adored my
friends. He didn't mind waking up to find that he had to tiptoe
through the living room if a couple of girls had stayed over.

The father of my child sounds grandiose. He was, actually. It
was a Chekhovian thing: I was in love with let's call him Mark.
He was in love with my friend Millicent, who loved herself.
Beyond that, she went from crush to crush. We were all twenty.
No idea what we were doing. After a party at my house one night
when my father was out of town, Mark stayed after Millicent
went off with a snotty law school student, a mouth-breather
already spotted as someone likely to go into politics. You'd
recognize the name but that's not part of my saga of getting
knocked up by someone who only liked me. Mark stayed to
help me clean up the glasses, ashtrays, empty pizza boxes, and
then we sat in front of the fire for one of our usual talks about
What Millicent Wants. The talk veered into our own plans. I
knew I would travel. I already was clearly on the writing path.
He'd applied for law school, like many of our friends, but he
lacked the ambition that marked our group. He'd always known
he'd go back to Richmond to take his place in the long family
line of attorneys with a vast local practice. I saw museum board
meetings, historical society, portraits in the dining room, him
growing stout. Not for me. But, oh, really, I saw his square
shoulders, face like the statue of David, the same pouty lips
and serene, confident gaze as he appraises Goliath. I wanted to
run my hands over his toned marble body. That I did, after we
split a bottle of wine, started singing camp songs, giggling, and
then he picked me up like Rhett did Scarlett and took me to my
childhood bed, where we made love like crazy three times. Mark
fell asleep until morning. Michelangelo should have carved a
sleeping David as well as the tensile standing youth. I lay awake

all night. In thrall. This was not my first time, but never had I experienced real lovemaking before. Such joy in our two bodies swirling and soaring. He would love me. My lips pressed his damp spine. Once in the night he turned and reached for me. It was the longest night of my life and that includes those in a concrete block hotel in Iraq with guns strafing and bombs in the streets.

After amorous protestations, amorous compliments, and several cups of coffee, he was off to class. Then, nothing. I only saw him one more time, seven weeks later. Meanwhile, Millicent reclaimed him. I dropped her as a friend. When I knew I was pregnant, I felt obligated to tell him. The father of a child. He was—well, you've already guessed. This can't happen, are you sure, why didn't you . . . His good breeding surfaced, if only slightly. He offered to help me "take care of it." Oxymoronic, I thought. He even would go with me.

So long ago, dearest reader. Era of coat hangers and chemical douches but abortions not unknown. I still can see my own stark face in the mirror as I faced impossible facts. Old story. Always new for the bearer.

With my novels, there were various ways a story could work out. In life, the conclusions are few. You keep it; you give it away. And isn't "it" such a clue. If "it" were Adam or Lucinda, the conclusion veers.

When Mark called the next day, I told him I had arranged the abortion. He dropped an envelope with eight hundred dollars through our mail slot. Easy peasy. I turned hard against him. How could I have "loved" such a callous twit? I never heard from him again.

I won't go into the agonies of my decision. I did not have the abortion. I dropped the group I hung out with, changed my way of dressing to loose tops, shapeless skirts, and always carried my notebooks clutched in front of me. That way, I finished the semester. In April, I confessed to my father, who dropped his glass of sherry onto his shoe. After graduation, which I did not attend, my father drove me to New York, where he'd found a studio apartment for me in the West Village. I got an unpaid internship at the *Village Voice*. Oddly, no one asked questions as I ballooned forth. Was I obligated to tell Mark that I was carrying the child? I thought he forfeited his right by wanting to get rid of it. I loved the work; the editors were impressed, really impressed. Later, after the baby came, they offered me a real job.

I have been unbearably lonely at times. That summer was the first of my frequent bouts of intense loneliness. Estranged from my mother, who was off in a new life with an East Indian man fifteen years younger, I had no one but my father to call. My other relatives would have been horrified, forever referring to me as "unfortunate" as well as their previous judgments (spoiled, cheeky, too smart for her own good, and stubborn). "She always was a sassy child," I once overheard.

I'd drink iced tea out on the fire escape and thumb through my address book. What friend to call? But (too smart for her own good) I knew this juicy piece of gossip could not possibly be kept secret.

I felt like Gregor in the story, who woke up and was a bug with six legs and a shell. Metamorphosis, indeed. Moving from wafer thin to bulbous. Except at work, I lost my core self. It was a summer of reading Elizabeth Bowen, Henry James (I walked by his house), and Betty Friedan's book explicating "the problem with no name." It was a summer of canned tomato soup, roast chicken for protein, protein, protein, and chocolate milk—I was still partly a child. I never thought that I could keep a baby, though my father offered to help me raise her or him, not it.

Through research resources at work I found a Park Avenue adoption service and interviewed them. In glass offices with Norfolk Island pines in pots and a wall of photos of adoptive parents gazing adoringly at little swaddled bundles in their arms, and no photos of the destroyed, bereft, or liberated birth mothers. I was shown, after an interview, folders of four couples. I lied and said I didn't know who the father was but that he was a Georgetown student. I regretted a promiscuous period after my parents split up. I figured few adoptions took place without a few protective lies. "Love lies," my mother called them. Lies you tell to protect someone or yourself from the truth.

I stipulated: well educated, fun, loving, smart, stable. I didn't have to say not poor because anyone paying their fee had to be well off. All four looked promising. I asked to look at others but in the end went back to the couple on top of the stack. She was a violinist with an open face that looked kind, straight tar-black hair, like Mark's. Maybe her jawline was oval like mine. She went to Colby, then Juilliard. The man was tall like Mark, with a high arched nose and eyes that looked as if he'd just delivered a witty remark. His profession intrigued me: naval architect. The father of my child. He could be. Pale like me, probably freckled as a child, he looked stalwart and dependable. I was looking for parents who physically could have been biologically connected to the baby. The name on the folder was covered over with white-out tape. Holding it in my lap, I deftly lifted up the tape with my nail while I chatted with the director about terms and conditions. Possibly that was my first move toward being an investigative reporter. I glanced down, smoothing my skirt. Edward and Amanda Knowles. I pressed down the tape and we worked out details. At the end of the meeting, I said, "Would you ask them to consider keeping the name I give the baby?"

"That's unusual but I will ask."

"Then, thank you. The baby has a good home."

Stay calm and proceed. But I was young, alone, and—I pictured a wishbone—something snapped in me. I went forward into an altered world.

• • •

TO MAKE SENSE OF THE info I found in Margaret's manuscript, I copied sections in my notebook, thinking that the words running through ink onto paper would help me understand her hidden life, and why she left the sheaf of crabbed writing and typing for me to find, or not. Did she somehow know she would not return?

(Problem with no name. Wafer thin. Rights. Judgment. Juicy gossip. Writing path. Portraits in the dining room. Run my hands. Love like crazy. Breeding. Swaddled. Pale like me. Altered world. Hideous to wake up as an insect.) (Ovid also wrote a *Metamorphoses*.)

MY OWN PREGNANCY, OPPOSITE OF hers. Mine made her story leap into life in a way it would not if I'd read this a few months after she abandoned the suitcase, when *my* pregnancy was beyond any possibility or even interest. Seared into my consciousness: the image of Margaret (I've seen early pictures of the young waiflike beauty and the knowing eyes) on a hot night, sitting cross-legged on the fire escape, drinking something cold and feeling large blank spaces around the edge of her mind. A little radio playing dance music inside. Music from a world she had to set aside.

LO STUDIOLO:

The Studio

CAMILLE LOOKS AROUND HER PAINTING room, noticing abruptly the transformation that has occurred. What began as an art space confined to a corner, with a generous work surface, simple shelves, a reading chair and lamp, has morphed into a humming hive of art books, museum postcards on bulletin boards, prints from museums, another worktable, three easels, tubes, brushes, and stacks of paper that she makes every week with Matilde. On new shelves, she has arranged small jars of tiny pearls, copper BBs, beads of aqua glass and faceted pewter, thin gold tesserae mosaics—how resonating the mosaics at Aquileia have proven—and minute semiprecious stones in jewel colors, a basket of an-tique ribbons bought at the Arezzo antique market, archival glues, a row of glass-tipped pens and ink bottles—lake blue, violet, bur-gundy, white. On one wall, where the light falls, hang her paper doors, glowing and vivid like the Book of Kells, the illuminated manuscripts she loves in San Marco in Florence, or even Persian miniatures. She especially likes marginalia, as the monks did. She references in every historical direction, yet the paper doors are unmistakably contemporary. The designs angle and divide; she uses squares of color in patterns that could be from Moorish Spain but for the jarring contrasts and crosshatching.

Eighteen and counting. Each as alive to her as a person. She loves the tactile paper and the light use of ornament for a different texture and dimension. The words, lines, designs are all intuitive, though years of teaching intro to art history give her a wellspring of images. The project keeps enlarging and pulling her along, even when she'd like to stop and try to paint a winter landscape or a still life of pomegranates in a glass bowl.

At Christmas, Charlie noticed. "You're putting your whole life into these," he said. And she'd made only two then. The visit opened up his own work and added a new, deepening layer to their relationship. Every few days now, one of them sends a photo and a process note. She feels closer to him than she has since he came home from college excited about his first semester of studio art, unrolling his enormous canvases on the floor, his eyes lit with that fire she'd also felt once upon a time.

Camille straightens her space, thinking not of her losses, as she has for many months, but of good fortune. A stab of happiness—to have raised such a boy. A lucky love, sweet home, health. And *this*—all her synapses firing. Looking around her room, she whispers, not to a god—but maybe to the nun NM, a muse, *I'm on my way.*

IN THE KITCHEN, SHE FINDS Julia reading by the fireplace. She's burnished gold in the firelight, her hair pulled into a topknot and tied with blue ribbon, and the rosy throw over her lap. Hard to imagine from the peace of this scene her starring role in such an ugly domestic drama. Blue early evening light shimmering at the window, yes, someone should paint this scene.

Late, and Susan still works outside, taking advantage of this almost-spring day. Camille watches her from the window. What's coming up? Susan already has reported that there will be major bulb action. Camille brews tea and brings the pot with biscotti over to the table in front of the fire. "Aren't you sweet?" Julia says, taking two of her own hazelnut macaroons.

"When Susan comes in, I want to show you both something." She drew up her feet and began to look at a magazine. "What are you reading?"

"Kit's poems. They are strange."

"Yes, I agree. But good strange."

"Absolutely. Where does this come from? We know her. She's like us. Younger, yes. But basically kind of normal."

"Maybe we're not, none of us!" Camille joked. "Really, the poems—they're the layer after you've peeled back two. Not that I can compare with Kit, but I look at one of my paper doors and what's there wasn't anywhere within reach *before* I began working. What I create comes out of the creating."

"Listen to this:

The cat goes boneless when she sleeps. But she wakes,
stretches taut. She stares out the window at birds. Her eyes
dart and dart. She has no idea it's a fallen world.

" 'Goes boneless,' she says, where I'd say 'relaxes.' Then something so simple and accurate. Then, whoa, that leap out into the cosmos. It's like she touches the language with a cattle prod and shocks it into life. Is that what making art feels like to you?"

"Must be what it feels like to *her*. I just get lost. Kind of a trance, if that doesn't sound too goofy. I used to love to play with my mother's tissue paper dress patterns with all the blue lines that looked like constellation maps. I'd trace the dresses and aprons on big sheets of paper, then color them in. Remember when women wanted a sewing room? Remember paper dolls? Did you ever covet the life of Betsy McCall?"

"*McCall's* magazine! Yes, I cut her little outfits out every month! Betsy Has a Wonderful Thanksgiving. Betsy Goes to the

Beach. She and her mom in matching suits. I wanted to be called Betsy, not Julia."

"Not me. I had a doll that wet—Betsy Wetsy. But the ways my project has evolved have much to do with paper doll Betsy! And all the foreign twins paper dolls I collected. The Polish children with black rickrack, the Dutch with square faces and wooden shoes, the American midwestern blonds in overalls and calico."

"Stop! Listen to us. Men would be claiming first influence from a mother playing Bach on the cello and an early encounter with Matisse's cutouts."

As they talk and Camille pours more tea, Susan stamps in at the kitchen door, slipping off her gloves and out of muddy boots. Archie shakes himself, sending the cats running. "We'll all be shocked in a few weeks. Bulbs are sprouting *everywhere*. Hyacinths! I can't tell what other kinds yet but this garden is going to explode." Camille brings a cup for Susan. Archie settling in front of the fire throws his legs in the air, and two of the cats leap on him. Ragazzo jumps onto Julia's lap, ignoring the fray.

"Time to take note, you all. Look at this kitchen." Camille points around the room. "Think of when we arrived. Now the windowsills are full of herbs and white gloxinias, there's a row of cookbooks on the mantel, Julia's jug of blue spatulas on the counter, a bowl of lemons, ceramic platters on the wall. Three cats, for Christ's sake, that rosy mohair throw, logs stacked, wine rack full. What do you think?"

Susan is quick to answer. "We've made it home. You're right, the kitchen was gorgeous before but now it's ours. Best kitchen I've ever cooked in. Did you know there's no Italian word for *home*? Only house, *casa*. I find that weird in a culture where home is everything."

Camille continued, "They don't have *pet* either, just something about animals you feed at the door. But wait, I want to bring up something. I was looking at my studio. I had not put the two images—now and then—together. I was struck—in less than five months we've changed *everything* from when we arrived. Spring-ing forward to now—the time changes tonight, by the way—look what we've done here. Are you as astonished as I am?"

Julia takes a dozen eggs out of the fridge. "Okay if we have omelets and salad tonight? The cupboard is bare; we need to shop tomorrow. Yes, it's totally true. The kitchen surely smells differ-ent! From scuzzy drain and mouse to flowers and herbs, garlic and melon. You're right, Camille. I'm thinking of my room, too, all my scarves over the coverlet rack, Susan's olive tree photographs I enlarged, my desk stacked up with recipes and guidebooks. What we've all learned! Finding the faded silk draperies at the market was a stroke of luck. Eau-de-Nil, didn't you say, Camille?"

"Yes, love that color, water of the Nile. They're decadent. You make Savannah proud. And learning Italian! That's the most dras-tic change. Not that we're fluent by any means. I'll never get that subjunctive."

They walk through the downstairs rooms, exclaiming over the changes. Into the previously blank entrance hall, Susan has dragged a round table where she keeps a grand arrangement of flowers. Here's where they leave mail and notes to each other. The top of the piano in the living room became another place for Susan's flowers. This is a morning room; early sun floods through the windows, lighting the brick floor with blocks of light. She's kept southern-style ferns growing on the broad stone sills all win-ter. In the storage room upstairs, she found a tapestry showing four dainty women prancing on horses with silky manes. Some-what tatty by now, it still looks regal over the fireplace.

"Who would have thought?" Camille asks. "I guess I expected we'd just move in, unpack, and live here as it was. A widening of the aperture, yes, but the whole panorama is a wild gift."

They've done little to the dining room, where the nun's fresco so dominates that nothing else is needed except food on the table. "Let's eat in here tonight." Julia opens the *madia* and takes out place mats and napkins. "This is my favorite room. Already many memories of our feasts. Remember when Rowan gestured at the fresco and his wineglass flew across the table?"

"Well, yes, since it landed in my lap. He recovered quickly with some wine quote from Catullus. I need to study the villa's garden scene, *com'era*," Susan says. As it was. She loves *era*, the big imperfect past of *was*, where everything remains in motion even when finished. *C'era una volta* . . . the fairy tales begin, *there was a time* . . . "Remember when a bird flew in and lighted on the table, looking at each of us then flew back out?"

"That was a visitation from our painter nun." Camille isn't given to flights into mysticism but half believes this.

JULIA SIGHS AND BEGINS TO grate the parmigiano, as Camille and Susan fall to their usual roles, feeding the animals, setting the table, and opening the wine. "Home. We are at home! We didn't know we could, would accomplish that. Do you have an instinct yet—will you want to stay? Can you imagine leaving this place? Or could you go home tomorrow?"

"We haven't been to Sicily yet. I'm just getting started." Camille thinks of the stack of handmade paper on her shelf. She misses Charlie—not Lara—and Ingrid, who sweetly took to Italy over Christmas and asks when she can come back. Isn't this better, she wonders. Introducing them to this country? Better than the Sunday brunch with a bought quiche at home in North Carolina, even the annual week at Bald Head Island? "The deeper level, though, is that we remain American. Can't help that! And southern. We've all stood in a cotton field at night, lightning flashing all over the sky, with electrical pylons thrumming like some music from the galaxy."

Julia frowns. "What?"

"You know what I mean. In Italy, we have to live *as if*. As if we belong."

Susan hands around the wine. "I'm fine with *as if*. Stay forever?

I could. I miss home less than I thought, but I feel pangs for my front porch and garden every single day. It's not as though I get to see my daughters that often anyway. And I know I was repeating the years, with slight variations. That's okay, nothing wrong with that. I just love waking up with a *what's up today* feeling, not an *already know what's in store*." She shows them the wild and earliest flower she found today. Annetta called it *bellavedova*. She gathered only a dozen, though they're all over the hills, mysterious small stalky irises of chartreuse and burgundy. "Here's the first gift of spring—the 'beautiful widow.' " She picks up Archie and twirls him around. "Our time here is not half up. Let's push this discussion of the future back for later."

Julia says, "I'll always want to have this in my life, some way or other. I love every minute here." She turns away and stares at the window running with steam. Tears. Always just out of sight, her shadow girl, now more missing than before. Whirlpool, snake pit.

She shakes back her hair. "Can you believe how *orange* these yolks are?" She whips the eggs into lemon-colored froth. How to answer Chris? She hasn't called back since he tracked down Lizzie's last residence. She stirs in the cheese, and a handful of thyme and parsley. A Jacques Pépin video taught her how to make the perfect omelet. "You all ready?" She maneuvers the flip and turns out the first fluffy, half-moon omelet onto a plate.

After dinner, Susan brings her laptop to the table. Camille and Julia moan, then laugh. When Susan does this, she's planned something. She types fast for a couple of minutes, then looks up. "Want to go to Florence?" Photos of a frescoed apartment appear on her screen. "I found a fabulous last-minute deal. It's still available. Look at this." They see the Arno, with ochre, sienna, and russet *palazzi* reflecting in the water. "That's the view from the living room. And I have more news. Nicolà and Brian asked me to evaluate a possible rental they're considering for their portfolio. We can all go to Capri at the beginning of April."

"I'm afraid something awful is going to happen. We keep spinning out into wider and wider circles." Julia imagines *awful*: Lizzie shaking pills into the palm of her hand, gulping them down, the weeks after she left for the last time—the gut-anguish that felt like drowning.

"What's the Italian saying? 'First roots, then wings.'" Camille, too, feels unentitled to such pleasures. She thinks of shopping, always buying her nicest clothes on sale or from catalogues. Charles liked the Lands' End sweaters and shorts. She reached more toward silky prints at Off Fifth and Neiman Marcus cashmere on sale.

"Nonsense. Just think of all the fat cats buying up regal property in London and letting them sit empty. You think any of them worries about being smote because of a weekend in someone's luxury rental in Capri? It's a woman thing. What do we deserve? This is our easy year. We're old. We deserve some levity. Get over it."

Julia and Camille love Susan for this.

Florence: Winter Banished

SPRING, NEAR. TUFTS OF BALMY air and the swollen river Arno running fast, toffee-colored. Few tourists, glamorous shop windows that cause you to vow to clear your closet, enchanting *palazzi* with massive doors you long to open: Firenze.

Julia pauses on the bridge, naming colors she sees. Cinnamon, curry, turmeric, sage. Sipping cappuccino, she lingers, smelling the turgid river, letting the morning breeze play with her hair.

Looking for signs of spring, Susan spends the morning wandering in the Boboli Gardens, which she finds grand and oddly depressing, parts so bleak and underplanted that she rests on a bench sketching her own version of how the park could look. Those megalomaniacal Medicis wouldn't have had such a stripped-down palette. She photographs the famous statue of the fat dwarf peeing, Neptune with a trident that looks like a big cocktail fork, and a wonderful horse rising from water, Perseus on his back urging him on. Walking quietly around the garden; what should be relaxing instead turns her brain into a swarm of possibilities.

She finds a shady bench where she spends half an hour studying prepositions. Susan's Italian is a force of nature. She's fearless. She speaks fast. Slow, no one understands you, even if you're grammatically correct. She studied diligently all winter and frequently meets Annetta for a walk, Nicolà for lunch, and Riccardo for drinks. With each she speaks Italian the whole visit. She knows it must be painful for Riccardo—translation is his métier—but they have good laughs at her bloopers and often he comes home for dinner.

She's learned even more by volunteering at the hospital. She only fills water glasses, helps postsurgical patients take slow steps down the hall, and sometimes, when someone asks, reads the paper aloud, much to her benefit and to the amusement of the person in bed listening. She gets corrected, and remembers the next time. She's known all over the hospital for the flowers that now greet everyone in the waiting room.

She glances up at Palazzo Pitti and nods. Yes, how stupid of me, she thinks. Of course! The garden design was meant to be seen from *there*. The perspective would be encompassing. She's a speck on the path, but the Medici clan had the godlike view without the inconvenient mud. She walks around a grand stone-rimmed pond. If we stay at Villa Assunta, she thinks, we need water. Not a plain swimming pool; certainly no lap pool. Something natural, a local *pietra serena* stone surround with, what, something tall at the end with cascading water. Draw and dream, wander and look.

Camille remains at the apartment, uncharacteristically blow-drying her hair into a light flip, attempting to use eyeliner and mascara, and dressing with care, even wiping every speck of dirt off her boots. She walks out in pursuit of a wild (for her) notion. At Prada, she stares in the window. She saw them yesterday. She's intimidated by the tiny sleek woman in black who greets her at the door and stays right beside her as she tries to look around casually. Susan has explained that hovering is service, not suspicion. They're being helpful. Something, she said, we're just not used to. Camille points to the shoes she admires, covets actually, in the window. "Thirty-nine?" she asks.

Ten minutes later, they're hers, dark red velvet shoes with a slender ankle strap and a quite high heel. Knee be damned. Now she'll have to invent an occasion to wear them. After the initial formality, seeing Camille's obvious excitement, the sales attendant became friendly and showed Camille a python-skin clutch purse the same color as the shoes. She bought that, too.

After her impulse purchases, she spends the morning in the vortex of American twentieth-century art, a just-opened exhibit of the Kandinsky-Pollock era at the Strozzi. Here's much of the art she's taught to undergrads. In this lofty setting, the synergy among the paintings hums. After months of renaissance art, this stark return to her own time startles her. She's stopped and mesmerized by the Rothkos, five of them so wondrously lit that they seem alive from inside. She spends an hour inhaling their seeming simplicity. One looks like the surface of the moon with space behind. Really, it's just gray and white, but how luminous and grainy and opaque and mysterious. She's happy. She stares long at a Helen Frankenthaler, one of the few women represented. She loves Frankenthaler. A serious boy of perhaps fourteen walks with the rented audio from painting to painting. He's intent on the Duchamps. She loved Charlie's years of awakening to art; this boy feels that quickening, too. Their eyes meet for a moment and he smiles. She smiles, too. A small exchange that makes her eyes sting with tears.

Laughing to herself over the exuberant art, the red shoes, the boy, the promising air, she walks to Mercato Centrale, where she meets Julia and Susan for lunch. Julia spent the morning at a cooking class there, though she didn't learn much. She's long since mastered pasta making, as well as the easy *panna cotta* and boring tiramisu.

The Mercato, a paradigm upscale food court, swarms with people, even off season. What a range—mini-shops serving hamburger, *lampredotto* (don't ask), truffled pasta, Sicilian pastries, divine mozzarellas. They move from counter to counter, taking little plates to a table, then visiting another enticing counter and dashing back. A good southerner, Susan opts for fried. She passes around her plate of crispy zucchini, calamari, carrots, potatoes, squash flowers, and balls of fried bread. Julia analyzes her cauliflower and guanciale pasta, a good one to remember for cold weather. Trying to move beyond her comfort zone, Camille surveys, with a bit of uncertainty, her order—black polenta with grilled octopus. She is afraid the octopus will taste like rubber bands, but it is delicious.

Back in their apartment, she unwraps the shoes. Holding them up in each hand, she waves them about in dance steps. "Cha-cha-cha!" Everyone tries them on. Camille feels a twinge in her knee just looking at them. "I'm going to lose five and get a black dress. I'm turning seventy in April." My work is burgeoning, she thinks. I'm taking a cue from Susan. More fitted clothes, brighter colors. And more rigor, like Julia. No more endless poring over art books. Work!

She's done shopping for now. Late this afternoon and tomorrow morning, she has tickets to the Uffizi, where she plans to feast her eyes and fill her notebook.

Susan takes off to explore artisan shops on the Oltrarno, the other side of the Arno. Having eaten too much, Julia announces that she needs a "renaissance nap."

A Letter to Mail?

MY APPOINTMENT IS QUICK. DOCTOR smiling and pleased! Oh, sweet! Colin and I are in Florence overnight. We will dine with our American neighbors. They're all set up in a river-view apartment Susan found. When she called, she said Camille has stepped far out of line—ordering octopus and shopping Prada. Her breakout in art has loosened other tethers. (Not to mention the still unexplained sex on the sofa she toasted on our trip.) As in Venice, they're all over town. Susan called from an "uber-trendy" café near the Pitti Palace that she spotted after leaving the Boboli Gardens. They were sitting outside drinking Campari Sodas at five in the afternoon. We're meeting at eight and I hope they're not wobbly!

After my appointment, Colin still had work to do. The *palazzo* restoration is stalled by the discovery of a fresco in a vast room slated to be divided into three rooms. The architect's nightmare. Now a pack of experts must evaluate the painting. At a glance, I'd say Colin is in for trouble; an entire wall looks to have ravishing depictions of Botticelli-like graces carrying a long flower chain toward the Virgin, who's reaching down for the blossoms as she ascends into the sky. Colin thinks to make that wall a long wide hall, reducing the size he's planned for the bedrooms. I think they've just added a bundle of money to the property value. (Architect Kit speaking, of course.)

I'm back in the hotel, thumbing through notes, organizing, and sometimes just gazing out at Piazza Tornabuoni. Such a handsome space. I'm at a level view with eight different styles of renaissance windows. In moments like this, I'm close to Margaret, who fiercely loved architecture. We used to sit in the sun at Caffè Rivoire overlooking Piazza della Signoria, ordering glasses of orange juice, talking about each building around that piazza that has seen everything from the burning of Savonarola to the installation of a brassy Jeff Koons statue next to the David (a copy). All the tourists in the world come there, but Margaret didn't notice. "Look up," she'd admonish. Or, she'd look straight through them. Energy streamed out of Margaret. Just sitting there like anyone else, she had a force that even the waiter recognized. Solicitous, he was, instead of abrupt. In all the time I knew her, until she died at seventy-five, she never changed an iota, except that her clothes became more eccentric. As I mentioned before, I thought she had a thing for Colin. She used to bring over a printout of a recent Renzo Piano or Zaha Hadid design and sit shoulder to shoulder with him, going over the specs and discussing whether the human element was subsumed to the design and how the light must play inside.

I TURN HER MANUSCRIPT TO the end, where she has tucked in a letter, addressed, stamped but not sealed. Calhoun Green. A law office, Green, Green, & Schwartz in Richmond, Virginia. She obviously—it's yellowed—didn't mail it. Should I?

Were the contents of the suitcase meant for me? She said she'd be back in the fall. After she returned to Washington, we heard less and less and then nothing, and then everything.

I read:

Cal, this is Margaret Merrill writing you. I'm sure you remember well. After so many years, I want to tell you that your child did not get swabbed out and rinsed away. I gave birth to a boy. Eight pounds. A shock of black hair, those blue eyes infants have that look like a deep summer night sky, little fists he waved as though fighting the air, a solid little loaf of sugar. I was twenty-one. I gave him up. Through an agency in New York, I selected a handsome naval architect, who looked somewhat like you but taller, and a musician who was rising rapidly in reputation. She wore her hair straight as a waterfall and had a lofty chin.

I know they were good parents. During the process, I obtained their names and then it was easy to locate their address on the Upper East Side.

I was working in the city. I would go to a corner café near their brownstone. Polished brass numbers on the door, seasonal flowers plugged into the small square by the steps. An iron fence around the plot. Careful people. Large brown eyes, her hair up now, sometimes escaping in wisps, the "mother" exited with the baby in one arm, the stroller in the other. How precisely she placed him, covering his feet with a soft white blanket, adjusting the cushion. She kissed his cheek. She was always smiling. She pushed right by the window where I sat.

Later, I'd see a nanny, a neat Filipino woman, walking with him along the sidewalk where he stopped to look at leaves and pointed at dogs, turning his open face up to the nanny to see if she recognized the wonder before them. He wore a yellow sweater with a boat stitched on it and polished oxfords, a little man, spirited, cunning and headlong. The nanny had to chase and grab constantly.

Twice I saw the father. The boy on his shoulder, bouncing as though he rode a horse. The father exaggerating his gait for the boy's amusement. I was leaving the café and came face to face with them. The boy and I locked eyes for an instant and he smiled.

The last time was two days after his fourth birthday. A sweltering day in Manhattan. I'd given up and stepped outside the café when

*I saw him down the sidewalk zooming toward me on a scooter,
propelling himself forward rapidly. He was an apparition. The
pedestrians parting before him, his long curls blown back, his foot
working against the pavement. The florist outside her shop called to
him, "Whoa, Colin!" The newsstand agent greeted him, as did a bag
lady. He passed by. He was out of a dream.*

*Four and a half years, then I was gone. Europe, reporting, some
private government work, my novels. Maybe you've heard. Through
my sources and later the Internet, I found snatches of information.
The concerts, a gala hosted, an article on advances in submarine
locators. Not much. Then, just last year, I was in Afghanistan
working for the Times. I came across this on the wire service.*

Colin Adams Knowles, 16, son of Amanda and Edward Knowles,
died on August 5 following an accident while rock climbing at Yo-
semite National Park. He was a student at Horace Mann School,
where he excelled in languages and literature. Adopted as an infant,
Colin was loved by his family and many friends for his humor, exceptional intelligence, and infectious joie di vivre. In the future, he
planned to study architecture. He was a talented pianist, enjoyed
tennis and soccer, and was in training to scale Annapurna with a
group of fellow hiking enthusiasts. His parents are joined in grief by
grandparents Carlos and Josephine Alcazar and Sandra and Phillip
Knowles, and by a younger sister, Josephine Amanda Knowles.

*There. You never knew. Now you do. He lived the years he had. I
live with him every day. Now you can have—and I don't mean this
ironically—the honor, too. Margaret*

Colin says I must mail it. How can I? She didn't. How can I
not?

Life can be surreal. I'm churning with this dilemma and at
the same time pulling up my chair at Cipolla Rossa and greeting
Susan, Camille, and Julia, all high on the frescoes in their apartment and new hairstyles they got in a fancy salon and pistachio
gelato and the Feltrinelli bookstore and the bunch of violets they

brought me. Everyone buoyant. I remain placid in my loose dress, tight shoes, my legs feeling pumped full of air.

COLIN AND I STROLL ALONG the river back to our room. Over us, the transparent full moon, a soap bubble blown by a child. The friends decided to go back to the piazza for a late limoncello. Tomorrow we'll all take the same train home to San Rocco. I'm amazed at the energy they continue to amass. They seem to have doubled in force since arrival. I'm walking back also with young Colin Knowles, cut short. My Colin turned silent for hours when he read the letter to Mark aka Calhoun Green. Margaret, why? If only she'd told us. How foolish I was to think she had the hots for Colin (thirty years younger), when she'd instead only taken what comfort she could by transferring a piece of her hurt and longing. Her lost Colin could have become a man like Colin. A writer is a namer. My *Colin*, architect, must have hit like a stun gun.

The letter unlocked dark Margaret: a child kept secret. And after, she carried secrets forward into her life.

OVERHEARD

WHEN THE KITCHEN PHONE RANG, we all looked at each other. What? I was at Villa Assunta for dinner (Colin in London until tomorrow). We moved into the living room for dessert. As I grow, I gravitate toward big soft chairs. This one reminds me of Tito, who used to warm his big feet at the fire as Luisa knitted scratchy red scarves. As I shift the cushion, I think I catch a whiff of his cigar smoke and the odd smell he gave off of freshly cut wood. We're discussing baby names. Lorenzo, Silvia, Flavia, Luca, Ettore, Lia. I like names with character. From a Trevor novel, I remember an aunt Fitzeustace, but who would dare saddle a child with that? They all like Della, which keeps sounding right to me, though Colin likes Junas, lofty and statuesque. (Not as romantic in English—Eunice.)

"Tatiana," Susan suggests. "She would be a dancer." On the eighth ring, Susan dashes to answer; no one ever uses the landline. "For you, Julia," she calls. At the door, she adds, "Man. With a southern accent. But not Cleve."

Julia grimaces as she takes the call. We continue to talk but overhear Julia's side of the conversation.

"This is Julia."

"Wade! How did you find this number?" She waves from the doorway, mouth wide open, shaking her head, gesturing a thumbs-down.

"I guess that's true. No place to hide anymore." She laughs without laughing.

"I'm listening."

"That's right. My friend went to check on her . . ."

"Well, he *made* it his business."

"A friend, a good friend. Anyway, that's not the point. He's willing to look further, but I haven't agreed yet."

"Wait. He doesn't *think* it's his business. He was willing to do it for me."

"Wade, calm down. You do what you will. He's trying to help."

"Well, go. You've made that trip how many times?"

"She's gone dark before."

"I said go. I'll tell Chris you're going."

"Yes, Chris. He has a name. I work with him, if you need an explanation."

"Of course if you go I want to hear back."

"I do not want Daddy making that trip. It's too much for him. You know how she feels ganged up on, how she makes it our fault for being there."

"The last address we had. And there was that friend who called us when she was arrested. You could look for her. Honor Blackwell, I believe."

"*What?* Wait, what? Wade, have you lost your mind?"

"This is beyond belief. I don't have any idea what to say, so I won't say anything. I am going to hang up . . ."

"The house? Well, that is totally up to Daddy. It's his house."

"Oh, please. What are you talking about? We lived there forever. He even paid the property taxes. You're *not* entitled to be reimbursed for maintenance. What's wrong with you?"

"No. No. And no. I'm hanging up." Julia clicks off the phone and comes back to the living room with her face in her hands. "Was he always without a clue? How did I not see him all those years?"

"You okay?" Susan asks. "What the hell is happening? We heard you. Probably should have shut the door but we were afraid. I knew it was Wade when I answered. We were scared of really bad news."

"Anything from him is bad news. I told Daddy what Chris found out. He ran into Wade at the club bar. They started talking and Daddy let him know that Lizzie is missing. Now Wade is all over going to California and searching for her. Once again."

"Well, let him go. Why not?" I ask. "Something may have happened to her."

"I don't doubt that and, yes, he's going. That's fine. She can smash his heart all over again. The other news—this is unbelievable—the girlfriend is pregnant. How tacky. Rose something. She's about half his age. How addle-brained can he get? Oh, second chance! He actually said that. What a cliché. Get this—he suggested that she move into our house, which doesn't even belong to us. Or that he move out and Daddy pays him back for all the improvements we've made over the years. And, oh, *she's* anxious for everything to remain friendly. Christ. Does that just beat anything?"

WHAT COMES TO MIND IS a quote from Wallace Stevens: *The world is ugly and the people are sad.* I refrain from throwing it into the fray. I'm thinking maybe the woman is in love. Rose—speaking of names, that one predisposes her toward innocence. Maybe she's thrilled. "Who knows what she's been told?" I say. "Handsome dude, Wade, even at sixty. I've looked him up online at his marine store. Hair blown back, strong hands on the rudder, shirt open. Looks like he stepped out of *GQ*. I'd turn my head to look at him.

I'm sure Rose is projecting and part of that involves a filmy *Can't we all be friends*. He does sound opaque." Or, as Margaret said, *If they're not sleeping with you, you're history.*

Julia plops down with a huge sigh. "Two steps forward. Three back. Now that it's sinking in, I'm glad he's going to look for Lizzie. And he's acting stupid but I know he also has a big hole in his heart. Now that Sweet Thing is with child, he's feeling huge guilt over Lizzie again. What a freaking train wreck. She's the lining in a coat I can't take off."

"Julia." I laugh. "Can I use that line? Now, seriously, I think something might happen. Allow yourself a sliver of hope." I say this because of the baby in question. I know what a powerful re-ordering takes place as soon as that swab turns pink. Sometimes change engenders more change. This I don't mention. Not the time. "You know," I do say, "now he's on a set path away. This frees you. Even if it's still painful, it cuts you loose."

Wide-eyed Julia looks at me. "Umm. Right. True. But how impossible to think, and I know this is irrational, that he *could* make a life without me. I'm the one he once drove twenty-two straight hours to see." She doesn't say, *I'm the one he licked from little toe to ear. He, who many times cried after sex.* "I'm always waiting for the scattered pieces to re-form into the shape they should have. I have this recurrent dream that I'm on a busy corner waiting for him to pick me up and we'll go home. I feel like I'm falling into a big relapse."

"No, that is not happening," Susan says. "He can't throw you like this. We just won't allow it. Why didn't he go to San Francisco and let you know later? He still wants you to suffer with him. And maybe he didn't mean to, but the whole pregnant-girlfriend info shouldn't have been part of this conversation. He's a man without borders."

Camille brings in a pot and pours big cups of American coffee. "Decaf," she says. "Drink up. Julia, you've been thriving. Keep at it. Right now, try to focus on what moves you forward. You've walked over coals for Lizzie. What happens to her now is her call. And Wade?" Her voice softens. "What you had, you don't have anymore."

"You are right. Now all I have to do is believe you."

"Let's move onto another square," I say. "Tomorrow, I want to take you on a walk that leads to a Roman bridge hardly anyone ever sees. We walk out from the spur of your land and straight down a rocky path across the valley into an overgrown area where this arc of a stone bridge crosses a *torrente* that must have once been wilder and more ferocious. This time of year it will be running."

Julia looks up. "Yes, get back on the horse. Shall we take a picnic? Are you sure you can walk on rough terrain?" She feels thrown from her gelding when she was twelve; she and horse flying over the jump, that moment in the air and then the fall. Lucky she only had a dislocated shoulder.

"Yes. There's a path out to the valley road. We can get Colin to pick us up. The walk back up isn't easy. Good night, you three. *A domani.*"

Yes, see you tomorrow. And I hope Julia sleeps.

$\mathscr{M}$ARVELS

NOT WITHOUT TREPIDATION, AFTER COMPLETING eighteen paper doors, Camille packs them to show to Matilde, who takes a break when Camille comes in holding two large boxes. She's teaching a small group of African nuns who want to repair damaged texts in church archives. Leaning over a single sheet, the five starched white habits look like petals of a large flower, their heads almost touching in the center. Matilde's students all fall in love with the process of papermaking and, as a bonus, some adore the more important work of her restoration projects, which are the *bottega*'s raison d'être. Stepping into the work in progress, Camille feels awkward. Shouldn't her own paintings dissolve into oblivion?

Matilde and Serena have dismantled the five-panel altarpiece from the San Rocco Duomo and spread the pieces on tables. Camille looks through the microscope at the intricate incised gold work around the figures. Matilde then shows her what a swipe of cleaner reveals about the color of Saint Jerome's garment: murky pond green turns bright viridian. "Humbling," Camille says, "that you can save this work. It feels like an operating room here.

What's the brown mark?" She's fascinated enough to forget her own meager paintings.

"Candle damage. That's hard. Not only wax, but see this?" Matilde shines the lamp onto the blackened spot on the saint's shoulder. "This damage goes down to the wood. I must repair the gesso. I use mordants, ugh, you smell them? Rabbit glue and fish glue." She recaps the odorous elixirs. On the wall is a large photograph of the altarpiece with name tags pinned to various sections. Serendipitously, the students of papermaking, who see her painstaking and loving work, are also saving this crucial piece of the Italian patrimony. Matilde has devised a plan so that a single person can sponsor a sector of the restoration. She stands in front of the photo, pointing to Mary's cloak. "Who wouldn't want to save that blue? Expensive ground lapis lazuli. See, only twenty-five hundred dollars for restoring a minor saint, but sixty-five hundred for an accompanying angel, and much more for a major saint. A class could go in together for a section. They're thrilled that their names will be listed on a plaque when the altarpiece is at last restored to its hallowed place above the altar." All this in Italian, which Camille somehow understands.

"Enough! What's in your boxes? You came not for a restoration lesson!"

"I wanted to show you what I've been working on. What becomes of all the paper I lug home. But you're busy . . ."

"Not at all. Let's look!"

At an empty table, Camille lays out her paper doors around the periphery. After only a glance Matilde's eyes widen. She walks around, examining and repeating, *"Dio mio,"* and *"Madonna!"*

Serena, coming downstairs, stops short as she sees the doors on the table. "Camille, what have you done? Where did these *come* from?" The nuns gather around, too, nodding, chattering in their language. Matilde stops swearing. Camille, arms crossed, frowning, stands to the side.

"These are marvelous. In the real sense. Marvels. Small miracles. I'm dazzled." Matilde keeps gliding around the table, murmuring and smiling. "I'm not sure how to think about this work because I've never seen anything like it."

Camille feels equally thrilled and wanting to disappear. She's unaccustomed to attention. Matilde is saying in English, "We must cause a show." Camille shrugs and looks shocked. For all his virtues, Charles never *insisted* that she pay attention to the work she was intensely engaged with when they met. Mutually, they fell into a lifestyle. Lovely it was, but how could she have displaced her own interests? Before Charlie was born, there were the trips to New York when she was newly wed and still determined. Oh yes, Cyrus. A classmate, former boyfriend at UVA, up there doing well. His friends, all committed and living in roach-infested cold-water dumps. The shock of shame she felt in every corpuscle after his show, when they went out to bars and then to his bare loft; Charles at home in their two-bedroom apartment, going over briefs at the folding table where they ate. What was she thinking? They laughed, smoked weed, and even though she privately thought his work was superficial, she praised his huge white canvases with slashes of built-up white impasto. He was selling to all the cool collectors. Mattress on the floor. The sex was inspired. Much more than his art. She went home. She felt she'd been on a moonwalk. She ran a fever. Charles's big hug and smile. He had made spaghetti and wanted to hear about her weekend. How could she?

Later, she knew she was pregnant. She did not know if Charles was the father. Agony. Cyrus calling. Come back! She never told him. And outrage—the IUD lodged inside her. Could she let a stupid night's indiscretion govern her life and the life of a child? He/she would be born, and she would be scanning the features? Who's the father? No. On her own, through a sorority sister who was a nurse, she arranged an abortion. She went alone to Charlotte, ostensibly to visit a college roommate. After the procedure, she spent the night at an airport hotel, crying and watching movies and eating nuts from the minibar. How could she betray Charles? She was untrustworthy.

She became trustworthy. All that tennis. Lavish attention to her classes. She barely could look at her own corner area of canvases and paints. She strove for perfection in her home, her marriage, her job.

"APRIL," MATILDE SAYS. "WHEN THE tourists return. The little gallery on the piazza. I will talk to them. Can you leave the doors here for a few days?"

"Yes, and I want to give you one. Please choose."

"No," Matilde answers. "You cannot give these away." Just the same response Rowan gave at Christmas. Rowan. Too long until he's back. Rowan *had* seemed transfixed. Matilde, too.

"Matilde, *grazie*. I'm kind of stunned. I'm totally excited that you like them."

"Camille, you have no idea how much. And I see a lot of original art."

CAMILLE WALKS HOME SLOWLY. THERE will be a show! Julia will throw a celebratory dinner. Susan will fill the house with flowers and maybe Rowan will be back. If I'd stayed, she thinks, *nothing, nothing* would have happened. She imagines her paper doors hanging on the walls all around the gallery off the piazza. People will wander in and out, sign a guestbook, opinions will form, someone may want to buy. But could I sell? How do artists let go of something so intimate? Or maybe the five nuns and my teachers at the *bottega* are anomalies and no one else will like the work. They'll be polite and I'll know. Wait, Rowan loved them, my friends do, Charlie did, even Lara. Why, when the goodies were passed around, did I not get a fucking ego?

How do I repair that? she mused. From the road, she looked out over the valley flushed with early spring greens, ripples of shadows like gray pleats in the hollows, and the fast-lowering sun falling into its own sifted gold light. She tries to pick out the secret Roman bridge Kit showed them, but she can detect only the white rush of falling water downstream. Kit has moxie. Kit presses on regardless. The others, too. Everyone feels more confidence in their new paths than I, she thinks. Regardless, I *have* moved into my art. I'm exhilarated. I just have to get used to the public part. Put it out there.

When she arrives home, she checks her messages. Matilde already has scheduled the local gallery, and she's contacted Rowan with jpegs of all the paper doors. He responded immediately that he will prepare a catalogue. He wants Kit to write an intro. She has three messages from him.

Julia meditatively stirs a pot of ragù while Susan has gone momentarily insane playing with the kittens and a piece of string. "Momentous news," Camille announces.

There's no one she'd rather celebrate with than Susan and Julia. After, she tells them what snagged her art. The *easy* abortion. Oh, yeah. The already dead embryo clutching the IUD. Going home to her sweet marriage. And, of course, about sex on Rowan's sofa.

PER SFIZIO:

For Fun

THESE WARMING DAYS, SUSAN ATTACKS the garden. She's been waiting to approach the *limonaia*, the lemons' wintering-over house,
though there are now no lemon trees. She intends to remedy that
as soon as she cleans out the long stone room. Grazia said to throw
away everything, but Susan will keep the rusty round table, the
battered tin watering cans, the arches that appear in the dining
room fresco, and the faded green metal chairs. She takes "before"
pictures for the garden design blog she's started. Lightly sanded
and given a clear opaque coat of protection, the vintage furniture
will look natural for summer dinners under the pergola. Leo says
the wooden table, rather rickety, easily can be fixed up for dining
among the lemons and oranges. Susan wipes down the surface,
deciding to coat it later with a light gray wash. Grazia has no idea
these things, even the watering cans, cost a fortune in French antique markets.

Leo, who remembers how glorious the *limonaia* was when he
was a boy, volunteers to help. "I used to walk in just to breathe the
perfume. There must have been thirty lemons back then, all in
the old-style pale terra-cotta pots. Tito and my father moved them

outside in early May, took them in before hard frost. In summer, they stood along the drive."

"*Facciamo ancora*," let's do that again. Susan hopes her Italian isn't atrocious because it has a sexy sound.

Also, Susan will not toss out the green glass wine demijohns still covered in woven osier. She slices off the rotten baskets to reveal sensuous emerald globes, curved like Kit's new belly. Leo shows her how to clean out the grotty inside. He puts in a couple of handfuls of small stones with soap, then squirts in water. The tricky part is sloshing the bottle around without it slipping out of your hands as the rocks scour the glass. He rinses several times. Susan will make one flower bed featuring these bottles. Some raised on stone bases at different heights, she decides. She sweeps, de-cobwebs with a broom, lugs dirty flowerpots outside and hoses them off. In her business, Susan has been on the hiring end of whipping property into shape. Oddly, she finds that she's loving this work. The three cats pounce on dust balls and sniff the corners of the *limonaia*. "Ah, you can move out here for the summer," Susan tells them. "You, too, Archie. Get *out* of that trash pile!"

Here's the worst job: she attacks the filthy stone floor, first with a push broom, then with hose and scrub brush. The cats run into the bushes. At this point, Camille and Julia, watching from the kitchen, take pity and change into jeans and rubber boots. Cleaning the *limonaia*'s front of iron and glass doors uses all the rags, window cleaner, and vinegar they have. The wavy glass shines. With the three of them working over three days, and Leo repairing a side wall of sagging shelves, the *limonaia* takes shape. The glass-fronted building becomes a garden room, potting shed, rainy-day spot for lunch. Susan points to the end section. "Camille, there's all this room. We could close off that last third for studio space. You could work with the doors open and step out into the garden when you want. The light is spectacular."

Camille opens the doors. "Are you serious! I will die and go to heaven!" Immediately, she has a premonition of working on large canvases.

Julia scrapes open the door of the pizza oven close to the kitchen. "Leo, do you think this works?" It was so overgrown with ivy they'd hardly noticed it until Susan had two men clearing last week.

"*Certo!*" Leo shines his phone light inside, pokes his head in to inspect the intact brick dome and the smooth floor of the oven. "Luisa used to make bread. We must build a fire to season it again before we start shoveling in the pizza. No one has used it in years but spiders."

Susan already has arranged for the delivery of three large, potted lemon trees, a kumquat loaded with fruit, and two oranges. They will live inside around the wooden table until all chance of frost is over. More citrus must come, she knows.

"UNBELIEVABLE," JULIA SAYS, AS THE nursery men arrange pots around the table. "This is just fabulous." Now the air is suffused with the divine fragrance of white, waxy blooms. "It's sixty degrees. Let's eat out here tonight. We can plug in a couple of our bathroom space heaters. I'll line the back ledge of the wall with candles. Leo, can you and Annetta come? I'll make the lemon pistachio pasta we all love."

"In that case, I need to fix that wobbly table leg."

FROM THE UPSTAIRS STORAGE ROOM in the house, Susan, up early, hauls down four mismatched dining chairs, handmade baskets, and wooden wine boxes to the *limonaia*. She stacks the boxes to make shelves for small pots, and hangs the baskets around the new outdoor dining room. Three green demijohns catch the light along the glass doors. Last night, she ordered an outdoor rug from an Italian website—wide gray and white stripes—to go under the table. The whole middle of the *limonaia* stays free for her workspace. She needs a potting table. She'll buy a new shovel, and shiny new clippers and trowels. Time to start seeds.

"JULIA, LET'S GO TO TOWN. Market day," she calls.

"Coming," Julia answers from the open window. She's talking to Chris, catching him up on the Wade development. "That's off your agenda. But thanks for setting this in motion. I'm glad he's going, and I'm not. Hope that doesn't sound selfish. I just can't. I've put my hand down on that hot burner too many times."

Chris texts his flight details. He'll land in Rome in three weeks, stopping in San Rocco for a couple of days en route to Venice, where he's meeting the Friuli group. "We'll reconfirm all the Friuli reservations and get some time to talk about the Sicily tour for next year," he says. "Mostly, I want to sit in the piazza with you and look around at those mellow buildings and hear you laugh." After Friuli ends, he's back in Tuscany for a few days before the usual Tuscany group arrives.

"It's been ages. Will we recognize each other? I'll take care of all the reconfirming—that's what you hired me for!" Julia is putting on her shoes. "I've got to go. Susan is dying to go buy a shovel."

"A shovel?"

"You will not believe what she's done with the *limonaia*. That woman is formidable. Talk later? Can't wait."

"Me, too. And I hired you for more nefarious reasons, as you well know."

Bougainvillea, Grapes, Prickly Pear

A PLACE TO HIDE. THE blissful climate imparts a godlike joy. Waking to the scent of orange blossoms and temperature that says, *You're mine, don't worry, I always will caress you like this*—the poems I am writing seem as natural as bougainvillea blossoms blowing into the hallway. The fragrant air alone makes me feel rocked in the cradle. Above me, the blue dome resembles a glazed, inverted china teacup.

Capri, a maze of paths. Soon I am on not a walk but a plunge, down, down, down, happily, scarily, vertiginously. One of Capri's primordial appeals—scale. In a lifetime, I could know the island as well as I know Colin's body. Know each carob, every stone wall with blooming capers, all the outbreaks of yellow broom.

THE HOUSES (CURVED ROOFS FOR catching water) offer views of corkscrew paths, a transparent sea layered with emerald, lapis, turquoise water. So clear that your mind seems equally clear. Move into one of the white houses and soon I would be painting the walls blue, setting a pot of basil by the door to keep out the bugs, and napping away the hot hours under an arbor. After six months here, I might emerge, finally, as a disciplined writer. I would develop iron calf muscles. Glamorous Capri, long a bolthole for outcasts and those fleeing scandal.

The surprise: the tourist-clogged island offers solitude. Away from the main scene, you're faced with *paradiso*. Lentisk, prickly pear, pine, asphodel, myrtle. Were they planted by the sirens who tried to lure Odysseus with their songs? He was so tempted that his sailors had to lash him to the mast and sail on.

WHAT COMPRISES THE ESSENCE OF this place? Guidebooks don't tell me. But the waves on the rocks tell me, the fisherman's blue shirt shouts it out, the delicate shadow of an almond tree on a white wall scrawls three angular black reasons. Capri—combing the island, inhaling the sunbaked scents of wild mint, lemon, and the sea, making love in a mother-of-pearl light, joking with the woman chopping weeds along her fence, memorizing a tumble of pink and apricot bougainvillea intertwining on a rough white wall, picnicking on a pebble beach, and Colin leaning to catch a hot grape I toss toward his open mouth.

WE'RE AS GLAM AS JACKIE in the round sunglasses, skinny Frank Sinatra, insouciant Cary Grant. Or so we feel. Colin in his rolled-up white pants, me in a billowing yellow sundress. The island lets you know that you live a charmed life. I see it in Julia, Camille, and Susan, putting their feet down to measure for sandals on Anacapri, then hailing a convertible taxi and letting their hair fly. Meeting them in the piazza where they've already ordered crazy drinks involving blood orange juice, bitters, and gin. Camille has put her streaky blond hair up into a twist. (I take a photo and send it to Rowan.) Julia has bought Carthusian monks' soaps shaped like lemons for Susan, who has found a shop that makes exquisite baby clothes. I suspect she has found something for our little voyager. Those three have the #1 quality of great travelers: curiosity. And they have fun.

WE ALL CAME DOWN ON the fast train from Florence to Naples, then over to the island on the hydrofoil. They're in a posh house Brian and Nicolà will be featuring on their rental site. Susan already has copious notes on what the Swiss owners need to do to upgrade it into a luxury rental. Get rid of the fake flowers. Better tableware. Who wants cheap white plates and straw mats at this price?

We are here for four nights in the blessed season before mass tourism descends. This will be my last trip before what they horrendously call "confinement." (I'm almost seven months now.) Colin was able to get away for this blissful escape. Even if you don't need a respite, Capri offers one. I've been before, only once and in July when the crush of humanoids around is pure hell. (But no one in the designer shops.) By four o'clock ferries tootle away, leaving a manageable crowd. At cocktail hour, you can convince yourself of your sophistication and beauty under any bar's awning on the piazza.

At their luxurious villa (*grazie*, Nicolà!) with a long terrace looking over the Faraglione rocks and a sweep of the sea, Julia is shelling new peas. She has found a local woman to work with her, and who will serve us at a table with a view so stupendous that I don't want to eat. Just stare out at the lights twinkling toward Naples. I walk over to the wall overlooking the waters, pulling my shawl around me, relishing the taut roundness of my body. To be pregnant with the person you love. What can compare? To stand over this grand sweep of water, to know that you love, you can love, you can live with your love. Colin rubs his face against my neck. "Are you okay?" Then he steps up to the evening, help-ing serve Julia's baked olives with capers, her mozzarella skewers layered with sun-dried tomatoes and basil, and after drinks, pasta shells stuffed with shrimp, peas, and three cheeses.

Camille comes out of the kitchen with two more bottles of the local, thin wine. "Colin, and you three gorgeous graces! We've come this far, as far as a pergola with bunches of dangling grapes. *Grappola*, a bunch. The tactile word makes you want to reach up and grab one." I see Julia reach for her pad and jot down the word, an entry for her *Learning Italian*.

"Yes, yes," Colin says. "Still, Kit and I have a long way to go. I'm thinking of the next two months. But tonight will be divine." Colin sets up his speaker out on the patio and plays all the versions of "Nessun Dorma" that we love. He's made a pitcher of lemonade with mint, and gamely drinks with me. I don't miss wine at this point; imagining Miss Priss getting high keeps me mindful.

We dance as the constellations perform their arrangements. The Seven Sisters, my favorite. The Big Dipper pouring blessings over this island. Colin must hold me almost at arm's length like nineteenth-century waltzers. My beach ball. Our churner in his own Blue Grotto. I love Capri. For good reasons we aesthetes and day-trippers migrate here for a whiff of the air gods breathe.

BACK AT OUR B&B LONG after midnight, I'm still awake. No moon, but the sky radiates a filmy white afterglow. Nightingales are calling from the shrubbery. From poems, I always imagined a piercing repetitive sweetness. What I'm hearing sounds like the station keeps getting switched. Someone must have counted the number of sound patterns and at what intervals they reoccur. One chatters like a squirrel, one sounds like hammering tacks, others do have that sweetness I expected. What a double-dealer. I think I'm laughing as I fall asleep.

• • •

MORNINGS I WRITE AND COLIN sketches ideas for a pavilion, café, and museum on the water in Key West, polar opposite of Capri. On our warm afternoons, Colin walks the steep paths and I lounge on our patio reading *South Wind* by Norman Douglas, a pederast who preyed on local boys. Creepy he was, but can he ever write an evocative description of the island. I skip around finding words and phrases to admire. Otherwise, easy to fall into a lovely siesta with the sun on my feet and bougainvillea blurring orange to pink to magenta in front of the distant Tyrrhenian Sea. The far-away slosh of waves repeats, repeats *Tyrrhenian, Tyrrhenian.*

ON THE FERRY BACK TO Naples, my back starts to ache in a strange way, as though I am being pushed. I'm only carrying a light bag; Colin juggles the two carry-ons. I'm hot, and no one else is. I found a seat and let the strong breeze blow on my face.

We board the fast train to Florence. In the bathroom, I feel weak. A streak of pale blood stains my underwear. When I return to my seat, Colin is deep into his files, but he jumps up. "What's wrong, babes? You look sick. Are you okay?"

"When we get to Florence, we need to go to my doctor ASAP. Could you call her?" I tell him about the blood. I'm by the window and can hide my face. I don't want to move. I cup my arms under my baby. Stay. *Stay.*

Colin keeps his arm around me and with his free hand starts looking up symptoms on his phone. "Are you sure your water didn't break?" I can see in his eyes the horrifying prospect of de-livering the baby on the train.

"No," I say, trying to be calm. "A little smear of blood. And my sides ache." Just then lightning bolts of pain shoot down my diaphragm into my legs. He leaves a message for the nurse. *Emer-gency. Will arrive around 14:30.*

Glancing over at Colin's screen I see *placenta previa* and *nor-mal start to labor.* The attendant offers drinks, and I order a Coke, thinking it might calm my insides. My mother's remedy. Shortly, I'm throwing up in the bathroom. Julia saw me pass down the aisle and followed.

"Are you all right?" She knocks.

I say fine, yes, fine, no, not fine, and unlock the door. "Something's weird. We've called the doctor." I tell her about the blood and the ache. I'm remembering the narrow-pathed climb to their aerie on Capri, hauling myself up steps and leaning on the rail, the fleeting thought that maybe I shouldn't, then descending late as we walked back to our place, a kind of extending that my knees and back seemed to rebel against. Later I was okay.

"You are going to be fine. These things happen all the time. I know it's scary."

"They don't happen all the time in the last three months."

"Uh, well, sometimes. And sex can cause bleeding."

"Let's don't go there."

"We'll come with you."

"No, Colin will. But how can you get to San Rocco?" Colin has left his car at the train station parking garage.

"I'll call Gianni right now. Not to worry. You'll let us know?"

THE DOCTOR'S EXAM SHOWED THE baby's rapid heartbeat. The bleeding stopped, then started up again with clots. I was hooked to an IV. (Will spare you my nightmares.) She kept me overnight at the hospital. Colin blamed himself, but I assured him that we are allowed to make love (though privately, something about that begins to seem a bit eldritch to me). When I woke up this morning I felt light cramps, like when you're about to get your period.

When Dr. Caprini calls around, she says I can leave late today if there's no more bleeding but that she wants me to stay in bed at home now. I can prop up in a chair, take showers, but, she warns:

no activity. We have to see if this baby wants out now. *Stay*, I will. Stay, bitty she/he. In place.

"LOOK ON THE BRIGHT SIDE," Colin begins.

I cut him off. "No, the bright side is *not* that I get to concentrate on writing. If this hadn't happened I could do that anyway. And you'll have to cook! We're going to be having a lot of grilled cheese." I'll willingly stay prone if it helps the baby come to normal term. I can read. Camille says she'll give me drawing lessons. I can work on my friend's project and on Margaret. I can watch Spanish *telenovas*, which is what I flat-out want to do. I'm shaken to the core. As Colin is whistling while he cooks, I'm weeping into my pillow.

COLIN'S CHICKEN ISN'T BAD, BUT it isn't good. "Julia will come through for us. She's already brought over six jars of her frozen ragù. When you have ragù, you have dinner. Said she'll be back later with minestrone.

"Immigrant energy!"

I FEEL OKAY BUT TENTATIVE. A day spent ordering my desk is a good day. No lifting, even dictionaries. In the stack of mail, I find a letter with a Richmond return address. Confident, blocky print. Real ink. Calhoun Green. Not sure I can take Margaret-drama today. I prop it on the windowsill and look out at my row of roses just coming into leaf along the tall stone wall. Albertine, my good coral pink climber; Queen Elizabeth, who can't decide if she's a climber or just unruly; decadent Eden, aka Pierre de Ronsard; and Albéric Barbier, the scrappy one that presents tight yellow buds only to open to the color of vanilla gelato. I must give

Susan cuttings of all these. When they're in full bloom, will I be walking my baby along the wall, little bundle in a blanket breathing in first-ever rose scents? Another life.

Meanwhile, I send out new poems to magazines, organize my Margaret files, and answer emails. Here's a tempting invitation to read in Nashville in October. Babe will be four months. Hard to commit when I have no idea what our lives will look like by then. London? Miami? Here? I pull my silky throw around me, stack two pillows, and turn on *Grand Hotel*. Fitzy usually practices Olympian disdain but now jumps onto the bed and stretches his silky white body along mine. Animal instinct. May his purr lull my restless *bambino*.

CHANGES CAUSE CHANGES

A LETTER DROPPED INTO A slot. A reply.

Dear Ms. Raine,

Thank you for sending the letter you found among Margaret's papers. You cannot imagine the impact. You must have struggled with whether to send such news to me, news withheld for many years. I could have never known of the existence of Colin. His birth, his life, his death, these have landed upon me with devastating sadness. Only a brief time has passed. How this all will settle, I don't know.

May I say clearly: letting Margaret walk out of my life was the mistake I will regret forever. In my hard head I knew she was more than I could manage. Mine was a destined life; I thought at the time, a clear and regulated life, one handed down like monogrammed silver. At twenty, I wanted that. I loved the place I came from and my family's values. She was born to rove, to think big, to risk. She was a rip-roaring girl, iconoclastic, challenging. She scared me then.

Now, this. I see how much stronger she was. That the feisty independence was much more than I understood. How brave she was. What a dolt I was. This is hard to write, hard to admit, but some part of me always wondered if she had gone through with the abortion. That word was revolting to me. Yet my own shallow self-protection kept me from doing the right thing. Doubling the shame, I was in love with her. Looking back, my head must have been in a vise; I don't understand the boy who could let her go off on her own like that. I tried two months later to reach her. When her father came to the door, he had no idea who I was. She hadn't told him the name of the bastard who let her down. He said she was indefinitely away traveling, that he didn't have contact information at the time. I didn't leave a note or number to pass on. I went on to law school, married a lovely local girl. We have no children.

Maybe you care about these details, since your note says you are writing about Margaret. I followed her books. She was as remarkable as I expected. Since I have behaved abominably, I never wrote even to say what a marvelous writer she was. Once, when she gave a reading at the National Geographic in D.C., I attended. My seat was in the back and she never knew I was there. Not to say I pined all my life; I didn't. Water under the bridge, and all that.

I obsess over the last line of her letter: "Now you can have— and I don't mean this ironically—the honor, too." You're a writer, so possibly if this had happened to you, you could express what I can't. I know my limits. I did take another course of action. I hope it addresses the word "honor," which Margaret obviously chose with care.

A week after I received the letter, I called Edward Knowles in New York. He and his wife, Amanda, agreed to see me. I flew up the next day. They knew the birth mother's name, even had followed her career sporadically. Weeks before his death they had told Colin about her in brief outline. He planned to get in touch with her. He wanted, they said, to know why she gave him up.

I saw photos, a portrait, baby book. Handsome boy. I read the school narratives on his performance. Brilliant in everything but French. I saw his room, still intact, with a closet full of climbing

*gear, rackets, snorkel and scuba equipment. Photo of a girlfriend
who looked eerily like Margaret. In short, I was introduced to my son
and believe me I was knocked over. The parents and their girl, also
adopted, adored Colin. He deserved all the lavish love they gave.*

*Ms. Raine, I will be humbled and saddened by this for the rest of
my life, and yet I am happy that I know of this boy who graced the
earth for sixteen years.*

Respectfully, Calhoun Green

Colin and I read it over and over. We're old to be new parents.
Yes, Calhoun was weak, but he was twenty, unformed. Margaret
was twenty and had to form herself. From all I know, this is the
defining event that shaped her life. The courage she had at that
time resulted in the bravado of her adult life. The jilt, the betrayal
gave her a twisted sense of trust. The loss gave her eyes their old-
soul depth. That the worst had happened gave her an insouciance
toward the future.

I dig out what she wrote about her marriages. Two more un-
derlines in the betrayal column! It's rather flip. *Can't catch me.*

She wrote:

I met Jamie Sonnenfeld the first night I got back from Europe.
My father was entertaining clients and asked me to go. Jamie
was the renegade lawyer in a Chicago firm. He took on the
diciest cases and according to Dad was known to be tough
and flamboyant in the courtroom. My kind of guy, I thought.
I acquired a tough intestinal infection, along with acquiring
Jamie over the summer. We married at his parents' mansion at
Christmas. I was depressed over the faux Louis furniture and his
mother's high trilling laugh. She walked like a swan on land. The
father looked like someone with his eyes open underwater. He
said to me quietly, "Jamie has bitten off more than he can chew."

Jamie, center of attention. At the table, it was assumed he'd hold
forth and we'd second the motion. He was witty and smart but
we couldn't be. He turned out to be a narcissist who thought my
writing was a temporary affliction like the persistent infection.

Why recount the saga? Are unhappy marriages always alike?
Eighteen months, curtains come down. *Valete ac plaudite*, as the
Romans said. Farewell and applaud. Exit Margaret without a
bow.

My second marriage was announced like this: Margaret Ames
Merrill wore a mauve silk suit when she became the wife of
Henry Elton Hodges, III yesterday at five p.m. at Saint Joseph's
Episcopal Church. Her pearls belonged to her late grandmother,
also of the same name. Her hat was a white cloche, enlivened
with a clutch of violets.

Is that funny? The clothes taking total precedence over
the groom, who's not mentioned again until paragraph three.
Predictive. Something always came first before Henry.

We were wed for two months. We quarreled on our wedding
night about train reservations and he cuffed me on the ear.
Shocked, I kicked him in the groin and got another room.
We partly reconciled the next day and boarded the train for
Florida. That did not go well either. Like Jamie, Henry was all
about Henry. Maybe it was the era. I soon was on the phone
to my father, who said what a fine family Henry came from.
He desperately hoped that after my youthful "troubles" and
"mercurial personality," I was on the road to normal happiness,
a state that also eluded him since my mother absconded with
the East Indian podiatrist she'd visited for bunions. Poor Dad. I
separated, leaving Henry's "personality in disarray," according to
his psychiatrists.

Both husbands were American Wasps; both studied at Yale.
My dad thought my independence was too much of a challenge
for both men. But he was wrong. Their psyches were too weak
for them to realize that my independence was a plus for them.

Aftereffects? The acceptance that my talents were not conspicuously domestic/matrimonial. Being alone became something I cherished. And endured. Articles about me always say "elusive," "rigorous," "independent." Not accurate. I'm just unwilling to submit to arbitrary control. I was back home soon, packing up again, this time for Europe. For good. I was finding American life to be, as H. L. Mencken said, "a powerful solvent." Bye-bye.

Not a word of connubial bliss. No French toast brought to her bed on a tray. No quotes from love letters. No *this hurt*. All razor edge. Take no prisoners. Margaret hits it hard, down to the subcutaneous truth: Their psyches were too weak for them to realize that my independence was a plus for them.

Tangos

THEY FELL INTO THE HABIT of sharing news over coffee in the mornings. Family troubles are avoided, as are politics—too upsetting this early. Only book reviews, art openings, food articles, travel, general news, and of course the small subjects: who's shopping, who's taking the cats for shots, and what was that website on ravioli with young nettles because they're springing up in the ditches.

They've neglected messages for the past week. After Capri, the mornings are slow. They find it sweet to linger over a second cappuccino, although Camille not only has work she wants to do, there are details to handle about her show. The gallery is simply for hire, with no staff involved. She must see to publicity (a few flyers around town and an email to everyone she knows), hanging her work, and finding someone to sit in the gallery during open hours.

Chris is due in this afternoon. Lighting briefly in San Rocco, he's booked at Luca and Gilda's hotel. In preparation for his arrival, Julia has begun to research places of interest near vineyards he's chosen in Sicily, and how a weeklong swing around the island might happen. She's fallen in love with *The Leopard* and hopes some remnant of that majestic and primitive Sicily still exists.

Susan scrambles eggs. Mostly they've adopted the no-breakfast habit of Italians, but she's ravenous. The prospect of a morning of work in the garden makes her hungry in advance. Now everyone wants eggs and toast. Sunday mornings with Aaron and the girls, newspaper spread out, the talk, the spills, Archie's predecessor as a puppy, sticky jam, windows fogged from the air conditioning, the blue velour robe she wore for years. She beats the eggs to a froth and whisks them into the hot pan. She serves the plates, then flips open her laptop. Molly! Her friend at Artful Dodge Antiques in Chapel Hill, oh, good, she's proposing what they should focus on for the next container shipment. Um. She reads this aloud:

> It would be a blast to acquire some of this together. I could pop over for a week and we could go grazing around Tuscany. Would that work for you? Say when. We'll catch up on all the news. Cheers, Molly

"Oh lord, a week." Susan looks up. "I guess it would be fun. It would be fun."

"What a coincidence. I just got this from my next-door neighbor in Savannah." Julia reads:

> Dear Julia, This will be a bolt from the blue. The girls are doing well. Bill and I, not. After thirty years, he is checking out of this marriage. With all your troubles, I didn't keep you posted about our decline. We attempted various strategies. Weekends away. I won't bore you. Tango lessons seemed like a romantic option. I guess it was. How degrading to have to say that he is running off with the tango teacher. I am not kidding. You can't make up this stuff. I wish you were near. Would you consider having me come visit for a couple of weeks this fall? I need to sort out and regroup. Everyone knows about

Wade and the young woman. Is it true that she's PG? How did all this transpire in our lovely neighborhood? Let me know and if it's not okay I will certainly understand.

Love, Alison

"The tango teacher! They're tangoing off into the sunset. That is humiliating." Susan shakes her head. "Fool! What is he thinking?"

"Old roosters wanting to crow," Camille laughs. "Oh, I know, not funny. But it *is* absurd. I guess you can recognize some things better when you're old: it is not going to work out with the tango teacher, it's just not."

"Oh, and this—more news." Julia reads:

Dear Julia, Greetings from Bodrum where I'm reposing after twisting my ankle about ten ways. I'll be fine but am considering a respite before I continue my project. You said to come visit. Would you be open to a week or so? I might look for a short-term rental to organize my files and even begin to work on a long article. Are you all settled and happy there? All the best, Hugh

Susan scrolls down and finds:

Dear Susan,

Hope you remember us—we bought the historic Baskins house on Franklin from you. I've heard of your interesting life change from your colleague Becka, who gave me your email. We are coming to Tuscany for a vacation, much needed. We'd love to stay with you for two or three days. Love to take you to dinner. It would be fun to catch up. Let me know if mid-June works for you. Arrivederci, hope that's correct! Terry and Bob Morain

"Speaking of absurd. Who *are* these people with this much gall? Catch up with what? I remember them as quite pleasant, but we never socialized after the sale. Whoa. They want to *visit?*"

"Kit says you never lack friends when you have a vacation house in a great place. Word's out. I'm surprised it took this long," Camille says. "I've got one, too, last week. Let me find it."

Dear Professor Trowbridge,

Remember me from Art 101? I'm going to Europe with Amy & Rick who were also in that class. It was a great class now we'll see the art in person. I hope this is still you're email and that we can stop by and visit. If you could put us up that would be awesome. We could help with the chores! We will be traveling all of July. Hope to see you. Your an awesome teacher.

Dylan Schultz

"Dylan was sweet. Never learned the difference between *your* and *you're*, but he loved the Dutch landscapes. Oh, that life were so that you could just say to all these people, yes, come, door's open, we've shopped and cooked and cleaned and there are flowers in your room. Stay. Stay as long as you can!"

"Seriously, we need a policy. Something like good friends three days, family fine if we plan ahead. This is one of the tricky areas of living together. You might not want my guests, or me yours." Susan is already answering Molly. "I'm telling her, if it's okay with you, that she should come here for a couple of days and then we'll go on a road trip."

"That's fine. At least the house is big. We can refer most to an *agriturismo*—they're wonderful and they have pools. And we need to hone our skills at saying no, something none of us is good at. So, no to the students, no to the historic house owners. But, Julia, you'll let Alison come, won't you? And Hugh, oh yes, it would be lovely to see Hugh."

"Yes, Hugh. He'll be no trouble and I'm sure after a couple of nights he'd be happy to move into town. But Alison, not for two weeks, no way. She's my friend, but since I can't inflict a guest on you for that long, I'll blame it on you! You work at home. Which is totally true. We all do; we are not just on vacation. The three-day rule. Then she's going to love Luca and Gilda's hotel. Spa, cooking class, wine tastings. I'm sure she'll still have that bozo's credit cards. He's guilty as hell. He won't peep. We'll have her over, of course."

"We've slapped into shape some good guidelines. We're only inviting three guests, plus I think Charlie will fly over for my show. Rowan and Chris, but they won't be staying here. We'll be fine."

"Oh, wait. My daughters. Here, Eva says they can't stay away. We'll deal with that later." Susan reads on to more drastic news. "Eva and Caroline are going to China to search for their birth parents. She wants to know where the adoption papers are and if I signed any privacy agreement." *Don't worry,* Eva assures her. *We just want to know. We'll be taking over our DNA results.*

She responds immediately.

> Cara *Eva—do come. Anytime. Keep me posted as there is much going on here and we'll have to juggle dates. You'll have to go to the safe-deposit box for the papers from China. The key is in my right-hand desk drawer and both your names are on the permission. I haven't looked at them in donkey's years. Password is Waretear. Let me know when you're going. I can get the house opened and aired. Xxxx*

Susan gathers the plates and loads the dishwasher. After all these years, why now?

"I've got to run. I'm getting a haircut. Chris wants to have a drink in town, then we're going to the hotel for dinner. Can I pick up anything in town?"

"Thanks," Susan says. "We can cook, my dear. Did it for years before we got you as a chef. I'm on a roll. Tonight I'll make my soon-to-be-famous Carolina meat loaf. Camille and I will revel in a quiet evening."

WITHOUT A BUMP IN THE sky, still the flight from California feels endless, the car rental desk always crowded, and the drive out of the airport, after nineteen hours of travel, not easy. Then two hours to San Rocco, radio blaring to keep him alert, with only one stop at an Autogrill for a double espresso. At last, the serene turn into Hotel Sant'Anna.

After kisses and hugs from Luca and Gilda and half the staff, Gilda orders pasta for him from the kitchen, which Chris devours. He starts to go over details for the Tuscany tour, but Gilda tells him that Julia already has nailed down every room selection, cooking school agenda, and pickup time. All he needs to do is show up.

Julia will be here at five. He already has asked Luca for a bottle of chilled prosecco and flowers in his room. Romantic for days, he's packed a few votive candles. Suddenly feeling pretty jet-lagged, he calls Julia. "I'm here. I'm waiting." He showers, rests for two blessed, deep-sleep hours, then meets Julia in the terrace garden. She's wearing a filmy orange top and white pants. What has she done with her hair? It's longer, pinned up on either side. He sees her before she sees him but when she does, her face lights, and then as if she knows how much, she covers her face with her hands for a second. Laughing, she opens her arms as he opens his and they crash into each other. "You know you smile with your eyes?"

"And you smile with your whole body." The last thing he

wants to do is drive, but he longs to sit in the piazza with Julia on this spring evening and talk and talk. Gilda has planned a spectacular dinner—ravioli with borage, pheasant braised with dried berries and thyme, asparagus, and Gilda's silken *panna cotta* with wild strawberries.

VIOLETTA BRINGS A TRAY WITH two flutes of prosecco to their table. She kisses and hugs Chris, then Julia, whom she's kissed and hugged earlier in the day. Violetta serves bowls of olives and chips. "Ever think there's maybe a bit too much kissing around here?"

"Better than pulling out guns all the time," Julia laughs.

First toast of many. "Here's to our ventures, all kinds of adventures." Chris clinks glasses with Julia. "Don't we love it all? Don't we love how the sun strikes the stones in the late afternoon? They have a sheen like wax." He gestures around the piazza.

"Yes. I'm always trying to figure out if there's some solstice or equinox marker, or if those Romans just sat out here drinking mead until they lost track of time. And let me right away toast you for making that trip to look for Lizzie. You were sweet to do that for me."

"Let's hope Wade finds her. Let's talk about your book! About me heading off to Friuli with a van full of wild women on holiday. About Susan and Camille. Rowan. Archie! Everything. Tell me everything."

Five months it's been.

Carpe Diem

"I GET TO BRING THE flowers. What flowers go with paper doors?" Susan asks.

"Do you want austere and sculptural or various and tumbling? Roses in glass bowls or huge renaissance extravaganzas?"

They're arranging the gallery, moving the table to the wall by the door, wiping down dusty windowsills, leaving four chairs in an alcove where people can pause and visit. The paper doors will ring the walls, not crowded. Along the center of the room six of Camille's favorites, suspended by transparent fishing line, will float in the air. Leo, who seems to be able to do anything, and Valter, who owns the frame shop, take measurements. Camille sees them looking at her work with a what-the-hell-is-this expression.

She unpacks her doors and Julia helps lay them along the floor the way she wants them hung. "I'm liking this do-it-yourself exhibit." Camille holds up two doors to see how they like each other. "Imagine just shipping your stuff off to New York and appearing when the caterers do."

"I'm the caterer and thrilled to be so. You're going to love my antipasti platters, which I am mixing up with a few southern goodies such as ham biscuits and cheese straws."

"I'll try not to be too nervous to notice. But I *will* be wearing my red velvet shoes. And Rowan is cutting his final classes to get here. Pretty gutsy, I think, since this is his last semester of teaching."

Susan takes three tablecloths out of a box. "Choose which one you want and I'll make the flowers work." She shakes out a cream Busatti, makers of the traditional Tuscan linen, then a peach brocade from Grazia's stash, and a renaissance-moment red and gold jacquard.

"Definitely the cream," Camille decides. Susan already knew her choice but had a small hope for the jacquard's drama. "Okay, now I'll have fun. Lunch break, let's go."

At Stefano's they order *penne alla Norma*. Camille asks Julia, "What was it like to see Chris again? Maybe I'm feeling iffy about Rowan's arrival. You and I both sort of fell in with them quickly, but I'm thinking now what if we look at each other and think, *What was that about?*"

"I doubt that. He's completely cool and arty. With Chris, this may sound unlikely, but we took up where we left off. We started talking about the tours and Sicily and his boy coming home to live. I feel like I'm already beginning to know his son, that everything will be quite natural, and if it's not, if we later wear out, that's not going to end my world. Maybe it's my damaged sense that this is a—I don't want to say posthumous relationship. That's too dire. But this *revised* life has to unfold in a serene and good way. He feels like a best friend, and I happen to find him crazy attractive, too."

"That he is," Susan agrees. She runs her fingers through her hair, raising the spikes. "Not that I have run into anyone other than Riccardo—and I think he's gay without even admitting it to himself—so this is theoretical, but it seems like you're both ferreting out what love is at this stage." She laughs wickedly. "Love in the time of chin hairs and vaginal moisturizer!" They start laughing so loud that everyone turns their way. "Anyway—you sound like you've totally got it straight. The relationships are nothing like what any of us has known before—that passion that makes you overlook flaws, the arc of a long marriage, the comfortable complacency that sets in, the decades and decades where being a part of something seems big and whole but also splits you into twos and threes." She slaps her hands against each other. "Over and done. Now it's *seize the day*. People who like to be side by side, as you once said, Julia. Didn't you say you imagined you and Chris walking down a foreign street arm in arm? I love that."

"Did I? You're so good and succinct, Susan. But does it make you feel—what? Lonely? That we have these part-time men and you haven't met anyone? Well, there's Riccardo; he's interesting— about saffron and roses and translation and the inner workings of the Vatican. You have a lot in common. Are you sure he's gay?"

"I don't care. Truly. He likes to have lunch and dance at par- ties and he's passionate about literature and gardens. He's a friend, a good one. Sex? Actually, he doesn't appeal to me that way. I seem to want to throw all my—as you know, considerable— energy into my interests. For now anyway. I'm glad you found, at least, great dates and maybe soul mates. Don't worry about me. I'm way past thinking I need a bicycle built for two. You all having dessert?"

Julia takes her at her word. Camille shrugs. Paper doors, she thinks. Always opening.

Pearls

ROWAN RENTS A FIAT 500X, surprisingly ready and waiting with his
name on it. He heads north, stopping only at a wine shop in Orte,
where he once spent a few days, and next at his apartment on
the edge of San Rocco. He made excellent time. He opens the
shutters, letting in sudden strong light. Although he knows it's
constantly rented, the place looks untouched since his exit. His
landlady, Marianna, scrawled *Benvenuto* on a piece of paper sack.
What a sweetheart—she left fruit, bread, cheese, and coffee. He
showers and changes, putting on the green sweater Camille gave
him for Christmas, then drives straight to Villa Assunta. He's
bringing a suitcase full of Paper Doors exhibition catalogues—
letterpressed, with one of the doors that Matilde sent him in a
high-res photo on the cover. She wrote the intro, staking large
claims for the brilliance and originality of the work. For Camille's
birthday, Rowan made something else, too, a hand-sewn book for
guests to sign. The papers are those he made at the *bottega*, with
a blue, heavier-stock cover embossed with Camille's initials and
a painted design of a mosaic hand. Immensely pleased he feels to
offer her these tokens.

He's an hour earlier than expected. No one's home. He walks around the transformed garden. The hillside behind the house is blowsy with hyacinths and the pheasant-eye narcissus his mother loves. Farther up, poppies and unknown other white and yellow wildflowers rampage along the road to Kit's. Lemon pots line the drive, a seigniorial touch, and the pergola is dripping with white wisteria. Camille told him about Susan's spaces created out of the junk-shed *limonaia*. Since the doors are all open, he peers in. What a great place for a fine-printing press. Light. He has a flash of working there, side by side with Camille. Sturdy stone floor— great for the heavy printing press. As of today, he's sprung from his teaching. Freedom is a powerful aphrodisiac. What great books there are out there for him to publish. After his brutal marriage in his twenties, and the two ultimately unsatisfying relationships after that, he's optimistic about his feelings for Camille. She's his age. He's not wanting a younger woman; too problematic, and if too young what a drag to force yourself to remain enthusiastic over things you really no longer care about. And the powerful desire they develop for children. He feels a stab of regret for the two difficult children he did not save. Could not. And another stab of anger at their mother.

Camille remains young because she's starting over. She has all the excitement and trepidation of a twenty-year-old, an excitement he feels today as well. She gets his references. She thinks and reads—reaches out to touch the paper. She's still damned attractive. An image rises of her breasts, full and surprisingly tipped with small pink nipples. Late, but he feels sure he's found unfettered love for the first time.

THERE AT THE END OF the *limonaia*, Camille's easels are already set up. The middle section houses Susan's garden tools and pots. He leans to read the tabs on the biodegradable trays where she's started seeds: cosmos, lysianthus, basil, trailing nasturtiums, echinacea. In Julia's charming outdoor dining room, she's already set the table for Camille's birthday celebration tonight with a vibrant tablecloth of chevrons, a green tureen spilling with yellow hyacinths and wands of quince. These southern women, a genius for hospitality, or maybe better named, for friendship. He won't tell that he shooed one of the thieves' cats (Ragazzo?) off the table.

An Alfa Giulietta, blood-red, pulls slowly down the driveway and a tall blond man unfolds himself. Charlie. Rowan knows immediately. His smile, like hers, a default and there more often than not. The same high patrician nose. "Hey, man! You must be Rowan." He's walking forward with his hand out.

Rowan smiles back. "Great you could get here for the show. Looks like no one's around. And really great to meet the wonder boy." What a fine-looking son. And an artist.

"You, too, man. I spoke to Mom from the autostrada. They'll be back any minute. Some last-minute hitch with hanging things from the ceiling, but I think they charmed the gallery guy into letting them. She said to go in. The key is under a pot near the kitchen door." Charlie felt a pang for his dad. Who's this hip older guy stepping in, maybe bonging his mom? But he seems straight up and present. Charlie knows about the fine printing and wants to hear more.

There are ten pots around the step, but Rowan guesses right the first time. "At least it's not the doormat. So much for thieves being fooled, huh?"

"I'm upstairs across from Susan." Charlie starts up with his bag.

"I'm not staying here. I have my same apartment from last year on the edge of town." Rowan looks around the kitchen, thinking of the lumpy velvet sofa at his place the night he and Camille came back from Bologna. How much has changed. The night with the stolen jewelry, when he held Camille while she slept, cried, cursed, and slept. What a magnificently lived-in house. Now, even lighter inside. Then he notices that all the bushes obscuring windows have been cut back. He can't imagine the three of them not here. He calls up to Charlie, "You want a drink? I stopped in Orte and bought some wine and a couple of cheeses. Hope they pass muster with Julia."

Charlie has a quick shower, combs his wet hair straight back, and bounds down, buttoning his shirt. At the same moment Camille flings open the door, meeting him at the bottom of the stairs with a big dancing hug. "Oh, you!" She sees Rowan in the doorway and grabs him, too, still dancing. "You're both here!"

"Yeah!"

"And Chris will be here soon. He's picking up some last-minute things. Charlie, can you grab those last two bags out of the car? Rowan, let's put on some music."

Susan and Julia walked from town. They're trying to clock three miles a day. Julia holds up a handful of wild asparagus. "We'll see! It looks stringy. This may taste like yarn."

I'M NOT ABLE TO GO to the pre-show dinner at Villa Assunta tonight. From my study window I can hear commotion below. Snatches of laughter, who's playing "Heart and Soul" on the piano? Then the speaker blaring out Pink Martini and Buddha Bar, some of my favorites. Colin will go to the dinner (is he glad to get out of the house of confinement?), and they invited others. Riccardo, Nicolà, and Brian, not sure who else. Under house arrest, I am sending a birthday gift. Even though Camille says she'll never buy jewelry again, she won't be able to resist Margaret's grandmother's pearls I found in the suitcase. I fancy that Margaret would be pleased to know of Camille's resurgence. An important birthday, and on the eve of her show. I want to celebrate both.

Tomorrow I am allowed to go to the opening. Colin got the doctor's permission to drive into the center (closed to traffic), letting me out at the door. Inside, there's a chair for me. I am purely an invalid but thus far it's working. No further alarms. The little charmer has calmed in his/her churnings, seems to sleep when I do. Thank you! Stay put. Grow. Hang on by your nails if necessary.

I've only seen five of Camille's miniaturist works. They're nothing like anything I've ever seen. I sense that she has an instinct that they're fine but not the confidence to believe such a truth. Her paper doors look mysterious, a mystery wrapped in a mystery. They remind me of Emily Dickinson. Who could imagine that a New England spinster, hiding herself in her family home, had such piercing, abstract, and hidden motives? Where did her work come from? From girlhood. It was there all along but given no exit. No gas ever thrown on the fire! Emily was more obvious in hiding her talent (those rolled fascicles of poems in a drawer) but a right parallel to a woman from down South, decades later, pushing back her gift, canvases literally stuck in the attic. Circumstances (for sure) different but across time, a woman hiding her passion, even self-suppressing. Late one night in Capri, Camille told me about her one fling in a New York loft that messed up her head. Her strict parents always told her to color within the lines, stay close to home, take no risk. (Venture / gain nothing.) The family motto seems to have been *You'll be sorry*. She grew up constantly being herded. Then that one crazy night and bingo. Oh, were they right! She was as pregnant as she would have been if she'd slept with dozens of men. Deeply shamed and terrified, she felt the heavy letter *A* around her neck. She wanted her life with Charles. What she never expected to do, she did. The ugly word abortion, also a big *A*. The guilt, the relief, the sickening feeling of betrayal—all seized her whole body. Charles never knew. She invited her mother to visit for two weeks. Her mother, who constantly said, *I wouldn't, don't, be careful . . .* Camille disliked the sight of her paints.

WE'RE EXCITED TO SEE THE exhibit, to see the work reflected off her face—how she sees the doors with everyone else looking at them. No matter what the work, some will stare blankly. At least no one will say their children could have done better. But this *is* Italy, with a long and wide cultural life, where the worker who finished ninth grade hums *Aïda* while he unblocks the toilet. The *liceo* students catch references to Persian miniatures and renaissance sculpture, and many others simply will respond to the intricacy and beauty hanging before them.

I wish I were at their table tonight. But I'm happily home, too, still grateful that nothing terrible happened. I relish time with my pillows, my books scattered around, and the delicious prospect of Colin bringing home news of the happy evening in their *limonaia* and, best, a promised tray from Julia. He wanted to go but wanted to stay at home, too. His stone room, now completed, draws him to his design table, where the exciting Florida project starts to take shape.

The firm has been hired by the City of Key West to create a sunset-watching pavilion with a café and bookstore on one side and a restaurant on the other, truly the best project ever for Colin. I told him about the song all Italians know, *"Una Rotonda sul Mare,"* inspired by the round dance pavilion built in the Adriatic town of Senigallia. Hearing the song and having a glimpse at the round white building in the shallow waves makes you long to have been a heartbroken Italian teenager dancing there under the moon. Colin is romantic enough to fall for such crooning now and then, and he's inspired by the architecture. (No way Key West can build in the waves.) Now he plays the song as he works. We know this project means we spend a lot of time in Florida, as soon as ground breaks.

Colin's late. Maybe I can't wait up for the delectable tasting plate. I read a few Neruda odes to artichokes, socks, potatoes, his exalted ordinary things. He gets away with lines like *I want to do with you what spring does with the cherry trees.* He always puts me in a soporific state. I let the book fall to the floor.

The Opening of Paper Doors

MATILDE SURPRISED CAMILLE. SHE HAD not said she was inviting artists from all over Tuscany, gallery owners from Florence, critics, and restoration colleagues. Camille thought she was "bringing a few friends." From my chair, I watch waves of chic, artistic people arrive, streaming in among the local crowd. The whole of San Rocco is here, spilling out into the street. Party time. Chris circulating with the wine bottles, Julia with plates of delectable bites. Everyone circles the room, leaning in to examine the paper doors, gesturing to companions, and talking with animation. Camille stands off to the side with Rowan and Charlie. She looks quite wild-eyed, gazing around the room as though something is expected of her but she doesn't know what. That son of hers, grinning and beaming, is super-looking. My age, give or take. I wonder if any of those young fashionista artists behind him could turn his head. (My impression is that he puts up with a wife hard to please.)

Matilde walks arm in arm with a man in an American suit. He's nodding. She's talking. The gallery heats up. Someone opens

the front windows. Susan passes more prosecco. Julia and Annetta bring out platters for the table and like a sailboat coming
hard about, the weight of the room shifts toward the food. Gilda
and Nicolà sit with me—thrilled for Camille, too. A small gallery in a small town, but the energy vibrates. Camille—her red
shoes! She owns this show. Head up, hair clipped back, classic,
like Grace Kelly. And a fitted white dress with cleavage. Seventy
looking good! I'd like to stand up and cheer. Margaret's long loop
of pearls looks stunning on her.

Colin becomes the court photographer. He arranges groups
with their arms around each other, individual shots, and close-ups
of the work. Camille smiles as widely as she possibly can. I wonder if anyone has told her yet that Sandro Chia is here. I know she
admires his work. Matilde brings him over and introduces me.
"Camille will be thrilled that you've come."

"My honor," he replies. "This is quite extraordinary what's
going on here. Signora Raine, I also admire your poetry." (Surely
Matilde prompted him.) He's pulled away by a Florentine artist I
recognize. He looks as though he should instead model for Dolce
& Gabbana.

I throw my arms around Matilde. "I love you for this—you've
worked a miracle for Camille. She's floating on a big cloud! What
a thrill for all of us."

"Good things are going to start happening to Camille very
soon. There are two critics here. And . . ." Julia holds out a platter to them and Matilde doesn't finish her sentence.

"Fantastic. You're getting a star in your crown, my friend."
Colin takes a picture of us, Matilde looking like a pre-Raphaelite
goddess, me looking like a large biscuit.

Everyone stays and stays. Still Julia rolls out the platters of
artichoke fritters, crostini, skewers of prosciutto and melon. Everyone eats, but the Italians peer suspiciously at the cheese straws
and biscuits. Charlie loads his plate with them and urges Rowan

to try a taste. As the room finally starts to thin out, I take Colin's arm and stroll around, taking in each paper door. "Let's buy one. Where's the price sheet? We could hang it in your new studio."

Colin crosses to the guest book and comes back. "No price sheet. Just a notice by the book that says to contact Matilde after the opening. What's that all about?"

"This is all new to Camille. I wonder if she doesn't want to let go of them yet. Which would you choose if you could choose?" We stop in front of the one I saw the Florentine man in the tight suit eyeing earlier.

We both love this—a series of four waxing moons, beginning with the slightest crescent. They're the thin blue-white of mother's milk on a sapphire background. The stacked papers invite the hand. I'd like to take this off the wall and hold it. The shafts of minute writing appear to run backward, and intricate geometric designs in slate and white run around the border. "The floor of some church," Colin says. "Not sure which one. Maybe on the island of Murano?"

"No idea, but there's something arresting about all of these. They send your mind in many directions, not just one. I'm remembering Galileo's drawing of moons."

Camille comes over and hugs us. "What I can't believe even more than this show is these." She holds up the pearls. "How could you give these to me? That and all this . . . Can you imagine? I cannot believe this is happening to me."

"Oh, believe it—you deserve this." Colin gives her two big kisses.

"We're overwhelmed. Really, Camille, this is astounding work. Is it possible to buy this one?" I ask.

"Absolutely not, I'm giving it to you when the show ends."

"No, you can't start giving away your paintings. You're a pro now. You're supposed to be saying, *Show me the money!*"

"You're coming to dinner? Stefano is saving us a table. I think Julia has ordered another birthday cake, when I'd really like to let this slide by without notice. With this many people in town, I'm glad we reserved."

"Oh, I can't go. I'm only out on a brief pass. Colin's going to take me home now. You all have a fabulous evening."

They did.

NICOLÀ'S DAUGHTER, HOME FROM SCHOOL in England for spring holidays, agreed to gallery-sit for the week. She has a stack of books and plans to catch up on reading assignments between hellos to visitors. Since she can't start until Monday, Camille and Charlie spend Sunday together in the gallery, a treat. Camille cannot remember having this much time with him. She turns on the lights while he walks across the piazza to bring back cappuccino and pastries.

"I get to have the place to myself," he says, walking slowly from one painting to the next. "What's damned amazing is how you stepped out. You've absorbed all the art here and let it soak into your brain. What's on these pages is traceable to your days here but combined in ways that are totally you."

"Thanks, and it feels that way but working alone you never know if what you do is good or rubbish. You *think*, but some nasty critical voice is always carping, always asking, *Who do you think you are?*"

"No, no, no. Forget that. You are soooo way beyond your parents—that's the voice you internalized—didn't they always put the lid on any risk? Don't try this, you'll regret that, you have teaching to fall back on, your husband needs you, on and on."

"They were afraid for me . . ." She's remembering how intimidated she was in New York and what that got her. The stupid night in the oh-so-cool loft.

"Let them roll around in their graves! You're rocking it, Mom. You know it."

Charlie now teaches part time at the university. Instead of

the class taking away from his painting, as he always assumed, he feels stimulated by the studio workshops, and more motivated with bright students around who talk, breathe, and sleep art. He tells Camille that he's also much happier with Lara, maybe not as focused on her dissatisfactions, and there are fewer of those anyway now that they're living in Camille's house. "What a luxury space is; the three of us were too tight in our house, neighbors breathing down our necks when we lit up the barbecue. Ingrid loves Spit Creek. She and her friends splash around, catch turtles, act like the kids they still are. Sometimes she goes down to Dad's cyclamen patch and reads on his bench. Dad, by the way"—his voice slows—"would be completely blown away by this show."

Camille nods, silent for a moment, then says, "The sad thing is, if he were still with us, there would be no show. I've been spinning my own web here."

"Yeah, you're right. This comes out of Italy. Italy brought it to you."

"Not to say I wouldn't prefer that things had just gone on as they were . . ." She trails off, suddenly, disloyally, wondering if that is true. "But maybe we would have found a way to shake up the norm." A big question. No answer.

"What about Rowan? I like him."

"Yes, he's thoughtful, solid. You'll adore his work. He's quite well known in the esoteric fine print world. Julia, Susan, and I were just talking about this late kind of love, or affair, or whatever it is. We decided that carpe diem should reign. I think I'll just go where I feel guided. No one's in any rush."

He can't think what to reply and says the rather expected. "You—they, too—deserve every bit of happiness that's out there." For Charlie, the idea of sex at seventy is disorienting, but he has a hunch it's happening. This late blossoming—explosion, more like it—a miracle for his mom, also loosens something tight in him. All his life she's poured her passion for art into him, and at some level he felt guilty that she deprived herself. No more. Since his visit at Christmas, he's had four solid months of progress. Always an abstract painter, he's turned for the first time to landscapes. Working en plein air has been unexpectedly easy. He's begun to wonder if ease means something.

The American man at the opening with Matilde comes in the door. "Open?" he asks.

"Yes, please come in. We'll try to be quiet. We're having a big catch-up visit."

"I'm Steven Blassman, a friend of Matilde. I wanted another look. The event was so crowded that I probably missed something. Compliments on the work. Really, most intriguing."

Camille and Charlie speak in low voices. Tomorrow he must leave. He's giving himself three days in Rome but then flies back to North Carolina on Thursday. "Who is this dude?" Charlie whispers.

"Probably someone here to take Matilde's paper class."

WHEN THEY CLOSE FOR LUNCH, Charlie goes back to the villa for a chance to collect himself from jet lag before he gets it again. Camille reopens the gallery and welcomes four women who're traveling and painting in Tuscany for a month. She's seen a couple of the women in the piazza with sketchbooks, one with an easel set up overlooking the olive groves sloping to the valley. She tells them that she's done this work since she arrived in October. They're beginning watercolorists, all remarking on how focusing on a painting sharpens your perception of what you see. They sit down and swap stories, admitting awe at the "stringent oddness," as one puts it, of Camille's vision.

Some local people who didn't make it for the opening stop by for a look. At four, Camille closes.

• • •

CHRIS DEPARTS TOMORROW, TOO; HE'S picking up his group at the Venice airport, starting out on the new Friuli tour that's practically back-to-back with his Tuscany trip. Tonight, Susan has reserved a table at a trattoria out in the valley. He hopes Julia will stay over with him at the hotel. He's hardly seen her after the evening he arrived, what, only two days ago. Since he already has the van, he picks up everyone. "Are you on the bus or off the bus?" he asks as they pile in, but no one seems to remember the Merry Pranksters except Rowan. Guess the South bypassed hippiedom.

When the trattoria owner greets them, Camille says, "He looks like Bacchus in the Caravaggio painting."

"He does!" Charlie asks if they can all have a photo together.

"Why not?" Enrico says, black ringlets tossed back. He kisses Susan, seats them, and begins describing his farming methods, the antique recipes, the lost grains resuscitated, the pure wheat, on and on. Susan and Julia are rapt. The rest think they're in for Food Science 101, but when he begins serving they fall into hushed awe. Crunchy fried artichokes light as angels' wings, the most delicate gnocchi on earth, the succulent, tender baby pig, his own strawberry gelato that makes you want to get up and dance.

"How did you all find this place?" Chris wonders. He thought he knew the area inside out.

Julia wishes she'd found it but admits, "Susan discovered it on one of her garden ornament expeditions. That's why she's getting the large serving of artichokes."

"Let's not tell anyone ever! Keep it to ourselves."

Enrico pulls up a chair at the corner of the table. Here comes another lecture on biodynamic wine. Like his grandfather years ago, he buries ox blood at the top of each furrow in his vineyard. Chris knows about the methods but never has met a grower. Julia sees him make a few notes because the wine is rich and full of life. Susan translates when the practices begin to sound like a witch's incantations. A stag's bladder stuffed with yarrow, ground quartz in a cow's horn, crushed valerian. When did Susan's Italian become fluid? She has to look up *quartz, yarrow, valerian*, but otherwise, she's on it. Enrico agrees when Chris observes, "It's all composting, basically." Over coffee, Susan and Enrico discuss seed banks and how he rotates crops.

Everyone's charmed. Charlie loves Enrico's homemade *digestivo*. A recipe similar to limoncello but made of fennel. Hand-gathered last August, of course. "Okay, not a doubt. I'm on overload. This place keeps expanding." Charlie polishes off the last bite of his gelato.

"No," Julia counters, "just another surprising everyday feast in the Tuscan countryside."

"I have plenty to ponder on the flight home. I can't believe I wanted my mother to move to Cornwallis Meadows."

VI

Full Term

THE PIAZZA ZINGS WITH ENERGY. Tourists are back. Sun's out, moving across the graceful ellipse where the Romans used to raise hell with their races. In three places, you can see grooves from the rims of carts' wheels rasping into stone. As at a bullring, you choose sun or shadow, only there's no fight, only waiters with trays aloft delivering cappuccino after cappuccino to the yellow-skirted tables, and visitors with their faces turned toward bright warmth. Colin says, "This is my idea of *paradiso*. After you die, you're installed at a summer table on a sun-drenched piazza in Italy, with only the day of freedom ahead. That's if you've been very, very good." When I ask myself why so many come to Italy to find a larger version of themselves, I wonder. Is it Italy, or is this where you come when you're about to bloom?

I'm free. Now close to full term, I can park myself at my favorite spot this morning and take in the day. Colin dropped me at the gate and with a great feeling of freedom, I slowly walked (waddled) to the piazza, joining first Susan and Nicolà, who's holding forth about the three friends buying Villa Assunta. "The price is right; you cannot imagine the opportunity you have. San Rocco now soars every three months. If the villa were over in Cortona or Pienza, the cost would be at least thirty percent more. This area, much less crowded, is gaining on those hot spots. Believe me, in five years—easy—you could double your investment."

"We probably could swing it. Anything divided by three seems a lot more feasible." Susan does the addition in her head. "I sold my beach house. Even after giving my girls a chunk, I've got profit. Plus assets from the company I sold. I'm not ready to sell my home. None of us can just spontaneously plop down a *sacco di soldi*, but, you know, we're *old*, we've been financially smart, we've worked, and I don't see why we can't fork over whatever it takes, if we decide to. Exactly how much do you think the villa should sell for?"

"I'll do some research. My initial feeling is that the price is low as it is. Grazia has consulted no one but her aunt, who hasn't sold anything since 1970."

I'm with Nicolà. I took my inheritance, risked it. All three of them have slaved away always; they're not pampered and entitled, though as Margaret would say, that doesn't exist either; trophy women pay through the whatsit and know their devil's bargains full well.

Go for it. I was at a much younger age. (Maybe blessedly naïve.) Much later I got the prizes and money from Margaret. Lucky, lucky. I didn't have to wait for husbands to die.

Nicolà needs to go, but Camille and the four visiting women painters she met at her show join Susan and me for a second cup. I am enjoying the pleasure of simple visiting; these resting weeks of involved writing and solitude have turned me inward. Even my little smiley face seems quiet this morning. Camille has invited the painters out to the villa for valley views, Susan's garden, details such as a white cat curled under an astrolabe, shadows of lemon trees on the grass, a window overlooking the smeary greens of the valley, front door half open, and light spilling into the hall. As they gather their supplies and head off with their satchels and easels, I notice an older man and a young woman sit down under an umbrella rather than in the sun. She's delicate and striking, the noble profile of young Virginia Woolf, but walks almost with uncertainty. The man guides her by her elbow. He looks familiar; someone who visits every year? The woman sits down and crosses her arms. Defensively? He's smiling, smiling, a stunner of a man, maybe with one of those trophy wives. No, she's pretty enough but doesn't have the aggressive quality of a young triumphant victor over the middle-aged wife. Riccardo then joins us, meeting Susan for conversation in Italian. "You're uncanny," he says to her. "You're going to knock me out of my translating job. I thought languages were supposed to be difficult after age twelve."

Brava, Susan. "True," I say. "You speak as well as or better than I do and I've been here thirteen years."

"What do y'know! I studied harder than I ever did in college. I've lived and breathed it. And I *love* speaking a new language. I feel like a new and different person. I think I'm funny in Italian. Weird how another part of your personality becomes emphasized when you learn another language."

"Maybe that part was waiting all along."

"*Dio mio*," Riccardo says, "I think I sound effeminate in English. Where does that come from?"

The morning streams along pleasantly. I'm on the alert for any twinge of pain. But no. Only a glorious day, the sun passing above the bell tower just as the deep gongs throw out massive reverberations that I hope young master now somersaulting in my body can feel in his bones.

Colin. Colin coming back with the shopping, coming toward us, toward me, toward little one, ready to take me home for a stroll through the rows of planted lettuces, basil, tomatoes, eggplant, sorrel, parsley, melons. All the promises of summer.

Cutting the Distance

JULIA SHOULDERING HER LADEN MARKET basket walks toward the piazza. 11:30. Chris due in today from the Tuscan tour. They had marvelous events in San Rocco, and even worked in a country lunch at Enrico's, a hit, and quite different from anything else they experienced. Then they were off to Montalcino and the Maremma. Julia checked and rechecked all the details. All Chris had to do was have fun and keep everyone happy. He's coming from Florence, after dropping them at the hotel. They fly out tomorrow, and it's all over until fall. He's arranged their dinner tonight at a totally overlooked trattoria on via Parione where the chef will be making filet mignon in a reduced and rich sauce of shallots and balsamic vinegar. They are going to love it. After, they take an easy stroll back to the hotel Kit and Colin love. And then Julia has Chris back.

She stops to say hello to signora Bevilacqua in the bookstore, stops at Armando's cheese shop to pick up a wedge of Sardinian pecorino. The sandals she bought in Capri rub on her right foot, and she leans to loosen the strap. As she stands up she catches sight of a man and woman at an outside table at Violetta's bar.

Her throat catches and she begins to cough. She straightens up and looks again. This sandal is irritating her instep. She runs her fingers through her hair, shakes it out, and looks again at the apparition of Wade and Lizzie drinking coffee in the piazza. She closes her eyes, looks hard, then turns down a shadowed *vicolo* of tiny shops. Her back pressed against the stone wall, she tries to will her mind to focus. Five minutes. Inhale. Exhale.

Julia, back in sunlight. Walking fast toward the piazza. Mirage, mistaken identity, Swedes on vacation, hallucination. No, Wade. Lizzie. Like anyone else. Taking in the morning. The girl, Lizzie, scoots back her chair and reaches into her bag for sunglasses. Now they see her, Wade rising, almost tipping the table. But Julia's eyes are on Lizzie looking up quizzically. Lizzie as herself. Julia rushes to her and almost falls forward as Lizzie rises, smiling, and Wade leans in to hug her, too. Julia tries, can't speak, but sits down gaping at her unrecognizable daughter. Lizzie without two layers of gray circles under her eyes, with shining, not lank and dirty hair. Lipstick. Her small teeth and winged eyebrows. Lizzie herself. "Lizzie, Lizzie, Lizzie," she says. "Am I in a dream?"

"Mama, it's good to see you. Not a dream. Not a miracle. A lot of effort. I'm doing well. Finally."

"Wade? You went?"

"We'll tell you the whole story. I thought it would be best just to show up, cut all the distance out of the picture."

"I'm stunned. Look at you both." *My loves*, she didn't say. Wade swims before her more godlike than ever, his fair hair streaked with white, his elegant, strong body more fit than ever. Something agrees with him.

"You look radiant." His smile, wider on one side than the other. "You know it, too, Hadley girl." When they were young he'd always been amused that she was known as "the Hadley girl."

Violetta comes over, a questioning look on her face. But Julia just says, "Meet Wade and Lizzie," with no explanation. She orders an espresso for herself and they want more cappuccino.

"Wow, you're speaking Italian!" Lizzie is looking at her; they're all gazing as though they've encountered each other underwater in diving gear.

"Well." Still blank. "How did this, when did you . . ." She trails off.

"We got into Rome yesterday and drove up this morning. We're staying right down the street." He points toward the Albergo Lorenzo. "We can't check in until two. We were going to ask around for Villa Assunta. I got the name from some of your lawyer's correspondence. That's all I had, no address, only San Rocco."

"Um." Julia was not going to justify her attempt to cut him off from her life. What does he expect? "Oh, Lizzie. You're here. You're here. I can't take this in."

"Hope it's not a bad shock. It's a shock to me, too. I'm trying to trust it. Where to begin?" Lizzie says. "I've been in a residential treatment house for a year. I'm sorry I didn't let you know. I just could not. I had to isolate myself from everything. I know you thought when I hit bottom, where I'm supposed to pull out of my habit or else, that I didn't. I fell right back. Even worse. Letting everyone down once again. In the hospital, the doctor thought I was sleeping but I heard him say to you that if I didn't kick it then, statistically I'd die before I was forty. That wasn't bad news to me at the time, since that's what I wanted anyway. But later, after I bailed on you in Savannah, when I got back to San Francisco and fell in with my group, I felt sick a lot. I was on some new opiate that was out on the street. I saw in the mirror that I'd developed this weird tic of fluttering my eyes. I looked crazy. I was in that nice yellow robe you gave me, all stained. My reflection was someone I hardly recognized and wouldn't want to know. In some way, that robe did it. When you brought it to the hospital, it was soft chenille, that hopeful yellow, and I knew you'd wanted something to comfort me when I took comfort from no one. I looked down at it. All nasty.

"Skipping a bit. Enter a social worker. She came to the house and told us about a new city program we could apply for. Out of pure boredom, maybe out of not recognizing myself anymore, I applied. At the time, I wasn't planning on quitting. Maybe finding a nicer place to stay, taking better care of myself. My fingernails were always bleeding. Everything wrecked. I still wanted to get high, only it didn't feel high at all anymore. And hadn't in a long time."

Violetta sets down the coffees, eyebrows raised quizzically. Obviously, something intense is happening. She brings, too, a plate of biscotti.

"First thing, hard and horrible thing was detox. I was rolled out of an ambulance and checked into a locked facility where I went through that once again. You well know what the process is. This time I just endured it and walked through the sessions. Maybe something was at work but I was strung out for so long that I think my synapses were all numb. Long story short, I walked out of that shithole, as I have before, exhausted mentally, with no clear thought that the detox would take. I was put in a taxi and sent straight to this new place for rehab.

"So then I find myself in a program with twenty other druggies—all women—at a huge Victorian in the Haight. Four to a room. Selma Hodges, in charge. She has her own theories. We made fun, laughed at her. Everyone had to work in the house. It was immaculate. White curtains in every room, starched. Quilts made by 'the girls.' We had kitchen shifts and had to learn to cook. We had eggs at breakfast. Cereal. No caffeine. She had us making soups and stews, muffins. Twenty mentally stunted women buttering muffins." She laughs and shakes her head. Julia feels breathless. Lizzie uttering something amusing!

"She required us to choose an activity and to spend three hours a day working on it. The basement was set up as a weaving and sewing room, a potting studio in the rear, a computer room upstairs. I chose potting. And I loved it. We had to commit to one online course. I signed up for, don't laugh, international relations. I guess something way outside my little realm was appealing. We had to volunteer at Golden Gate Park one morning a week, weeding and picking up trash like prisoners. Later we worked in nursing home kitchens, school lunchrooms, in libraries shelving books, and then graduated to part-time jobs. Mine was making hot fudge sundaes at the chocolate factory on the wharf. I never want another bite of chocolate in my life. But, Mom, I'm good at pottery. Bowls anyway. My plates are wonky and the cups' handles always break. But I'm selling a few small bowls at Selma's friends' shop."

"How about a rock of a cookie instead?" Wade passes the plate of almond biscotti. They are tooth-cracking hard.

Lizzie continues. "At night, we had the usual sessions. I've always looked down on those as dumb-ass and reductive. Drama queens starring in their pitiful plays. My name is so-and-so and I'm a royal screw-up and you're a royal screw-up but in a different screwy way. Selma Hodges, though, had a touch. Maybe she was hokey but she probed, she listened, and she has a sense of humor, something I hadn't experienced with any of the many fuckers who tried to save me from myself by telling me to make lists of my goals. She also has a shit detector and sometimes just cut people off with a *Rethink that* remark. I can't explain everything. Against all odds, I started to feel comfortable. The old saw, *One day at a time*. But months have passed. This is condensed. Upshot—I have been off drugs for eleven months and I have every intention of remaining clean, clean, clean."

Julia, guarded, feels that guard start dissolving. Almost a year. A long time. Lizzie—articulate, if foul-mouthed. Looking normal. Dear and remembered. The sweet curve of her jaw, sweet oval face, sweet smile. The girl who used to decorate her sand castle with shells and wanted to find fairies under mushrooms. She's clear and present, the ironic smirk gone.

Wade reaches over and puts his hand over Julia's. "I know

you're hit with a stun gun; I was dumbfounded. I went to the house where your friend Chris went and Lizzie's friend maintained that Lizzie was 'lost in space.' A damaged guy with a tattooed face knew where she was because a girlfriend of his checked into the same place and dropped out after a month. Said it was too artsy-craftsy for her. Too politically correct. Too-too."

"That's Sandy. He doesn't look like a Sandy anymore but he must have been one a long time ago." Lizzie pushes up her sunglasses, now that the shadow has reached their table, and Julia gets to see her eyes, the same pond green as Wade's.

"Anyway, let's move on to lunch and we can finish the saga. There's too much to say. I just didn't want to call and drop this on you. Wasn't sure you'd believe me. Where can we go?" Wade tosses money on the table, more than enough, a habit Julia used to admire.

Julia stepped to the edge of the piazza and left Susan a message. "You will not believe this. I'll tell you everything later. Sit down if you're standing. I'm with Wade and Lizzie. In the piazza. Shock. Lizzie is totally okay. It's like someone stood up out of the grave. We're going to lunch. Lunch! Just letting you know. Lunch. Like ordinary people." She texted Chris: *Call you later.* Her throat felt parched. She drained the bottle of water in her bag. Lunch. Crazy.

She chose Angelo's trattoria, where she's only been a few times. If she went to her usual Stefano's, she'd have to introduce everyone and she's not ready to do that yet, though she knows all of San Rocco soon will be talking about the appearance of the ex-husband and the daughter no one has heard of before.

Angelo, the owner, confusing her with Camille, congratulates her on the art show. They're seated in the courtyard under a white umbrella. The pallid light beneath makes them all look spectral. Lizzie looks directly at Julia. "I haven't given you a moment to tell me what you are doing here. I don't even know quite how you *got* to Tuscany or who your friends are." Lizzie takes the menu and regards it with interest. Julia hasn't seen her eat a bite in years, and this is the first time in memory that Lizzie has expressed a particle of interest in her. An ugly aspect of addiction: *me, me, me.* Angelo plops down a carafe of wine, not ordered but welcome. Lizzie asks for water.

"Your dad probably has told you that I left Savannah. When I was house-sitting for my professor in Chapel Hill, I met two women. We had such rapport—fun, really—and we had some common issues. We'd all lost our husbands. Not that mine was dead! Sorry, Wade. We cooked together, spent a lot of time walking on the beach. It was exhilarating to make great friends. We brought out the visionary in each other. Over the summer, we got a wild idea and here we are." How much does Lizzie know about Wade's escapades and his forthcoming daddy status? Skip for now. Well, no. Not at this stage. "Things at home were complicated by your father's romance with another woman." *He fucked up everything*, she didn't say, but bit the inside of her jaw and tasted blood.

Glad the waiter speaks no English.

Wade looks up, seemingly unperturbed. "She knows about Rose. We don't need to get that far right now."

Julia feels a sweep of anger—who is he to decide?—but she takes a sip of wine. "Okay. *Va bene.* Onward," she says, just a slight edge to her voice. "You all come out to the house for dinner, see the villa. Susan has made the garden a showplace. Camille has her art studio. We have the most beautiful kitchen with marble tables and a huge sink and copper pots everywhere. I'm taking my Mulberry experience to another level. I'm trying, no, I am actually writing a book called *Learning Italian.* I'm combining my study of the language with Italian cooking, real Italian cooking. I took a course where we each had a pig to dress and cook." Open-mouthed, Wade looks at her.

"That's fabulous, Mom. You're loving it, I can tell. In a funny way, it sounds like Hopesprings House. That's where I am."

They share a laugh. The first one in a dozen years. "Cool

name. I hope it does! I am happy every day here. We're traveling
a lot. The other thing is, I also have a job. Helping plan wine and
culture tours for a California vineyard owner, Chris Burns. He's
just finishing our second tour of the year. I do research and handle
details and help plan. Love it! And Chris and I have become close
over the past few months." Let it all out.

Lizzie nods, scarfing up the pasta and reaching for bread.
Whether she knows how destructive her addiction has been for
her parents, Julia has no idea. What a wake of flotsam and jetsam
she left behind.

"Back to you, Lizzie. What I'm doing is not as monumental as
your big changes."

They're eating. As a family. Watching this good Lizzie-twin,
Julia is barely able to swallow. Had she totally given up? She thinks
she had. The story of the yellow robe undoes her; cry later.

Angelo brings over platters of grilled meats and potatoes.
"What do they do to make such simple food so good?" Wade asks,
stabbing a second sausage. His dazzling smile, as though nothing
ever went wrong. She's not immune to his beauty, even as he bites
into a hunk of sausage. Pretty herself, she's always privately ac-
knowledged his prerogative. He wears it lightly, almost unaware,
but the first time she saw him she thought of a line from a poem
she just studied in school. *He walks in beauty like the night.* The poet
said *she*, but the line applied. How many everyday mornings has
he walked into the kitchen, tousled from sleep, and in the middle
of frying pancakes, she's caught her breath. He didn't fight for me,
she thinks. He took the course of least resistance, like lightning.
But here *she* is, Lizzie, my girl.

"It's the water and the sun." She smiles. "Be right back." In the
bathroom, she turns on the water full blast and cries. Not for the
last time.

If they notice her flush and red nose, they don't say. "You can
check in now. Why don't I come back in a couple of hours and
pick you up. Walk down that street"—she points—"and I'll meet

you at the gate at four. We can take a walk and talk more, then I'll make dinner." She gathers up her packages and rushes out the door; she practically runs home. The confusion she's escaped during these months of walking on air crowds her body. Lizzie: possible again. Wade: former body and soul love, now impossible. She feels as if she's about to go under anesthesia.

At home, she lies down in the grass under the pear tree and falls deeply asleep.

Somewhere, Someone

SIXTH SENSE? WHEN I SAW the extraordinarily handsome man—though *handsome* doesn't seem quite accurate—and the pink-rose young woman in the piazza, something about them caught me. They stood out from the general flow of tourists. Maybe an electrical energy emanated. The next day, Susan stopped by and filled me in on the identity of the prodigals Julia greeted in the piazza. I connected the dots quickly. He was the Narcissus, she a nymph surfacing from a deep pool. I didn't get to meet them. Julia invited us for dessert last night but we came home from my visit to Dr. Caprini (everything fine) too late.

As a writer, I wonder about his decision, deus ex machina, to surprise Julia. Easier for her? Or for him? Did he want to present himself as the glorious rescuer? Look at the wounded bird I have brought to your doorstep? It's more understandable from Lizzie's point of view. Just *Here I am, take me back* instead of a phone call or letter.

Now they've gone. Julia must feel like something washed up on shore. Liz, as she now prefers, goes back to the Hopesprings

House for an indefinite time, Wade back to his new life. Liz mentioned eventually moving home to Savannah and trying to enroll in ceramics at the art school there. As Julia took them to the train, Wade pulled her aside at the station door and apologized, mouth against her ear, saying what a serious fool he had been, but that he'd put himself into a situation he now had to honor. *You know you carry my love always.* That, to me, is a knee-weakening line, but Julia told him the important thing was Lizzie, and that she, too, was way down the line from any reconciliation. They hugged, and Julia hugged Lizzie long and hard. Lizzie wept.

Susan, Camille, and I were shedding a few tears for all of them. And for Chris, who had to be headed off from the drama. He decided to dine at Hotel Santa Caterina with Camille, Susan, and Rowan, all exiled from the villa.

At the station, Lizzie unzipped her bag and pulled out a tissue-wrapped gift for Julia. A bowl, sky blue with concentric ridges and a few flecks of malachite to catch the light. Something to hold. On the marble kitchen table at the villa, as it glows under the light, they all regard it with awe.

ACCORDING TO DR. CAPRINI, DILATION will begin soon. The baby's room is ready. I am ready. Colin is set to take off two weeks. Meanwhile, he works in his new barn space on designs for the sunset-viewing pavilion for Key West. May it inspire poets, moon-viewing poets as well as those worshipping the sunset. Sometimes a single building can transform a place; I think this will be one, and in a good way. Colin and I disagree; I think the Louvre glass pyramid desecrates the severe and historical aspect of the Louvre, especially now that it has the atmosphere of a nice subway station. And what they've done with the British Museum—I won't go there again. The Key West district where the pavilion will be situated is funky. It is what it is. What Colin builds has to win over hearts and minds. I've never seen him as enchanted with a project.

I'm thinking of Julia and send her that message. She replies: *The reprieve feels as though broken bones all over my body have mended but I can't yet walk because they don't know how. See you soon.* I mull over that and read Akhmatova all afternoon, some poems aloud in case Leaf/Della might hear.

COLIN AND I GO OUT for pizza. He works way too late out in his new studio. With Fitzy on my feet, I finish rereading Margaret's last, luminous novel. I read and aspire.

AFTER THE LASSITUDE OF MY bed rest, I'm charged. I feel like a bolt of lightning trapped in a jar. I'm riding waves of energy, followed by dips when I want to sleep. But the surges inspire me to invite the three women, Chris, and Rowan for a simple supper, and Matilde, too, since she told me in the piazza that she has news for Camille and would love to surprise her. It's Susan's birthday, the big sixty-five. Colin will throw some steaks and vegetables on the grill, and I'll make a salad. I have pecorino Leo brought me from the mountains. Rowan offered to pick up gelato in town. Julia dropped off a pan of gingerbread, saying she was feeling nostalgic and wanted to bake something from her mother's recipe box. She looks wild. Her hair's gone frizzy; she's blank-eyed and startled. At least she's coming. I'm setting the table outside now, in case I lapse later in the day. I walk the land, gathering an armful of wildflowers to poke into a copper water pitcher.

Everyone knows to bring sweaters or shawls; these early summer evenings turn chilly around nine. I'm planning to serve dessert in the kitchen.

Matilde arrives dressed simply in teal tight pants and a retro-patterned fitted T-shirt. Her red-bronze hair seems ornament enough, flying out in tiny waves around her face like some Annunciation angel's. Matilde is someone Margaret would have loved.

They share the taste for lush fabrics and romantic embroidered blouses and vests and platinum velvet skirts and fringy scarves and earrings that jangle. (Margaret also had a severe black-suit, clenched-jaw style as well. Matilde works in a lab coat.) Matilde, too, is decidedly single, claiming to have no time for anyone who must be accommodated. Matilde, ugly name in English, but here it resonates from the Tuscan queen of that name.

"Oh, but you are huge!" she greets me. "You're looking quite ready for the big event."

"Past ready. I've even got the crib made up."

"This is for the nursery wall."

She hands me a gift, a framed manuscript page with painted bees and tiny wildflowers in the margin. I'm overwhelmed. "It's astonishing. What a lucky baby. But how can you part with this?"

"I think we should expose new ones right away to art, don't you? I've looked at it for years, now new eyes can try to focus on it. See, the monks got bored with the lettering—those figures are really doodles in the margins."

The others arrive: Susan bringing a stuffed elephant (looks like me?); Camille in her red shoes again, even though this dinner couldn't be more casual; Rowan, holding a shoebox. "I didn't want to be upstaged by the baby. I've been busy over the winter." He takes out a copy of *Somewhere, Someone*, the poems I gave him over Christmas, now bound into a chapbook. The title comes from a line in a John Ashbery poem, "Somewhere, someone is traveling furiously toward you." I wrote the clutch of short poems in the first shock of pregnancy. The binding made of swirly blue marbleized paper must have taken him weeks to make. The hand-pasted-on label runs sideways, with the two large title *S*s looking scored like music. Classic and careful.

"Colin," I call, "you will not believe this." I feel a hard jab of elbow or foot scrape across my stomach. "Feel that, Rowan. He/she approves. What a joy. I love the typeface, everything. Those sinuous *S*s are dramatic. I hope the poems are decent."

"Oh, yes."

Camille comes over to see. "Oh, Rowan. It's as beautiful as my guest book. Let's toast." She passes the book around as Colin fills glasses. This is what it means to be happy. I can do this. (Twinge of pain.) The downside of a vivid imagination is that you always have the capacity to visualize the worst. For weeks I dwelled on the worst things that could happen. We would both die. The baby would be one of those *fetus in fetu*, the small fetus contained inside the body of another baby. Or some undeveloped baby attached to the body of a normal-sized baby. I'd wake up hollering like a haint and scaring Colin out of his wits. My doctor wondered, when I told her, if I needed counseling. I confessed to her that I always imagine the plane going down, the elevator falling, the tumor when I have a headache. I'm just wired that way. At last I feel perfectly normal; this is a normal state, not that I am an alien host, or a cocoon for a butterfly who will rip out and fly.

"*Cin-cin*, here's to a new book in the world!" Camille clinks with everyone.

"And here's to the someone who's coming furiously," Rowan says.

"To summer," Susan adds.

"To Lizzie," Julia says.

"Yes, to Lizzie."

"But not to Wade," Susan whispers to me.

Chris, frowning, smiling, keeps close to Julia, talking quietly to her. Colin takes away her prosecco and puts a full glass of sauvignon blanc from Friuli, her favorite, in her hand. Perhaps she is feeling a layer away from things, something like the image I dreamed: a shutter bangs in the room you never added on.

"How is Julia?" I ask Camille quietly.

"Getting over shock. The double whammy of Lizzie back from the dead, the two of them appearing out of nowhere in the piazza, and the finality of Wade—it's way too much. We've just been quiet at the house, playing good music. Susan planting ever more flats of double pink impatiens and white begonias. Julia has been baking, studying Italian. Chris has been around, calm and sweet. Since he's tired from the two tours, all's been low key. Rowan and I are going to the Marche for three days—Fabriano, where there's a long history of papermaking—and Susan will be on the coast with Nicolà and Brian for part of the week. She'll have a chance to absorb and regroup. I hope you don't have the baby this week!"

"Who knows?" Actually, I'm feeling strong lower-back pressure right now. "Let's sit. I think we're ready to eat. You all, sit anywhere. There's no way to go wrong with this group."

Everything's on the table at once, which is non-Tuscan, though the big Florentine steaks could be from nowhere else, and the vegetables are smoky browned. We bring out gifts for Susan—a palm tree that thrives in this climate, a hand-forged trowel, and a straw hat with style. She models it and admires the woodwork on the trowel.

Matilde, seated by Camille, takes a letter from her bag and hands it to Camille.

"What's this?"

"You'll see."

"Matilde! Who's it from?" Camille opens the envelope and reads. Conversation around the table stops. "What! This is some mistake." She reads again, looks around the table, then leans into Matilde laughing and saying over and over, "This is impossible."

"Tell us!" Rowan implores.

"Matilde, you read it. I can't."

Matilde stands up. "Friends, Romans, countrymen . . ." She's laughing, too, and waves the letter in the air. "Seriously, I'm going to read it!"

Dear Camille Trowbridge,

What a pleasure for me to attend your show in San Rocco. I am indebted to my dear friend Matilde for alerting me to your

work. *We met too briefly at the opening, and in the gallery the
following Monday, when I had a chance to have a second look, which
confirmed my first impression of the unique vision exhibited in "Paper
Doors" and the original use of materials for the expansion of the
paintings' reach.*

*Let me congratulate you on a fine and auspicious entry into the
public phase of your career. I am writing to invite you to participate
in an exhibition . . .*

Applause and whistles break out around the table—Rowan
raises his thumbs *yes*, and Susan with glass raised leaps around the
table in a whooping, bizarre war dance.

"Okay, okay, listen up!" Matilde continues:

*. . . an exhibition titled Six New Artists: Vision/Revision at MASS
MoCA, where I am a curator. The exhibit will take place next year from
1 June until 1 August, and then will travel to the Walker Art Center
and the High Museum in Atlanta. (Details to follow.) We would be
delighted to include you in this important exhibit of newly discovered
artists. Please let me know via email if you will consent to be a part of
an exhibit that promises to contribute significantly to the appreciation
of the art of this moment. When I have your decision, I will link you to
further information about the exhibit and the participants.*

I look forward to hearing from you.

My very best,
Steven L. Blassman

Julia hugs Chris, then Camille. Her shock forgotten, she's
herself again. "This is *al di là*—beyond the beyond. Not that you
don't totally deserve this, Camille. But that it truly is *happening*,
when it easily could not, if this friend of Matilde's hadn't trusted
her word and made the journey. Here's to him. A prince!"

"Here's to luck!" Camille toasts. She's dazed, her mouth open.

"No, you make your own luck," Rowan says.

Hard thunder shakes the table as rain begins. We grab our glasses and dash inside. Everyone's crazy about the gingerbread. It's out of context here but a memory-lane treat we all remember. And it goes nicely with tangy lemon sorbet. Really, in my life, I've never known a group of more simpatico people. A balm to me, having lost my parents early, having lost my mentor, Margaret. Colin and I, private and obsessed with our work, never have had such a close family of friends. That October afternoon when I saw them tumbling out of Gianni's van in their bright jackets, I couldn't have dreamed their lives could enhance ours so abundantly. There's not a word in English or Italian for those in our lives who are between friends and family.

CLEARING UP LATE AND QUITE exhausted, I drop a glass on the floor, water spreading on the bricks. But, wait, there wasn't that much water in the glass. I grip the sink. Unless I somehow have wet my pants, water is running down my legs. For a long moment, I'm dumbfounded. "Colin," I shout, "Colin, my water has broken! What time is it? Can we call the doctor this late? Oh, look, it's midnight." The base of my spine catches in a tightening vise. "Back labor, I've read about it. Is the baby backward?" Am I shrieking?

He leads me to a chair. "Everything's fine. Are you sure? Yes, we're calling the clinic, but do you feel contractions now? Sit, sit. Wait. Everything's fine." His hand is shaking like a palsy victim's.

A CALM NURSE ASKS ME about pain. I describe my lower backbones that are about to shatter. "Take a warm shower. Walk around slowly, then try to sleep and if you wake up with contractions, monitor them. Since you've been on bed rest, we want you here when your pains are twelve minutes apart. We'll get your room ready. If you don't have contractions by morning, we'll want you to come in and see Dr. Caprini."

So normal and soothing. This is what happens. It's *not* a sign of preeclampsia or anything dire that the water broke before labor started. I follow the instructions and manage to feel comfortable propped on pillows. Colin sits on the side of the bed with his face in his hands. I hope he's not going to be one of those fathers who faint in the delivery room. Still dressed, he rolls in behind me and says, "I won't let anything happen. Sleep, sleep."

"You know, I'm excited. Scared of the labor. But this baby is embarking!"

"The first of many voyages. This may be our last night of just us."

"Oh, please don't get any ideas!"

"Don't worry. I don't even see how that would be possible unless we were contortionists."

I WANT TO LIE AWAKE in the dark. Colin's breathing slows and he seems to sink into the covers as he always does, no matter what. He has a talent for sleeping that I don't. Girl or boy? I'm glad we don't know; we've loved imagining each. Annetta says it's a boy because I've carried it high. Violetta says it's a girl because I've carried it high. I'm missing my parents. Margaret, too. They never envisioned this, especially my dad, who left us abruptly when the semi, brakes gone, driver drunk, rammed him from behind. The car sailing into the water. I've always wondered what that long flight must have felt like to my daddy, what image he saw, what thought he had, as he crashed into the waves. I've hoped he saw us as he had when he drove off, Mother and me on the front porch, sipping our usual blackberry lemonade and innocently waving good-bye.

Hours seeping by, a few fleeting stabs of pain; is it mainly exhaustion from all the work of throwing a dinner for only eight?

My carry-on stands by the bedroom door, ready to go. Finally, I bought baby clothes and friends have brought over many little outfits and onesies—solids, dots, stripes, all white, yellow, red. No gender-identifying pink or blue. When I was born, my mother stayed in the hospital for a week. She always maintained that the days gave her energy for the tough days ahead when she had an infant and no help at all. I'll be home before Colin even can get the kitchen back in order. (That is if I don't have preeclampsia, C-section, or if . . . Stop that.) The clinic is forty minutes away. In an emergency, I could go to San Rocco's, where happy babies are born underwater in a warm pool. Because of my age, I chose the specialist route but I'm game for the water birth.

MORNING. I WALK AROUND THE house, send my neighbors news that I'm going in today. Susan walks over immediately and starts cleaning up. I'm useless. Just drinking tea. She's had strange news. Her daughters had DNA tests in anticipation of looking for their birth parents. The results show that they are sisters.

"We adopted them from the same orphanage, two years apart. They told us nothing. Maybe they didn't know. They must have! After two years, they contacted *us*. Another girl was up for adoption. At the time, we flattered ourselves that we'd seemed like outstanding parents."

"Well, you were. It's good news for them, but I guess it kind of points to the parents as making a habit of this." Susan takes a tray out to the pergola and brings in greasy plates of bones. I try to imagine handing over a baby to an orphanage, the desperation of that. Margaret losing her brand-new Colin. Or Camille lying down to erase that new beginning. "Sit down, have some tea with me. You don't need to do that. How lucky your two girls were, to have you and Aaron."

"Don't worry," Susan said, opening the already full dishwasher. "I've got excess energy this morning. I wish they were here to talk about it. Face to face is not at all the same as Face-Time. Yes, I suppose they were lucky but not as lucky as we were. What joys they were, and still are. Sisters! Yes, amazing. I wonder if I should go with them to China."

"Up to you, of course, but I'd think that might make the search more awkward for them because their loyalty to you would keep coming up."

"Kit, you're right, and I was thinking I'd make it easier. And, frankly, the trips there were nightmares. I'm not raring to go back. Now how are you feeling?"

"Some intermittent cramping, not any hard pain."

"Call if there's anything. Anything at all." Susan gives me a hug just as Colin walks in half awake. Fortunately, he's heard voices and stepped into running shorts.

He stands behind me with his hands spread on my grand belly. "Come out, come out, whoever you are," he chants. Susan takes off into her day.

A Parabola of Light

AT THE CLINIC, DR. CAPRINI listened and looked and questioned. "You are dilated but only about three centimeters. Why don't you go have a light lunch somewhere and come back around two? Or sooner, if necessary. Leave your things in your room because you're definitely staying here tonight." My room is small but airy, with gauzy saffron curtains billowing at the open window. Most thoughtfully, a daybed for Colin, not a recliner. Fashion magazines on the coffee table must remind the new mother to get back quickly to *la bella figura*. I wanted to crawl in immediately, but Dr. Caprini insisted that it's good to keep moving.

THE FIRST BODY-SHOCKING PAIN STRUCK as we drove back to the hospital after lunch. In the parking lot, another hit hard. Really? Like this? I bent over at the door of the clinic and heard a growl come out of my mouth. What happened to the gradually increasing contractions I was expecting? Colin called out and someone with a wheelchair pushed it under me and rushed down the corridor. Contractions five minutes apart. "You're not wasting time, *Signora*," the nurse said, simultaneously helping me into a gown and hoisting me onto the bed.

FIVE HOURS OF THIS AND I wanted to die. Some prehistoric beast was mauling my body. This cannot happen to a human, this thing that is ordinary and happens and happens. Then, I'm infuriated—the pain clenched, contractions hammering constantly. Thunderous avalanche, skis akimbo. Speedboat smacking down hard in high waves. Worse.

An old story, the oldest story (Eve yanked out). I will skip to the hours-later ending, when I am wheeled into the whitest room, where silence reverberated and masked people peered down at me, the one whose body is riven. They urged me on. (Wrung-out washcloth over the sink. Wrung and wrung.) Colin kneeling at my side, white as the doctor's coat but steady. Holding my arm, whispering—what? I couldn't tell for the din of pain.

The noise level increased. Everyone bustling. Dr. Caprini smiling over me like a lurid clown in a convex mirror. "Crowning," I heard, and thought of a tiara I wore with my pink tutu and ballet shoes, my mother clapping in the front row. "You were wonderful," she says at the moment the baby pushed out like a pea from a shooter, was lifted, bloody cord dangling, a little face, fists, a parabola of light blazing in my face, I was crying, laughing, Colin stony, shocked, Dr. Caprini saying, *You have a lovely boy* as he wailed (I will hear that first cry my whole life) and she placed him on my chest and I'm to push again and, as something else slid out, I hallucinated a jellyfish, I looked into the deep-space eyes of my son.

In my room, I got to see him, clean and swaddled and, miracle, looking around at the new digs. I think he focused on Susan's red and purple anemones by the bed. We undressed him to see his fierce small body, took turns holding him, analyzing his scrunched face, downy black hair, and pursed mouth. Lips, defined lips and ears, all the whorls. What I recognized and I recognized clearly was that he has my father's upside-down V eyebrows, the shape children draw of birds in the sky over the iconic square house with the sun shining overhead.

"He's our boy," Colin says. He put his finger on the eensy hand and the baby squeezed as though saying, *I'm with you*. At that instant, I think Colin's face underwent a permanent transformation.

ON JUNE 20, THAT'S HOW life swung from its trajectory and headed toward a different star. We could not have been happier. (They say the pain fades but I goddamn know it won't. I was cleaved, an ax in a melon.) The next day, as we drove home, I was hyperaware of the menace of cars and I began to understand my mother always saying, *If you have a child you are a hostage to fate*. My new worry, my glorious new worry. Colin keeps grinning. He is such a Mozart lover that we almost decided on Amadeus. I flirted with Fulvio. We named him Lauro Raine Davidson.

Garden of Earthly Delights

SUSAN STEPS OUT OF THE shower and opens the window to let out steam. Even the bathroom has a view of a medieval tower placed to anchor your gaze across the valley. Farther in the distance, a shining green dome, and a scattering of farmhouses that look as though they've been there for all eternity. In full-on summer, Susan expected to miss her family beach house on Figure Eight. This time last year, she spent weekends at Sand Castle with Julia and Camille at the start of their friendship. She remembers poignantly the weekend Julia told her story of Lizzie and Wade. Opposite of that, she remembers happily the dinners, the walks on the beach, buying shoes and ice cream in downtown Wilmington, Camille's watercolor of water and sky. In memory, Aaron in his debilitated state fades more and more, leaving in the forefront the confident, sexy hunk she lived beside for decades. She has missed nothing this summer, except her daughters, and she's used to missing them. The days roll out one after another full, hot, crowded with joys large and small. She's out early. Coffee in one hand, she wanders around the garden, deadheading roses, pulling up stray weeds, pausing to admire the astrolabe. She scoops leaves out of

the amphora she has fitted with a burble of running water spilling onto a pebble surround. She stoops to pick a handful of gauria
and white sage for her bedside. Archie follows her. The three cats
piled on a chair look on with regal indifference.

Could I leave this? she wonders. Would I want to? Would
Grazia extend our lease? She scans the hedge of blue hydrangeas
along the shaded wall, and the sunny splotches of color falling
away from the house and down the slope. She wonders, now that
we have improved the villa and the garden drastically, will Grazia
try to turn that to her advantage? The recession, when properties
lingered for three years on the market, is over. Nicolà describes
San Rocco as "hot." What are Julia and Camille thinking? Our
situations are different, since they have Chris and Rowan in their
lives. Those are newish relationships—would they commit to extending our time at the villa? We've had glorious times but how
long can this go on? We get along well. Because we're different
but, luckily, complement each other. Would Julia pack up and go
to California? Live a two-country life with Chris and the tours?
Sounds fun. Their trips can expand in endless directions. I'm almost sure Camille would not go live in Berkeley. Not even sure
Rowan wants to stay there after his mother passes on. Camille
is thriving here and is more of an inner person than Julia. Just
as I can see Julia in a California vineyard, I can imagine Camille
happily alone. But now Julia possibly has Lizzie returning to the
nest in Savannah. Would she be pulled back, living in her parents'
house with Lizzie? Wade across town crowing in a new barnyard.
That's mean. He's lost Julia, and however he justifies, at midnight
he's got to know that's the mistake of his life. Summer is rushing on. We need to make decisions soon. *Flessibile.* Flexible, that's
what we've learned. How better it is to be *flessibile.*

Everyone's back from their jaunts. Susan adores her investigative trips, this last one on the Argentario coast. Nicolà and Brian
came and also invited Riccardo and the Irish expats Brendan and

Sally. Sun and seafood, card games, and sweet nights on the terrace just getting to know each other. Hot days, swimming off the rocks in cold pellucid water, returning to the airy house for drawn-out lunches of caprese, cheeses, tomato tart from the village, prosciutto and melon, white wine. Naps and books. They rearranged the furniture, bought table linens, spruced up the desolate pots on the terrace, and threw out stacks of damp magazines. The place looked revived when they left. She discovered that Riccardo likes to dance. She loved his Italian playlists. Was it too much vino or did he nuzzle her neck when they slow-danced to Prince?

Next week, Nicolà has arranged another free four-day mid-week trip to Cinque Terre for all. After that, Susan wants time at home to work more on the downslope area of the garden and on her blog that is starting to get great feedback from landscape designers she admires. Her links to Artful Dodge Antiques work, too.

Cinque Terre will be Kit's first trip with Lauro, though she's out and about in San Rocco. She bemoans her doughy belly, but she looks completely like herself again. The last month of her pregnancy she ballooned alarmingly. We thought she would float into the heavens if we cut a tether.

"We're ready," Julia calls. "Kit's at the top of the road." We all walk into town together in the mornings and as soon as we enter the gate, people come running out of their shops to admire the baby, no matter they've done the same routine yesterday. We've taken to forming a phalanx around the stroller so he won't be frightened by faces zooming in at him. But this is also what we relish about Italy, yes? The compliments flow; he's adored; his attributes are lauded. Everyone loves the name Lauro, laurel, though it's an old name not often chosen anymore. Alessandro, Matteo, and Lorenzo currently reign in town, with an occasional Luca and Marco, and one recent Ettore (Hector).

We are loving the early mornings in the sunlit piazza. Lauro faces us. We pull up the hood to keep him from staring into the sun. Violetta brings us tall glasses of fresh orange juice, a tray of pastries, and long coffees. Sometimes Chris and Rowan join us. Colin, never. After two weeks of little sleep, he's had to return to London for four days a week. His firm greenlighted his Key West project. Susan heard disturbing talk from Kit of them leaving for several months.

Lauro rivets everyone's attention, his every squeak or squirm. That little darling. He laughed. He swung his head to the side and a pure giggle came out of his mouth. Isn't it good to witness the first laugh of someone only in the world for three weeks? Isn't it amazing that someone just recently arrived seems totally present and essential?

Camille sips her juice, sketching, and reveling in the sunlight. Scudding clouds travel fast overhead, casting us in and out of shadow. She keeps glancing at Palazzo Monferrato's Gothic arch around the inset door with a fanlight that looks like half a compass. Her sketch superimposes an imagined completion of the compass over the stalwart wood doors below. She's homing in on the two giant lion-head knockers, drawing them enlarged on the checkered marble portal. She's fracturing, architecturally extending, and making some elements outsized. All this Susan sees in glances over her shoulder.

Since the invitation to the American museums, Camille is spurred into even more intense action. On the morning walk to town, she's relaxed and leisurely, but the minute she's home, she throws together a sandwich, picks up one of the cats for company, and disappears to the *limonaia* until Rowan appears late in the afternoon. He's working with Matilde on oversized papers for a one-copy book by an American poet and a Cuban artist. He's obsessed, as a major collection—he won't say which museum—already has expressed interest in acquiring it. Camille, in her new glory, teases him by saying she'll put in a word for him at the High

Museum. She thinks they'll all travel to see his new one, wherever it ends up on display.

"Which did you like best?" Susan asks Julia. "Fall, winter, spring, or summer?"

Both Camille and Julia reply together, "Summer."

Susan agrees. "There's never in my life been a string of more divine long, long days. Every day lasts a week."

Italic Hours

I CAN'T NAME A SEASON I like best. I like all of them best. But this, Lauro's first summer, I'll remember as a blissful time I'd like to bottle and put away for harder days sure to come. (Fatalist!) Memorable, lying on a quilt, writing under the pear tree with Lauro on his back finding out he can kick and wave. Fitzy liked to flick his fluffy tail over Lauro's face, causing pure giggles, which I videoed, but mostly Fitzy preferred sitting on what I was trying to write. Memorable, Julia's blackberry crisps with deep summer tastes, all the platters we served forth of fried sage leaves, crisp zucchini and squash blossoms; garish Popsicle-colored sunset walks with the sun wobbling down slowly, then quickly swallowed by the horizon; Leo's melons, their musky-rose perfume wafting through their kitchen. (Cantaloupe: song of the wolf. Probably named for a place name near Rome.)

Memorable—seeing my friends' astonishment over the brilliant fields of sunflowers splotching the landscape, each flower six feet tall with a round, brown face surrounded by golden spikes. They stand shoulder to shoulder, these crowded pilgrims wanting to march to the sun. That they swivel with the solar arc baffles me. (Though I do the same.) I can't help but anthropomorphize the flowers; they look like sentient beings, especially when they droop before harvest, heads bowed down, shamed to be denied the immortality of the sun gods. Memorable—warm nights with black-flame shapes of cypress trees against the sky, and the Milky Way streaming over the house like a molten river of diamonds. (Diamondiferous sky. Not a good word for a poem, as it sounds exaggerated. But who can exaggerate the beauty of Tuscany?) In Florida, I never saw the Milky Way, diamondiferous gift to us on earth.

Memorable, the dramatic summer rains I love when the cypresses bend and bend in the wind, and I watch from my study, hoping once to see the tip of one touch the earth and spring back. I saw Lauro's first fear during a morning thunderstorm. The crack hit loudly; he stiffened and his eyes widened. He discernably frowned. Did he feel vibrations throughout his body? I fancy that he looked for us. The lightning did strike the modem and we had to get a new one. These violent storms clear the air, letting the next day dawn sweet and transparent, with a favonian breeze and cottony clouds drifting high. One morning the sky appeared to be lined with glass. Colin and I were out in a field with Leo as he trained his new falcon. The bird, fierce and scary, soared up and up, wheeling against the blue as though it could fly forever up until it shattered that blue dome and slivers of glass would fall like rain. The reward for returning was a live quail for the falcon to dismember and devour. Colin and I had the same thought at the same moment. The falcon on Leo's arm, Lauro in a sling around Colin's neck. "Leo, it won't . . ."

"No, *cara*," he assured me, but I grabbed Colin's arm and pulled him to the road.

Sometimes the land seems magnetically powerful. I try to write about its pull, its felicitous effect on the body, even to risk metaphors that can lead to personification, that most irritating and egotistical gesture in writing. (But see my sunflower description above!) The sky never smiles. The rain is not weeping. Better to find the more imaginative figurative image, like D. H. Lawrence's: *As we have candles to light the darkness of night, so the cypresses are candles to keep the darkness aflame in the full sunshine.* Reading that changes cypresses forever.

Iconic, the curvy white roads, fields of poppies and sunflowers, cypress trees, stone walls. All touch me but I'm not going near. Not my bailiwick. I am working on a falcon poem.

I am wrapping up my monograph on Margaret, too. The father of her Colin has written to me again. He is coming to Italy next year and asked if we could meet. He wants to hear about Margaret's life. I wrote back, saying yes, if I'm here, though he will go away disappointed. Margaret remains a cipher.

Before she left for the last time, she seemed to prefer Colin to me. (Now I know that she got to say his name, and to imagine her boy in Colin's shoulders, hands, mouth, voice.) She planned a couple of months' stay in Washington for meetings, to get her yearly checkups—she had a tingling cough she couldn't shake—and to research a new novel she had formed in her head without yet writing a word. (Or so I thought. The manuscript in the suitcase turns out to contain a near-perfect one-hundred-page novella.)

After a month in Washington, she wrote that she'd been diagnosed with cancer and she was *not going to put up with it* if the initial treatments didn't work. Esophagus. Nasty one. She said when she would begin radiation. Without telling her I flew home and turned up on her doorstep the first morning of the treatment. She was awed and weepy. Was sure no one ever had made such a gesture for her. She seemed fine with the treatments. I stayed until it was a routine, then came back home. Later, surgery, a brutal treatment that involved swallowing platinum, and the news that she would no longer be able to eat solid food. She was full of gallows humor. *I look like a gargoyle*, she wrote. *Don't come. My hair is a moth-eaten fright wig and I'm not up to seeing anyone.* A caretaker made food for her in a processor. *At least it's not Gerber's.* After a few weeks, the humor stopped. *Shouldn't happen to a dog.*

Then another round of chemo. *I can't talk. When you can't talk, can't eat, what's left, and don't tell me I always can write.*

I'm coming to see you next week, I wrote. *I'll do the talking for once!* I bought my ticket, guilty, guilty that I'd not insisted and gone sooner. She wrote back, *Don't come. I don't want you to see me like this. I don't. I mean it. I don't want you to come. Stay with your pretty boy.*

"What should I do?" I asked Colin.

"Sounds like she means it. *Stay with your pretty boy.* Man, she can still dig, can't she?"

As we know, he who hesitates . . . I canceled.

A WEEK LATER SHE SLIT first a wrist then her throat in the bathtub. On the bathroom door, she'd taped an envelope for the cleaning woman she expected the next day. *Do not open the door,* she instructed. *Call 911. My apologies.* Also inside the envelope, she left five thousand dollars. (Strangest tip I ever heard of.) I'm haunted by the final gestures: her hand on the faucet, turning on the bathwater, as though preparing for a nice soak, placing the knife and straight razor in the soap holder, stepping in. Too hot? Then, painful to contemplate, what thoughts ran through her as she leaned back in the tub. That moment. I will not ever move off that moment. Margaret. Her iridescent brilliance. Gleam on the knife blade. Cut the cancer. Margaret, always on point.

THEN THE REALITY OF MARGARET gone. Off the planet. Left no other note. I'm sure she thought her reasoning was obvious. And I began to have to live with my failure as her friend. I could have . . . I should have . . . The recriminations never stop.

Her lawyer/executor informed me that Margaret wanted

cremation and no funeral but she'd asked if her ashes could be scattered in my olive grove and in the Tiber she overlooked during her Rome years. Yes, of course.

A week after her suicide, a postcard arrived. Addressed to me. *Think of me on a long voyage where I am gathering information for my finest book. Kit, you are a rare friend.* Ci vediamo dopo, *Margaret.*

Ci vediamo dopo, see you later. Kind of slangy for a final farewell. Tacked above my desk, the photo on the postcard I see every day is of Vesuvius shooting out fire and lava. Last rite, last gasp, last straw, last words.

MY FIRE-AND-LAVA FRIEND. HER CHILD. Lizzie. Charlie. My child. The insouciant Chinese daughters searching out the birth mother. The miscarried and aborted embryos of Susan's and Camille's, never to be. I've been writing all along this year about *quest,* about questions of arrival and departure, about creative explosions in later life—my tapestry of abundant life and friendship. Now at the end I see I have been writing about the force unleashed on your life when you become a mother. (I'm at the beginning.) This from a Robyn Schiff poem I came across today: . . . *the most powerful jaw in the world is the one that sucks.*

True, mothers. (Did my mother know this?) Learning about Margaret's Colin, hearing the sagas of my three friends, I stepped into a new awareness I never had in the era of the tipped uterus.

Margaret, my friend. (How sweetly Susan's white roses weave themselves among the gnarly wisteria vines.) What do you have to do with Susan, Julia, Camille? With me, at this juncture?

I gave them your novels. They were fascinated, excited, moved by them. Camille wears your pearls. My freedom to write I owe to you. (You made sure I couldn't thank you.) I'm your doppelgänger (root: double-goer. I like that. I go now for you). Both of us self-exiled from a young age. After four excruciating years of my mother failing to thrive, I arrived here poised for change. As you once said of yourself, *I entered Italy like a bride in her dress enters the church.* You were the friend of sharp retort, the one who still flirted with waiters, and sat alone in the piazza at one a.m. smoking cigars. You wrote till all hours, then went out walking in the dawn to calm down. I remember a night at Vassaliki's when I came in late and you were dancing alone with your long scarf. Everyone watching. Our Scheherazade. If not for you, would I have had the gumption to say to a stranger, "Do you have time for a drink?" As you continue to goad me onward, I in turn do the same to Julia, Susan, and Camille. The friend you were to me, I became to them. Spirals of friendship. What else do I have to offer? I can write your names, the colors of your eyes, your slips of the tongue, your jokes, the moons of your nails, your leaps into bright water. I write in ink.

A FEW WEEKS AFTER MARGARET'S suicide, I was stunned when her lawyer informed me that she left me the proceeds from Casa Gelsomino, her future royalties (if any), and a stash of stocks and investments, some of which she inherited from her father. Everything else and her papers she left to Georgetown.

The least I can do is write the damn book on her work. At least I can forgive the irrational stab at my reading in Washington when she piped up about the Italians not liking for foreigners to write about them. *My Italy and you can't have it!* I'm petty to have kept smarting from that.

She could be petty, too. She could be magnanimous. She could be crude (*the worst side effect is the butt-stinging diarrhea*). She could be sublime, as in her fiction. She was a friend like no other friend. What a grand piece of luck to have met her. Memorable, Margaret. Especially in this most idyllic summer of my life, polar opposite of her unimaginable exit from this world.

. . .

WHAT I AM WAITING TO reveal to my friends is the now-set news. We are leaving for ten months. At least. This is the great opportunity Colin has craved. Not a renovation, not a hotel or service building like a hospital wing, or even a lecture hall at a university. The pavilion is a game changer for Key West. A career changer for an architect. The chance for the city to erect something symbolic of the place, a lasting monument for residents and visitors. *Monumental* is not the adjective architects often hear from clients. Colin grasps all the implications.

After some juggling, his firm has offered to lease my parents' house, allowing us to live there while the project is under way and for other architects working in the Miami office to live there later. Back to my home. Lauro in my childhood room. Me set up in my father's study. The circadian rhythms of Florida nights and days taking us over. But the bottom line: we'll be back before the pavilion is playing music on a spring night, people gathering in late afternoon to count down the minutes until sunset.

Before we leave, my project with my friends will end. Will they leave? How do they go forward? What does this year suggest about the next?

My own question now has an answer. I'm leaving. I'm coming back.

Assumption

"DOES ALL OF ITALY GO on vacation in August?" Julia sets down a basket of plums. She leans on a kitchen chair at Annetta and Leo's. At the sink, Annetta runs long bloody tubes under the faucet. Julia is not sure at all that she'll include this in her *Learning Italian*.

"If you didn't get the kitchen painted or the drain unclogged or the tile ordered, don't bother to try now." Annetta throws the blubbery tubes into a pail of cold water. "The person you need is at the beach."

"Or even just at home throwing parties but definitely not answering messages," Leo adds. "You reach the peak on the fifteenth of August. That's Ferragosto, Italy's biggest holiday."

Julia knows that's when the Blessed Virgin Mary was scooped up into the sky. San Rocco prepares for days for a community feast in the piazza. Three hundred seated for dinner, and no, not with paper plates and plastic cutlery—white plates, real knives and forks. "What is this? I thought you were preparing goose."

"Of course, goose," Annetta tells her. "The goose we eat in

the summer." Her sister rinses the pail, spreads the tubes on a towel on the kitchen table, and begins plucking out pinfeathers on the goose carcasses.

Julia looks puzzled until Annetta's sister, Flavia, motions to her throat. "Oh! You're going to stuff the necks." She doesn't remember the word for neck and uses *gola*, throat, instead of *collo*. She's remembering a disturbing video of someone force-feeding a goose. At least these are dead. "What do you put inside?"

"Oh, anything, meat, sausage, potatoes, whatever you want. We're using the livers, *odori*, pecorino, eggs, bread crumbs, garlic. You tie the top, put in the stuffing, and tie the bottom. I poach it for a while. You've never had this?" She looks at Julia incredulously. No stuffed goose neck? You poor thing.

"After, they go in the *forno* outside. Leo already has the fire ready. They will be sliced and much appreciated."

Okay, Julia thinks. Always something new but old under the sun.

"There are thirty of us making these for tonight. Maybe next year you will. The penne will be served with goose ragù and next the roasted goose with potatoes. Everyone is supposed to bring a salad or vegetable. For dessert, the summer tradition, wedges of watermelon."

Julia already has prepared platters of roasted eggplant, tomatoes, zucchini, and peppers. Next year, she wonders, will the three of us pluck those pinfeathers? Where will we be on Ferragosto in a year?

At four this afternoon, Gianni will deliver Hugh from the Rome airport. Since the flight from Istanbul is quick, Julia thinks a brief rest is all he'll need before being introduced to San Rocco's intense summer social life. He wrote that he will be looking for a perch for a while. Terrorist bombings in Turkey don't deter him, but his broken (he finally admitted) ankle does.

• • •

SAN ROCCO'S SAGRA DELL'OCA, FESTA of the Goose, not only represents the culmination of summer, the celebration is the major community gathering of the year. The *sagra* marks the end of Tuscans' favorite season. As Nicolà explains to Susan, "It's when we best come together. The *contessa* will be dancing with the garbage collector, the postman with the *marchesa*, boys will be asking their classmates to dance for the first time. The communist councilman dances with the far-right doctor. It begins with prosecco and dancing in the piazza, proceeds to feasting together, with wandering accordion players, pauses for speeches everyone ignores, segues into more dancing—this time uninhibited—and ends with fireworks." Chris bought tickets yesterday since this is always a sell-out event. The endless table for three hundred stretches half the length of the piazza. Along the edge, long serving tables are set up, and grills for sausages and some fish for those tourists who inexplicably don't eat meat. Susan reserves places with their names. Already, midmorning, it's not easy to find adjacent seats but she does, noticing that several friends are nearby. She knows Julia is excited; everyone else is privately thinking *that's a lot of goose.*

LAURO IS GOING. HE SHOULD, shouldn't he, be exposed to the intense love of community we all feel on such a night. I hope I never miss the *sagra* in my lifetime.

We gather at Villa Assunta for preprandial antipasti. Susan's late summer garden: the allée of lemon and orange trees laden with fruit, sinuous borders of white begonias interspersed erratically by dwarf dahlias, hedge of hydrangeas mostly blue though a few reverted to white, great swaths of lavender, santolina, and rosemary along paths, and swaying artemesia gone rogue along with bolting phlox. I love her harsh pink gauria softened by purple-haze catmint. We luxuriate here. "I'm working on transition spots"—

she points down the spur of land—"where the garden gives over to views." Already she's convinced Grazia to plant six cypresses, slender as ten-year-old ballerinas, that step off into the distance, guiding the eye.

Walking with a cane and a limp, Hugh emerges after his rest and meets everyone. "This garden is Eden after Istanbul, which I adore but it's seriously chaotic. This place slows my heartbeat just to look at it." He's thin as a twig but carries well the privileged academic elegance—loose linen shirt and white pants, gray suede espadrilles (ankle still bruised and swollen), his white hair slicked back like a '30s movie star. Colin says to Rowan, "Just let me look like that when I'm in my mideighties."

Chris arranges a tasting of white wines in the *limonaia*. He has wrapped each bottle in a dish towel and we're to guess the grape and the maker.

"Good luck," Camille says. "This one tastes like how chalk smells, and, oh, like rosewater. And green—herbal."

"Great!" Chris says. "What's the grape?"

"Malvasia, made by that vineyard in Friuli, what, Istriana."

Chris is astonished. "Raccaro Malvasia Istriana. That's the hardest one."

"I remember it with that berry tart."

The next one puzzles everyone but Julia, who guesses right away her house wine, sauvignon from Livio Felluga. "Damn," Susan says, taking another sip. "We all should have known that down to the moment of bottling. How many bottles have I lugged to recycling bins?"

Chris's hopes soar but after that, everyone misses everything but the pinot grigio. He reveals the bottles, then everyone just drinks and strolls around the garden.

After almost a year of none at all, even white wine tastes strong to me. A few sips. Colin and I agreed it's time to tell everyone our plans. Julia brings out what we've craved all summer, the fried zucchini flowers and onion rings. We gather around the table. Colin begins. "Here's a toast to welcome Hugh." Everyone raises their glasses. "And another to thank you all for making this summer incredible for us."

That glass sky is about to crack. This one moment will shift the action, set change in motion. I take Colin's sleeve. "Wait, wait, wait."

"Kit, we need to say it."

"I know but I don't want to."

"Remember the pavilion. It's not forever. We want this. They'll be fine."

"Okay. Let me." I notice that Susan is looking at me with a wary expression. "You all! Bombshell to drop! We have news. You know that Colin has a fantastic chance . . ." I talk about his ethereal design and the timetable for it. "I think it will be seminal for Key West. By now, you already know where I'm headed. We have to go. We'll be leaving in a few weeks for maybe as long as a year . . ." From his sling around Colin's neck, Lauro lets out a piercing scream. Everyone laughs.

"Lauro, that's what we all want to do," Julia cries. "When?"

"You will miss the olive harvest?" Susan asks.

"What about your house?" Camille wants to know.

"What about Fitzy?"

"Hell, what about us?"

"Do you have to?"

"Where will you live?"

"Will you really come back?"

We're answering as fast as we can.

"We'll live in my parents' house."

"Colin will fly down to the site. It's quick."

"Fitzy will go, too."

I hold up both hands. "Stop, you three! What about you? We'll be back. Will you still be here?" The three women look at each other, at us, at the sky.

Irrationally, Camille says, "We have three cats."

Hugh puts his arm around Julia. "Have I entered a moment of crisis?"

"No, we, we need to talk, but not now. We have to get to the dinner. Can you dance with that ankle?"

Rowan says, "Another toast? Here's to Kit and Colin. We're coming down to Key West to cut the ribbon and watch that sun go down. Till then, we'll miss you. Good luck!" Rowan has made a decision, too. He's rented his apartment for six months, though he'll have to go back to California for November to care for his mother while his sister is away. He and Camille are happy with the current status. No more sex on the creaky sofa; they've graduated to a *matrimoniale*, queen size.

WHY IS IT THAT ITALIAN men can dance? None of that reluctance and slow stepping regardless of the music. Since they know what they're doing, you follow easily. Chris and Rowan seem indecisive, moving their feet around whereas the Italian men dance from the waist up. Their shoulders move, the hand sits firm on the partner's back, guiding. The band from the valley plays the traditional music from wheat threshings, weddings, and baptisms. Strings of lights crisscrossing the piazza flicker, then stay on as summer dusk falls and surrounding shops glow, each one candle-lit, as are the windows in the *palazzi*. Down the table from us, I wave to the expat group and Guido, Amalia, Luca, Gilda.

Eugenio, *carabinieri* chief, holds out his hand to me. He dances, greatest of ease, as though he's spent his life in ballroom class. Colin is happy to wait with Lauro and watch me twirling around the piazza with Riccardo, Leo, Gianni, Stefano. I'm who I used to be, a girl who partied hard. Julia, Camille, Susan, too. All dancing. Camille, those red shoes, held by Leo. Susan in an orange fitted sundress and Julia wearing something pink and drifty. The man with Down's balters about with his mother. Chris, arms waving over his head, raves on. Riccardo is good! He's sweeping Susan all over the piazza and they're laughing. Hugh, at our space at the table, seems to be holding forth to three Italian women. Is he speaking to them in Latin? What an intriguing man. Julia says he wants to stay. I wonder if he'd like to live at our house? It's always good to have someone at home to keep Gypsies from invading and leaving you three cats.

Everyone serves themselves antipasti and pasta. What you brought, you put on the tables. After that, volunteer women serve the goose and potatoes because who wants to get up twice or three times? The menu is the same every year. I always love the stuffed necks but best of all, the potatoes crisp-roasted from goose fat. Even during dinner, the dancing continues, as it will until three in the morning. Blissed-out Lauro snoozes away in his stroller at the end of the table.

Hugh waves a big goose leg. "This is incredibly good!" He passes around the roasted onions and peppers Julia enlivened with pinches of Aleppo pepper and slivers of Leo's hot pepper from his garden. "Darling, these are a stroke of genius with the goose."

When the band pauses to eat, Lucio Dalla blares from a loud-speaker, making anyone with a shred of romance in their souls want to get up and dance under the moon, making anyone who has lips want to press them close to the ear of someone they love. Many around the table join in singing along, especially "Caruso" and "*Tu non mi basti mai*," and at the end of every song all the older local guys stand up and raise their glasses, shouting *Grande Lucio*. He hits the emotional notes, operatic at times, but you can hear the peasant harvest music in his voice, the music your mother played on the radio while she rolled out pasta, and the beach music from your youth. When "Caruso" starts a second time, it's a duet with Pavarotti. Chaos erupts; everyone standing and swaying and sing-ing. I see tears in Chris's eyes. Big romancer! Rowan pulls Camille into the piazza and proves he *can* dance if motivated.

The music, yes, the songs many heard when they first fell in love, yes, but the long table crossing the piazza means more.

Here's where we come together, putting aside trouble, gossip, and difference, to this grand living room for all of us who live in this small place that could fit in the cupped hand of the Madonna who on this day did or did not ascend into the sky. Fireworks begin, to honor her big whoosh up into the heavens—armfuls of lights cascading down, dandelion puffs of gold, Venetian chandeliers purple and green, silver rockets spewing, pops and bangs over the valley, children running with sparklers. With or without words, we all feel every past *sagra*, and we also feel a future when we are no longer here, a century hence, two centuries, knowing some track of falling light tonight recorded that *we were together, you and I were here in this place under this sky.*

The younger band starts up, sending the young out to dance without touching, to gyrate and nod and send up hand signals. We gather at the watermelon table and the gelato shop that makes only for tonight a special olive oil ice cream. Everyone to greet! Grazia embraces us. Looks like she has a date, bald guy with hooded eyes and Halloween wax lips. She looks happy, flashing her fluorescent smile. Kids kick soccer balls against the wall of the church. Candles extinguish in the windows, and some have closed the shutters as the bells strike midnight. Chris reverts to Fresno disco dances with Violetta and Annetta. I overhear snatches of Julia and Hugh deep in conversation about Turkish food. Eugenio's wife, pregnant again, sits stonily as he wows everyone he dances with. For some, the night is young. For us, time to go home.

Let us come back, I say to the billowing skirts of the Madonna as she disappears into the sky.

Leap Before You Look

THE FACT OF CINQUE TERRE is the sea. Marled swirls of clear turquoise to blue waters. Camille prefers Corniglia over the other Cinque Terre towns. Wedged above the sea, the village looks from a distance like an opened pan of watercolor paints, blotchy rectangles of aqua, copper, pink, rose gold, pomegranate, cream, stacked upside hills of grapevines.

Yesterday, Susan drove Nicolà's Land Rover, the Fiat way too small with me, Lauro, and all the baby paraphernalia. Hugh stayed at the villa. We dropped the car at the station and hauled all the stuff onto the local train that plies the villages. What a fiasco juggling the portable bed, the stroller, the bags, et cetera, et cetera. And Lauro can wail. Everyone packed lightly, as there is nothing to do at the five lands other than hike, walk, swim, eat. Of course Susan's here to check on Nicolà and Brian's future rental, an independent white house with wraparound views. The rest of us tag along. Julia's birthday, #60, is on Friday, so we're lugging gifts for her as well. From the train, getting to the house, we had to climb hundreds of steps dragging everything. We were panting at the door. Inside, instant balm. Susan opened all the glass doors, letting in the sea air and views of blue, blue, and more blue. Nicolà's cleaning woman stocked the fridge with basics. Soon we're on the terrace with an icy pitcher of a blood orange drink that came in a Tetra Pak but tastes delicious. Susan holds up Lauro for his first view of the sea. Camille breaks into "Eddystone Light," a camp song everyone knew but me. By the time I went to camp we were singing "Stayin' Alive." What provoked "Eddystone" was a verse about the father falling in love with a mermaid. Looking at these limpid waters and gnarly rocks, you believe they slither up to comb their tresses.

BECAUSE I'VE BEEN HERE BEFORE (and Lauro gets heavy), I want to forgo hiking and to take this time to write. Although there are level stretches, inevitably you meet steep inclines, stairs, and unfortunately at this time of year, crowds. Too many people. We're crazy to be here at the end of August. Thank you, Nicolà and Brian—a quiet house away from the fray.

CAMILLE AND SUSAN TREK OUT early. When Camille decides to find a local café and read, Susan heads on toward Vernazza. Rowan's new project with the poet gave Camille the idea of making paintings inspired by Italian writers. I told her that Eugenio Montale had a house in Monterosso. She wants to spend a couple of hours reading his poems about Cinque Terre. Is she going to find only sea views and flowers? Well, maybe that would be fun to try—spontaneous sketches in red chalk or ink. Meanwhile, she has an almond pastry and cappuccino, the book open, her gaze drawn out to sea.

She thinks of October, when the lease expires on Villa Assunta. She imagines packing her clothes, dismantling her studio and *limonaia* workroom, saying good-bye around San Rocco, the puzzled looks from Violetta and Stefano, Leo and Annetta throwing a final dinner, a farewell lunch with Matilde. Home to Carolina. Oh, let Charlie stay in the big house. He has workspace there, his uptight wife is happier, and Ingrid has space to breathe when things are tense, which Camille suspects might be often. Ingrid is studying Latin. Camille can take her on tours of Rome in the summers. One of those end units at Cornwallis, with corner views and a porch with a swing, now that we've had our fun. Charlie and family coming for the chef's Sunday brunch. Rowan? He'll come to see her. They'll meet in Istanbul or San Francisco or, where? Copenhagen. She has not seen Scandinavia.

She tries to focus on the poems. They're elusive. Reading them feels like socking a pillow. Who's in them? There are no people, only nuances of some "you" who begins to seem like the poet himself. Camille sighs and comes up short. *Now that we've had our fun?* She hears herself thinking that. *Our fun?* I've been asked to exhibit by important museums, and I call that *my fun?* Must I always pull back into some I-don't-deserve corner? She bites her thumb knuckle. I deserve to give up my house and move to a corner unit on the—what did they laugh about—the luxury cruise down the River Styx? I am *stupido!*

The waiter smacks down the check. Is she taking the table for too long? She stares up at him angrily, orders another coffee, and stuffs the Montale book in her bag. She remembers sensuous Keats from "Ode to a Nightingale," *oh for a beaker full of the warm south.* The longing. A big swallow of time and place and heat. That's what today feels like, end-of-August sun bearing down on one of the most enchanting places on the globe. Multitudes, many on their phones, oblivious, surging down the streets and paths. No wonder Montale floated above them, she thinks, and focused his attention on cicadas and tamarisk trees and sunflowers.

FLUSHED AND SWEATY, SUSAN DOUBLES back to the café and orders a large beer. "Great place to hike, great! But we're not the first to think of coming here. The trails are crowded; it's like a forced march. We have to come back in April or November." She takes wipes from her fanny pack and swabs off her face and neck. "Let's get back to the house."

They're charged with picking up ingredients for dinner. "Tonight will be fun for Julia," Camille says, gathering her bags, "with a basket of what's just caught from the fishmonger. Maybe he'll have some of those razor clams."

"Where is Julia?"

"I think she was going to the beach in Monterosso. She's still reeling, you know."

"Yes. She's better. Everything that *was* suddenly turned upside down and shook out. And it's real. Did you see the photos Liz just sent of the three gray vases she made?"

"There's talent. I'd love to have a few for the villa. Ah! Wonder if I could commission a couple. Not gray. A sage green looks pretty with any flower."

"They should have grocery delivery by drone here." They're hoisting two bags each.

"Wouldn't that just work—the skies as crowded as the streets."

JULIA TAKES THE TRAIN TO the beach at Monterosso. She finds a spot for her towel. A couple of women who would be in cover-ups at home lounge in their two-piece suits on plastic chairs next to her. One on her phone, the other knitting. Julia sits down and rubs sunblock on her nose. The knitting woman asks where she's from and they chat for a few minutes. They are two widows from Viterbo. When Julia decides to swim, she asks them to keep an eye on her phone and bag.

From all the bodies sprawled on beach chairs and the sand, she is afraid the sea will be warm, but no. The water feels luxurious and fresh. She swims out beyond children and the ones cooling up to their waists. Only cold salt water can instantly infuse such a great rush of energy. She's a natural in the water, having grown up with summers on Tybee, a sailboat, and camp swim teams. She remembers the pride of receiving the Junior Life Saving badge from the Red Cross, a medallion her mother sewed on her swimsuit. She flips and surfaces like a seal. To somersault, backstroke, kick, to bind yourself tightly to yourself and roll on top of the water—this is a joy we were born for. Fresh and deep, the water limpid, unlike the turbulent blue-gray Atlantic she loves, with the wild surf and the hard-sucking undertow she was warned against, it seems, on the day she was born. She practices the sidestroke, her mother's preferred way to swim, remembering summers with her parents, Cleve always up for racing into the waves, letting the cresting foam smack them down over and over, taking off his suit underwater and rinsing out the sand, bouncing her on his shoulders, running up a beach white as flour, Julia wrapped in a big towel, shivering. Treading, Julia sees tall rocks rise abruptly to the left. A boy poised at the top leaps, plunging into the water that must be forty or fifty feet below. She wades into shore and shades her eyes. Another boy stands on top looking down, his two friends urging him to jump. He's shaking his head, backing up. How high *is* that cliff? Julia walks over to the path up. A girl of about sixteen in an ounce of fabric scrambles up just ahead of her. "Are you going to jump?" Julia asks.

"Yes. It looks so fun. Are you?"

"No. I'm just going up to see what it's like." This would never ever be allowed in the U.S., Julia thinks. But here, people make their own fates.

Julia scrapes her knee on the rocks, looks down. Already dizzying. At the top, four kids are standing around working up their courage. One says, "You have to leap way out."

From above, the water is dazzlingly blue. If you jump and you're not lucky, you could bust your head like a watermelon falling off a speeding truck.

Julia creeps up to the edge. How sublime the water looks.

Limpid. Clear to the bottom. Fear rises in her like thermometer mercury from a feverish child. The girl who said it would be fun to jump backs off, after looking down. One boy goes, arms flailing. Just to test, Julia steps to the edge. She looks down at the small figures on the beach, out at the horizon. *Via, via,* one of the boys says. Go. Go. She feels a quick shock of surprise.

She rises on her toes. And jumps.

CAMILLE AND SUSAN FIND LITTLE new potatoes, huge juicy tomatoes, lustrous black eggplants to roast with peppers. Last, they pick up sorbet. Tonight, they get to stay "home." The wine is a pain to lug back to the house but they manage everything, plus a jug of fresh orange juice and a bag of lemons.

Walking back, Camille says to Susan, "I've been sitting on that stupendous terrace imagining going back home in October. What that would be like."

"Are you crazy? I'm not going anywhere. This is home now. My life is much more *interesting* than I could have imagined. We have fabulous friends. Look what happened to you here! Italy! Tonight we should talk, really talk."

Susan has been searching online at comps for her house in Chapel Hill. Her girls agreed when she sold the beach house, but would they want to give up the house where they were raised? They love coming home to pound cake, peanut butter cookies, dinners on the screened porch, their rooms, one blue, one yellow. Even so, if Susan stays, they'll love coming to Italy probably more: the new replacing nostalgia for the old. They're in China now. No one yet has responded to the large ad they placed in the newspaper with the earliest photos of themselves, dates, where they were found, and the name of the orphanage, which still exists but will not release further information. Susan doubts they have any, since they did not at the times of the adoptions. Eva was left on a bus, Caroline outside a shrine. Both had their birthdates pinned to their blankets. Susan has always imagined the mothers writing those dates, preparing to leave the house, imagined them at the moments of abandonment. Fleeing the scene, what she must have felt. A crazed relief? If Eva and Caroline find out anything, it will be subject to DNA testing. How amazing if they locate some wide-eyed, tragic parents. Do people who abandon children out of whatever desperation come forth because of an ad? Can they read? Wouldn't the shame keep them silent? Huge random chance, statistically against the girls. She thinks of their rooms, intact since college, the canopy beds from her grandmother's house, a southern heritage tacked onto their origins, of their minimalist apartments in California, their devotion to their jobs. And each other. No other relationships seem to arise, a puzzling fact but Susan can't intrude on their privacy. She stares out to sea. She's their mother.

Susan could sell her home, buy a small condo for visits. She remembers the man with narcolepsy, the willowy Catherine who planned to leave the North. Why buy anything? Why not cut the cord? If she wants to go back, she can rent a temporary base. Bridges have burned.

LAURO LIKES IT HERE. WHO wouldn't? The breeze makes you want to say *halcyon*. He's peaceful, knocked out after nursing, a milky haze descending as he nods off. I parked him under a purple passion vine, a live mobile, while I worked, moving from one project to the other all day, pausing only for cheese and fruit. *Meriggiare*, to rest in shade on a hot day.

Nicolà has an enticing rental. At least the basic furniture is colorful. Sparseness suits Cinque Terre, where delivery of heavy items must be a nightmare. Susan plans to rearrange beds to capitalize on the views and to recommend updating the tiny showers and '70s kitchen. More tumbling vines and pots of herbs. We're all happy here. Such simplicity gives the feeling of unburdening.

Blue is good for the soul. Florida girl, I'm always best when I can see open waters.

Julia returns last. Susan and Camille lugged food up all those steps and decided to read in their rooms. I suspect they are sleeping. Julia opens the fridge and takes out melon and cheese and a leg of the roast chicken we had last night. "I'm famished," she says, bringing a plate out to the terrace. Her hair hangs in salt-dried clumps, her shoulders the color of plums, painfully blistered. I offer some after-sun lotion. "I'm fine, thanks. I think I fell asleep on the beach for a few minutes. You won't believe what I did but I'll tell everyone later." She falls on the chicken, smiling and licking her fingers. "This is good-good. Want some?" She spears another piece. "What I need is a shower and a nap. Something good happened to me today. I'll not only tell you, I'll *show* you. How is our sweetie over there?"

Lauro makes little sounds as though he's talking back to the mourning doves that coo in the pergola next door. The woman there sunbathes nude. Through the grapevines, I can't help but glimpse her impressive breasts like two rounds of pizza dough rising.

A bit surreal. I just hope she doesn't burn into the color of a sweet potato. Her husband (clothed) reads the newspaper, then lets it drop over his face when he falls into a snoring sleep. Part of the panorama! Julia and I giggle. Why is snoring always funny? Is he lying at the opening of the cave, scaring away bears? Below us, a woman hangs out wash, flowered sheets fluttering. This village is a hive, each house a honeyed cell.

JULIA KEEPS IT SIMPLE. SHE'S the maestro, directing Susan to sauté the potatoes, me to set the terrace table. (Let's hope our neighbor doesn't dine nude.) Camille is one of those who peels tomatoes. In Liguria, the Genovese basil grows huge and pungent, with curly leaves. Susan found fresh burrata in Vernazza on her hike. Little clams over pasta shells to start, then the fish baked with thyme, olive oil, and lemon.

The wine is light and easy. Out on the terrace while the fish bakes, Julia empties a bottle into a glass carafe she sets in ice. "Quaffable, don't you love that word? Chris never says *quaffable*." Everyone's showered, wet hair, fresh shorts, and barefoot; Lauro sleeps, snug in his small bed. Julia takes out her phone and searches for a photo. Camille pours and passes the glasses around.

"Here's my news." Julia holds up a photo of a woman falling straight as an arrow from a cliff into water. She's midway down, toes pointed, arms tight by her sides. They pass it around.

"Scary," Susan says. "That's, who is it? That's *not* you, Julia?" She hands the phone to Camille, who looks closely.

"That's your bathing suit or at least it's blue like yours."

I'm leaning into Camille to see. "Julia. I know that cliff. Did you jump? You wild thing."

"I did. I can't explain it. I just found myself climbing up, looking down. I did it. Maybe I wanted to do something to shake me out of the state I've been in since waltzing into town and finding my whole past sitting there in the piazza. It was all unconscious, but . . ." She pauses and sips some wine. "Oh, it felt good. Going down I thought I might fall forever, plunge to the bottom and surface on the other side of the world. It must have been only a moment but it felt long, falling. Then to hit the water like a pane of glass. I went way under but somehow had remembered to take a breath at the last instant. Coming up, up through the water, I had my eyes open. The water was so transparent that I felt I could breathe it like air. The biggest shock—shooting up, breaking the surface, taking a big gulp of air, then swimming to shore. The two women who sat beside my towel applauded. One of them had watched me. She took the picture. I'm glad to have it!"

"Send it to Lizzie!"

"Hell, paste it on your résumé."

"No big deal, you all. Those kids were doing it without think-ing."

"Yes, but you were thinking!"

"I came up feeling washed clean. Well, I'll just say it—spiritually. The fear was intense but the leap was renewing. I felt buoyant—oxygenated. When I walked out of the water, I shed a skin there."

"Is it the southern thing, immersion? Like baptism in the river?" Susan pauses at the kitchen door, the oven timer buzzing.

"Honey, it means time to move on," Camille says.

"Again? We just did that." Julia leans against the wall, facing her friends.

"Julia, Miss Icarus, this looks delicious. I'm starving. Are you all?"

The caprese may be the paradigm example of caprese for all time. The pasta with clams tastes like a milder version of the sea. Julia closes her eyes and savors the briny succulence, wishing briefly that she could give a bite to Chris.

I decide to broach the subject. "I am going to miss you all. If you travel back, come down to Coral Gables. I think you'd love my mother's kitchen, Julia. My dad cooked. My mom sat at the counter with a Mojito and they talked. We listened to José Feli-ciano, 'Light My Fire,' over and over. Mexican tile floors, dated maybe by now, but really open to the outdoors and a screened porch—the only way you can eat outside without mosquitoes lift-ing you out of your chair and depositing you in an alligator pond. We could grill some great seafood—as good as Italy!"

"It will be strange without you—even just walking into town in the mornings."

"My table at the bar is your table." (As it was Margaret's.) I venture, "Isn't your lease up soon? Will you try to extend?"

Susan speaks unequivocally. "I want to stay. I love it here. The adventures we've had! The villa is out of a dream. I've made a garden that . . . that defines me, who I am. Or, who I want to be. Everything's unexpected! I've never had a better experience."

"Camille, you're modest, and most spectacularly successful. You earned it! Now are we going to acknowledge the dead cat on the table? What do you want to happen?"

"I've thought about it all day. I know we've been skirting the subject for a while. I think we were waiting for you to settle into yourself again, Julia. You all know I have a terrible lack of confidence, but the sheer fact of being chosen for the American museum exhibits keeps knocking down my throwback once-rejected-by-arts-council responses. It's clear to me—I'm involved with Rowan—but, really, we're going to forge ahead with a relationship that suits us. He has ties in California, business and family. I'd like to visit now and then. What we three decide about the villa isn't going to be an influence or deal-breaker. One pleasure of being old, I realize, is that you're free. Beyond caring what the neighbors might think."

"I'm the same with Chris," Julia says. "He's dear. Fun. And thoughtful, like no man I've known except my dad. But 'I do' and all that—no. I was squashed like a frog in the road when I left Wade. I never ever expected I could love being independent. Love it! I think a mature love can be different. Kit, you must feel that being with Colin is a freedom, not a binding."

I nod. I do. He's my *lux mundi*, light of my world.

"Getting off topic." Susan serves the fish and passes around the carafe. "Take a vote, talk more? I say we buy the villa. It's not that drastic—speaking as a real estate broker!"

"Seems drastic to me," Camille laughs, "but many things seem drastic to me."

"We can always sell if we decide to move on to Thailand! Ask Nicolà. They're not making these villas anymore. They're one-offs. They'll always be valuable. Not to talk you into it—the decision is really, really personal."

"My divorce settlement will soon be sitting in the bank. I

could do it. My dad's keeping the house for Lizzie if she moves back to Savannah. I have my savings, too."

"Nicolà and Brian said they'll negotiate with Grazia for us. I don't think my Italian is up to it." Susan already has investigated all costs and procedures. She's surprised at how straightforward the process is when there are no required inspections or lawyers involved.

"Invite Grazia and her aunt to dinner," I advise. "Most San Rocco transactions occur with a handshake."

"Wait, don't race ahead. I don't want a handshake yet! I'm nervous about this. I should think about it, talk to Charlie."

"Take your time, sweetie. Ha! Take a week. Then we have to decide."

"I have a toast, if I can remember it. Get some vino. It's a couple of stanzas from a poem by W. H. Auden.

> The sense of danger must not disappear:
> The way is certainly both short and steep,
> However gradual it looks from here;
> Look if you like, but you will have to leap.
>
> A solitude ten thousand fathoms deep
> Sustains the bed on which we lie, my dear:
> Although I love you, you will have to leap;
> Our dream of safety has to disappear.

Julia blinks back hot tears, her eyes already red from salt water. "I did leap." She smiles. "I can leap."

That "leap" grabs attention in the last stanza, but what strikes me is the profound realization: the lovers lie on ten thousand fathoms of solitude. Yes, we do. Love and friendship are the mitigators.

Camille puts her arm around Julia's shoulders. "Hey, we can do what we want."

Charles rises viscerally through her body, his solid presence. Always the first image to surface: her mouth against his shoulder in bed, the immense security of his body. The image hurts and she knows why. She is leaving him behind, a colossus in memory. A resin urn of ashes that she must scatter in Spit Creek and among his wild cyclamen.

"Sleep on it, you three," I say. "Gloria Steinem said dreaming is a form of planning. What's the plan? Let's have some of that lemon *sorbetto*. And Julia, you have gifts to open."

Something I Meant to Say

THE AIR IS FULL OF SOUNDS; *the sky of tokens; the ground is all memoranda and signatures; and every object covered with hints . . .* So wrote Emerson and he is right. The world is at all points sentient. That's my religion. Pagan, I guess. I imagine him writing this beside a window in his Concord study on a sweet early autumn day. Maple leaves are falling and mockingbirds call through the brilliant trees. Someone has left him a gold-lettered book with a gray cover. As a reader (and I suppose cooks, architects, musicians, or furniture makers reach back to their predecessors like this, too), I often feel a synaptic connection (beyond meaning) with words I am reading. Not just, Mr. Emerson, an *I'm with you.* More, *I know you.* I read of his sounds, tokens, signatures, as alive today as on that faraway morning. I feel the pulse of *I rise up as a poem* (Marina Tsvetaeva), or even reaching way back: *Flectere si nequeo superos Acheronta movebo: If I cannot move heaven, I will raise hell* (Virgil, *Aeneid*).

The leaping poem by Auden I quoted that night in Cinque Terre came whole, right out of my mouth. I was in the ink that flowed from his pen. *A solitude ten thousand fathoms deep / Sustains the bed on which we lie* . . . You feel that at the cellular level—but try to articulate *how*, and you can't.

Writing their pilgrims' progress story, I came to know that precise same link with Julia, Camille, and Susan.

For how many people do you feel such a connection? Not just *I've got your back and you have mine.* I bring this up near the end because I want to express what real friendship is like. Also, it's what I hope for if on a summer day someone reads this story I've told in the yellow flowered blank book (not much blank space now) with the vellum spine (now a little soiled). May some voltage run through the words so the reader feels *I'm with you.*

Remember, this book began long ago on a fall day when I was gathering twigs for a fire. As the year carried us in its arc, I wrote our stories. (Margaret still waiting for her book.) That the novel is true, not fiction, only I know. Colin hasn't seen a word. (Someday maybe they'll tell me how I did with imagining their thoughts.)

What have I failed to say? *The whole of everything is never told.* (Henry James.) And shouldn't be, I might add. This is where the last pages of the book can be torn out by someone who doesn't want to know the ending (or perhaps by a collector who is making a book only of last pages).

But if I can plant a few small flowers into the crevices of my stone wall, here's where I'll add:

* Their whole names? Mary Camille Acton Trowbridge. Susan Anne Frost Ware. Julia Lee Hadley. As a child, Camille was called Mary Camille. Susan was called Suze, and Julia was ever only Julia. Mine? I am Catherine Elizabeth Raine, Kit since Cathy didn't work out even at two months.

* San Rocco is unrelentingly beautiful. (I didn't say that enough.) On the town hall clock face, a tinny skeleton holding a scythe taps at the passing hours, a not-subtle reminder that

time will overtake everyone. Chiseled below in 1600: *VOLAT HORA PER ORBEM*, *time wings through the world*. At the other end of the piazza, the bank in an ancient *palazzo* has two clocks—one marks hours, the other minutes. This I prefer. Try to keep both small and large time in mind, I think it means. The inscription there is the old "time flies," but in Virgil's more profound original phrase *FUGIT INREPARABILE TEMPUS*, meaning *irretrievable time flees*. (Time presses against this story, since the women are older than those who usually star in books.)

San Rocco is made of gold-hued stone, thin Roman bricks, and stuccoed façades with grand windows. Because of the oversized piazza, sky plays an active part. Not chopped or angled off by buildings, the long blue dome completes the whole. Late afternoon, sitting out with your *aperitivo*, you're aware of sky not as backdrop but as the miraculous event of clouds, shifting and re-forming all day; you're aware of weather coming, sun scraping over stones, and the play of light shadowing and revealing doors, passageways, ghost outlines of former windows and arches. Rays highlight a hand pulling back a curtain, the silver glint of cutlery as Stefano brings out lunch, the electric field around the fur of a ginger cat sleeping by the post office door. How the sky is part of architecture, Colin. Have we ever discussed that? Martyrs and saints were found to have precious stones in their hearts. Rubies, I think, with intaglio images carved into the surface. For those of us who live here, each carries close the jeweled silhouette of San Rocco.

* *Vagitus*, the first cry of the newborn. I heard it and Colin heard it, too. For us Lauro made the sound of the earth whirring around the sun. Lauro, only glimpsed so far. I'm fitting him into the last pages: a delectable bundle of complicated energy with a what's-happening look in his mystery-blue eyes. Unlike us palefaces, his skin has a dusky cast—Colin's Nicaraguan grandmother sending her love from León, where she rocked in a courtyard surrounded by tropical plants into her ninety-fifth year. Lauro's feet, a small wine-stain birthmark on the back of his left heel, as though a wing might have been clipped. Flour from my sack. Who will he be? We don't know yet. I am his mother. They say soldiers dying horribly or tortured prisoners call out for their mothers. (I might, too.) Forever, I am someone's mother. He's as fated as I.

* The process of writing a novel: the stone house becomes a transparent house and I can write on the glass.

* Coming up for them: Sicily for all. Chris and Julia's research trip extending around the island. They'll end in my favorite Sicilian town, Siracusa. Susan's daughters arriving later for travel in Puglia. They found no parents in China, texting merrily to Susan, *Couple of leads dead ends. Guess we're stuck with you!* Friends from home will visit and visit. The oldest agricultural cycles pull toward the olive harvest, the chestnut and mushroom season, the dark of the year, everyone going *pazzo* over two inches of snow in the piazza.

Hugh plans to house-sit for us until the new year. He's invited everyone for American Thanksgiving. Camille and Rowan will go to Venice. Camille! How she vaulted over her own expectations! Now she's casting for a new project. I've seen her wonderful rendering of the famous leap into blue water. Julia will travel to see Cleve, then both go to California to visit Lizzie (briefly—a year is not long enough to have cleared out two decades of drugs from the brain), then to meet Chris's son and see the vineyard. They begin the life I know and Margaret knew: *va & torna.* Go and return. All good. For now, the gods allow them to play in the freedom of their later years.

* Coming up for us. Unpacking in my other home. A grand
chance for Colin. (His pavilion on the ocean, he hopes, will
look inevitable and defining, not like some architectural hy-
brids that smash onto the landscape like meteors.) In south
Florida, there will be no green nest in the garden for making
love. If we tried such folly, we would be sucked dry by mosquitoes, crawled over by lizards, and might disturb the ep-
ochal snooze of an alligator. The screened porch with a daybed
is hidden by banana trees and elephant ears. By the grace of
overhead fans and the scent of ginger lilies, love will happen.
(Birth control, a new issue.) Because I have few friends left
in Coral Gables, and Colin will travel to Key West a couple
of days a week, I'll teach a writing class at the University of
Miami in the spring. Priority: finish Margaret's tribute. Lauro
will sit, crawl, walk. Until we return, I will miss my friends
in Villa Assunta every day.

More to say but the ink is drying, like a *culaccino*: the circle
left by a wet glass on the table. The end belongs to them.

My words slide off the page and float over the desk, rearranging into what I meant to say.

First Night

WHERE ELSE WILL THE BANK have ceiling frescoes of Bacchus in grapevine headdress? He looks lewd, about to tip his glass of wine onto customers standing in line, waiting to deal with the intricacies of withdrawing money. Susan knows she's in for red tape, as her, Julia's, and Camille's money for the house has been wired into her account.

Two hours later, every *centesimo* has been transferred to Grazia. Yesterday they sat at the notary office and listened to the endless contract read aloud, a remnant from days when many couldn't read. As of this moment, free and clear, Villa Assunta belongs to Julia, Camille, and Susan. Grazia cried, even though she wanted to sell. (Should we always cry when we get what we want?) They all went out for celebratory prosecco after everything was signed and she cheered, even got a little drunk, then cried again. She'll be coming by later today to pick up the few items she wants. From the big storeroom upstairs, she chose nothing. Susan looks forward to delving into the packed boxes, surely filled not just with musty curtains but with treasures. The room gives them a new space to invent, but it's destined to become another bedroom for guests and family. Three owners will be juggling the visitor issue for years.

When Susan worked at Ware Properties, she had a tradition of sending three dozen roses to new owners when they moved in. She ordered red ones for Grazia, and has long-stemmed yellow ones for Villa Assunta. From the garden, she already has vases of her late roses around the house, even in the bathrooms. Julia has dinner under way. Later in the week, a party with Chris, Rowan, all their Italian friends, and the expats to say good-bye to Kit and Colin and to christen the house as theirs. But tonight, just the three of them.

JULIA'S PREPARING MERINGUES TO SERVE with a berry coulis. Camille organizes the wines and glasses, and sets the table with one of Luisa's (now their own) linen tablecloths. She has gift sacks of lemon soaps and bath gel for each place. "This silver! Can you believe it? All ours now. If we ever sell, we should offer it again to Grazia. She might change her mind."

"Let's don't talk about selling on the day we bought!" Susan arranges her massive bouquet of yellow roses.

"We've crossed the divide." Julia whips the whites with fervor. "Forever after, we'll be saying 'before we bought,' 'after we bought . . .'" The aromas of baking zucchini tarts and roasting ducks with pears fill the kitchen.

"Feels drastic, exciting, I'm still nervous," Camille admits. She's looking at her playlist but doesn't select that favorite Yo-Yo Ma playing Ennio Morricone, for fear of breaking down into a torrent of tears. *The Mission* gets to her on a calm day but on this one of rocketing emotions, no. Best not. She chooses opera instead. The Three Tenors blast forth. "This house was meant for listening to great arias. Oh, I am totally speechless; this is major. Are we geniuses?"

"Imagine, we've done this. I wish I believed that Aaron is looking down from a cloud admiring us."

"Charles would be quite astonished."

"Can we listen to 'Georgia'? I kind of have to hear it tonight. Who knows what Wade will think and who cares?" The syrup-thick lyrics take them back, especially Julia. Susan switches links and here comes Louis Armstrong. Bright blessed day and dark sacred night . . .

"Let's get ready and celebrate." Susan dashes upstairs.

In their rooms, they dress for dinner. Julia in a metallic gray silk top, Camille in navy linen pants and blouse for the last gasp of summer; Susan already moving into fall in a copper shirt and taupe skirt. They take turns photographing each other on the threshold of the house, remembering when they opened the heavy, creaking door almost a year ago and saw clear through to the back window where the linden tree's last leaves blazed yellow in the late evening light. In the photos, each holds up in turn the iron key. "Paper door!" Camille says. "Wasn't it a paper door!"

In the dining room, under the auspices of yellow roses reflected in a round mirror, and the nun's felicitous fresco, and the great gold-leaf mirror above the fireplace, they pull up their chairs to the table. As they touch glasses, the mirrors catch sparks of light from the clear wine, the clasp in Julia's hair, flickers of candles, the old silverware.

Where this story stops, they look into a mirror reflecting a mirror where the story begins and reflects a mirror where the story continues.

Acknowledgments

MY WARMEST THANKS AND GRATITUDE to my agent, Peter Ginsberg, at Curtis Brown Ltd., and to the fine Crown/Hogarth staff: my editor, Hilary Teeman, publisher Molly Stern, and editorial director Lindsay Sagnette. Special thanks also to Jillian Buckley, Elena Giavaldi, Cindy Berman, Rachel Rokicki, Rebecca Wellbourn, and designer Elina Nudelman.

I'm lucky to be represented for speaking engagements by the Steven Barclay Agency. Such a great group!

Robin Heyeck of The Heyeck Press taught me about letterpress printing and papermaking. My enduring thanks to her for that and for publishing my first books of poetry so beautifully.

For grand times at Figure Eight, I'm grateful to Emily Ragsdale, Franca Dotti, and Frances Gravely.

To Lee Smith, who read a draft, *mille grazie*.

Edward Mayes, my husband, gave me one of his poems for my character Kit, and made the writing of this book even more of a pleasure. I'm buoyed, too, by my family—Ashley, Peter, and William. Will always solves any computer problem with a few quick strokes. My nephew, Cleveland Raine Willcoxon III, now deceased, was on my mind throughout the seasons of this book. His name made its way into the text. *Cin cin*, Robert Draper, for introducing me to Cormòns in Friuli.

The character Margaret is a tribute to Ann Cornelisen and Claire Sterling (both deceased), two gutsy writers I met when I first lived in Tuscany. Although Margaret is fictional, she was inspired by their brilliance and independence.

Women in Sunlight comes from one of the major joys of my life—my friends. On every page, my love goes out to them.

About the Author

In addition to her worldwide bestselling Tuscany memoirs *Under the Tuscan Sun*, *Bella Tuscany*, and *Every Day in Tuscany*, FRANCES MAYES is the author of the travel memoir *A Year in the World*, illustrated books *In Tuscany* and *Bringing Tuscany Home* (with Edward Mayes), *The Tuscan Sun Cookbook* (also with Edward Mayes), and her most recent memoir, *Under Magnolia*. She has published a novel, *Swan*, set in the South; *The Discovery of Poetry: A Guide for Readers and Writers*; and five books of poetry. Her books have been translated into more than fifty languages. She divides her time between Tuscany and North Carolina. Visit her at www.francesmayesbooks.com.